THE SPLENDID HOUR

A MEDIEVAL ROMANCE

BY KATHRYN LE VEQUE

DE LOHR DYNASTY SERIES
—AND—
PART OF THE EXECUTIONER
KNIGHTS SERIES

AUTHOR'S NOTE

Welcome to Peter de Lohr's novel!

Strange how I never saw Peter having his own novel until he joined the Executioner Knights. Then, it wasn't "if" he'd have his own, but "when". Peter is on the young side for an Executioner Knight – and he hasn't had this vast lifetime of experience like some of the older members – Maxton, Kress, Achilles, Sherry, Cai, etc. – but he's the next generation of greatness and they recognize that. I think that's why they embrace him. Not because of who his father is, but because of who *he* is. He's Peter. And he's definitely destined for greatness.

Now, let's talk about when this book is set. We're right after when the Magna Carta was signed, during a very turbulent time between King John and the rebel barons. The Magna Carta (and I've read it) is a very complex document that is mostly about the relationship between the king and his barons rather than a document between the king and ordinary people. It completely serves the warlords, but there are a lot of elements in it that were the founding of many governments, including the United States of America.

Specifically, this story starts in August 1215 A.D. John signed the Magna Carta in June of that year, so it's two months later and nobody seems really apt to adhere to the terms of the charter – warlords included. The rebels hold London at this point (remember the siege of London in *Lord of the Shadows*), and per the Magna Carta, they were supposed to surrender the city if John agreed to their terms. He agreed, but they didn't trust him so they didn't leave, which means John pulled in the Pope to punish them. For once in his life, John wanted the help of the Catholic Church, which he'd had a terrible relationship with for all of his reign.

Enter William Marshal and his agents and allies. William Marshal had a very turbulent relationship with John. He was in favor, he was out. In, out. At this time, he is in – and he is siding with the king, but for very specific reasons. Christopher de Lohr, however, is not. That puts him and The Marshal on opposite sides and puts the Executioner Knights right in the middle of it.

Interestingly, as John engaged in a contentious relationship with the Catholic Church, he was one of the few monarchs that had a decent relationship with the Jews of London. The history of English is rife with the poor treatment of the Jewish population, mostly at the hands of the monarchs, but John was a surprisingly rare exception. During the reign of Henry II, John's father, the Jews became powerful both financially and politically, and Henry had a decent relationship with them also.

John recognized what his father had – that the Jewish merchants and bankers were necessary – and skilled – at generating income, so he afforded them a great deal of protection. However, that didn't sit well with his Christian warlords, many of whom were Crusade veterans from Richard the Lionheart's Great Quest and had bigoted beliefs towards Jews. It was just one more conflict between John and his warlords in a sea of conflicts. It's of interest to note that John wasn't tolerant of Jews because he was benevolent – it was really only financial and, at times, political. The Christian warlords knew this and, not strangely, one of the conditions in the Magna Carta limits the power of the king and his Jewish bankers over Christian debtors' estates. So – the history of John and his relationship to the Jewish population of England makes for very interesting reading.

Now, there are some issues addressed in this book about the Christian and Jewish relationships. Really, there weren't any unless it was financial or some other kind of professional relationship. What they call "intermarriage", a marriage between a Jew and a Christian, was forbidden by the Torah, although by this time in history, the situation was relaxing a little. It wasn't forbidden any longer (meaning the offenders weren't put to death), but it would be virtually impossible for an English knight, who'd swore an oath to God and Christianity, to be married to a Jewish woman without someone having to convert. That means the situations you will read in this novel are not contrived. Were a relationship between our hero and heroine really to happen, the difficulty would be very real and choices, for the sake of the time period and the culture, would have to be made. There was really no such thing as just "accepting the situation".

Now you're prepared to read it!

On a completely different note, let's talk about Christopher and David de Lohr. They are in this tale because they are part of the Executioner Knights, but also because they're some of my favorite secondary characters. They just pop up everywhere. I've you've read *Steelheart, Shadowmoor,* and *Silversword,* you get a glimpse at David, his son Daniel, and Daniel's son, Chadwick in these stories, but in *Silversword,* there are clues about when Christopher and David passed away. I sat down and did the math and realized that Christopher and David had the same longevity as the de Wolfe Pack boys – William, Paris, and

Kieran. If you've read de Wolfe Pack Generation stories, then you know that William, Paris, and Kieran are extremely elderly. Well, guess who else ended up being extremely elderly? You guessed it – Christopher (b. 1156 – d. 1249) and David, who outlived everyone (b. 1159 – d. 1260). That makes them 93 years and 101 years at their death, respectively. Not bad for knights when their average life expectancy was 31 years old (disease and battle will do that to you). But there were exceptions, as there always are – and we see several in my universe.

Now, the usual pronunciation guide:

It has occurred to me in all of the books I've written that I've never clarified how "papa" and "mama" are pronounced. If you're an American, it's "PAH-puh" and "MAH-muh". However, for Medieval England, it's "puh-PAH" and "muh-MAH". Different emphasis on different syllables.

I think the only name in this story that might need clarification is the heroine's – Liora – Lee-OR-uh

Lastly, a list of the de Lohr siblings to refresh your memory (because they pop up in here):

Peter (Christopher's son with Lady Amanda)
Christin
Brielle
Curtis

Richard

Myles

Rebecca

Douglas

Westley

Olivia Charlotte (the future Honey de Shera)

And with that – enjoy this very different but very adventurous tale!

Hugs,

It's Christopher de Lohr's bastard son, Peter, in a tale that could change the stars of the House of de Lohr forever…

When religion and politics don't meet, it's an explosion that could tear the Executioner Knights – and England – apart forever…

Peter de Lohr is the illegitimate son of the greatest knight in the realm, though he has been accepted by his father. Not only accepted – embraced. Peter is well-loved by everyone, an enormous and powerful knight in the image of his famous sire.

He is also an Executioner Knight, and one of the very best. A great marriage is expected of him, it is presumed, to the daughter of a high-placed warlord.

Until he meets Liora ben Thad.

Petite, raven-haired and blue-eyed, Liora is the exquisite and glamorous daughter of a very prosperous goldsmith. She is also a Jewess, her father being a jeweler to the king. It is a time of great prosperity for the Jews of London, with King

John being surprisingly fair to them, far more equitable than to some of his own barons.

When Peter sees Liora, all other women – and quite possibly his plans for the future – cease to exist.

But that comes at a price.

The high-placed warlord and his daughter will not go quietly and they certainly will not relinquish a prize like Peter de Lohr to a woman of lesser social status. So begins a plot to separate Peter from Liora, a sinister plan that will threaten the House of de Lohr and the Executioner Knights… and everything they believe in.

One that puts Peter right in the line of fire.

Will two cultures, and two religions, and a royal order keep Peter and Liora apart?

Or will their love find a way?

Watch the Executioner Knights take sides in this delicious – and unusual – love story.

House of de Lohr Motto

Deus et Honora
God and Honor

LIST OF EXECUTIONER KNIGHTS/SPIES FOR WILLIAM MARSHAL
As of 1215 A.D.

(Note: some later Executioner Knight tales take place years after this story is set, so as of 1215 A.D., this is where these knights serve and/or are in command of. Also note that while some Execution-er Knights may be mentioned, not all appear in this story.)

William Marshal – Earl of Pembroke, Pembroke Castle and Farrington House

Christopher de Lohr – Earl of Hereford and Worcester, Lioncross Abbey Castle

David de Lohr – Earl of Canterbury, Canterbury Castle, Bellham Place

Peter de Lohr – Lioncross Abbey Castle, Lord Pembridge/garrison commander Ludlow Castle

Gart Forbes – Dunster Castle, Devon

Caius d'Avignon – Richmond Castle, North Yorkshire – also Hawkstone Castle

Maxton of Loxbeare – Chalford Hill Castle, Gloucester

Kress de Rhydian – Seton Castle, Scotland

Achilles de Dere – Caversham Manor, Berkshire

Susannah de Tiegh de Dere – a Blackchurch-trained knight, wife of Achilles

Alexander de Sherrington – Lioncross Abbey Castle/garrison commander, Wigmore Castle

Bric MacRohan – Narborough Castle, Norwich Castle, Norfolk

Dashiell du Reims – Ramsbury Castle, Wiltshire – also Thunderbey Castle, East Anglia.

Sean de Lara – King John's personal bodyguard

Kevin de Lara – Canterbury Castle (in the service of David de Lohr) – also Hyssington, Caradoc, and Trelystan Castles – Welsh Marches

Cullen de Nerra – Rockingham Castle, Northamptonshire

Cole de Velt – formerly William the Lion's personal guard, now at Berwick Castle

Addax al-Kort – service to Christopher de Lohr and William Marshal

Essien al-Kort – service to Christopher de Lohr and William Marshal

Morgan de Wolfe – in service to Caius d'Avignon, Richmond Castle

Gareth de Llion – in service to William Marshal

Rhys du Bois – in service to Christopher de
	Lohr/after 1201 living in France under an
	assumed name

Keller de Poyer – in service to William Marshal at
	Pembroke Castle/Netherworld Castle (Keller
	is more of a knight for William Marshal than
	he's actually a spy)

Garran le Mon – technically, he's believed to be
	dead after 1201 A.D.

Marcus Burton – Lord Somerhill and Dunnington,
	Somerhill Castle

REBEL WARLORDS AND OTHER NOTABLES

This is only a partial and mostly fictional list, as appearing in this novel.

"The Northerners" (this was actually a term for warlords from the north who rebelled against King John)

Juston de Royans – Bowes Castle

Ajax de Velt – Pelinom Castle and Berwick Castle

Yves de Vesci – Earl of Alnwick

Alastor de Bourne – Castle Keld

Marcus Burton – Somerhill Castle

Allies of The Northerners:

Christopher de Lohr

David de Lohr

Duke of Savernake, Bentley de Vaston/Dashiell du Reims

House of de Lara (Kevin, Sean)

Maxton of Loxbeare

Alexander de Sherrington

Caius d'Avignon

Siding with John (though still secretly allied with
de Lohr and the rebellion):

Daveigh de Winter/Bric MacRohan

Valor de Nerra/Cullen de Nerra

William Marshal, Kress de Rhydian, Achilles de
Dere

THE WARRIOR'S PRAYER

(Origins unknown – suspected Viking prayer, 9th century. Note that there is a similar warrior's prayer in the epic poem, Beowulf, and there are several versions of it throughout history.)

Behold, I see those I love, and my relatives who have died before me.

I see my father seated in the golden halls with an empty seat beside him.

I see the greatest warriors who have ever lived, surrounding my father, calling to me.

Death is not the end, but the beginning, for a true warrior never dies.

He takes his place of greatness among those who are worthy.

Mourn not the glorious dead but rejoice in their legacy.

They wait for me, not in this life, but in the next,

Where their legends shall live forever.

PROLOGUE

~ CAVE SORS (BEWARE OF FATE) ~

September
Year of Our Lord 1215
London

H E'D SEEN HER coming.
        Christ!

Lady Agnes de Quincy was out looking for him. He knew that. Oh, she pretended she was out on the dirty, crowded streets of London for another purpose, but the truth was that she was looking for him. The woman lusted after him like a predator lusted for prey. She was *in love* with him, or so she swore to anyone who would listen, but he was certain her father was more in love with him than she was because a marriage between his *darling* Agnes (and he could only hear that name in his head with the man's lisping drawl) and Peter de Lohr, the new Lord Pembridge, would cement a great alliance between two Marcher families. The House of de Lohr and the House of de Quincy from Astley Cross would be forever immortalized in flesh and blood, and pomp and circumstance, as befitting two great families.

Well, he wanted no part of it.

He had to hide.

It wasn't exactly easy, however. Peter was assigned the high-visibility security detail for the coming conference between King John and the warlords who hated the mere sight of him, his father included. Christopher de Lohr, the Earl of Hereford and Worcester, had been leading the pack against a man he'd hated for thirty years. His father, who had been Richard the Lionheart's champion, grossly hated the stench that John Lackland's name brought to his very sense of being, a distaste that went bone-deep.

Peter knew it. Everyone knew it. For years, Christopher had sided with William Marshal, a solid and unbreakable alliance, but that alliance was showing cracks with The Marshal's tempestuous relationship with the king. One day the man was out of favor, the next day he was in. Christopher could no longer put up with John's corrupt ways and the wavering relationship with The Marshal. When he finally took a stand and broke with William Marshal, he took many warlords with him. That also meant The Marshal's circle of secret agents, the greatest spy network the world had ever seen, had fractured.

For the moment.

But men could still love one another and not exactly be on the same side.

The Executioner Knights, as the men from The Marshal's spy ring were called, still functioned as a group for the most part. They still served their missions, tasks required by The Marshal. It simply meant that the situation was a bit fragile these days.

But Peter, of course, served his father more than he served the spy ring. In the end, he was his father's son, and that's where he found himself today. He was playing escort for some of the great barons who were arriving in London and making sure nothing got out of hand. Too many warlords in close quarters was often a recipe for disaster. He was enormous, powerful, skilled beyond measure, and brave beyond reason. He could handle the most difficult warlord with finesse.

But the sight of Agnes de Quincy had him running for cover.

Peter was in the city proper, near Milk Street

as he headed to Aldergate because they were anticipating a large party coming in from Norfolk. The House of Summerlin was a warring house, one with fine knights, but they weren't at peace with the Earl of Lincoln at the moment, who was also due. Several de Lohr men were spread out in the city, escorting arriving barons, so Peter was alone at this point. As he'd told his father, he didn't need help escorting anyone, so he was riding solo and that, unfortunately, left him vulnerable when he caught sight of Agnes and her father.

Two against one, as it were.

Quickly, he bolted into one of the smaller alleyways that lined Milk Street, which was in the Jewish quarter of the city. Nearby was the Street of the Jewelers, comprised of stall after stall of some of the finest jewelers the world had to offer and in that section of the city, all of them were Jewish. But here on Milk Street, the homes were fine and well-appointed, the streets better maintained than most. When Peter ducked into an alley, it was a surprisingly clean one. He slid off his expensive Belgian rouncey, a type of horse that was big and showy, and peered around the corner of the building like a child hiding from bullies.

Agnes and her father were heading away from the Street of the Jewelers, which is where he suspected they had been that morning. Agnes was a woman with expensive tastes, as she displayed every single day in the copious amounts of finery she wore, so there was little doubt in Peter's mind that her father had taken her to buy her more loot. The woman was up to her eyeballs in loot and looking for a rich husband.

She wanted to get her hands on the de Lohr fortune.

Perhaps there was more to it than that, but Peter wasn't going to make it easy for her.

He should have been smarter about trying to avoid her because she seemed to turn up wherever he was. He swore she had spies on his tail, something his father laughed at, but even as Christopher thought his son was being paranoid, old Walter de Quincy was trying to convince Christopher just how perfect Agnes would be for his firstborn son.

A bastard son, but firstborn nonetheless.

And now this.

Agnes and her father happened to be near the Street of the Jewelers just when Peter was heading in the same direction. This wasn't coincidence; it was witchcraft. Agnes had pulled out her cauldron to once again locate the man she'd set her sights on.

Damnation!

He could see the pair lingering at the mouth of Milk Street and Lombard Street, one of the main east/west avenues through London. Fearful that they really did have spies on his tail, Peter headed back into the alley, looking for a place to hide. Milk Street ran between Lombard Street and Catte Street, so he could head to Catte Street and escape them by taking another route, but the problem was that he would be visible if he made an appearance out of the alleyway.

It wasn't worth the risk.

But he heard voices, people drawing closer. He could hear the clops of horses. Nearly in a panic, he pushed open a big gate that bordered the alleyway and entered into a neat kitchen yard. He wasn't at all concerned with whose yard he was actually in as he shut the gate and leaned against it, listening as the voices seemed to grow louder. He couldn't be sure that it was Agnes and her father, so he listened carefully. Someone was definitely traveling up Milk Street.

And he waited.

"What have we here? Don't tell me that you are the new livery servant."

The voice came from behind him and he whirled to see a woman standing several feet away. She had clearly just come out of the house, a basket in her hands, but she was looking at him with curious amusement. No fear, no anger. Just… amusement.

For a moment, Peter was actually speechless.

He was looking beyond the amused expression to the woman who wore it.

A woman of unearthly beauty was gazing back at him. She had black hair, silken and curled, and a face of porcelain. Her black eyebrows were delicately arched over eyes of an exquisite cornflower blue. She had a pert little nose and lips that were shaped like Cupid's bow, lush and pink. And the rest of her… he found himself looking her over from head to toe, from the top of that dark head, to her full breasts, to her tiny waist and generous hips, all of it clad in a dark blue dress that was finely made but simply constructed. She wore it like a goddess.

Nothing about her was imperfect.

In fact, he had to blink his eyes to make sure he wasn't dreaming.

"I… I am the *what*?" he sputtered. "What did you call me?"

Her blue eyes twinkled. "Livery servant," she said. "But I suspect you are not."

He shook his head. "Nay," he said. "Are you disappointed?"

"Possibly. Who are you?"

He couldn't believe the woman wasn't terrified of a fully armed knight in her kitchen yard. She wasn't showing an ounce of fear. That impressed him until he realized he was about to make a fool of himself with his answer to her question. Given that he couldn't think of a lie fast enough, it would be better to face the truth and hope that glimmer in her eyes didn't turn to disappointment.

Somehow, he wouldn't like that.

"Hiding," he finally said.

Her dark eyebrows lifted. "From what?" she said, growing serious. "Are you in danger?"

He grinned; he couldn't help it. Standing away from his horse, he put his entire armored body on display.

"Do I *look* as if I could not handle another armed man with a weapon?" he asked as if her question had offended him.

She shook her head, that silky hair licking at her neck. "You look like a highly skilled, highly honored knight," she said. "But why are you hiding?"

He sighed heavily. "If you must know, and since you found me in your yard I suppose that you have a right to, I am hiding from someone I do not wish to see."

Her gaze lingered on him on a moment before her expression suggested she understood what he meant. "Ah," she said. "You are hiding from your father?"

"Nay."

"Your mother?"

"Nay."

"A nasty cousin with foul breath?"

He chuckled. "Nay," he said. "Keep going."

She cocked her head, sensing a game afoot. "Someone you owe money to."

"Nay."

"Someone who owes *you* money?"

He started to laugh. "Why would I hide from someone who owed me money?"

She shrugged. "I would not know," she said, fighting off a grin. "I'm simply going through all potential choices since you are being so mysterious about it. Are you hiding from an annoying sister?"

"Nay."

"A frustrating brother?"

"*Nay.*"

"Then I give up," she said, finally letting her smile bloom. "Who has you hiding out in a stranger's yard?"

He grunted. "You would not believe me if I told you."

"I would believe it."

He cocked his head. "Very well," he said. "I am hiding from a woman I do not wish to see."

She cast him a long look. "You are correct," she said. "I cannot believe that. A lad as comely as you, hiding from a woman? Astonishing."

He puffed up at the suggestion that he was comely. *He* knew he was handsome and he was glad she knew it, too. Already, he was glad that he'd hidden in her yard, if only for the chance to speak with this exquisite and witty woman.

It made the awkward situation worth it.

"It is true," he said, sounding exasperated. "Everywhere I go, there she is. Even today, she is in this quarter of London on the same day I happen to be here. I do not wish to burden you with my troubles, but that is why you find me here. I promise I will leave as soon as I am certain she will not find me. I will not vex you any longer than necessary."

The woman shook her head. "You are not vexing me," she said. "You are welcome to stay until your trouble has passed."

He smiled at her, a genuine and warm gesture, and he swore he felt a flash of something pass between them. It was... vibrant. Shocking. Like the flash of lightning from a summer storm, titillating and exciting.

He wondered if she felt it, too.

"Thank you," he said. "I am Peter de Lohr. May I know your name, gracious lady?"

"I am Liora, daughter of Haim," she replied. "Do you live in London, Sir Peter?"

He shook his head. "Nay," he replied. "Though I spend enough time here that I may as well live here. I serve my father at his castle on the Welsh Marches."

"That is far away."

"Have you been to the Marches, then?"

"Nay," she said. "But my father has. He has business associates in Hereford. I know that it takes him weeks to travel there and back again."

Peter looked her over again. A woman that fine should be in the highest social circles with the right familial connections, but she wasn't. He'd never seen her before. She was a petite little thing, but more than that, he noticed that she was wearing a cap sewn with gold thread that matched her dress. Her hair was gathered in an elaborate braid that also had gold ribbon woven into it. The house itself was a wealthy one; he could see that. She was clearly wealthy from what she was wearing. But the way she'd introduced herself had him curious.

"What business does your father engage in?" he asked.

"He is a goldsmith," she said. "A jeweler. In fact, he is the jeweler to our king. He has supplied John with his fine jewelry for years and before that, he supplied Richard, although Richard sold many of his pieces to pay for his wars."

A jeweler. Peter knew what that meant and, abruptly, he realized what she was and why he hadn't seen her before. "Then you are a Jewess?"

Liora nodded. "I am."

Peter nodded as if a good deal suddenly made

sense to him. "I see," he said, looking at the structure. "I've never been on this particular street before. Your house is very fine. In fact, all of the houses on this street are fine. Is everyone here Jewish?"

Again, she nodded. "They are," she said. "Mostly jewelers, but there are some merchants as well. It is a nice, quiet street."

"And a good one to hide in," he said, grinning. "You will forgive me for asking questions. I have never met a Jewess before."

"And I've never met a Christian knight hiding from a woman before."

He broke down into soft laughter. "I'm not such a coward, I promise," he said. "I come from a long line of fearless knights. My father is the Earl of Hereford and Worcester, a man once known throughout the kingdom as the king's champion. Therefore, bravery is in my blood. But this woman... she would frighten the heartiest barbarian, I assure you. Aggressive is where she begins. Where she ends, no one knows."

Liora fought off a grin. "Mayhap she is simply misunderstood," she said. "Why does she pursue you? Have you asked her?"

He snorted. "She pursues me because her father wants her to marry well," he said. "*She* wants to marry well, but she is a woman of expensive tastes, haughty manner, and general arrogance."

"How do you know? Do you know her well?"

"Well enough," he said, distaste on his features. "The first time I met her was a few months ago when I came to London with my father. I met her at Westminster Palace when there was a great feast. My father always told me that the true test of character of any man or woman is how they treat those beneath their social rank. If they are kind to those who are inferior, that speaks very well of them. They are people of good character. I have always remembered that and try to behave accordingly. The first time I met Lady Agnes, she cuffed a serving wench on the ear because the woman accidentally brushed against her. That told me all I needed to know."

Liora was listening seriously. "Your father sounds like a wise man," she said. "It is a pity when great men or women cannot be great to those who serve them. There is something ignoble in treating the less fortunate no better than the dirt beneath your feet."

"True," he agreed. "And that is why I avoid her."

Liora set her basket aside. "I do not blame you if that is the measure of her character," she said. Her focus lingered on him and Peter swore he saw a flash of warmth in her eyes, like that lightning he'd felt earlier. But it was quickly gone. "But I am sure you do not wish to hide from her all day. Would you like me to go out onto the street to see if anyone is there?"

"Would it be too much to ask?"

"Of course not," she said. "Stay here and I shall return."

He did. He watched her turn back into the house, noting the way her backside curved beneath that blue dress. He had been quite enjoying the view, even lingering on it, when he felt a sting to his right cheek. He put his hand up to see what had touched him when he felt another sting to his temple. Perplexed, he looked around the yard in time to see a young boy several feet away with a hollow piece of straw in his hand. When he saw Peter looking at him, he stuck out his tongue and ducked behind the chicken coop.

Peter returned his attention to the open rear door where Liora had vanished, but his senses were attuned to the hooligan lurking in the kitchen yard. Now that he knew the boy was there, he listened for the rustling as the child moved about. It seemed that there was a game of cat and mouse going on in that kitchen yard that he hadn't even been aware of until now.

He was being stalked.

He could hear the child moving around behind him now, by the small outbuilding behind the house. Quietly, he tied off his horse, which left his hands free, and he began to back up towards the rear of the horse and pretending to check his hooves. But all the while, he was waiting and listening. He wanted to be able to move one way or the other if the little boy decided to shoot projectiles at him again. He didn't want the lad startling his horse, which could be quite snappish when provoked.

As he stood next to the big, round buttocks of his horse, he heard noise behind him and turned his head in time to see movement. As a purely reflexive action, he threw up his hand in front of his horse's rear end and managed to stop a pebble that had been aimed right at the horse. He whirled around in the same motion, just in time to see the little boy within arm's length as he tried to reload another pebble into his straw.

Peter lashed out an enormous hand and grabbed him.

"Let me go!" the boy howled. "Let me go or I'll fight you!"

Peter cocked a droll eyebrow. "Fight me? You already have. I have won."

"I'll *kill* you!"

"With what?"

The boy was all fire and fear – fear because he'd been caught and fire for the same reason. He tried to kick Peter in his protected shins.

"My feet and my hands," he said, trying to

kick with all his might. "I'll kill you with my hands and feet. Then I'll get a big sword and I'll cut your hands off. Then I'll cut your legs off. Then I'll chop your head off and throw it in the river!"

Peter frowned. "Christ, that was graphic," he said. "Who taught you to say such things?"

The child was beginning to sweat because he was struggling so hard. "My friends and I will throw you to the fishes!" he said. "They'll eat your eyeballs right out of your head!"

"Asa!"

They both heard the gasp from the back door, looking over to see Liora standing there, aghast. She rushed out and grabbed the child by the ear as he howled, but he didn't fight her the way he had fought Peter. In fact, he whined and cried as she dragged him over to the kitchen door, swatted him on his behind, and shoved him inside. Cha-grinned, she turned to Peter.

"I am so sorry," she said. "He… he is young and foolish. Please forgive him."

Peter fought off a smile. "He is young and fearless and frightening," he said. "Is that your brother?"

Liora nodded sheepishly. "Aye," she said. "His name is Asa. He has only seen seven years, but you would think he's seen thirty from the way he talks. He has a group of friends that are older and quite rough."

"Ah," Peter said. "The same friends who are going to throw me to the fishes?"

"The same."

He chuckled. "I am fearful for my life now," he said, but soon sobered. "Did you notice anyone on the street?"

Liora was glad to change the subject. "Nay," she said. "You are safe."

His smile grew. "Thanks to you," he said. "You were quite kind to a stranger when you did not have to be."

She smiled at him, a gesture that was more beautiful than anything Peter had ever seen in his life. The woman was such a magnificent beauty that every new gesture, every new expression, was like seeing her again for the very first time. Something told him that he wanted to see her again.

It had been a most interesting afternoon.

"You are welcome to hide here any time you feel the need, Sir Peter," she said. "I am happy to have made your acquaintance."

He was moving back towards the front of his horse, but his eyes never left her face. "Thank you," he said. "I am happy to have made yours, also. I was thinking that I have never seen you around the town, at feasts or festivals. Do you never go away from your home?"

She shrugged. "Not too often," she said. "I

help my father in his stall sometimes, or my mother here at home. We attend the Great Synagogue weekly."

"But you mostly stay to home and your father's business."

"I do."

Peter wasn't naïve. He knew why. Although the king enjoyed a good relationship with the Jewish population of London because the Catholic Church hated them, and he hated the Catholic Church, there were many Christians who did not like the Jews. There was prejudice in the veins of men and women who professed to be loving Christians. Peter didn't make it a habit of interacting with people of the Jewish faith because he'd never honestly had the need to, but he knew that there was a definite divide between the Christians and the Jews, as there had been throughout history. He wasn't oblivious to that, but he had to admit that he never understood why there was such bigotry on the part of the Christians when Jesus Christ was, in fact, Jewish.

It made no sense to him.

Even more so as he looked at Liora.

"And that little hoodlum of a brother," he said after a moment. "He does not stray, either?"

Liora shook her head. "My mother tries to keep a tight rein on him, but you can see that it is nearly impossible."

"There is just you and your brother?"

"Just us two," she said. "And you? Do you have brothers and sisters?"

Peter untied his horse's reins from the post he'd secured them to. "I have several," he said. "Five brothers and four sisters."

Her eyebrows lifted. "God's Bones," she said, impressed. "That is a great many. And do your brothers behave like Asa?"

He snorted. "I am the eldest," he said. "After me, there is Curtis, who has seen ten years and two. He is what my mother calls an 'old soul'. Richard is next and he is outgrowing his annoying phase, fortunately, but Myles and Douglas are still of an age where they need daily beatings. They make Asa pale by comparison, but my mother is certain they will grow out of it, too. Most boys do."

She giggled, putting a hand over her mouth. "Then mayhap there is hope for Asa yet."

He smiled at her, feeling the need to linger but knowing he had to go. He had tasks to attend to, but he'd never wanted to veer from his duties so much as he did at this moment. He wanted to stand in that smelly, cold kitchen yard and talk to Liora for the rest of the day. But he could not, so it was an effort to move his feet towards the gate.

"It seems that I must take my leave of you, Demoiselle," he said. "Thank you for a pleasant diversion while I waited for the unpleasant one to pass."

Liora didn't accompany him to the gate. She remained standing in the middle of the kitchen yard, watching him unlatch the heavy iron panel.

"You are welcome," she said. "And I wish you well, my lord."

He paused, the smile still on his lips. "As I wish you well, also," he said. "If… if you are ever in need of assistance, please do not hesitate to send word to me. It took my father five years to build it, but we now have a manse a few miles out of town, along the Thames. It is called Lonsdale and my mother has taken great care to furnish it, much to my father's distress. He does not like to spend money, so they had great rows over the empty rooms. He thought building it was enough, but my mother assured him that it did indeed need a few beds and tables. You may send word there should you ever have need of my services."

He was laughing as he said it, conveying the fact that that situation itself was humorous. The wildly wealthy Earl of Hereford and Worcester built a house at great expense but then was loath to actually spend additional money to furnish it.

Liora laughed softly.

"The poor man," she said, gently mocking the earl's pain. "But… well, I do appreciate your generosity, but it would not be seemly for me to impose upon you for any sort of assistance. I do thank you kindly for your offer, however."

He knew her reluctance was because of their different religions, and different social statuses, but he chose not to recognize that. Before him, he saw a beautiful woman and that was all, and he hastened to reassure her of his position on the matter.

"It is not a random offer, Demoiselle," he said. "It is because I owe you a favor and I like to pay my debts."

She forced a smile, but he could tell that she wasn't convinced. He was thinking he may have to persuade her otherwise, but not now. He didn't have the time, but the curiosity of this magnificent woman had his attention.

It was a challenge and he liked challenges.

With the gate open, he swung himself into the saddle and gathered his reins. His helm, which had been affixed to his saddle, went on his head and he secured it at the neck. It was a great helm, or bucket helm, but it had a face plate he could lift and the design was new and sleek. He lifted the faceplate and dipped her head in her direction.

"Thank you again, Liora, daughter of Haim," he said. "I do hope we meet again."

Her smile turned genuine and she gave him a little wave as he departed the kitchen yard. With thoughts of that lovely woman on his mind, Peter was halfway down the alleyway when he heard something ping off his helm. Asa may have been trapped in the house, but he hadn't surrendered. Not in the least. That kind of spirit did indeed remind him of his youngest brothers, demon children that they were.

A second ping hit him in the neck, but he didn't give Asa the satisfaction of a reaction.

He did, however, laugh all the way back to Lombard Street.

It had been an afternoon well-spent.

CHAPTER ONE

Hollyhock House
London seat of the House of de Winter

T HERE WERE TWO distinct sides.

Christopher de Lohr, the Earl of Hereford and Worcester, was sitting on one side of an enormous table that stretched from one end of an equally enormous chamber to the other. With him were many rebel warlords, including the men they called "The Northerners". These were warlords from Yorkshire, Northumberland, and Cumbria, powerful men who held the borderlands between Scotland and England. They were also the warlords that were the most opposed King John and his rule. Being far from London and the politics therein, they were almost in their own world up in the wilds of the north and they deeply resented a king that no one could stand. In truth, many of them owed debts to the king, so there were some financial issues, as well.

But that didn't make their stance any less dangerous.

Three months earlier, the rebel warlords of England as a collective whole had forced King John to sign a document known as the Magna Carta. It was a long and complicated document outlining their grievances and demanding concessions from a monarch who had thus far in his reign been at odds with most of the men who were supposed to be loyal to him. The Magna Carta was a last-ditch effort to force John into behaving as if his vassals meant something to him and were not, in fact, his enemies. It was an attempt to corral a king and force him to behave fairly, for not in the entire history of England to this point had a monarch behaved with such willful deceit, corruption, and selfish ambition.

The Magna Carta had been the rebel warlords' attempt to exact fair and equitable treatment from the man they so freely hated.

But it had been a battle – literally.

Even now, the warlords opposed to the king held London. They had captured it in the siege of London earlier in the year and although the terms of the Magna Carta had called for them to surrender the city, three months later, they still occupied London and controlled it. That was why the king had come – tensions, three months after the signing, were not any better.

Something had to give.

The gathering of the king and his warlords was being held in the home of Daveigh de Winter. His father, Hugh the Elder, had passed away the year before, leaving Daveigh head of the house. This wasn't the larger group of barons who rebelled against the king, but a smaller and more powerful core. It was the only neutral territory that they would agree upon even though the House of de Winter was siding with the king in this matter. It wasn't that they agreed with John or had any particular love for him – it was simply that, without fail, the House of de Winter supported the king. It always had, it always would.

It was their legacy.

Some warlords even referred to de Winter as the "royal army". Daveigh and the de Winter war machine was one of the most powerful armies in all of England and a close friend and ally of Christopher de Lohr, who was on the opposite side of the table this day. It was the only time in Christopher's and Daveigh's lifetimes that they had been on opposite sides.

In fact, it was the first time that many of them had been on opposite sides but, above all, love and friendship held steady. Even if Christopher would not fight for John, he would not take a stand against Daveigh. It made for an incredibly complex and sad situation because, once, Christopher had been the right hand of King Richard. There had always been an extremely complicated relationship between Christopher and John because of it. More than de Winter even, the House of de Lohr represented the Crown.

But no longer.

John was aware of this. He had arrived just before the nooning meal, escorted by de Winter and royal household troops. The de Winter troops were led by Bric MacRohan, an Irish legacy knight who hated John more than anyone in England, so to see him riding escort for the king was truly something to witness. Bric was joined by the House of de Nerra, the hereditary Itinerant Justices of Hampshire, including Cullen de Nerra, who was very much part of William Marshal's stable of agents. But Cullen's father, Val de Nerra, was the current Itinerant Justice, an appointment that came straight from the king. Were Val to side with the rebels, he would undoubtedly lose his position and everything else that went with it, which made for a difficult decision on Val's behalf. He very much allied himself with de Lohr and the rest of them, but he wasn't willing to jeopardize his legacy.

There was a good deal of alcohol flowing on

this day and even at this early hour, it wasn't watered down. It was full strength because the men in that chamber were going to need the reinforcement for what they were about to discuss. No one was happy, on either side, so much like Runnymede and the signing of the Magna Carta, this meeting had the potential to blow up.

The stronger the alcohol, the more fortified the man.

Christopher was sitting with his brother, David, the Earl of Canterbury, along with his allies, men who had fought under William Marshal for many years. Edward de Wolfe, Earl of Wolverhampton, was one of the most important, followed by Bentley de Vaston, Duke of Savernake. The Earl of East Anglia, Talus du Reims was present along with his eldest son and heir, Dashiell du Reims, who used to serve Savernake.

And then, there were "The Northerners" – Ajax de Velt, the warrior known as The Dark Lord, perhaps the most feared warlord in all of England, and his son's father-in-law Alastor de Bourne of Castle Keld. The de Bournes were descended from the Kings of Northumbria. Juston de Royans, a mentor to many of the men at the table, had a place of honor next to Christopher, along with Caius d'Avignon, Lord Hawkstone and commander of Richmond Castle. Gilbert d'Umfraville, Lord of Prudhoe Castle was sitting towards the end of the table along with Maxton of Loxbeare, one of William Marshal's premier assassins.

But the last Northerner baron in the room was perhaps the most legendary of all. A man who had gone to The Levant with Christopher, David, and many other legendary knights, a man who was as mysterious as he was deadly, but always in support of Christopher. Marcus Burton, Lord Somerhill and Dunnington, usually spent all of his time in the north and although he allied with William Marshal, he was considered a retired Executioner Knight. But that didn't mean he wasn't looked upon with reverence and awe. Marcus, Christopher, and John had a long and sometimes violent association.

Having the three of them in the room was like looking at history repeating itself.

The sides of the table were lining up with one notable absence – William Marshal himself. Christopher passed a questioning expression across the table to Daveigh, who lifted his shoulders slightly. The Marshal was supposed to be in attendance, but still hadn't arrived. However, unwelcome men who had arrived were Peter des Roches, a man recently appointed the king's Justiciar whom the warlords detested, and several of John's personal guard, men who had served alongside John's greatest guard, Sean de Lara, until Sean's fall from grace earlier that year.

Sean had been one of William Marshal's premier spies in the battle to keep John on an even keel and for nine years, he'd performed flawlessly until his cover was blown. Even now, he was recovering from near-mortal wounds received in the siege of London and Christopher knew his counsel would be sorely missed. If anyone knew John, it was Sean de Lara.

But they were going to get along without him.

"Good lords, I am sure you know that our king is a busy man and that you respect his need to be brief in this meeting," Peter des Roches began in his heavy French accent. "If you are agreeable, we shall come straight to the point."

Christopher looked at a man he hated a great deal. Peter was not English, but French by birth, and was now in a position of extreme power in the court of the king. Peter was arrogant, reckless, and calculating, and he hated the English with a passion. He rubbed nearly every warlord in England the wrong way. For a Frenchman to have such power in the English court was an insult to Englishmen everywhere. Christopher's gaze lingered on the man for a moment before addressing John directly.

"Your Grace, we are agreeable to this meeting, but not with that trained dog as a mediator," he said. "Remove him and let de Winter mediate."

Des Roches flared. "*Espèce de bâtard arrogant*," he hissed. "*Comment oses-tu…!*"

David, always quick to temper and especially when it came to his brother, slammed his gloved hand on the table to shut des Roches up. "Speak to him like that again and I will cut your vile tongue out of your filthy mouth," he growled, leaping to his feet. "No one will weep over one less French pig in the world."

Des Roches began to shout, which brought John's bodyguards to the table. David was already on his feet, but Maxton of Loxbeare shoved the Earl of Teviot out of the way in order to get across the table to John's henchmen. Caius d'Avignon, a massive man of enormous power, rushed to Maxton's side as Christopher himself leapt up to pull his brother back over the table. Juston and Talus were pulling on Maxton and Caius until Marcus Burton bolted to his feet and gave a good yank on Maxton, pulling the man back from the brink of hand-to-hand combat in Daveigh's hall. They all saw, very clearly, when Bric, standing with John's men, grabbed des Roches by the neck and yanked the man back so hard that he nearly snapped his neck.

That was no friendly grasp from the fiery Irishman.

It was Marcus who finally threw up his hands

and boomed.

"Enough!" he shouted, immediately silencing the chamber. He pointed at Maxton and Caius. "Sit down, both of you. David, if you cannot behave, I will personally escort you outside. And you – des Roches – insult the Earl of Hereford and Worcester again and I will turn every man at the table loose on you and I can promise that you will leave your share of blood on the floor. Mayhap they didn't teach you manners in Paris, but it is extremely bad form to insult a warlord who could overrun your holdings, kill your family, and destroy everything you know. If you value your life, you'll keep your damnable mouth shut. Is this in any way unclear?"

Des Roches was a proud man who, most of the time, didn't know how to shut up. He took pride in having command over English warlords, wielding John's power like a dagger. He was rubbing his neck where Bric had grabbed him, his mouth working furiously, but the king put up a hand to him, silencing him. Even John knew how badly this could go if his courtiers misbehaved. With des Roches silent, he looked to Christopher.

"I do not think we need a mediator, de Lohr," he said. "You and I have known each other a very long time. This is not the first time we have been at opposite sides of the table and it will not be the last."

Christopher was regaining his seat. "Nay, Your Grace," he said. "Let us come to the point before we destroy Daveigh's chamber."

John opened his mouth to reply but was interrupted when Peter and his brother-in-law, Alexander de Sherrington, entered the hall followed by William Marshal and Pandulf Verraccio, the papal legate and representative of the pope in London. While Peter went to stand on his father's side of the table, William lingered at the edge of the table with Pandulf.

Right in the middle.

Everyone was looking at William and the papal legate with confusion. It wasn't unusual for William to be here, as he had been expected to be present during this discourse, but it was well known that John and the Catholic Church had a contentious relationship. No one had any idea why the papal legate had come – at least, Christopher and his allies didn't. They were looking at William as if the man's expression might give them a clue, but William's expression was like stone. He wasn't sitting on John's side of the table, but he wasn't with Christopher, either. He simply stood at the end of the table, looking at everyone involved.

"I hope I am not too terribly late," he said, then looked to John. "I have brought Verraccio, as you requested."

John perked up in his seat, motioning the papal legate forward. "Excellent," he said. "Your timing could not be better. I have a feeling that your message to my warlords will end this conference quickly, so please speak freely to them. You have my permission."

Clad in heavy ecclesiastic robes of a dark brown color that were fine and silk-lined, the papal legate looked every inch the representative of Rome. Pandulf was a short man, thin and fragile like a woman, but with dark, intense eyes that conveyed the man's power and intelligence.

Christopher knew of the man; they all did. He was very sharp and reasonably fair, not at all like the sometimes political-minded clergy that held high positions in the church. Therefore, they had some trust in him, as much as there could be with a papal representative, but Christopher and the others were more than curious about the man's presence and now, evidently, with a message he bore. What was even more disturbing is that The Marshal, with no great love for the church, had brought the man.

Something told Christopher and the rest of them to be on their guard.

"My lords," Pandulf spoke in a heavy Italian accent. "As you have heard, I was summoned by your king to deliver a message from the Holy Father."

Christopher held up a hand. "No offense, but I find it extremely unlikely that the pope would have any message for the warlords of England," he said. "It is not as if the king and the pope are bedfellows, so tell us from the beginning why you are here and make clear the origins of the message you bear."

Pandulf wasn't offended because he knew de Lohr. The man was fair and likeable, most of the time, but his contention with John was well known. He wanted truth, not the twisted stuff John sometimes came up with, and was making that very clear. Any royal meddling with this situation would only make it worse.

"I understand, my lord," he said. "I have been in England for several years. I am well aware of the relationship between the king and most of his barons, so I assume you would at least give me respect in that regard."

Christopher, and most of the others seated with him, nodded. "Of course," Christopher said. "Continue, please."

Pandulf eyed John before returning his gaze to the warlords. "You are correct when you state the obvious, my lord," he said. "Our Holy Father and the king are not exactly bedfellows. Many is the time I have had to give the king absolution for something he has done, so I am not his bedfellow, either. Will you acknowledge this?"

Christopher and the others nodded. "Without question," Christopher said.

Pandulf nodded shortly. "Good," he said. "My duty is to God and to the church, in that order, so the message I bear has no bearing upon the king, but upon the rightness of your rebellion against the lawful king. Nay, I do not simplify this situation by calling it simply a 'rebellion'. It goes deeper than that and I am aware, but rebellion is the closest word to the situation that I can choose. I pray your forgiveness if it is not the right one, but for the sake of argument, I shall use it."

No one seemed to give him much of a reaction. They were listening closely, so he continued.

"Then let me come to the point," he said, fixed on Christopher. "The king has declared himself a crusader, a warrior for God, which affords him papal protection. I received a missive from our Holy Father a few weeks ago instructing me to relay the following to you – as rebels against the rightful king's rule of England, a man who has sworn his sword and army to God, any warlord resisting John's rule shall be excommunicated from the church. Be advised that Stephen Langdon, the Archbishop of Canterbury, has been removed from his post because of his alliance to the rebellion. That was why I was late to this meeting, my lords. Langdon was removed, as all of you shall be excommunicated if you do not swear your allegiance to the king and surrender London, which you still hold for your rebellion. Our Holy Father considers your actions against the king illegal and unjust, as the king swears that he was forced to agree to your terms. He did not agree willingly. He has therefore appealed to the Holy Father for assistance and he shall receive all Rome can do for him in this matter."

It was a shocking ultimatum, one that had not been expected. Though the pope had gotten involved in the signing of the Magna Carta somewhat, these revelations on what John had done, and the consequences with the church, were astonishing. John had made it well known throughout his reign that he disagreed with the church. There was no love lost there. So to hear what he had done in order to force the hand of the rebelling warlords… it was truly astonishing.

Christopher's gaze never moved away from Pandulf.

"Nearly ever warlord in this chamber went on crusade," he said evenly. "We were all warriors for God. Where is our support from a man we killed thousands for?"

"You are not the king."

"The king never killed in the name of God," Christopher snapped. "*We* did. The king only took a crusader's oath to circumvent our opposition. You *know* this, Pandulf."

Pandulf did, but he was in a bad spot. Pandulf eyed John, who was gazing at him expectantly, knowing the pope was on his side. For Pandulf, it was a sickening moment.

"I am afraid I cannot make any decisions, my lord," he said. "I am only the messenger. You have until the autumn harvest to make your decision so that I may report your choice to the Holy Father. Until then, you are still honored members of the church, but only for now should your decision be otherwise."

Christopher's eyes narrowed. "Then let me make it plain to you and to the king so there is no question as to what will happen should we refuse your offer," he said. "He loses our armies. He loses tens of thousands of men who would heed the call should it be needed – for example, for a crusade to The Levant to fight for Christendom. Hundreds of churches would lose their patrons. They cannot survive without their patrons and you know this to be true. My wife and I are patrons to a dozen churches along the Marches and all monetary support would be removed. Shall I go on?"

Pandulf knew the threat wasn't an idle one. But he also knew he had a position to take and that was with the Holy Father. He had no choice. Slowly, he shook his head.

"It is not necessary, my lord," he said. "I understand that such a move, for both factions, would be… devastating."

John, who had been listening to the conversation, was incensed that Christopher and his allies hadn't immediately cowered at the suggestion of excommunication. Pandulf had been his secret weapon in his battle against his barons, but they didn't seem overly impressed by the threat and that outraged him.

"Do you understand that without the church's support, you would have nothing, de Lohr?" he said, aghast. "You would be a man without an immortal soul. Your family, your children, would be excommunicated as well. You have young sons. They could not be knighted in the usual sense. One of your sons is here, now, in young Peter. Peter could not hope to marry an eligible woman from a good family with his father excommunicated, a rebel leader, a man to be scorned."

Peter heard his name. Standing near The Marshal, he didn't like the way the king was browbeating his father. His father was the most righteous, decent man he knew and John's bullying didn't sit well with him. He opened his mouth to defend his father, but Alexander was standing next to him. He must have sensed Peter's inclination to respond given he was the subject of discussion and the moment he flinched, he felt Alexander's grip on his arm, pulling him away from the table.

Sherry's instincts were better than most.

Even so, neither Christopher nor John noticed. They were still focused on each other.

"I will be no more scorned than a disfavored king," Christopher rumbled threateningly. "In fact, you risk making all of us martyrs against an unjust king. At the moment, you only have the animosity of your warlords, but if you excommunicate us, you'll have the animosity of your people as well. Therefore, we *will* survive. We always do, so if your threat is a real one, be prepared for the consequences."

John was genuinely stricken that the threat from the pope hadn't immediately turned the tides of the meeting. The warlords were sticking together. But there was someone who hadn't entirely sided with them and his gaze moved to William Marshal, standing at the edge of the table.

John and William had suffered through a tumultuous relationship over the years. John knew that William ran the most elite spy ring the world had ever seen. At times, that ring had supported the king but at other times, it had been against him. It had been an odd relationship between the king and The Marshal's spies, preserving the monarchy of a king they disliked. John knew that most of the men at the table were part of that ring, or at least had been at one point. Christopher and William Marshal were as thick as thieves even if they were on opposite sides this time, but the situation was salvageable, in John's opinion.

He would make it so.

His attention moved to Daveigh.

"I must speak to Pembroke alone," he said, using William Marshal's official title as the Earl of Pembroke. "Show us a private chamber."

Daveigh did and everyone watched with curiosity and trepidation as John and William disappeared into a nearby solar. That had Christopher on his feet, pulling the men at the table with him. Instead of remaining indoors, they went outside, into the wide street that fronted Hollyhock House. It was a major thoroughfare through London, just south of Westminster Palace, now mostly blocked off with the escorts of the men attending the meeting.

It was the safest place they could be at the moment.

"Thank God," Marcus muttered as he came up behind Christopher, who had stopped in the middle of the street. "I was starting to suffocate in there. Any air John breathes is like poison."

As Christopher nodded, David piped up. "Why are we out here?" he said.

Christopher wiped a weary hand over his face. "Because we have more privacy out here than we did in that chamber," he said. "Anything I say to you, someone is going to overhear, but out here –

there is less chance of anyone from John's horde hearing us."

"Even The Marshal?" Maxton muttered softly.

Christopher looked at Maxton. "Even The Marshal."

Maxton shrugged.

Christopher's gaze lingered on the man he shared a semi-like/hate relationship with and had for many years. They were both dominant males, both thinking and acting very much alike. Maxton had always thought Christopher was too arrogant for his own good and Christopher simply didn't have any love for Maxton and his brooding ways. They butted heads frequently on many issues but, oddly enough, they would both kill or die for each other, hence Maxton's charge over the feasting table to get at des Roches. Christopher would acknowledge that at some point, but not now.

He had more important things on his mind.

He looked around the circle of men, now gathering out in the middle of the street – Wolverhampton, Teviot, Ajax de Velt, East Anglia, Caius, Maxton, Savernake, d'Umfraville, de Bourne, Canterbury, Dashiell, Sherry, Peter, and Marcus. So many fine, trusting, seasoned warriors.

He looked directly to the older men.

Men who had forged a nation, who were legendary in English history, and warlords the likes of which would probably never be seen again.

The first one he focused on was Ajax, his old and dear friend. De Velt was the original barbaric knight, The Dark Lord who still struck fear into the hearts of men. He was quite elderly as far as fighting men went, but no less fearsome.

The man was truly ageless.

"Jax," Christopher addressed him. They had long since gotten past any formalities between them. "In all of the brutal things you did in the past, did you ever run up against the church excommunicating you?"

Jax fought off a grin. "They were too frightened to," he said, watching the others snort. "In a serious answer to your question, nay, I was never excommunicated, or if I was, I did not know about it."

"Then what are your thoughts on this?"

Jax glanced at the older men around him – Juston de Royans was one. They were longtime acquaintances, only allies in their later years, but the respect of decades of experience was there. He glanced at Talus du Reims, too, whose father had fought during the anarchy between Stephen and Matilda those years ago. Older men with a good deal of knowledge, who had dealt with John's father, Henry, at length. John's father, who had upended the monarchy from time to time.

His attention returned to Christopher.

"It is my sense that John's decisions are often based on his own selfish wants, of course, but also on spur of the moment judgments," he said. "He has gone to the Holy Father to side with him in the hopes of forcing you into submission and from the expression on his face, he was surprised when you did not immediately capitulate."

"He'll push the excommunication," Juston said as Jax nodded in agreement. "He'll make sure we're all excommunicated but he will not realize the long-term results until well after the fact. Excommunication changes nothing. Most of us have our own chapels and we will worship in our own way, so it changes nothing except John will have divided this country more than it already is. Excommunication gains him nothing, but he does not see that now."

Christopher nodded slowly. "He's using it as a threat."

"A threat that will turn on him in the end."

"But he is right in one way," Marcus said quietly. "It will complicate things for our families, our children, our relatives. My eldest daughters are already married, but I have five sons and two more daughters who will need spouses someday. It will lessen the choices if we are excommunicated."

Christopher looked at the man who had been his best friend for many years. "And you cannot find enough attractive choices between all of us who will be excommunicated?"

Marcus scowled, but it was with humor. "I do not want any de Lohr offspring tainting my bloodlines," he said. "De Royans, either. Pah."

The men were chuckling. "That is good," Christopher said. "Because I certainly do not want any of yours, either. I'd rather my children marry puppies. In any case, know that I, for one, do not intend to negotiate or submit to a threat from a man who corrupts his holy power as he sees fit. Pandulf is a fair man, but his superior is not. The Holy Father can excommunicate me if he wishes to, for it will not change my mind about the rightness of what we are doing and the goals we intend to accomplish."

"Are you certain there is not a grudge against the king that is clouding your judgment?"

The question came from Talus du Reims, an excellent warrior from a long line of warriors. He and Christopher had known each other for many years, including the history of Christopher's relationship with the royal family.

But Christopher simply shook his head.

"There is no grudge, I assure you," he said. "There never has been. I was Richard's champion, once, but that was a very long time ago. John was a spoiled, conniving prince at the time and he is a spoiled, conniving king now. That has not changed. But I tell you now that any sense of surrender to him will be a sign of weakness and, at this moment, we do not need to be viewed as weak. If we do not stand together, mark my words, John will pick us off one at a time."

CHAPTER TWO

"**I** MUST PICK them off one at a time."

The words came from John, spoken in a hissing tone that had weight and petulance behind it. The Marshal found himself facing a monarch he'd once called a necessary evil, a man he shared his own tempestuous history with. He continued to stand by the door of Daveigh's small solar, perhaps to be able to rush out should he need to. Being shut up in a chamber with the king was not something he was comfortable with.

"Pick them off?" he repeated. "I do not understand."

John threw up his hands. "Like a hunter selects his prey," he said. "It is like shooting boar – in a group, they are strong, but if you weaken that group one at a time, it will eventually scatter."

"And you compare your warlords to boar?"

John sighed sharply. "I have done everything they've asked of me," he said. "I was coerced into signing that document at Runnymede, but I have no intention of honoring it."

"They know that."

"The Holy Father himself says that it is illegal and immoral for them to do such a thing."

"They did it because you govern England like a fat man governs a feast," William said. "You pick and choose your favorites, throw away those who displease you, and turn the dogs loose on others. Your Grace, I have lived through three kings. Though you are the rightful king, your methods could be better. Those men out there had no choice."

John's eyes narrowed. "You dare to insult me?" he spat. "Careful, Pembroke – you are only here by my good graces. I do not need you."

"Aye, you do," William said, refusing to be intimidated by a spoiled man he hated to his bones. "If you did not need me, I would not be here. You want me to control the warlords. De Lohr, Burton, de Royans, and de Velt. All of them. That is the only reason you have brought me here – to control them. To bring them onto your side. I am the most valuable man in your kingdom at the moment, so let us dispense with the threats. You brought me in here for a reason. What is it?"

John postured angrily for a few moments longer, but the truth was that William was right. He had brought him into the chamber for a reason. But he wasn't ready to give in so quickly. He didn't like the feeling that The Marshal was one step ahead of him, though it had always been true. Throughout their decades-long history, William Marshal had almost always been at least one step ahead.

But not this time.

To get what he wanted, John was prepared to bargain.

"It seems that the threat of excommunication did nothing," he said. "Are they really so arrogant in the face of God?"

The Marshal shrugged. "Not in the face of God," he said. "They are pious men. They are fair men. But you do not seem to like that they are fair and pious."

"Why do you say such things?"

"If you did not treat them so poorly, you would not have this problem," he said, growing bolder. "Your Grace, I have fought since the time of your father. I was his favorite knight and you are well aware. You have abused me, cast me aside, called me back, and now I stand in a chamber with you while you clearly have something more you wish to say to me. I have always been your servant, but not your trained dog, as de Lohr called des

Roches. I will do all I can to further England's cause, but I will not do it at the cost of those good men out there. Yet here I am, on your side, because you are the king. Now, *what* did you want to talk to me about?"

John was somewhat taken aback by that speech. He couldn't decide if he was enraged or in agreement. Indecisive, he backed off, finding a cushioned chair to sit in as he pondered his next move. Finally, he looked at William.

"Giles de Broase and Walter de Lacy have angered me for the last time," he said. "They have both escaped to Ireland, leaving a good portion of the Welsh Marches in my hands. Ludlow Castle in particular. Hugh de Mortimer has been discovered to have been expanding his castle without my permission and as of last month, I have sent his neighbor, Fitz Walter, to claim it. It is now mine."

The de Lacy and de Broase news wasn't of any great surprise to William, whose own lordship was in Pembroke, Wales, but the comment on Hugh de Mortimer had him listening carefully.

"Ludlow and Wigmore are under Crown control?" he asked.

John nodded. "Aye," he said. "So are Knighton and Risbury Castles. De Lohr should know some, if not all of this, especially about Ludlow that has been in my hands for a while now."

"And why do you tell me this?"

John leaned back in the chair, his dark eyes fixed on William. "Because you will go to de Lohr with a proposal," he said. "You will offer him Ludlow and Wigmore in exchange for his support."

The Marshal had a feeling this proposal was coming and he was prepared. "He will never give you his support for those properties."

"I will add Risbury and Knighton."

"Never."

"Then I will give all four of them to des Roches and he will bring his French allies to the Marches," John said flatly. "How will de Lohr like it when the Marches are overrun with French warlords?"

It was a brilliant, nasty move. The Marshal could see that and he had to admit that he was impressed by it. But it was incredibly dastardly, as befitting John. He knew better than almost anyone how to make deals and how to coerce men into his bidding but, in this case, it wasn't going to work.

It was going to end him.

The Marshal took a long, deep breath.

"Then I hope you are prepared for war," he said quietly. "De Lohr will not take that and well you know it. He'll bring his allies in and they will erase des Roches and whoever he happens to bring into those properties, and then he will send you their heads. I suspect he will also ally with the Welsh warlords and then you will have a massive war on your hands. If you think to keep the Marches with this proposition, it will be your undoing, Your Grace. De Lohr, his allies, and the Welsh will not stand for it."

"And you?"

"I will not stand for it, either."

That forced John to rethink his strategy, which he was loath to do. He wasn't a man who liked to be forced into anything, but he knew he'd pushed. Perhaps a little too far.

But it was still salvageable.

"Then do this," he said. "Tell de Lohr I will give him all four castles if he, and the other rebels, will pull out of London. I speak not of excommunication or the illegalities of the Great Charter – but I want the rebels out of London. If he will do this, I will give him the Marcher castles."

That was a little more reasonable, but still possibly difficult. Christopher was a leader of the rebels, but he didn't make unilateral decisions. There were others involved.

"The castles for London?" William repeated, stroking his chin thoughtfully. "It is possible he will accept that," he said. "But you have the papal legate here threatening to excommunicate these men if they do not declare the charter you signed as invalid. That is not going to simply go away,

Your Grace. What will you do about that?"

John held up a finger. "One step at a time," he said. "Get de Lohr to agree to pull the rebels out of London and I will give him those properties."

"The other rebel leaders will want concessions, too. You cannot gift de Lohr and not expect the others to obey when there is nothing in it for them."

He had a point.

John frowned.

"Then I will prepare a list of gifts for the leaders of this… this *travesty*," he said with disgust. "I will promise them all something in exchange for removing their armies from London. Properties in Ireland, in Wales… I will make it worth their while. Will you tell de Lohr?"

William wasn't keen on any of this, but he, more than anyone alive, knew how politics worked. Bargains, bribes, and promises… nations were made in such a way.

So was peace.

"Very well," he said after a moment. "I will tell him. But I suggest you remove des Roches and your guard before there is another flare up between David de Lohr and someone who looks at him in a manner he does not like. Heads will be rolling before we can blink an eye."

John stood up from his chair, smiling at The Marshal. "My true and faithful friend," he said.

But it was all for show. He didn't mean it. "I knew you would see the reason in all of this. But just so you are aware, de Winter his hosting a feast tonight and I have been invited, as a guest of honor. Truth be told, I invited myself so he could not deny me, but tell de Lohr and the others that I should like them to attend as well. Mayhap we will be able to speak further under more pleasant surroundings."

The Marshal looked queerly at him. "You are inviting your enemies to sup with you?" he said. "Your Grace, that cannot end well."

John shrugged. "It will because you will tell them they must come," he said. "You will tell de Lohr of my proposal and he may come and discuss it with me. I am not unreasonable, Pembroke. They will see that."

It was untrue. So much of that was untrue. Even as John spoke of peace, he had French mercenaries preparing to sail for England. Some already had. When he spoke of des Roches bringing French warlords to the Marches, he wasn't joking. He meant it. While he pretended to want peace with his warlords, his actions spoke of another wish altogether. He didn't want peace – he wanted surrender.

And The Marshal knew it.

Still, he didn't contradict him. He simply nodded and John snorted in a way that suggested he felt that he had gained the upper hand. He proceeded to follow the king into the hall where all of the warlords were missing, but he knew they hadn't run off. They had simply left the chamber when the king had, which was wise. Without The Marshal or the king's presence, tensions would flare if someone said the wrong thing.

As John instructed his guard to depart, The Marshal looked to Daveigh and Bric to discover where the warlords had gone to. It was Bric who took the lead, silently beckoning the man to follow him. But along with The Marshal, Daveigh and Cullen de Nerra came, too. They had all been part of The Marshal's spy ring and in a normal world, they still were. When The Marshal saw that he was being followed, he wasn't troubled. He let them.

Better they hear John's proposals from his own lips.

It was something that would affect them all.

CHAPTER THREE

"I F I ACCEPT Ludlow, then I keep it out of John's hands," Christopher said to David. "Wigmore, too. That castle is strategic and it is enormous, so I shall give one castle to Peter and the other one to Sherry. I'll garrison the whole damned southern Marches to keep John from it. If he thinks giving me these properties will cause me to change my mind about him, then he has gone mad."

David couldn't disagree. It was well into the night at the feast at Hollyhock House in the same hall that only hours earlier had seen the unhappy king and his rebellious warlords face off. At this feast, however, with the presence of women, the men were behaving themselves. Female presence always made the men behave themselves.

Which was why Christopher had sent word to his London townhome for his wife and daughters to join them.

Dustin, the Countess of Hereford and Worcester, arrived in the company of her older daughters. Christin, Lady de Sherrington, was one of them. She was married to Alexander and, for a time, had been one of William Marshal's best spies. A beautiful woman with dark hair and her mother's gray eyes, she had retired from the spy game in order to have children, but she was still as wise and cunning as ever. When she entered Hollyhock House, her husband was quick to claim her upon his arm. He hated to be far from her and her appearance at the feast was a welcome event.

Two years younger than Christin was her sister, Brielle. Named after Marcus' wife, Gabrielle, Brielle de Lohr had blossomed into an astonishing beauty. She looked exactly as her mother had in her youth – a thick mane of blonde hair, buxom and petite, but instead of Dustin's gray eyes, she had deep brown ones when no one else in the family had. She was unmarried yet, and considered quite an eligible young woman, but for years she and Jax de Velt's youngest son, Cassian, had their eyes on each other. Even as she entered the manse with her mother and sister, Cassian wasn't far behind.

He'd ridden escort all the way from Lonsdale

House.

No one would look at Brielle for fear of Cassian's wrath.

Cassian had gone to foster at Lioncross Abbey Castle, seat of Christopher de Lohr, at a young age, so he and Brielle had essentially grown up together. Jax was a very large man, as were his elder sons Cole and Julian, but Cassian had undergone a growth spurt when he was about nineteen years of age that made him taller than anyone. He'd sprouted up, bulked out, and become a beast of a man, and all of him a slave to a little blonde who equally adored him.

Unfortunately, Christopher wasn't yet ready to acknowledge anything between Brielle and the youngest de Velt son, and the mighty beast of a man who was Cassian was fearful to push his suit, so he bided his time… and stayed close to Brielle, wherever she went.

As Cassian entered behind the women, his father was there to greet him. With Jax and Cassian embracing, Christopher pulled away from Marcus and David and went to greet his wife.

"My lady," he said with a warm gleam in his eyes. "You look ravishing, as usual."

Dustin de Lohr was a truly spectacular female specimen who had seen forty years and two. But to her husband, she was an ageless beauty who was much like a fine wine – the older she became, the better she looked, and Christopher was as smitten now as he was when he'd first met her. But she was also willful, stubborn, opinionated, and fiercely protective of her husband and family, which was why he wanted her at the feast.

The situation, for them, could possibly be changing.

He needed her counsel.

"Thank you, my lord," Dustin said coyly, fighting off a smirk.

Christopher lifted her hand and kissed it. "You are welcome," he said. "But did you wear that gown to seduce me? You know what happens when you wear it."

He was referring to the dark blue silk that displayed her full, white bosom most ably. She chuckled at her husband of over twenty years. "I do not need to wear this gown to seduce you," she said. "If I wanted to do that, I would have worn nothing at all beneath it like I did in our younger years."

Christopher fought off a grin. "I do remember you doing something like that back when we only had five children."

"Now we have eight and I have stopped doing that for a reason. Every time I do, we have another child."

Christopher burst out laughing, kissing her hand again and finally her cheek. When he was finished, she removed her cloak, handing it over to a nearby servant as her gaze moved about the hall.

"Where is Keeva?" she asked, referring to Daveigh's wife. "I've not seen her in a very long time."

Christopher looked around for the de Winter's Irish-born wife, spying her flame-hair inside the hall near the hearth.

"She is over there," he said. "But give me a moment, if you please. I brought you here for a reason."

Dustin lifted an eyebrow at him, her gray eyes fixed on him. "Not simply to shine?"

He grinned. "Not entirely," he said, looking over the heads of those crowding the entryway and the doorway to the great hall. He spied Peter, Alexander, and Marcus just inside the door and he emitted a low whistle, catching their attention. "I must speak with you and Peter and Marcus and Sherry."

Peter and Marcus started gravitating in his direction, followed by Alexander and Christin. Since Christin was savvy in the politics of England, Christopher didn't mind that she joined the group as he took them into Daveigh's small solar and shut the door. She was as astute as her husband, brother, and father, so her opinion was respected. Christopher was about to speak when the door abruptly opened and David entered.

He shut the door behind him.

"I want to be part of this," he said to his brother. "Have you told Peter yet?"

Christopher shook his head. "Not yet," he said, looking to his eldest son. "I will make this brief. The Marshal has informed me that John wishes to make a bargain with the warlords holding London, starting with me. It would seem that de Broase and de Lacy have fallen out of favor, forfeiting several of their properties to the Crown, the larger ones being Ludlow Castle and Wigmore Castle."

Peter's eyebrows rose. "Ludlow?" he repeated. "That massive place? And Wigmore? My God, those two are enormous. They hold a huge chunk of the Marches."

Christopher nodded. "I know," he said. "John has offered me Ludlow and Wigmore along with Knighton and Risbury. That would nearly double my empire. But this comes at a price."

Marcus, who hadn't heard any of this yet, was understandably wary. "What price, Chris?"

Christopher looked at him. "That the rebels pull out of London," he said. "I am not the only warlord he will be making an offer to, but I am the first. And, it seems, mayhap the biggest offer. He'll grant me all four properties if I pull my army out and convince the other warlords to do the same."

"And if you refuse?"

"Then he'll give the properties to des Roches so the man can bring his French barons to the Marches," he said. "We'll be crawling with French bastards and God only knows what else. Either I accept the offer or I will spend the rest of John's reign defending my borders and my vassals from des Roches and his scum."

Marcus usually kept his emotions in check, but even he was shocked at what he was hearing. "That is no choice at all," he said strongly. "He's threatening you."

"He is, indeed."

"What do you intend to do?"

Christopher shrugged. "What can I do?" he said. "It's a strain on manpower and finances to keep five hundred men here in the city and I know it is a strain for the other warlords who continue to keep men here, so pulling them out would actually be a relief."

Marcus was thinking through to the long-term consequences. "And royal troops take the city once again."

Christopher nodded. "London belongs to the royals," he said. "It always has, it always will. We held it to gain leverage against John so he would sign the Great Charter and he has."

"But he hasn't held up any of the terms."

"Nor have we by not pulling out of the city when we said we would."

He had a point. The barons had agreed to withdraw from London as part of the terms of the Great Charter. Marcus snorted. "Then we cannot exactly condemn the king for doing what we are doing."

Christopher shrugged in agreement and Marcus shook his head, turning away as he pondered the situation. Christopher's focus moved to Peter and Alexander once more.

"It is my intention to agree to John's proposal," he said. "Peter, you shall be the garrison commander of Ludlow Castle. It will belong to you. Sherry, you will be the garrison commander of Wigmore. You both shall keep all of the tolls and taxes from the properties, paying me a quarter of the total yearly take. That will make you both quite wealthy. You are not, however, allowed to raise taxes without my approval, but we will discuss the terms more in detail before you assume your posts. Do you have any questions so far?"

Peter and Alexander were somewhat stunned by the turn of events. Ludlow and Wigmore were without question two of the largest castles on the Marches, so this was a lucrative post for them both. It was Alexander who spoke up.

"Who occupies the castles now?" he asked.

"Fitz Walter," Christopher replied. "When he turns those castles over to me, he will take the men he brought with him. It is my understanding that de Broase left some of his army behind, so there should already be a contingent of men, but we will reinforce that with de Lohr men. Understand me well – once I get my hands on these castles, John shall not get them back, no matter what happens. They are mine and will remain mine until the end of all things, so your task will be to hold those castles for the House of de Lohr. Forever, if need be."

Now that the shock was wearing off, the pleasure was evident on Peter and Alexander's faces. "Who shall man Knighton and Risbury?" Peter asked. "Those are substantial garrisons."

Christopher stroked his chin. "I realize that," he said. "I was thinking of sending Cassian to Knighton and possibly Addax al-Kort to Risbury. You remember Addax and Essien, Marcus? The Kitara princes?"

Marcus looked at him sharply, disbelief in his expression. "Are those two serving you now?"

Christopher grinned. "Those young men we took under our wing and helped train on the sands of The Levant those many years ago have never lost their loyalty to England because of us," he said. "They were serving a Flemish count before they ended up with de Velt. When I heard about that, I demanded they come to Lioncross and serve me, and they've been there ever since."

He was speaking about two young men from a

country far to the east of The Levant who had fled their country in a hostile takeover. Their father, the king, had been killed, so Addax and Essien were forced to flee. They made their way to The Levant via a merchant caravan and ended up under the care of Christian knights – Christopher de Lohr and Marcus Burton. When the wars were over, they were separated from their Christian mentors and traveled to Ghent where they were trained and knighted. They were brilliant men and fine warriors, and Marcus was quite pleased to hear that they had turned up again.

"That is excellent news," he said. "I have always wondered what became of them. I'm very glad to hear they have made their way to England."

"And I," he said. "They are excellent knights, both of them."

"I look forward to seeing them again, soon."

"They will be quite thrilled to see you, also," Christopher said. "Addax will make a fine garrison commander, so I will send him and Cassian to the smaller garrisons. Truly, this situation may work out better for us in the end. We could never hope to hold London for any length of time, anyway, so accepting those four castles in exchange for pulling out my men… I have the better end of the bargain."

Christin, who had been listening intently,

spoke up. "Do you intend to only allow my husband to be a garrison commander?" she said. "Or will you give him the property someday? He deserves that, Papa. So does Peter."

Christopher looked to his ambitious daughter. Not that she wasn't correct in her declaration that both men were deserving, but he didn't want to make any commitments at the moment. "Aye, they do," he said. "But I also have six sons who all must have a piece of my legacy, so do not push me into making any decisions today. Be pleased that you will soon be chatelaine over such a fine castle."

Christin opened her mouth but Alexander shook his head at her, faintly, a silent husbandly command that forced her to keep silent. As she made a face, unhappily muzzled, Christopher turned his attention to his wife who had, thus far, remained silent during the exchange.

He looked at her, the woman who had been by his side for so many years. She was strong beyond measure, wise and clever. He wanted to make sure she understood the greater implications of what was to happen.

A husband who was taking on more responsibility.

"I know this is a good deal to take in, but I wanted you to know what had transpired this evening," he said. "I suspect we will be returning home sooner than we had planned because of this latest development. There is much to plan for."

Dustin was clearly mulling over what she'd been told. "It is a great deal, to be sure," she said. "I am not astonished at the scope in which your legacy is growing. There is no one in England who deserves it more. But that is not why you invited us here tonight."

Christopher's eyebrows lifted. "What do you mean?"

She cocked her head. "I know you too well, my love," she said. "You said that the king is going to be here tonight and you would not invite me to be in the same hall as that man unless you needed me badly. What do you need me to do?"

Dustin and John, not surprisingly, had a history as well. There had been a time, many years ago, when the then-prince had abducted Lady de Lohr for his own nefarious purposes. Christopher had saved her, of course, and ever since then, he'd made sure his wife and daughters were nowhere near John.

But Dustin was correct.

He needed her for something.

"Astute as always, Lady de Lohr," he said with a glimmer in his eyes. "I do believe Peter needs your assistance."

Hearing his name, Peter perked up. "Me? What do I need?"

Christopher looked at him. "If I am not mistaken, Agnes de Quincy and her father will be here tonight," he said. "Agnes is on your scent like a bloodhound and I thought your mother might be able to give the girl a moment of pause when it comes to pursuing you. I do not like Walter de Quincy, but his lands border mine. It would be a fine lordship for you, Peter. You know the family is quite wealthy."

Peter put up a hand to stop his father from continuing. "I want nothing to do with her," he said flatly. "Everywhere I go, there she is. She's petty and mean, and she is not someone I wish to know much less be married to. If you want someone to have the de Quincy lands and Astley Cross, then marry her to Curtis or Richie. I am not a good candidate."

Christopher fought off a grin. "I know," he said. "Which is why I brought your mother in. She can discourage Agnes and her father as I cannot."

Everyone turned to Dustin, who simply shrugged. "I will do my best," she said. "Are you certain this is what you want, Peter?"

Peter went to her, taking her hand and holding it sweetly. Even though Dustin had not given birth to him, she had loved him from the moment she'd met him and he loved her. She had always taken a special interest in him and made the bastard of her husband, born well before she had married or even met him, feel like one of the family. At least, she had always tried to.

There was a deep bond there.

"Please, *Ange*," he said, calling her what he'd always called her – the French term for angel. "We do not want a woman like that in our family and I certainly do not want to be married to her."

Dustin smiled at him and patted his cheek. "Then I will do my best," she said. "Or, my worst as far as Agnes is concerned. Have no fear."

With that, she headed for the door, pulling her husband and David, and even Christin and Alexander with her. Like a queen, she emerged from the solar with her entourage in tow. Marcus started to follow, but Peter called to him quietly. When Marcus paused, Peter motioned for him to close the door after the others.

He wanted a moment of Marcus' time.

In fact, Peter had fostered at Marcus' castle of Somerhill for many years and he was almost closer to Marcus than he was his own father. Marcus hung back, looking at Peter with curiosity.

"What is it?" he asked softly.

Peter had been planning this for the better part of the afternoon. He needed someone to talk to, someone who wasn't his father or his brother-in-law, someone who wasn't a family member and perhaps had a broader view of things. He trusted Marcus, a man who was noble and trustworthy, at least to Peter. He knew that in Marcus' past, the man had sometimes been less than scrupulous when working for something he wanted or something he believed in.

Marcus Burton was a man who would let nothing stand in his way.

Peter had heard the rumors of the days when Marcus lusted after Dustin. He'd even been married to her at one point because it was widely believed that Christopher had been killed in battle, but that was all a very long time ago. Marcus and Dustin and Christopher had been young and passionate and sometimes foolish in their judgment, all of them, so the actions of a man from long ago had no bearing on what Peter thought of him. For as long as he'd known Marcus Burton, the man had only been kind, wise, and noble.

Peter trusted him.

"I had everything planned out that I wanted to speak to you about, but now that the moment is upon me, I am somewhat tongue-tied," he said, grinning nervously. "I suppose I wanted to ask you a few questions."

Marcus cocked his head curiously. "What about?"

"What do you think of the Jews?"

"The *Jews*?"

"Aye."

Marcus was looking for more of an explanation, but when Peter wasn't forthcoming, he simply shrugged. "They worship the same God as we do," he said, puzzled. "Are you asking me what I know about the Jews or what my opinion is?"

Peter nodded. Then he shook his head. "God's Bones," he muttered. "I do not know what I am asking. All I know is that I saw the most beautiful woman I have ever seen today and she is a Jewess. I've never known any, so I do not know if... do you think my father would even let me court such a woman? If I liked her enough, I mean. Do you think he would permit it?"

Now the situation was starting to come clear a little and Marcus' dark eyebrows lifted. "I see," he said. "You have met a woman you are attracted to."

Peter sighed with relief now that Marcus understood what he was saying. "Aye."

"And she is a Jewess."

"Aye."

"Where did you meet her?"

Peter tried not to look too embarrassed. "While hiding from Agnes de Quincy," he said. "I hid in her kitchen yard over on Milk Street."

Marcus cocked his head thoughtfully. "That is over in the business district," he said. "Over by the Street of the Jewelers."

Peter nodded quickly. "Her father is the jeweler to the king," he said. "I am sure that means the family is quite prestigious and wealthy. Their house is very nice. She was very… nice."

Marcus looked at him when he said it, a smile spreading across his lips. "Captured your attention, did she?"

Peter nodded as if he could hardly believe it himself. "I spoke to her for a short time," he said. "She was witty and intelligent, and her beauty… I have never seen anything like it in my life, Uncle Marcus. The woman is a goddess. Were she Christian, she would be the most popular and sought-after woman in all of England. I've honestly never given a thought to the Jews one way or the other, but she… she has me thinking about them."

Marcus watched the emotions ripple across Peter's fair face. He was dashingly handsome with his blond hair and dark eyes, and being a de Lohr, that made him one of the most eligible bachelors in England. Agnes de Quincy knew it, which was why she was pursuing him so voraciously. There were other families who had approached Christopher about a potential betrothal, but Christopher was being quite selective with his eldest son. Peter was a prize and Christopher intended to treat him like one and broker the most advantageous marriage for him, but Marcus was fairly certain that did not include a Jewess.

It was simply the way of things.

"Well," he said after a moment, clapping Peter on the shoulder. "I cannot speak for your father. I do not know what he would allow or what he would not. Personally, I have no quarrel with the Jews. I know many crusading knights cannot say the same thing, but the ones I have known have been congenial and fair. But you do realize that they lead quite a different life from what we do."

Peter lifted his shoulders. "As I said, I've never given them a thought, really," he said. "I remember someone saying, once, that they have horns underneath their skull caps and that they feast on rats."

Marcus rolled his eyes. "Rubbish," he said. "They simply worship differently than we do, and their customs are different, but that is where it ends. If I were you, I would educate myself on Jews before I go any further with these thoughts. And do not mention this to your father, Peter. He has enough on his mind at the moment without his son asking about a religion that may or may not feast on rats."

Peter nodded as Marcus opened the door to the solar and the entryway and great hall appeared beyond. But he paused before he stepped through the opening.

"Uncle Marcus, would you let Michael marry a Jewess?" he asked.

Marcus paused next to him. He was speaking

of his eldest son, a young man who was blossoming into a spectacular warrior. Michael was just
entering manhood, looking and acting very much
like his father. Marcus had five sons in total, the
youngest one being three years of age, but Michael
was the apple of his eye. Still, he pondered Peter's
question seriously.

"I do not know," he said honestly. "All men
hope for advantageous marriages for their sons, so
I do not know. I would want him to be happy, of
course, but I also would not want him to marry
foolishly."

"And you believe marrying a Jew would be
foolish?"

Marcus shook his head. "As I said, I have no
quarrel with them," he said. "But that is not the
first place I would look for a beneficial marriage."

"But why?"

"Ask yourself that question. What can she
bring to a marriage? Is it more than you can? Is it
less?"

Now, Peter was the one pondering the question. "She's beautiful and smart."

"So this is only about her being beautiful and
smart?"

Peter could see where he was going, but he
didn't like it. Marcus was trying to force him to
look at the marriage from all angles, not just
because she was pretty and smart.

Not just because she had a face that mesmerized him.

"Would you say the same thing to me if she wasn't a Jew?" he said after a moment.

Marcus nodded firmly. "Absolutely," he said. "This has nothing to do with being a Jew. But you must understand that their world is very different from ours. They don't necessarily fit into ours and we do not fit into theirs. You would be bringing a woman into a world that she knows nothing about. But let us discuss this more later, Peter. Your father is expecting us, so let's focus on the present."

With his hand still on Peter's shoulder, Marcus headed out into the crowd, taking Peter with him. Even as Marcus ran into Juston de Royans and struck up a conversation right at the entry to the hall, Peter was thinking on what Marcus had advised him.

I would educate myself on Jews before I go any further with these thoughts.

It was good advice. In fact, he knew just who to ask.

If she would even help him.

In any case, it gave him a reason to see her again.

The feast was crowded on this night with a good many de Winter allies which, incidentally, didn't include anyone who sided with the king other than de Winter and de Nerra. These were all rebel barons, all former allies of de Winter who were now simply friends. And friends supped together and drank together, without speaking of politics for the moment, and everyone seemed to be relaxed and enjoying the evening.

Peter had every intention of enjoying himself along with them. He could see Christin and Alexander speaking to Maxton and Caius, men he liked a great deal. Even though Peter was quite a bit younger than they were and had never experienced life and death on the sands of The Levant, Christopher had and by virtue of his father, Peter had been accepted into their closely knit circle. When Peter proved himself by being a fearless, skilled knight, that cemented further bonds.

Peter was an Executioner Knight and very proud of it.

Someone who seemed to be missing on this night was William Marshal. The king had yet to make an appearance and Peter wondered if The Marshal was with the man and would perhaps arrive with him. Ever since the signing of the Magna Carta those few months ago, the dynamics within the Executioner Knights had changed slightly. No one really addressed it other than to say they were all still faithful friends and loyal to The Marshal.

Still… times like this felt very odd.

Inevitably, his thoughts drifted from The Marshal to memories of the afternoon and the brief time he'd spent with Liora. When he should be focusing on the situation at hand because his father was in the middle of a very dicey situation, he found himself thinking of the raven-haired beauty with the wicked little brother. Oh, he could handle little brothers. He had been doing so for years. But the beautiful lass with the cornflower blue eyes… he wondered if he could handle her.

He wondered if he'd even have the opportunity.

As he stood with Christin, Alexander, Maxton, and Caius, he caught sight of his mother near the dais as she spoke to Daveigh's wife, Keeva. It occurred to him that she wasn't speaking to Agnes or Walter de Quincy, both of whom he caught sight of in the same glance. They were near the dais, too, and when they saw Peter looking in their direction, Walter waved and took Agnes by the arm, heading in Peter's direction.

Peter bolted out of that hall as if his arse were on fire.

He didn't care that they had made eye contact. He didn't care that they were smiling and waving at him, greeting him from across the room. Through the smoke and warmth and people crowding the hall, Peter used them like a shield as he made his escape. He slipped past Caius and Maxton, Teviot, his father, and the rest of them as he found himself practically running for the exit. Once outside, he rushed to the group of de Lohr men and horses, finding his trusty steed and mounting swiftly.

And with that, he took off towards London city proper.

He made his escape.

Peter traveled swiftly, passing Westminster Palace and the Thames, and many of the great London manses of warlords that were both siding with the king and against him. He came to the city gates, now being manned by rebel troops and not royal ones, and he was admitted into the city because they recognized his de Lohr tunic. Even in the dark of night, when they usually kept the gates sealed up, they admitted him.

Odd how he seemed to know exactly where he was going.

He was fleeing, indeed, but with a destination in mind.

The moon overhead was cold and bright as he slowed his pace once he entered the city. Even if de Quincy was following him, he might not get past the gate guards and even if he did, Peter was confident he could lose himself on any one of the dozens and dozens of streets and alleys. He was becoming weary of being followed all the time and decided that if his mother couldn't call off Agnes and her father, then he would have to do it personally. He just couldn't keep running like this every time Agnes reared her head. They would have to understand that he simply wasn't interested – and he would have to make sure his father supported that decision.

Truth be told, he wasn't sure if his father did.

He ended up on Lombard Street, heading towards the Aldergate part of the city, when he came upon Milk Street. The little street was quiet and mostly dark at this hour, and his horse's hooves against the dirt echoed softly off the walls. He made his way to Liora's home, a four-storied structure that reached into the sky.

Peter found himself looking to the upper floors where the bedchambers would be. He didn't know which window belonged to Liora, so he didn't chance the usual throwing-pebbles-at-the-window ploy to get her attention. He didn't want to awaken that terror, Asa, or worse, Liora's father. If that happened, things would be over before they had a chance to start. Therefore, he moved around to the small alleyway that ran next to the home, the one that contained the gate leading into the kitchen yard.

For a moment, he paused in the little alley, a smile on his lips as he thought of his encounter with Liora. Such a perfectly angelic woman, beauty beyond compare. He could admit that her beauty had him smitten, but it was her wit that had him hooked. He'd seen beautiful women with the manners of a boar, so it wasn't *all* her beauty.

Well, mostly not.

He spent a few minutes reliving his conversation with Liora before finally deciding he couldn't remain here all night, as much as he wanted to. Begrudgingly, he turned his horse around when a window on the third floor suddenly opened up. Terrified he was about to be seen by Liora's father or even her little brother, he was preparing to ram his spurs into the sides of his animal and take off when a head with long, dark hair appeared.

"Sir Peter?" Liora whispered loudly, incredulously. "What are you doing here?"

Peter found himself gazing up into Liora's beautiful face. Her hair was braided for sleep and she was wrapped in a shawl against the cold night air. When he was over the surprise of realizing she had made an appearance, he smiled weakly.

"How did you know I was here?" he asked.

She cast him a long look. "Because I have ears," she said. "I heard you ride up and you did not ride away, so I peeked from the window and saw you. *What* are you doing here?"

There was that question again, the one he had avoided the first time. He felt like an idiot.

"You would not believe me if I told you," he

said. "I am hiding again."

Liora frowned, but it was one of those frowns that suggested she was trying not to smile. "Good heavens," she said as if he were quite foolish, indeed. "Don't tell me that Lady Agnes is chasing you again."

He nodded slowly and deliberately. "Along with her father," he insisted. "I was only now at a feast where the king was due to arrive and those two chased me right out of the hall. I am fearful they are following me, so I came here. You hid me successfully once before. I was hoping you would do it again."

She shook her head reproachfully, but her smile broke through. "Truly, Sir Peter," she said. "Are you always such a coward when it comes to women?"

"When it comes to *that* woman."

She covered her mouth with a pale hand, chuckling but not wanting him to really see it. Still, he knew, because he was grinning also.

"I cannot admit you to the yard," she said. "My father would be very angry if he found out."

He shrugged, as if he'd known such a thing all along. "Then I suppose I shall have to take my chances," he said. "But I was hoping to at least speak with you again. I very much enjoyed our conversation earlier."

Her smile faded as she looked at him. "That is

kind," she said. "You were in trouble and I gave you shelter. It was the right thing to do."

"I am in trouble now. Will you not give me shelter?"

"I am sorry to say that I do not truly believe you are in trouble."

Peter realized she evidently wasn't as glad to see him as he was to see her. That was a blow to his pride, but it was also a blow to the attraction he felt towards her. He'd been so sure it had been mutual and it was a shock to realize that it wasn't. He struggled not to feel foolish, but in that realization, he thought he should make his intentions clear. Perhaps if she knew, she might realize that he was here because of her – not because he was allegedly being chased by Agnes.

He had nothing to lose by telling her the truth.

"You are correct," he said. "I am not. But I really did run from Agnes on this night. She and her father are attending the same feast that I am, and when I saw them, I ran. But I did not have to come here. I came because I wanted to see you again. My apologies if you do not feel the same way, but never in my life have I seen a more beautiful, witty woman and I simply wanted to talk to you again. Forgive me if this is an imposition, Demoiselle. All you need do is tell me to go away and I shall. I shall not return."

It was a surprisingly little speech and Liora

simply looked at him. In truth, she didn't know what to say. What had been an unexpected but very pleasant encounter with a Christian knight earlier in the day had now taken on dimension and she wasn't quite sure how she felt about it.

How she *could* feel about it.

Peter de Lohr was nothing short of magnificent. With his blond hair, shadings of a beard, and piercing dark eyes, he looked like an archangel. As if he'd just stepped out of the halls of heaven and ended up in her kitchen yard. He was completely out of place in this district, the *kvartal*, and the fact had not been lost on Liora. But he was so glorious and golden that she did what she probably should not have done – she spoke to him.

But she couldn't help herself.

In her world, there were no knights, no great and shining examples of nobles or lords or ladies, so Peter had been an anomaly. Something she'd hardly had any experience in. He was funny, sweet, and the way his eyes glimmered at her made her heart leap strangely. She'd never experienced anything like it in her life.

And just as swiftly as he'd appeared, he'd departed.

But the truth was that she had been thinking of him since she'd met him. All through dinner, helping her mother serve savory soup and boiled beef, she had been thinking about that English knight. Asa had blabbed it to her father, who was curious about it and nothing more. Liora explained what had happened and Haim, who was much more accustomed to knights and lords because they were his customers, simply brushed it off and went on to the next subject.

But not Liora.

Peter had lingered in her mind.

And now, here he was, confessing something that took her completely by surprise. Had she had an ounce of sense, she would have bid him a good evening and shut the window, but she couldn't quite seem to do it.

I simply wanted to talk to you again.

It was enough to make her feel giddy all over again.

"You are always welcome in my father's home," she said, thinking she probably shouldn't say it, but she couldn't stop herself. "It is very late and I am afraid I cannot come out to commiserate with you about Lady Agnes, but I shall be returning from the market early tomorrow morning should you wish to continue this discussion."

Peter grinned. "I do," he said quickly. "But I do not wish to speak of Lady Agnes. *Anything* but her."

Liora smiled, revealing lovely white teeth in a

smile. "Then surely we can find subjects that are more pleasant," she said. "Good evening to you, Sir Peter."

That smile made Peter's knees go weak. Truly, he'd never seen anything so beautiful. "Good evening to you, my lady. Sweet dreams."

Her gaze lingered on him a moment before she pulled the shutters and closed the window. She had the very rare feature of actually having a glass window that opened, so she closed it and pulled the oil cloth. As Peter watched, the faint light in the chamber was snuffed out. Like an idiot, he grinned all the way back to Lonsdale, never giving a second thought that he should probably be heading back to Hollyhock.

But he just didn't care.

With what he had to look forward to tomorrow, he didn't give a lick about anything.

CHAPTER FOUR

"**Y**OU DO NOT seem to understand, Lady Hereford," Walter de Quincy said. "Agnes is very fond of Peter and he is very fond of her. Your husband has all but confirmed that."

Seated at a smaller table below the dais in the very crowded hall of Hollyhock House, Dustin didn't believe Walter for an instant. She'd only met him on a few occasions, when there were events on the Marches that required a gathering of the allies, so her experience with him wasn't vast. But it didn't have to be. Within the first five minutes of the conversation with Walter and his daughter, Dustin could see that the man was a liar and a schemer. For a woman who didn't take well to liars, schemers, or politicians of any sort, it was a struggle for her not to call the man out and insult him to his face.

Desperately, she was trying to be tactful.

"I am quite certain that my husband has not confirmed Peter's interest in your daughter nor his fondness of her, my lord," she said steadily. "In fact, he has sent me on his behalf to speak with you on the matter."

Walter's eyebrows lifted as if he were completely surprised by her attitude. "My lady?"

Dustin held up a hand to ask for his silence and attention. "Please, allow me to finish," she said. "You must understand something about Peter, my lord. He is my husband's eldest son and his marital prospects are great, but I suppose you already know that or you would not be pushing so hard. Permit me to remind you that the harder you push, the more you risk pushing him away."

Walter's expression bordered on insulted. "Push? I am certain I do not know…"

Dustin cut him off. "Stop following him," she said pointedly, looking between Walter and his plain-faced daughter. "Stop sending spies out to find him. Stop following him everywhere he goes. Stop sending him notes at all hours of the day and night. Two nights ago, he received no less than ten messages between sunset and sunrise and it was most disruptive to my household. Truly, you need not pursue him so hard because it is turning him away from the both of you. Did you not see him earlier, running out of the hall when you tried to capture his attention?"

She was mostly looking at Agnes, whose face had flushed a deep, dull red. The girl could hardly look Dustin in the eyes, instead, looking to her father for support and direction in all of this. It was true that she sent Peter notes constantly, but she didn't know that was public knowledge.

Walter tried not to appear too chagrinned.

"We only wished to greet him," Walter said, almost defiantly. "We like Peter a great deal, my lady. Surely you can understand that. And as allies, the House of de Quincy is a staunch supporter of the Earl of Hereford and Worcester. A marriage between our children would cement a great alliance and it is only right that Peter and Agnes come to know one another."

Dustin could see that they simply weren't understanding her. Or, more than likely, they were, but refused to capitulate. What had started out as a polite conversation was becoming increasingly tense. Like a dog with a bone, Walter wasn't going to give up something he clearly considered his due with Peter de Lohr.

She was going to have to be brutally honest.

"Peter has many more opportunities that can make a much more advantageous marriage than your daughter, my lord," she said, all of the politeness out of her manner. "May I be frank?

You behave as if your daughter is the only eligible woman in England and that Peter, and the de Lohrs, somehow owe you something, but that is not the case. Not in the least. Continue to push and behave boorishly, and I promise you that Agnes will not marry Peter. But if you behave as if we are doing you the honor of considering your daughter, I shall say no more about it. It is your choice. However, know this – continue on this path and dear Agnes will have to marry the next fine young man who comes along. Am I making myself clear?"

The Countess of Hereford and Worcester was nothing to be trifled with. Neither Walter nor Agnes liked being spoken to in such a manner, but there was nothing they could do about it. At least, nothing at the moment. Therefore, they had no choice but to agree.

"You are clear, my lady," Walter said, his manner strained as he struggled to remain polite. "You will forgive our eagerness. Peter is a fine young knight and we merely want him to understand our regard for him."

Dustin wasn't falling for the false apology. She simply nodded her head and stood up. "There will be more opportunity for Peter and Agnes to speak, but on our good graces," she said, smiling thinly at the pair. "Heed my words, de Quincy, and back away. Now, enjoy your evening as I rejoin my husband."

Walter politely bid her a farewell, watching her until she was out of earshot. Then, he turned to his daughter.

"The base-born bitch," he muttered. "She cannot speak to me in such a manner. She'll be very sorry for that."

Agnes took a gulp of her wine. She was quite fond of her drink, brought on by a painful lack of self-confidence and an overbearing father. "I told you not to follow him," she hissed. "You sent your men out all over the city to follow him. Did you think he would not know that?"

Walter sneered at her. "I will do what I have to do in order to keep Peter de Lohr close to you," he said. "You're not a beautiful girl, Agnes. Were you prettier, I would not have to go to the great lengths I must go to in order to secure you a husband, so do not blame this on me. This is all *your* fault."

Agnes looked at her father in horror, tears welling in her eyes. "That is a terrible thing to say to me!"

"It is true, God forgive me." Walter listened to her break down into quiet tears, feeling the least bit guilty he'd been so hard on her. The daughter he never wanted, but the child he was stuck with. "Quiet, Agnes. I did not mean it, really. It's simply that Peter *does* have greater prospects than you, so we must give you an advantage that the others do not have. I could lavish Peter with gifts, of course. I have been thinking about that. Mayhap a fine steed in your name? A fine cloak or dagger?"

Agnes wiped at her nose. "All men like fine horses," she said. "They have the horse market here on Saturdays. Mayhap we should select one and have it delivered to Lonsdale?"

Walter sighed heavily, his gaze moving over to the de Lohr clan on the other side of the hall. "We shall have to," he said. "I am not going to let Peter get away from you, Agnes. We will have to do everything within our power to see that he does not."

Agnes simply nodded. She wanted Peter badly, but her father wanted him more. The man had never forgiven Agnes for being born female. He always viewed marriage as his opportunity to welcome a son to the family.

A de Lohr son.

Things were about to get interesting.

CHAPTER FIVE

PETER WAS UP early.

He knew the markets in London were open before dawn, so he was up before the sun rose, heading into London along a cold, dark road that began to turn shades of blue and purple as the sun peeked over the horizon. The road was surrounded by trees, so the birds were up early, making noise and swooping down into the grass along the side of the road in search of a meal.

Not strangely, Peter had lain awake most of the night, wrought with anticipation. He'd pretended to be asleep when his family returned late from Hollyhock House and his mother even checked on him to make sure he was well. He pretended that she had awakened him, assuring her that he was quite well before pretending to go back to sleep.

But he didn't.

He lay awake most of the night, thinking about that magnificent woman with the raven-black hair and the blue eyes, thinking more and more about the Jewish religion and what he didn't know about it. History was rife with persecution of the Jews – he knew that from his early education from the priests in the village of Somerhill where he fostered – but beyond being told they had "killed Christ", he just didn't know that much about them. All he knew was that they were perceived as being different and that didn't sit well with him. When he looked at Liora, he saw a beautiful woman and nothing more. He'd called her a Jewess as one would call him a Christian. It was simply an identifier of religion and culture.

Something he was becoming increasingly interested in.

Of course, he'd only just met the woman. It wasn't like he was determined to marry her tomorrow. But he could only imagine how proud he would be with a magnificent wife like Liora who, according to custom and protocol, wasn't even afforded the honorary address of "lady". That was only reserved for the Christian nobility, not the Jews. He'd called her "Demoiselle" as a polite form of address, but that was the limit of what he could call her.

Somehow, it didn't seem fair.

Liora had told him that she would be back home after her shopping trip this morning, but he couldn't wait that long, hence his trip into London in the early morning hours. He knew that the Jewish market was on Poultry Street, something he'd never been to but, knowing London as he did, he was aware of the districts. It was his intention to head over to Poultry Street and see if he could spy the woman with hair as dark as night. Perhaps the mystery of her had his attention just as much as her beautiful face.

In any case, he was eager to see her.

Peter reached Poultry Street as the sun continued its ascent, bathing the land in its golden glow. Poultry Street, as he immediately saw, was packed with people at this early morning hour as shoppers and vendors converged. It was quite the madhouse and Peter paused at the edge of the lane, knowing he couldn't take his warhorse through the crowd. It would be awkward and perhaps even dangerous for anyone who came too close to the horse, who was battle-trained. Strangers were the enemy. Quickly, he went in search of a livery and found one two blocks away. Paying the man well, he left his horse tethered in a stall as he ran back over to Poultry Street to begin his hunt.

Because the avenue was so jammed with

people, Peter made his way to a small alleyway behind the businesses on the west side of the street. He knew he stuck out like the proverbial sore thumb in a district full of people of different dress and religion. The alley was mostly void of people except for a few vendors throwing aside crates or baskets. The southern end of the market was full of livestock and poultry, but only cows and goats, chickens and turkeys. There were no pigs that he could see. That portion of the road was sectioned off from the rest of the street by a small pathway, and to the north of the pathway were things like vegetables and fruits, and further up towards Catte Street were things like cheese and other food items.

Peter kept a sharp eye out for that dark-haired beauty as he made his way up the rear of the stalls. He kept peering around corners or through slats in the walls, looking at all of the people making their purchases for the day. There were a lot of children running about and as he reached the midway point on the street, he thought he saw Asa with some bigger boys running through the crowds.

Sensing that Liora must be close by, he continued making his way up the street by way of the back alley. When he reached a spice vendor, with the very air filled with the heady smell of a thousand different spices, he thought he caught sight of black-haired lady. He snuck around the spice vendor's shack only to see that, indeed, it was Liora.

His heart leapt at the sight of her.

The sun was rising in the sky and the area was better illuminated now. Liora was with an older woman whose head was wrapped in a tight wimple and another much older woman who was clad in a variety of veils, all of them black. There was a servant following them around, carrying two big baskets that were already half-filled with items. They were heading south, towards the area with the cows and chickens, and Peter followed.

He began to stalk her.

Peter ignored the odd stares he was getting from the people around him as he followed Liora and her little group. He was waiting for just the right moment to reveal himself when he felt a sting to his neck. Something told him that Asa and his boy gang had found him and he whirled around, seeing the boys and their peashooters made from hollow pieces of straw.

Immediately, he set out after them.

When the boys saw the enormous knight bolting in their direction, they scattered. Asa was too slow to move, however, but he managed to release a scream as he slipped in the dirt, regained his footing, and then tore off as fast as he could. Peter was in motion, running around people in the crowd, as he bent over and scooped up some pebbles in the gutter all while he was still running. He managed to fire off three or four of the pebbles at the bigger boys who were running from him before firing off the last one at Asa's head.

"Ow!" Asa yelled as the rock hit him on the back of the neck.

They had just rounded the corner on Catte Street and the boys were running at top speed. Peter came to a halt, watching them dash down the street.

"If I catch you, I will hang you by your feet and throw rocks at your heads!" he shouted after them. "You had better keep running, you foolish whelps!"

They shouted something at him but were too far away to be heard. One of them came to a halt and stuck his tongue out at Peter before continuing on. When they disappeared from view, Peter shook his head with disapproval at the naughty boys and returned to Poultry Street. He could only hope those little ruffians hadn't caused him to lose sight of Liora.

He hurried back to where he had seen her and was relieved to see she hadn't gotten far. She was by herself now, looking in the baskets of a vegetable stall while the women she was with were down the lane a short distance, looking at other things.

Peter saw his chance.

"*Psst!*"

He poked his head around the stall and hissed at her. He did it twice and the second time, she lifted her head, looking around to see where the sound was coming from. She didn't see him, so she looked at her vegetables again until he hissed a third time, loudly, and her head snapped up. She looked right at him and their gazes locked.

Peter smiled broadly and crooked a finger at her.

Surprised, Liora's eyes widened at the sight of him and she looked around to make sure the women she'd come with weren't watching her. Hesitantly, she came around the stall and into the small alleyway behind it where Peter was hiding. She looked at him, shaking her head, perhaps in disapproval.

"What on earth are you doing here?" she said. "I told you that I would be home in a little while. You could have come to the kitchen yard later."

He was smiling at her. In fact, he couldn't seem to stop smiling at her. "I just had to see you," he said. "I did not want to wait. Since I am sure you have no time to speak right now, I was wondering… there is a lovely meadow outside of Cripplegate. Do you know it?"

She cocked her head. "The meadow?" she said. "I do not think so, but I know where Cripplegate is. Why?"

The smile never left his face. "Because I was hoping… my lady, I beg you with all that I am, to meet me at Cripplegate this afternoon and we can take a walk in the meadow and talk." His features were alive with sincerity. "I have so enjoyed speaking to you and that is not usual for me. It is rare that I meet a woman I feel comfortable with conversing and mayhap you will think that I am foolish, but I was hoping we could simply talk. Mayhap you will tell me about your life and how you live it. I am very interested in it. In you. Will you do me the honor?"

Liora was hesitant. That much was clear, but he had asked so sweetly. It wasn't often that she had such a lovely request, from a handsome young knight no less. In fact, it had really never happened and the romantic in her, the young woman who was burdened with a rigid life and little joy, was both intrigued and touched by it.

Truth be told, she had been looking forward to seeing him today, too.

But it was wrong. She knew it was wrong. He was a Christian and she was a Jew, and in that aspect, what he was asking wasn't proper. It was simply a harmless little flirtation between them until he came back for more. Liora was a young woman ruled by reason because it had been drilled into her from a very young age. Reason, responsibility, faith, and duty. That was all she'd ever lived by. But a sweet, handsome knight was appealing to the part of her that longed for something beyond her narrow world.

So much of her wanted to go with him.

"I… I do not know," she finally said. "It is so kind of you to pay attention to me, but mayhap I should not have encouraged you to come and see me again. It was wrong."

The smile faded from his lips. "Why is it wrong?"

She looked around nervously, making sure her mother and grandmother weren't hunting for her. "Sir Peter," she said plainly. "You are an utter delight. When you stumbled into my kitchen yard, I was quite happy to talk to you. It was an enjoyable experience, and when you asked me if you could see me today, I should not have given you encouragement. You realize that we cannot do anything more than we already have. We cannot become… friends. You *do* know that?"

Peter could see that this was going to end before it really got started and that wasn't what he wanted at all. In fact, the mere thought was disappointing him far more than he realized it would.

"Why?" he said. "Because you are a Jewess? All I see is a beautiful woman I want to know better. Whether or not you are Jewish is of no matter to me but, clearly, it matters to you. Given our conversation yesterday and how you behaved towards me, it did not occur to me that it would. I thought you saw the man, not the armor."

Liora could see that she'd offended him. "I did," she said. "I do not care if you are Christian, Jewish, or Muslim. I do not see your religion, Peter, but my parents would see it, as your parents would see mine. So would those around us."

Peter looked at her, realizing that she was trying to force him to see something he didn't want to see. Deep down, he knew that he was being ridiculously blind to it, but he didn't care.

All he saw was a woman he wanted to know.

"Don't you think it only matters what *we* think?" he asked.

She sighed softly, a look of genuine regret on her face. "I wish it were that simple."

"It is if we say it is."

"I think you know that is not true."

He did, only he refused to admit it. He'd never met a woman that he was attracted to that he couldn't have. He was coming to wonder if her forbidden status might make her even more attractive to him. Men always wanted what they could not have but, in this case, he didn't think her forbidden fruit was sweeter. It simply made him more disappointed that it wasn't meant for him.

… or was it?

"Will you do something for me?" he said after a moment. "It will be painless, I assure you."

Liora couldn't look into that face and continue to refuse him. But she couldn't seem to make herself walk away. "What is it?"

"For a moment," he said softly. "For a brief and glorious moment, can we simply be a man and a woman, and have a lovely conversation? It is clear that we can get along well. We saw that yesterday. It is obvious that I am attracted to you and when I want something, I usually get it. Will you put aside your religion for just an hour? Just one hour is all I ask. Let us pretend there are no obstacles at all. I am willing if you are."

She grunted hesitantly. "Sir Peter, I…"

He cut her off, though it was not harshly. "Please, listen to me," he said, lowering his voice. "I told you that my father is the Earl of Hereford and Worcester. At the moment, he is leading the opposition against King John and I am at his right hand. Do you know what that means? I have seen battle after battle as of late and even now, my family is packing up Lonsdale so that we can return to the Marches. My future, at the moment, is nothing but death and war. There is nothing pleasurable that I have to look forward to. If you would simply give me a memory of something sweet and innocent and delightful, something to look upon when the days are dark and the nights darker, then I would be grateful. My world is nothing but warfare, Demoiselle. Will you at least give me a little light to shine upon it, if only for a moment?"

Her hesitation was gone. Of course, he was a knight. She knew that. She'd also known his father was a great earl but hearing him describe the life he lived was heartbreaking. This sweet, handsome man was facing gloom and doom. She barely knew him but, already, she didn't like the idea of what he was facing. The danger he would be in. She knew from her father that the king and his barons were at war against each other, but this was the first time she'd had a face put to that war.

That face was Peter de Lohr.

"At Cripplegate?" she said softly.

A smile tugged at his lips. "Aye," he said. "I will be there at midday. If you will come... I will be there. And if you do not, then I thank you for at least considering it."

She smiled at him, briefly, and quickly turned away, hurrying to find her mother and grand-mother before they realized she was gone and tracked her down. Peter watched her go, wondering if he'd be waiting by himself all afternoon or if she'd make the decision to meet him. At this point, it was all up to her.

He could only wait and see.

CHAPTER SIX

B Y MID-AFTERNOON, PETER was forced to face
the possibility that Liora wasn't coming.

He could have kicked himself, truly. He'd
been so overwhelmed with her beauty and charm
that it took him a while to realize that he'd done to
her what Agnes had done to him – following her
and trying to force a relationship.

He felt like a fool.

Cripplegate was a smaller gate in the walls of
the city of London, but there was a guardhouse
manned with Bigod men who knew him and his
father, so he waited with them inside the
guardhouse, rolling dice and winning a goodly
sum. No one seemed to ask him why he was
spending so much time at Cripplegate, but they all
knew of the king's offer to some of their lords,

properties or titles in exchange for pulling armies out of London. Word traveled fast. Gossip was as important as breathing and according to the Bigod men, several lords were already preparing to pull out, following de Lohr's lead.

Peter learned a lot as he rolled the dice with the men-at-arms.

Even so, his thoughts and his mind were on the gate itself and every person who came or went. He started losing because he was paying so much attention to the people outside the guardhouse that he simply wasn't keeping track of the game. When he finally lost everything that he'd won, he decided to quit and just sat back as the guards continued to play. Shifts came and went as men who were outside came inside, and still, Peter continued to sit and watch the activity even as his mind was on the gate. It took him several hours to realize that she wasn't coming.

Disappointment filled him.

Excusing himself from his new friends, he headed out of the guardhouse, thinking ahead to collecting his horse and heading back to Lonsdale. Mostly, he blamed himself for his misery. He'd pursued a woman who wasn't interested and that was his own damned fault. He tried to console himself with the fact that he never really got to know Liora, so there was no great loss. At least, not really. But he wondered if he wouldn't look back on this time in terms of what could have been. The life he could have had.

The wife he could have had.

But there was no use lamenting what had never really gotten started.

Crossing in front of the gate, he was heading towards White Cross Lane where his horse was stabled. He was just passing out of the line of sight of Cripplegate when he heard someone shouting his name.

"Sir Peter!"

Curious, he stopped in time to see Asa and several other boys heading in his direction. Eyes narrowing, he reached down to pick up a handful of dirt and pebbles from the road, prompting Asa and the boys to come to a halt. Asa held out his hand to him.

"Wait!" Asa said. "We've not come to fight! Lee-Lee has sent me!"

Peter was a half-second from firing off a barrage of pebbles, but Asa's words had him holding his fire. At least for the moment.

He frowned.

"Lee-Lee?" he repeated. "Who is that?"

"My sister."

Peter eyed him and the pack of wild dogs behind him posing as children. "This had better not be a trick," he said.

Asa shook his head. "No trick," he insisted.

"Liora sent me to tell you that she'll come in a little while. She has to help Ima."

"Who is Ima?"

"Mother."

Peter still had the hand with pebbles cocked and ready. He looked over the boys for a moment, his gaze returning to Asa.

"She told you to come and find me?" he asked suspiciously.

"Aye."

"But why?" he said. "I'm sorry to say that you do not seem like the trustworthy type."

Asa frowned. "I can keep a secret," he insisted. "I'm a Maccabee! I will not betray my sister or my friends!"

The child seemed irate that he'd been called untrustworthy. Peter lowered his hand. "What's a Maccabee?"

"A warrior for God," Asa insisted. "Don't you know anything?"

"I know a lot of things, but I don't know about a Maccabee," Peter said sarcastically. "Why should I? My education was Christian. Yours was Jewish. We know different things."

Asa edged a little closer, followed by his gang. Peter was well aware that they were moving closer and he braced himself for an ambush. The pebbles in his hand were still at the ready.

"I saw you when you came to our house," he

said, looking him up and down. "You were dressed like a knight."

"I *am* a knight."

"Where do you come from?"

"From my home, Lonsdale. It's just outside of London, to the west. Next to the river."

"Have you seen a lot of war?"

"I have seen a lot of war."

"Is Lonsdale a castle?"

Peter shook his head. "Not Lonsdale," he said. "But I have another home on the Marches called Lioncross Abbey Castle. It's a very big and powerful castle belonging to my father, an earl. Do you know what that is?"

Asa made a face as if he'd just asked something stupid. "Of course I do," he said. "That's a great lord."

"It is."

"Are you a great lord?"

Peter dropped the pebbles in his hand. "I am a lord, but not a great one," he said. "I am Lord Pembridge, soon to be the garrison commander of Ludlow Castle, one of the largest and finest castles on the Welsh Marches."

Asa digested that, looking him over. "Why do you want to talk to my sister?"

"Because I think she is nice."

"She *is* nice," Asa said. "But she already has a *shaverim*."

"What's that?"

Asa pointed at him. "Like you," he said. "A man she talks to."

Peter's eyebrows lifted. "She is betrothed?" he said, aghast, but realized that Asa didn't understand him. "She is to be married?"

Asa shook his head. "Nay," he said. "Just a friend who is a man. He comes around to talk to her, too. He tells my father he wants to marry her, but Lee-Lee does not want to."

Thank God, Peter thought. "Who is this *shaverim*?"

"A merchant," Asa said. "He sells horses. He is rich. I've heard my father say so."

Peter was getting quite an education about Liora thanks to her little brother. He really wasn't surprised that she had a suitor, although it made him want to track the man down and threaten him. Still, he wasn't surprised to hear that he had competition. With a woman of Liora's beauty, he wouldn't have expected otherwise.

That simply made him want to fight harder.

"As I said, she is very nice to talk to," he said as neutrally as he could. "What does she do all day? In fact, what do *you* do all day other than run around with ruffians and throw rocks at people?"

He thought he was very clever, bringing Asa into the conversation as if he were curious about him, too, and not just Liora. But Asa and his friends started posturing threateningly.

"We protect our street from Saul's Army," he said. "It is my duty."

Peter frowned. "What is Saul's Army?"

"From Wood Street." A bigger boy spoke up, freckles all over his face. "They live on Wood Street and they come to our street and try to steal eggs. We have to fight them off."

"God's Bones," Peter muttered. "Are these grown men?"

Asa shook his head. "Nay," he said. "They are like us, but they bring clubs and try to hit us. We must defend our street."

Peter fought off a grin when he realized the boys were dealing with another boy gang of thieves. It seemed that the Jewish quarter of London was just as bad as the rest of England with battles and enemies.

"I see," he said. "Keep aiming rocks as you do and you should have no trouble chasing them away."

Asa's gaze moved to the big broadsword hanging on Peter's left thigh. "Can we borrow your sword?"

Peter shook his head. "It is as heavy as you are," he said. "It would not do you any good. But the next time Saul's Army comes to steal eggs, send word to me. I'll come and fight them off."

That brought a strong reaction from Asa and

his friends. Their eyes widened and they looked at each other, shocked by the offer.

"A *goy*?" Asa said, surprised. "You would do that?"

"What's a goy?"

"A Christian."

Peter shrugged. "I suppose I would," he said. "But don't call me a goy. It sounds like a disease."

"What do I call you, then?"

Peter did grin, then, unsheathing his broadsword in one smooth motion. "I am *Saint* Peter to you," he said. "They called him the Rock and that is exactly what I am – the Rock. The greatest knight in all Christendom. And don't you forget it."

He swung the sword in a very controlled, very skilled move, one that terrified and impressed Asa and his friends. When Peter ended up pointing the sword in their direction, they took off running frantically in the opposite direction.

Peter just stood there and laughed.

⚃

SHE THOUGHT SHE'D never escape her mother and grandmother.

Liora had spent the day with them, preparing for the Sabbath feast as they always did on this day of the week, but today was different.

She had somewhere to be.

Her mother had put her on kitchen duty, directing the servants as they prepared the bread and roast chicken for the Sabbath, so she'd been stuck in the kitchen for most of the day. As the sun began to make its journey across the sky and afternoon came, she thought she might be able to slip away, but her mother and grandmother were busy with their own tasks and making sure she was tending to hers.

At one point in the afternoon, she managed to capture Asa and told him to go to Cripplegate, to the knight who had been at their home the day before and tell him that she would be delayed. Asa was many things, but flighty he wasn't. He also wasn't a tattletale, at least where his sister was concerned, making him an oddly dependable messenger. As Asa headed off, Liora continued with her duties, hoping that Peter would understand her delay. It was only later in the afternoon, with a few hours before supper yet, that her mother and grandmother went to lie down for a while, resting from the busy day.

That's when Liora bolted.

Truthfully, Cripplegate wasn't very far away from her home. Clad in a gown of deep amber with a golden tassel belt around her slender waist and a silken yellow scarf draped over her head and shoulders, Liora moved quickly to Cripplegate, staying clear of the carriages and wagons and groups of people moving about their business. She was out of the Jewish district now and feeling nervous, so she kept her head down and the scarf across her mouth to shield her features. Though it was traditional for Christian, unmarried ladies to let their hair flow and keep it uncovered, Jewish law required that Liora cover her head when she was out in public.

It also kept her somewhat shielded from the Christian rabble around her. Although she'd never had trouble with the great population of London, the truth was that she spent almost all of her time in the Jewish quarter, so venturing out was a little frightening. She kept her focus on Cripplegate as it came into view.

At this time of day, the gate was still open and people were coming in and out. To the north, on the other side of the gate, were mostly farmlands and moors. There were a few churches and monasteries north of the wall, set in fields that could be glorious and green when the sun was shining, but turned into giant swamps with the rain and the cold. Though Liora didn't know that personally, she'd heard her father speak on it.

Truth be told, she had lived a rather sheltered life.

As she approached Cripplegate, she noticed movement in the shadows near the gate itself and turned to see Peter emerging from the shadow of the wall. She came to a sudden halt as he headed right for her.

"Demoiselle," he greeted with a warm glimmer in his eyes. "Your message was received. Asa and his band of misfits found me and told me."

Liora had been nervous, hesitant about meeting Peter until this very moment. Gazing up at him, she realized that she was glad to see him. Something about that big, muscular, golden god of a man had her heart thumping madly.

"I am glad," she said. "I told him not to shoot you with a pebble to get your attention. Did he behave himself?"

Peter nodded. "Surprisingly, he did," he said. "I must admit that I was a little concerned that you sent him after me. I'm assuming you do not wish for your parents to know that you had an appointment with a Christian knight. And you are sure he will not tell them?"

She shook her head. "Asa and I have a special bond," she said. "Moreover, pay the lad a pence and he'll do anything, including keeping his lips shut."

Peter snorted. "He's a born mercenary."

"He is, indeed." A short, slightly awkward silence followed. "You said you wished to walk in a meadow?"

Peter had been staring at her, dreamily, completely forgetting that he had an agenda. All he wanted to do was look at her. But her question had him on the move.

"Aye," he said quickly, reaching out to politely take her elbow. "Shall we?"

Liora let him escort her out of the gate, into the wide-open space beyond. To the east were the moors, a swampy area that contained water run-off from the lands to the north, all of it draining against the wall. In ancient times, before the Romans built the wall, it was a natural drainage slope to the river. Because of that depression, however, the lands near Cripplegate were unfettered with water or marshes, and there was an attractive field between the wall and a farm to the north.

It was September, a time just past the heat of summer and heading into the cool, rainy autumn season. The weather was surprisingly fine and the grass of the meadow was fat and green. Autumn wildflowers popped up near the road and in bunches across the field, small blue dots beneath the clear sky.

"Well?" she said as they walked casually along the road. "What did you wish to talk about?"

Peter looked at her, smiling. "You," he said simply. "I want to know about you."

"What do you wish to know?"

"Everything," he said. "Anything. Did you

foster as a child?"

Her brow furrowed as she pulled the scarf away from her neck because it was growing warm in the sunshine. "Foster?" she repeated. "You mean when you are educated somewhere other than your home?"

"Exactly."

She shook her head. "I did not foster," she said. "But I am educated. My father saw to that. The rabbis at the Great Synagogue educate children. I can read and write in several languages. I can also do arithmetic and I am very good at geography."

He looked at her with great interest. "Do you paint? Or sing?"

She shrugged. "Not really," she said. "But I am very good at sewing."

"What do you do for entertainment?"

She clasped her hands behind her back as she walked. "I like to read," she said. "I read quite a lot. And I have friends next door, girls I grew up with. We spend a good deal of time together."

"Asa told me that you have a suitor."

She looked at him sharply, her pale eyes studying him in surprise. He looked at her, realizing her eyes were such a shade of blue that they were almost lavender. It was astonishing.

"Why would he tell you such a thing?" she asked. "Did you ask him?"

He shook his head. "Not at all," he said. "That would be prying and it is none of my affair. It simply came up in conversation. Are you betrothed to the man?"

Liora seemed to get a little defensive. "If I was, I would not be here with you," she said. "You must not think well of me if you think I would be caught alone with one man when I was betrothed to another."

He came to a stop and faced her. "That could not be further from the truth," he said frankly. "I think very highly of you. I was simply making conversation but I see that you have taken offense. Forgive me."

She eyed him before continuing on. "I should not have snapped," she said. "If you must know, I have known Gideon ben Ehud for many years. But that is where it ends, at least for me. He, on the other hand, does not seem to share my view."

"I see," he said. "Then his attention is unwelcome?"

"Not exactly," she said. "He is a nice man and he is wealthy. He buys and sells horses in London. But I do not want to marry him."

"He has asked?"

"Many times."

"And you have refused?"

"Many, *many* times."

Peter walked alongside her, pretending to be

looking at his feet as he walked, but he kept glancing over at her when he thought she might not be looking. He was rather glad to hear what she thought of this Gideon and the fact that she was keeping him at arm's length. Gideon's failure was his joy.

"Were you educated together?"

"Nay, because he is older than I am," she said. "Now, that is enough talk about me because, truthfully, I am very dull. Nothing exciting ever happens in my life, but you... *you* have a very exciting life, I would imagine."

He shrugged, lifting his head and looking off across the field towards the east. "I am not certain I would call it exciting," he said. "Unless you are speaking of being chased by a woman I cannot seem to get off my scent. That is not exciting – it is annoying."

Liora grinned. "Was she still hunting you last night after you left my home?"

He shook his head. "I went straight back to Lonsdale and avoided the situation altogether," he said. "However, I did get a bit of interesting news yesterday."

"Oh?" she said, looking at him. "What is it?"

He glanced over at her. "You must not repeat it."

"I will not, I swear it."

Peter came to a halt, planting his feet apart

and resting his big fists on his hips. "It seems that my father is being given more property from the king," he said. "I told you that my home is in the Welsh Marches, did I not?"

"You did."

"Do you know much about the Marches in general?"

She shrugged. "Only what I have heard in passing from others," she said. "My life has been spent in London. In fact, other than a journey to Oxford a few years ago, I have never left this city."

His eyes glimmered at her. "Then you have missed a great deal," he said. "There is a whole, big country out there, and a good portion of it borders with Wales. That is my father's domain and my domain, and as of last night, my father has been given four important properties on the Marches and I shall be the garrison commander of Ludlow Castle, one of the largest castles in England. The place is massive."

Liora appeared suitably impressed. "How very proud you must be," she said. "I congratulate you. It *is* cause for congratulations, isn't it? If it is not, then I take it all back."

He laughed softly. "It is cause, indeed," he said. "The appointment alone will make me a wealthy man. I will command a thousand men."

"Is that what you meant earlier when you said your world is war?"

His smile faded. "Aye," he said. "The entire country is at war against itself and along with my father, I am part of that."

She cocked her head curiously. "I have never been around a fighting man much less a knight," she said. "Of course, we see them riding through London constantly and many of them are customers of my father's business, but I have never actually met one until now. The life you men lead… it is puzzling to me."

"What confuses you?"

She lifted her shoulders. "All of it," she said. "You swear an oath to fight for England, yet you make war against your own king. Why?"

He folded his enormous arms across his chest. "That is a question without an easy answer," he said. "John is not a good king. He is greedy, petty, and dishonest. Is that the kind of man who should sit upon the throne?"

"Nay," she said thoughtfully. "But it is his right."

"Is it his right to cheat his vassals?"

"Of course not."

"Then you must consider that men like my father and I are standing up for justice," he said. "We believe the king should be fair to everyone and John does not want to be fair. That is a very simplified reason for taking a stand against him, but it sums it up well enough."

"Then you are not trying to take his crown?"

"Of course not. As long as he rules fairly, that is all we ask."

"And if he does not?"

"Then men like my father will do what needs to be done."

Liora considered that, looking over her shoulder to the city and its enormous walls. "I remember when the warlords laid siege to the Tower of London earlier this year," she said. "We were very frightened. There were so many armies in London at that time. I do not think we came out of the house for an entire month. There are still armies here, but not like there used to be."

Peter looked at the city because she was, but his gaze moved back to her. That creamy complexion, pert nose, and striking coloring was enough to turn him into a giddy squire. But that sharp mind was the one quality that had his true attention.

"The armies will be pulling out soon," he said, somewhat quieter. "I told you earlier that we are returning to the Marches. My father is pulling his army out as we speak."

She turned to look at him. "And you are going, too?"

"Aye."

"Will you return to London soon?"

He shook his head. "Nay," he said. "I will be

assuming command of Ludlow as soon as we return, so I do not know when I will return to London at all."

She almost said something in response, but evidently thought better of it. Peter was rather hoping she might say something that could possibly suggest she might be sorry he was leaving, but she didn't. She simply forced a smile.

"Then I will pray for your safety and health," she said. "You are a warrior for good, Sir Peter, and that takes a man of noble character and great bravery. Even if you do run from a woman."

Peter snorted at the last part. "It is not cowardice in that case, but intelligence," he said. "It is a smart man who avoids Agnes de Quincy at all costs. But I will always be grateful to her for one thing."

"What is that?"

"I would have never met you had she not been after me," he said. "In a sense, she has introduced us."

Liora laughed softly. "That is one way of looking at it."

Peter opened his mouth to reply, but a bell pealed in the distance and they both looked towards the city, listening to it ring off four peals, denoting the hour. It was nearing the supper hour and Peter sighed faintly.

"I suppose I must take you back now," he said.

Liora nodded. "I suppose," she said. "The Sabbath is tomorrow and our evening meal will soon be upon us."

"What is the Sabbath?"

"The holy day in the week."

"Do you go to mass? Or, the Jewish equivalent of mass?"

She nodded. "Aye," she said. "It is a day of rest, mostly. Chores, even cooking, are forbidden, so tonight we eat well and tomorrow, we will eat things that do not require cooking. You do not have a day like this?"

"Sunday is church day for us," he said, turning her back for the gate. "We can cook and feast, and we do. It seems as if Jews have many rules."

"Enough," she said. "But having been raised in the faith, I am used to them."

"Do you ever wonder what the world is like outside of your faith?"

"Nay," she said. "I am happy in my faith. Are you happy in yours?"

Peter thought of Pandulf at that moment, the papal legate who had threatened to excommunicate the English warlords last night for their opposition to a king who used the church when it suited him.

That reflection gave him pause.

"I'm not sure," he said honestly. "Sometimes there is a good deal of politics involved in the

Catholic Church, like now."

She looked at him curiously. "Oh? Has something happened?"

He didn't want to repeat what had happened last night. That wasn't common knowledge, so he wasn't going divulge that to a woman he'd just met, no matter how infatuated he was with her.

"Nothing unusual," he said. "I do not know how the Jewish religion is, but sometimes Christianity has its… issues."

"Like Richard's great crusade to the Holy Land?"

He shook his head. "That whole country is a chaotic mess," he said. "The Muslims held Jerusalem and the Christians went to purge them. But the Jews live there because, historically, Jerusalem belongs to the Jews. So much fighting over that sandy, hot land. My father spent years of his life there. He said it was futile."

Liora thought on her hereditary homeland. "There have been troubles there throughout history," she said. "Before the Christians and Muslims, it was the Romans and the Egyptians. But I would still like to go there, someday, and visit the Great Temple. It is a pilgrimage for every person of the Jewish faith."

Peter had ended up walking closer to her, reaching out to take her elbow as he walked. It was a polite gesture, although a bold one, but he simply wanted to touch her. He couldn't help himself because something told him that after this day, seeing her might not come easily again, if ever.

He wanted to remember it.

"I thought that I might like to journey there, as well, to revisit the places where my father fought battles," he said. "Truthfully, it seems like a great adventure, but I know it wasn't as glorious as some men make it out to be. My father said it was hell most of the time. He lost many friends there."

They were nearing the gate at this point and Peter slowed his pace. He simply didn't want to take her home any sooner than he had to. If Liora noticed, she didn't let on. She slowed down right along with him.

"It is not the land that is hell, but the men who make hell on earth there," she said. "No land is inherently evil. It is the men who are evil."

"Very true," he said. "But men like my father are not evil. He goes to battle to fight evil, in response to a wrong or a terrible action. My father is the most noble man you will ever meet and, someday, I hope you do."

She smiled up at him. "I would like that," she said. "Mayhap someday there will be an opportunity."

They were passing through the gate now even as Peter slowed his pace even more. They entered the city with its inhabitants going about their business. Since night was approaching, there were less people on the streets. Peter finally came to a halt and let go of her elbow, facing her.

"I cannot tell you how grateful I am that we had a few moments to speak," he said. "I am very sorry that it must come to an end."

Liora was still smiling up into his handsome face. "Sabbath is beginning," she said. "It was all the time I could spare."

"And you were most gracious to do so," he said. He hesitated a moment before continuing. "Demoiselle… as I told you earlier today, I will be heading back for the Marches very soon, to a future of uncertainty, and this time with you has been some of the better time I have ever spent. Any hour with you is a splendid one."

Her smile softened at his sweet words. "You are very kind to say so."

"It is not kindness I give you, but truth," he said. "You have indeed given me something to remember when the days and nights are dark and dismal. But I was hoping… and mayhap it is a foolish hope… to see you again before I go."

Liora looked at him with much less resistance than she'd displayed earlier, but it was still evident. "Why?" she finally said. "I told you that we can never be friends. What we are doing now is greatly frowned upon. We should simply part and remember a few pleasant moments well spent."

He was nodding even before she finished. "I know," he said. "But I do not want this to end. Demoiselle, if you were a lass from a good Christian family, I would be speaking to your father at this very moment about courting you. You're unlike any woman I've ever met before. You're wise and bright, and beautiful beyond measure. I have alluded to his before, but now I will state it plainly. I want to call upon you, Liora, daughter of Haim. I want to come to know you better."

Her eyes widened as he spoke and by the time he was finished, she was backing away. "You cannot," she said, clearly upset. "Sir Peter, you…"

"Please – *just* Peter."

She sighed sharply. "*Sir* Peter, what you ask is impossible," she said. "You *know* it is impossible. It is my fault for agreeing to see you again. I should have never done that because it has given you hope where there is none. What you are asking can never be."

He watched her move away from him. "Will you answer one question for me?"

She was several feet away, but at least she'd come to a halt. "I do not know until I hear the question."

"That is fair," he said. "Then here is the question – do you find anything attractive about me?"

Her eyes widened again. "That is a bold question."

"Answer it. Please."

She was shaken, off-balance. She began moving away from him again. "I will *not* answer it," she said. "You have no right to ask it and I will not answer it."

He watched her as she took more steps away from him. "Then I will not ask it again," he said. "Clearly, I am the only one who feels any attraction between us and I am very sorry if I have made you uncomfortable. That was never my intention. Liora, I wish you a good life. You deserve the best of everything, for always, and I hope you find a husband who will worship you as the goddess you are. And I hope you will remember me with pleasant thoughts and not aversion. Forgive a man who was so smitten with you that it overwhelmed his common sense."

With that, he walked past her, heading for the livery where his horse had been stabled. It was one of the hardest things he had ever had to do. He simply kept walking, feeling disappointment as he'd never felt in his life. He knew she was right; what he was asking *was* impossible. But Peter simply didn't believe in the impossible. If there was a will, there was a way, but she had to want it, too.

Clearly, she didn't.

He was simply going to have to accept it.

He gathered his horse at the livery but as he emerged from the stable, he saw Liora standing near the corral. Surprisingly, she had followed him, but he wasn't sure he wanted to hear what she had to say. She had already been quite clear. He paused a moment, his gaze lingering on her, before going to meet her.

"Can I be of further service?" he asked neutrally.

Liora was looking at him with those eyes. The woman could positively hypnotize with them. "I..." She paused, swallowed hard, and started again. "You asked me a question and I will be honest with you. When I first saw you, I thought you looked like an archangel. You look as if you have just stepped out of the halls of heaven and to think someone like you should pay attention to someone like me... I still cannot grasp such a thing. Nay, Peter, you are not the only one who felt the attraction between us. I feel it, too. I feel it greatly. But you are a Christian knight and I am not meant for you."

Her words restored his soul. At least, most of them did. "Please," he murmured. "Let me speak with your father."

She shook her head. "He would only send you away. It would not do any good."

"May I at least take the chance?"

She was greatly torn. "It is not that simple," she said. "We are from two different worlds and…"

He cut her off. "And I am perfectly willing to learn about yours," he said. "I am willing to do what it takes so that I may see you again. I will…"

She put her fingers over his mouth to silence him. Peter couldn't help it; he grasped her wrist and kissed those fingers. Soft, warm, gentle fingers.

It was enough to set him on fire.

"Please," she whispered, trembling at the feel of his lips against her flesh. "Go home and think rationally about this. I must think, too. If you are very serious, then I must speak to the rabbi about this before you can speak with my father. People in my culture do not court simply to pass the time. It is with a purpose in mind."

"Agreed. It *is* done with a purpose in mind."

Her eyes widened when she realized what he meant – marriage. It was absolutely shocking but completely, utterly wonderful. And pure madness, were she to think on it. None of this made any sense.

He didn't make any sense.

But she was coming to like that about him – this impetuous, sweet, golden boy.

"I do not know how this is possible," she said, growing animated. "You have only just met me.

How can you even suggest such a thing?"

"Because I know what I want. I do not need a week, a month, or a year to decide. When it feels right to me, that is all I need."

"And this... *me*... feels right?"

He smiled. "You do. And that is why I want to see you again."

He couldn't have been plainer, but still, she struggled with it. "Intermarriages are discouraged to say the least."

He kissed her fingers again and removed them from his lips. "Discouraged, but not impossible," he said. "I want to speak to the rabbi, too. May I come with you? It is true that I do not understand about your culture, so may I come so that I may understand?"

She closed her eyes, grunting softly at his gentle persistence. It was breaking her down. "Let me think about this tomorrow," she said. "Please do not come around. Just let me... think."

"And then we will speak?"

"Then we will speak."

He seemed satisfied by that, but he looked at her seriously. "I told you that I do not know when we are heading back to the Marches," he said. "If it looks as if it will be in the next few days, I will be back sooner rather than later. Do you understand?"

She nodded with regret. Not that she didn't

want him to come back, because she did. But she very much needed to think clearly about all of this. The handsome knight and his charming manners were overwhelming her and she needed to gather her wits without him hanging over her shoulder.

Being with the man seemed to suck the wits right out of her.

Peter winked at her and mounted his steed, indicating for her to head home. She did, but he plodded along behind her, making certain that she made it to Milk Street safely. When he saw her head towards her house, he whirled his horse about and headed to Lombard Street, which would take him out of the city.

She had some thinking to do. Frankly, so did he. The infatuation had turned into something else, something that could potentially get him into trouble, but he didn't care in the least.

Perhaps that was the biggest problem of all.

CHAPTER SEVEN

Lonsdale House

BUILT FROM WHITE granite and gleaming like the heavenly halls along the blue ribbon of the Thames, Lonsdale House was a jewel in the de Lohr crown.

Seated on a bend in the river, Christopher had designed the house so that all of the bedchambers and most of the living chambers had a view of the river. There was also a river gate so lord and ladies could anchor their river barges and visit, but there was still a great deal of security with tall walls and turrets for viewing. Nothing was left to chance.

The Earl of Hereford and Worcester made sure his family would be amply protected.

The front of the house faced the road that went all the way from London to Southampton. It was a well-traveled road and travelers greatly admired the great white-stoned de Lohr bastion, from its imposing gatehouse with the lion-head corbels to the four-story manse it protected. There were those in the inner circles who chuckled about the manse because it was well known that the de Lohrs already had a very nice London townhome called Bellham Place that David de Lohr, the Earl of Canterbury, had mostly taken over. Lonsdale was Christopher's response to Bellham to show his brother that he could do it bigger and better. In response, David had added a massive wing to Bellham that was very nearly done.

It was the battle of the building brothers on the outskirts of London.

Evening had softly fallen on the day that had seen Peter and Liora walk near Cripplegate and Peter had made it back to Lonsdale with time to spare before the feast that night. After leaving his horse to be tended in the stables, he entered the massive, heavily fortified front door of the manse only to run headlong into Marcus and Alexander, who were standing before the hearth in the entryway, speaking softly.

"Where have you been?" Alexander asked. "I've not seen you all day."

Peter wasn't sure how much to tell them. In fact, he wasn't sure he wanted to say anything in front of Alexander, as much as he loved the man.

It would be one less person to tell him he was doing something foolish. Therefore, he tried to brush it off with a half-truth.

"In London," he said. "I've been thinking about having a new dagger made for Papa for Christmas. Where is the old man, anyway?"

That was sort of the truth. He'd spoken about it before, in the past, but he'd not done anything about. He still hadn't, but it was a good cover. In answer to his question, Alexander pointed towards the grand solar that had a view of the entire bailey.

"In there," he said, lowering his voice. "He has the documents from John for Fitz Walter to surrender Ludlow, Wigmore, and the other two."

Peter looked at him in surprise. "John actually did what he said he was going to do?"

As Alexander and Marcus nodded, Marcus spoke up. "It seems that most of the major warlords received offers today. John is serious about holding up his side of the bargain to get us out of London."

Peter wasn't naïve. He understood the greater implications of the move. "And he's allowing his rebels to gain even more properties to fortify against him," he said. "I wonder if he ever stopped to think about that?"

Marcus snorted. "Probably," he said. "But we know he has French and Teutonic mercenaries arriving in England, so I am sure des Roches is telling him that pawning off a few castles is not going to hurt his cause. And that is where he would be wrong."

Peter looked at the man. "And you?" he said. "What do you get?"

Before Marcus could answer, Christopher was standing in the doorway of his solar. "I thought I heard you, Peter," he said. "Come in here. I must speak with you. Marcus, you and Sherry come as well."

All three of them headed into Christopher's solar, which was the last chamber in the entire manse that Dustin hadn't been allowed to furnish. She'd had fifty-seven other chambers to furnish, including children's rooms, ladies' rooms, kitchens, a feasting hall, smaller halls, and on down the line, but when it came to Christopher's solar, he'd drawn a line in the sand that she wasn't allowed to cross.

Therefore, the furnishing could be called spartan.

It was a two-storied chamber, with a gallery above, shelves for Christopher's maps and documents, and a stone hearth that had two great lions carved into it. The hearth was as tall as a man, an enormous thing, and the chamber itself was quite grand with the paneled walls and wooden floor, but there was a table in it, a couple of chairs, and that was about it. No rugs, no wall tapestries, no nothing. That solar was the butt of many jokes for the man who had spent a fortune to build it but refused to spend more money to properly furnish it.

"Papa," Peter said as he ended up sitting on the floor because Marcus and Alexander had the only two chairs in the chamber. "Will you please let Mama have more furnishings made for this room? I'm a grown man and I must sit on the floor like a child because you will not have enough chairs in here."

Christopher fought off a grin. "You *are* a child," he said. "You are my child. And sitting on the floor is good for your bones."

Marcus and Alexander started to chuckle. "Just admit you are too cheap to spend the money," Marcus said. "I've known you most of your life. You were always miserly, but it is no more readily apparent than it is now. For the love of God, Chris, buy a few more damned chairs."

Christopher was over by the table, eyeing the documents that the king's messenger had brought over earlier in the day. "Nay," he said flatly. "I do not want men to come into this chamber and be comfortable. I want them to feel edgy and unwelcome."

Marcus cocked an eyebrow. "Well, they do," he said. "You have accomplished your goal."

Christopher looked up from his table. "That is

not true," he said. "*You* are still here."

In response, Marcus kicked out his legs and settled back on the chair like he was going to sleep in it. Christopher couldn't help but grin at his cheeky friend as he returned his focus to the documents on the table.

"Peter, I thought you might like to know that I have the document instructing Fitz Walter to turn control of Ludlow over to me," he said. "I will send you to Ludlow with this document to present to him. Or would you rather I go with you?"

"I can go," Peter said. "I am capable of standing up to Fitz Walter should he resist, but I intend to take a thousand men with me. Will you spare them?"

Christopher nodded. "I can," he said. "But I would feel most comfortable sending Sherry and mayhap Maxton with you just to make sure Fitz Walter doesn't kick about it. He'll be less apt to do it when he's faced with more than one Executioner Knight. When Ludlow is secure, then the three of you can go over to Wigmore and follow the same process."

"Have you decided who you intend to put in command of Knighton and Risbury?" Peter asked.

Christopher nodded. "Cassian will make a fine commander of Knighton," he said. "Remember that Jax has five castles along the Welsh Marches that are still his properties, so having Cassian at

Knighton will further ally us with his father, securing the border even more than it already is. And Addax will do very well at Risbury. He is a brilliant commander and an excellent communicator."

"I'm curious, Chris," Marcus said. "Addax and Essien are clearly not indigenous to England and I've not seen them in many years, but I would assume they get along with everyone. If you are going to put Addax in command of a garrison, I would guess that he has been well-accepted by all?"

Christopher knew what he meant. The Kitara princes had dark hair and eyes and lacked the pale skin that was prevalent to those with Norman or Anglo heritage. They spoke with an accent whose origins were from their native language, something that made them different from the traditional English knight. But he nodded in response.

"Absolutely," he said. "It does not matter that they were not born here. They have proven themselves time and time again, and The Marshal has even used them as part of his spy ring because they are quite cunning, especially with women. I cannot count the number of women Essien has seduced. That is why they came to England, you know. They were serving a great Flemish lord but an angry father forced their liege to send them away, if you get my meaning."

Marcus grinned. "Essien was always a silver-tongued devil, even as a lad," he said. "Addax, too, but he had more sense than his younger brother had. Mayhap I shall travel back to Lioncross with you so that I may see them before I head north."

"Come along if you wish," Christopher said. "You have a property to inspect, too, do you not?"

Marcus nodded. "My offer came this morning," he said. "John is proposing to gift me with Selby Castle, a small castle outside of Leeds. I seem to recall that it is in a terrible state, so it may not be as big as Wigmore or Ludlow, but it comes with a good deal of land and several villages. It is quite lucrative. I can reinforce it and make an excellent garrison out of it."

"One more castle to hold against John."

"Exactly."

"I fear we are going to need it, especially in the north."

Marcus nodded slowly. "More than you know," he muttered. "Chris, de Velt and de Bourne, and de Longley have been in discussions with the King of Scotland for his support against John. Did they tell you this?"

Christopher nodded. "I knew of it," he said. "Jax mentioned something about it. But I've not been told if that alliance is firm."

"Did de Velt tell you that he is willing to

return Berwick to Alexander in exchange for his support against John?"

Christopher's eyebrows lifted in surprise. "He's not told me that," he said. "I expect him and the others later this evening and we shall most definitely discuss it. Berwick Castle, you say?"

"John is willing to bargain with properties and so are we."

Peter sat on the floor, back against the wall, listening to his father and Marcus discuss the coming crisis. While John was still at odds with the rebelling warlords, he put on a public face of negotiation while secretly, he was bringing mercenaries to England's shores. Or not so secretly; the warlords knew what he was doing and they were preparing with properties John himself was giving them, apparently now with the added support of the King of Scotland.

That was going to change the situation quite a bit.

As Peter listened to his father and Marcus and Alexander discuss the coming implications, his thoughts inevitably turned to Liora. His father was making plans for his future, sending him to command an enormous castle on the Marches, something that would take all of his time and focus. He didn't mind going, for this was what he'd been trained for his entire life. He knew that the name de Lohr brought great expectations. But what he didn't like was the fact that it would mean leaving Liora just when he was coming to know her. Hell, he didn't know her at all and he knew that, but he was loath to surrender the momentum of the moment.

Off to the wilds of the Welsh Marches and leaving behind the blue-eyed beauty he was so smitten with. He debated about keeping silent on it, but the more he listened to his father and Marcus speak, the more he realized that he didn't want to keep silent. He was feeling something he'd never felt before and he needed advice.

Something inside him had awakened.

He couldn't seem to keep it quiet any longer.

"May I interrupt?" he asked, watching his father and Marcus and Alexander turn to him. "Forgive me, but I have something on my mind that does not have to do with the king and rebellions and warfare and I am afraid if I do not speak of it now, I may never have another chance. Will you hear me?"

Christopher looked at him curiously. "Of course, Peter," he said. "What is it?"

Now, the focus was on him and he was sorry he'd spoken up. But then again, he wasn't. He didn't know what he felt, only that he felt compelled to speak of what he was feeling. He wasn't impulsive by nature but, in this instance, he was. There was something inside of him that needed to be heard. Looking at his father, he said the first thing that came to mind.

"I've met a woman," he said simply.

Christopher stared at him a moment before a smile spread across his bearded lips. "Is that so?" he said. "You? I do not believe it."

"It's true."

"Then I'm intrigued. Tell me more."

Peter tried to think of how to follow up that brilliant first statement. He wasn't very good at talking about what he was feeling, although it had come rather easily with Marcus because Marcus wasn't his father, who could be an emotional man. He looked to Marcus, who was gazing back at him with an expression that suggested he wasn't pleased that Peter had spoken up. He'd told Peter not to bother his father with this infatuation because Christopher had enough to deal with, but Peter couldn't seem to keep his mouth shut.

"I met her yesterday," he said. "I was riding escort to some of the warlords entering London for the conference at Hollyhock, but I caught sight of Agnes de Quincy and her father and that sent me running for cover. I ended up in a kitchen yard belonging to the most beautiful woman I have ever seen. Papa... she has hair the color of a raven's wing and eyes the color of the sky. I have never seen such magnificence. She is witty, intelligent, compassionate... she is perfect."

Christopher was very much enjoying his son's confession, a welcome respite from all of the war chatter. Peter, who swore repeatedly that he had no time for women and was most resistant to any suggestion of a betrothal, was apparently not so oblivious to women as he pretended to be.

"I am pleased," he said. "What is her name?"

"Liora."

"Family name?"

Peter avoided the question. "She has a little brother named Asa who runs with a gang of little street toughs," he said, chuckling. "The boy is about seven or eight years of age. Douglas and Myles could learn something from this lad. He shoots pebbles with surprising accuracy and evidently has enemies in a similar boy gang on the next street. I've not met her father or mother yet, but they live in London. That's actually where I was today... I was with her. We were simply talking, of course, but just being in her presence made me feel like a giddy squire. I've never felt that way in my life."

Christopher was still grinning, listening to his son speak of an infatuation that clearly thrilled him. "I seem to remember feeling that way in my life," he said. "As if you are walking on clouds."

"I have been walking on clouds since yester-day."

"Do not keep me in suspense, then," Christopher said. "Who is this woman's family?"

"She's perfect, Papa."

"I understand that."

"She is also Jewish."

Christopher blinked and the smile faded from his face. "Jewish?" he repeated. "You know this for certain?"

"Her father is King John's jeweler."

Christopher's smile vanished completely. He didn't say anything for a moment, but it was clear he was mulling things over. "The king's jeweler, if it is the one I am thinking of, was Richard's jeweler also," he said. "I only know this because Richard once sent me to collect something from the man many years ago. Haim ben Thad is the name, if I recall correctly. Is this the same man?"

"It must be because she said her father's name was Haim," Peter said, but he could see that his father wasn't so thrilled with the conversation any longer. "Papa, I know this is not ideal and given I have only met her yesterday, I should not even be speaking to you about her, but she's different from the other women I have known. She is not spoiled by fostering in great homes where they teach the girls how to be petty and selfish and vain. She can read and write several languages, so she's scholarly. She is warm and humorous, and her beauty... Papa, you've never seen such beauty in your life. Everything about her sings to me and, like the siren's call, I am drawn to her."

"*Drawn* to her?" Christopher repeated, frowning. "That's all well and good, lad, but men like you do not cavort with the jeweler's daughter. You enjoyed the company of a pretty woman today, so leave it at that."

"But I don't want to leave it at that," Peter insisted. "Why should I have to? She's a cultured, elegant, beautiful woman. Why *must* I leave it at that?"

Christopher leaned forward on the table, looking at him without a hint of warmth. After a moment, he simply lifted his eyebrows. "Surely you cannot be serious about this," he said. "What more do you want?"

"To court her."

Christopher shook his head firmly. "A Jewess? Lad, you know that the Christians and the Jews do not mix, or if they do, they do not mix well. Her religion, her heritage, is entirely different from yours."

"That does not mean I cannot learn about it," Peter said, pushing himself up from the floor and standing on his feet. "That does not mean that I cannot understand it and understand her."

"And then what? Do you really think that simply understanding her and her religion will make for a good marriage?" Christopher shook his head again, his annoyance growing. "Let me be perfectly clear on this matter, Peter – religion is of no matter to me, but it matters to a great many people. I would rather see you marry a godless woman of good character than a Christian woman with an immoral soul, so do not think I hold any prejudice against the Jews because it would be untrue. I knew many during my time in The Levant and they were kind, welcoming people. But they are also very devoted to their religion and they do not marry outside of their faith. If you pursue this infatuation, then you will find that out."

He wasn't being cruel about the situation, merely factual. Peter felt that he was discouraging him, not wanting to see his son hurt.

But he wasn't ready to give up.

"What if one of us converts?" he said. "What if she converts to Christianity or I convert to the Jewish religion? What then? Would that solve the issue?"

Christopher's annoyance was growing with his son. "Ridiculous," he said flatly. "If you become a Jew, then you lose everything. There are no Jewish knights, Peter. The knighthood is based on service to the Catholic Church, so you would have to renounce everything. And then what? What would you do to earn money? Become a mercenary? Who is going to hire you? No Christian overlord in England will, so where will you go? What will you do? Or do you just intend to live on my good graces for the rest of your life?"

He was hammering at him and Peter was feeling increasingly defensive. "So she can convert to Christianity, then."

Christopher threw up his hands. "You would force the woman to leave everything she knows and bring her into a world that is completely unfamiliar to her?" he said. "How happy would she be? How happy would *you* be? You would have a miserable wife on your hands who would more than likely grow to resent you. Is that really the life you would want? I can say with certainty that it is not the life *I* would want for you."

It wasn't usual for Peter and Christopher to be at odds. They adored each other, as father and son should, so the lack of parental support for Peter was difficult to stomach. Christopher gave no sense that he would even be willing to help, which thoroughly upset Peter. He wasn't very good at hiding his feelings with his father against him.

"Then I thank you for your advice, Father," he said, struggling not to become angry. "Forgive me for troubling you and speaking about my feelings. It will not happen again."

With that, he turned on his heel, storming out of the solar. He heard his father call after him, but he ignored the man. He was positively furious. Just as he reached the mural stairs that led to the upper floors, someone grabbed him by the arm. Peter balled a fist and whirled around to throw a punch, but Alexander held up his hands.

"Ease yourself, Peter," he admonished softly. "Your mother would frown greatly if you spilled my blood over her floor, not to mention the fact that Christin would probably come after you with a dagger. Do you dare provoke my wife's wrath by striking me?"

Peter immediately relaxed and lowered his fist. "I do not want to discuss it further, Sherry," he said. "I know you mean well, but I really have nothing more to say."

Alexander looked at him, studying him in the weak light. "She sounds astonishing," he said quietly. "Liora, I mean. Am I to assume she feels the same way about you?"

Peter sighed heavily, seeing that he was going to have to talk about it whether he wanted to or not. "I suppose," he said. "Truthfully, I do not really know. She looks at me with such... power, Sherry. I do not know how to describe it, but when she looks at me, it as if the world around me ceases to exist. All I see is her. Yesterday, we had a short but perfectly wonderful conversation and today, it was like I'd found a missing piece. Being with her, talking to her, seemed to fill a gap inside of me that I never knew I had. I am not sure I can describe it any better than that."

Alexander was a wise man. He had a way about him that naturally drew men to him, a command authority that was comprised of a strong presence, intuition, and intelligence. Everyone in the family was extremely fond of Alexander and Christin most of all. She adored her husband. Peter had to admit that he did, too. He was the big brother Peter had always wished for.

"I will not discount what you are feeling even though it has been a very short amount of time," Alexander said. "Infatuations can be like that sometimes. Mayhap you should give it a little time and see how you feel in a few days."

Peter shrugged. "That was what Liora said."

"She is right."

Peter scratched his head wearily. "We may not have all the time in the world, you know," he said. "Papa has some of the warlords coming here tonight, including The Northerners, to discuss pulling out of London and the king's proposals. For all I know, we could be heading to the Marches tomorrow."

Alexander put a hand on his shoulder. "All I am saying is not to rush into anything," he said. "Sleep on it. Think about it. I am always here to talk to if you need someone to listen. Your father… he is bearing the weight of a country on his shoulders right now and may not be the best person to speak to. His concerns are great, Peter.

You know that."

Peter nodded. "I know," he said. "I do not mean to burden him but, to me, this is a serious situation. I only wanted his thoughts on the matter, not his condemnation."

"He did not condemn you," Alexander said. "He did, in fact, give you his thoughts."

Peter's gaze lingered on him. "You think he is right, don't you?"

Alexander shrugged. "In many ways, he was exactly right," he said. "Do not forget that I spent time in The Levant with your father, too. What he said about the Jewish people and their dedication to their religion is exactly right. They are a people who keep unto themselves."

"But there have to be times when they marry outside of their faith."

"Probably. But not without great sacrifices from one person or the other."

He was saying what Christopher essentially said, only kinder. It gave Peter something more to think about, but it didn't discourage him.

"I want to speak with a rabbi," he said. "I want to find out what kind of opposition there is. I want to know why I have found a beautiful woman who makes me feel faint every time I look at her and I cannot marry her."

Alexander could see a passion in Peter that he'd never seen before. That told him that, perhaps, this was something more than an infatuation. "The Great Synagogue is in London," he said. "Surely you could go there and speak with one of the rabbis."

Peter had hoped to go with Liora when she spoke with her rabbi, but he was coming to think it might be better if he were to speak with a rabbi without her. He wanted facts, and truth, and he didn't want Liora there to feed his emotions. Already, she fed them and in this case, that was only working against him. As he stood there with Alexander, he knew what he had to do.

And he'd keep his father out of it.

"Thank you," he said, reaching out to put a hand on Alexander's arm. "You have given me something to think about without making me feel like a fool."

Alexander smiled faintly at him. "Do not think too badly of your father," he said. "I suspect he is sad that he angered you, so keep that in mind. I am sure he did not mean to."

Peter shrugged, forcing a smile at Alexander before continuing up to his chamber. There would be a gathering that night and more discussions with the warlords, and he would be part of it, but right now – this moment – was his. He had plans to make and things to do.

No matter what his father said, he wasn't going to give up.

CHAPTER EIGHT

*C*LICK... *CLICK... CLICK, click, click...*

The tick of the abacus filled the air of the shop on the Street of the Jewelers. Haim ben Thad's stall was like all the other stalls on the avenue, which was essentially a small fortress unto itself. As with all jewelers and bankers, they had a private security force that protected them from thieves and robbers. These men were usually Jewish and very well paid. Some of the shops were built from stone, making it more difficult for clever thieves to break through walls, and Haim's shop was one such stall.

It was the strongest shop on the avenue.

Haim inherited the shop from his father, and his father before him. He received direct shipments of jewels and purchased his gold from the goldsmiths on down the avenue. Every shop seemed to specialize in something different on the Street of the Jewelers, although some of them overlapped. Most everything was custom made, though there were a few pieces made specifically for sale to rich lords who didn't want to wait for something to be specially made.

Haim had it all.

He had two lesser partners who helped with the stall, salesmen, and four jewelers who did the most exquisite work. Haim himself also worked as a jeweler and he was one of the very best. He had more business than he could handle but, most importantly, he had the business of the king. In fact, he was making a massive golden belt for the king which, he'd only been told two days ago, the king wanted to turn into a necklace. There were twenty-seven gold links, each link set with a jewel, but the gold alone made it extremely heavy. Still, it was becoming increasingly fashionable for men to wear those heavy gold belts and once London saw the king wear such a belt around his neck and shoulders, it would become all the rage.

On this day, Liora was sitting on the second floor of the shop, at a table overlooking the street below. Her father was an excellent jeweler, but his business sense was often lacking, leaving it up to his wife and daughter to manage his books. Since Liora's mother, Ruth, was busier with the household and raising a wild son, Liora had taken over handling her father's financial affairs.

Today, she was determining the accounts for the month and how much her father was owed.

Click... click... click, click, click went the abacus.

Then she would write the figure down in the ledger.

Unfortunately, she'd made a few mistakes this morning because her mind wasn't completely on the ledgers. Try as she might, she couldn't seem to stop thinking about Peter. She'd thought about him all night, making it difficult to sleep. Every time she closed her eyes, she pictured Peter kissing her fingers at the livery and it was enough to cause her heart to leap. He'd been so sweet and gentle and romantic, something she'd never experienced in her entire life and something she was most definitely drawn to.

For better or for worse, she was drawn to him.

It seemed so surreal, however. She still couldn't believe the events of the past couple of days, events she had never believed she would ever experience. Her entire world was her family, her religion, and her way of life. It just didn't seem possible that something out of the ordinary should alter that.

But something was.

It was both terrifying and thrilling.

"*Zeeskeit?*"

It was her father, coming up the stairs to the second level. *Zeeskeit* was a term of endearment, like the Christians would use *sweetling* or *dearest*. Her father lavished all manner of attention on her, a kind and generous man who had been near his fifth decade when she was born. Haim ben Thad had married late in life to a woman half his age, and he adored his family. Liora turned to see him at the top of the stairs, an earthenware bowl with a lid on it in his hands.

"Your mother has brought you something for the nooning meal," he said. "You did not go home to eat, so she has brought it here."

Liora hadn't even realized the time. There was an hourglass on the other table and she looked at it, seeing that it was empty. She hadn't flipped it over as she usually did.

She set down her quill.

"I suppose I did not realize what time it was," she said as her father pushed aside the ledger to put the bowl on the table in front of her. "Thank you, Papa. Will you not sit with me while I eat?"

Haim was a big, round man with a bushy beard and hair that was mostly white. In his younger years, it had been black, like his daughter's hair color, and his eyes were the same color as hers. Father and daughter resembled each other quite a bit.

He sat down in the nearest chair.

"What is keeping you so busy today that you forget to eat?" he asked. "You have been very busy up here."

Liora smiled weakly as she took the lid off the bowl to reveal chicken soup with dumplings. She picked up the wooden spoon her father had brought along. "Many people owe you money this month, Papa," she said, spooning up one of the hot dumplings. "You sell a great deal, but you do not collect your money right away. That means we must send your guards out to collect."

That was usually how Haim, and other jewelers and bankers, collected their money if the customer didn't come to them. They would send out their paid guards, like henchmen, to collect. Sane men would not refuse to pay an armed guard. But Haim waved a hand at her.

"They will pay," he said. "They always do. In fact, the belt for the king is finished and I will take it over to Westminster later today. He will pay me well."

Westminster reminded Liora of Peter. Palaces like Westminster were full of English knights and lords, and according to Peter, his father was in the middle of England's politics these days. She sipped her hot soup.

"May I come with you?" she asked, trying to sound casual about it. "To Westminster, I mean. It has been a long time since I have accompanied you on a delivery."

Haim lifted his shoulders. "I do not know," he said. "Let me think on it."

"But why can't I go?"

"Because that world is no place for you. Women with painted faces and men with big swords."

He said it so dramatically that she grinned. "You've known knights and lords in your time, haven't you?" she asked casually. "Men who serve the king, I mean. In fact, we seem to have a few who owe you money."

Haim cocked his head to get a look at her ledger. "Who owes me?"

Liora pointed to a line on the page. "Matthew Fitzherbert is one."

Haim nodded, remembering that particular debt. "He will pay," he said. "He bought a necklace for his wife for her day of birth."

"Last year, Papa."

"He will bring me the money when he can."

Liora looked at him. "With all of the turmoil with the king and the rebelling barons, do you really think he will remember?" she said. "There is much unrest, Papa. Remember all of the knights and lords that came through London two days ago?"

Haim nodded. "I saw them," he said. "They

will not bother us. They are only interested in bothering each other."

"Do you know some of them?" she asked, spooning more soup in her mouth. "Some of the rebel warlords, I mean. You have lived through three kings, yet you never speak on some of the things that England has suffered through. Like the men who stand against the king these days."

Haim yawned. It was growing close to the time when he would nap in the afternoon. "Because it does not matter to me," he said. "In all of the wars the Christians have waged upon each other, it has never affected my business. They always seem to find money for their finery."

"Do you know any of the great warlords?"

"Like who?"

She shrugged. "I have heard the name de Lohr," she said. "He's an earl."

Haim held up a finger. "He didn't use to be," he said. "I know who he is. I met him once, a long time ago, when he was a knight for King Richard. He wasn't an earl then."

Liora ate her soup, listening to her father speak on a subject she was very interested in. "What do you know about him now?"

"I hear things," he said, shrugging. "He's a good man, a fair man, men say. But he does not buy jewelry from me, so what do I care?"

Liora grinned. "Papa, have you ever known

any of those knights to take a Jewish bride?"

Haim scratched his beard thoughtfully. "Why? Do you want such a man?"

She snorted, caught off guard by the question. "Don't be silly," she said. "I was just wondering. Do they all marry Christian women?"

"All of them," he said. "They are not part of our world and we are not part of theirs, which is a good thing. It keeps us out of their wars. Although I do seem to remember Abel ben Alon, who was a friend of your grandfather, with a sister who married a knight for King Henry."

"She did?" Liora tried not to sound too hopeful or too curious. "Did he become part of the faith?"

Haim shook his head. "I think she became a Christian," he said. "It upset her mother so much that the woman died of a broken heart. I seem to remember hearing that they moved to Oxford where people did not know them so they would not know she was Jewish. One cannot run from one's religion. It is who you are."

"But it *has* happened."

"It has," he said. "It used to be forbidden, meaning they would put you to death for it, but they do not do that any longer, not since the time of Henry. But you may as well be dead if you deny who you are to marry a Christian."

Liora didn't ask any further questions because

she didn't want her father to become suspicious. But the fact that he knew of someone who had married a Christian was encouraging to her. Sort of. But the fact that they had to move away so no one would know that the bride used to be Jewish was concerning. She'd told Peter she would speak with a rabbi about a marriage to a Christian and she would. At least now she had an example to refer to when discussing the subject.

"Well," she said after a moment. "I think it is silly that we cannot marry whom we want to marry, regardless of faith. God made all religions, did he not? They all worship the same god, so I do not understand why a Jew cannot marry a Christian freely."

Haim yawned again. "Because dogs do not marry cats," he said. "Fish do not marry birds. We are all different, that's why. Now, finish your soup so you can go home and help your mother. I have invited Gideon to sup with us."

Gideon was the man who wanted to marry her, the owner of the livery over by the Great Synagogue. Liora rolled her eyes.

"I will *not* sup with him," she said. "Papa, you know how I feel about him. Why would you invite him to eat with us?"

Haim cast her a long look. "I think I should have him sup with us if you are asking about marriage," he said. "That means you are interested in marriage, does it not? He is a good man, *zeeskeit*. He would make a good husband for you and provide well."

Frustrated, she pushed aside her half-finished soup. "He is a good man, but I do not love him," she said, returning to her ledger. "I do not want to marry him and I do not want to have children with him."

"Who, then?"

She picked up her quill. "I do not know," she said. "But *not* him. Please, Papa… do not make me eat with him."

"I have already invited him."

"Then I will be ill tonight when he comes."

"I will let you go with me to Westminster if you sup with him."

She looked at him, frowning, but he only grinned at her. He was a sly fox, that one. Seeing that she'd been backed into a corner, Liora nodded begrudgingly.

"Very well," she said. "When are we going?"

"Soon," Haim said, standing up. "Within the hour. Will you be ready?"

Liora nodded eagerly. "I will," she said. "Let me go home and change my clothing and I will return shortly."

"Everything covered, *zeeskeit*," he said, motioning to her chest, shoulders, and head. "Make sure everything is covered."

"I will."

Haim headed back downstairs as Liora excitedly finished up her last three accounts. She carefully sanded the ledger to dry the ink, blowing it off and examining her figures. Satisfied, she closed the ledger and set the abacus aside. Standing up, she put everything on the table into neat piles by the window. As she leaned in to close the shutters, she noticed a bit of a commotion down below as two knights neared her father's shop astride their enormous warhorses. She recognized one of the horses, having seen it hiding in her kitchen yard two nights before.

Liora's heart leapt into her throat as she realized Peter had arrived.

☙

IT WAS ANOTHER fine September morning in a week that had been full of them as Peter headed into London, his destination being the Great Synagogue.

But he wasn't alone.

Alexander thought he was being clever by following him into London, but Peter knew he was behind him. Alexander was an excellent spy, an exceptional assassin, and was proficient at following someone without being seen, so Peter could only assume Alexander wanted Peter to know he was there.

Peter finally pulled his horse to a halt and waited for Alexander to catch up with him.

It was a chilly morning and Alexander was wrapped in a cloak as he came up behind Peter, looking at the man with a hint of a smile on his face.

"Well?" Alexander asked. "Where are we off to this morning?"

Peter rolled his eyes and spurred his horse forward. "Wherever it is, I do not need an escort."

"I beg to differ," Alexander said. "If you are heading into London, I suspect I know where you are going, so you may as well confess."

"Where do you think I am going?"

"To see the jeweler's daughter."

Peter snorted. "That shows how much you know," he said. "I was *not* going to see her."

"You weren't?"

"Nay."

"Then where are you going?"

Peter sighed heavily. "Being married to my sister does not give you the right to interrogate me."

"That is where you would be wrong," Alexander said. "It gives me every right in the world. I know a thousand techniques to get information out of a man, so if you refuse to tell me, I may have to use one of those techniques on you."

That was very true. In the spy business, Alexander had learned some harrowing techniques over the years. Even Peter knew that. But he started laughing.

"I'll scream," he said. "I'll scream like a woman and then I'll tell my mother. You may survive my wrath, but you will not survive hers."

Alexander fought off a grin. "Just tell me where we are going," he said. "I will not leave your side, so you may as well tell me. I will find out sooner or later."

Peter looked over his shoulder at the man before finally shaking his head. "We are going to the Great Synagogue," he said. "Are you satisfied now?"

Alexander's brow furrowed. "Nay," he said. "I am more confused than ever. Why are we going there?"

"Because I wish to speak with a rabbi."

"What about?"

"About a Christian knight courting the jeweler's daughter."

Alexander lost some of his humor then. "I see," he said. "And what if you discover it cannot be done?"

"I will not accept it."

Alexander shook his head with regret. "And *that* is why you need an escort."

Peter didn't try and chase him away. In fact,

he was rather comforted to have levelheaded Alexander with him. The truth was that he'd lain awake all night, tossing and turning, frustrated that he couldn't court a woman he was so attracted to. There was so much about this situation that was disappointing.

So incredibly disappointing.

"It's just not fair," he muttered as the horses clip-clopped along the well-traveled road. "There are so many things in life that will keep a man and woman apart – social standing, wealth, family honor – but religion was something that never occurred to me."

Alexander's gaze was sweeping the road for any threats, a natural instinct for a knight. "I do not know anyone who has had an easy time of marrying his wife."

"For example?"

He looked at Peter. "You know a few," he said. "Maxton's wife was a postulate for the church, which was not an easy road for Maxton. You remember that whole mess, Peter. Kress de Rhydian and Achilles de Dere also had troubled paths – Kress married a woman he was escorting to wed another man and Achilles married a Blackchurch-trained knight. You know that his wife used to be an Executioner Knight."

Peter knew all of that. Kress and Achilles were original Executioner Knights, men with great reputations but men who, at this point, were not in London but stationed at their own garrisons and away from the bedlam that was London these days. He looked at Alexander.

"And you?"

"And I married Christopher de Lohr's eldest daughter in spite of the fact that I was twice her age."

"And a killer."

"And many things. Do you think your father made it easy for me?"

Peter cracked a smile. "I know for a fact that he did not."

"Exactly," Alexander said, returning his attention to the road. "Not that I expected him to welcome me with open arms. I've never been welcomed with open arms anywhere I've ever been, except among my own friends, of course. So, you having your eye on a Jewish bride is nothing unusual when it comes to the Executioner Knights but, in this case, you may run into more opposition than usual."

Peter thought on that, realizing that almost every man he knew had a difficult time when it came to the courtship of the women they eventually married. In that realization, he didn't feel so alone. But for him, it was more than not feeling alone in a sea of comrades who'd had to fight for the women they love.

For him, there was also the matter of blood-lines.

That alone, at times, had made him feel as if he did not belong.

"I know I am the eldest de Lohr son and that has been the great attraction for so many of these fathers wanting a husband for their daughters," he said. "But when they find out I am my father's bastard and will not inherit the title, most of them have ceased their pursuit. Without the title, I have little attraction."

Alexander knew that. "Your father has never made you feel any differently than the rest of his children, though. I see every day how he treats you. He loves you very much."

Peter agreed. "My father treats me as if I am his eldest," he said. "I know he is proud of me. More importantly, so is the woman I call my mother. Dustin has always treated me as if I were her flesh and blood and I love her dearly for it."

"Do you remember your birth mother?"

"I do," Peter said. "I was nine when she was killed in an accident, so I remember her well. She was a gentle woman, pretty and kind."

"Do you miss her?"

"Sometimes," he said. "I wish she could have seen the man I grew into and what I have achieved. Do you want to know something? Even though I have never been treated any differently by my father and Dustin, I have nonetheless felt different. I know I *am* different. It is all of my own doing, but I cannot help the feeling. Does that sound foolish?"

Alexander shook his head. "It does not," he said. "My own family ties are quite complex, so I understand that feeling very well. My father, Phillip, and I were not close. In hindsight, that was all my fault. Phillip and I never did see eye to eye, so I was raised by my grandfather, who also raised my cousin, Estienne, whom I considered my elder brother. For years, I called my grandfather my father, because he was. But my true father, Phillip, raised my two younger brothers. It was like having two fathers and two families – my grandfather and my own father. And I felt misplaced with both of them."

Peter looked at him. "I've heard you mention Estienne before," he said. "You did not get on with him."

Alexander shook his head. "Nay," he said. "He was older than me and he never let me forget it. Estienne was an imperious, arrogant arse who essentially stole my grandfather's properties when he died. In fact, I no longer consider him my brother. I haven't for years."

"What did your father say about his actions? Was he not your grandfather's heir?"

"He was, but he had his own lands that had

belonged to my mother," he said. "That is one of the things we did not see eye to eye on – I wanted him to fight for Broxburn Castle, which was his right. Upon his death, it would have belonged to me, but my father was a man of great peace. He didn't believe in aggression. When I became a knight and was quite proficient in battle, that further drove a wedge between us. He did not understand me and I did not understand him."

"What happened to Estienne?"

"He chose to remain in England when I went to The Levant with my younger brothers, who were killed almost immediately after arriving," Alexander said. "I felt so guilty about that, as if it were my failure, that I did not see my father for many years. By the time I returned home, he had died. I'm sure Christin told you about that."

Peter nodded. "She did," he said. "She said he remarried and, thinking you had been killed in The Levant, named his son with his new wife after you."

Alexander nodded. "He did," he said. "So, as you believe your own past and parentage to be complex, it is nothing compared to mine. You are your father's bastard, Peter – what does it matter? You are not the first bastard and you will not be the last. Chris has never treated you differently, you are deeply loved, and he has given you a title and now Ludlow Castle. You have more than a man could ever want, so stop feeling sorry for yourself. Be grateful."

Peter realized he was right. Odd how it took a man he'd known for years, a seasoned knight with decades of death and destruction in his past, to remind him of just how rich he really was. Alexander really had experienced a time of it with his complicated family relations, which made Peter feel better about his own.

Perhaps he was glad Alexander had accompanied him this morning, after all.

"I am grateful," he said. "I did not mean to make it sound as if I were not. But the fact that I am not my father's heir is… disappointing. Do not get me wrong; I adore my brother, Curtis. He will make an excellent earl. But there are times when I wish it was me."

Alexander looked at him, smiling. "If it was you, it would be much more difficult to pursue a marriage to a Jewess, so if I were you, I would be thankful for small mercies."

Peter chuckled, nodding his head in agreement.

He had a point.

The day began to grow brighter as they came to the outskirts of London's city, with Westminster Palace in the distance. They could see Westminster Cathedral, a massive stone icon of religion and civilization, and the River Thames as the sunlight reflected off the water. The heavy forested areas had cleared out and now they were in the farmlands that surrounded London. People were out in their fields, using oxen or simply manpower to harvest the last of the summer crops, which at this stage were mostly onions and turnips. The fields were full of onions that had been plowed up and were waiting to be put in baskets. In fact, the air itself smelled onion-y as Peter and Alexander headed through Ludgate.

Entering the city, Peter immediately felt a sense of anticipation. Last night as he'd lain awake, he'd planned what he would ask the rabbi. He decided to be succinct and to the point, and he thought he might even offer to pay the rabbi to broker a contract with Liora's father. Surely the synagogue was looking for monetary donations just like the churches were. Perhaps he could even convince the rabbi that a marriage between a Christian knight and a Jewess was perfectly reasonable. But something told him that he couldn't buy a rabbi, or convince the man that an interfaith marriage would be a good thing, but he chose to ignore that part of his common sense, at least for today.

Today, he would get the answers he sought or go down trying.

Once entering the city, they cut north to the main street that ran from one end of London to the other. It also intersected Milk Street and, a little further east, the street that contained the Great Synagogue. As they traveled, they happened to pass by a section of the city that was famed for taverns that catered to lower-quality clientele.

However, they could smell the bread and food from those taverns even at this early hour, causing their stomachs to rumble, and they ended up stopping at one called The Farmer's Prick to get something to eat. They came away with hollowed-out trenchers full of fish, battered and fried in fat, in a sauce made of eggs, vinegar, and pickled onions. They quickly ate, plodding down the street on horseback, and devoured everything including the stale bread bowls.

Fortified with fish and pickled onions, they pushed on.

Unfortunately, they didn't make it very far because they passed Milk Street and Peter stopped his horse, looking up the avenue and seeing a portion of Liora's house midway up the street. He didn't see her, nor did he really expect to, but he pointed it out to Alexander, who told him to keep moving. He was preparing to do just that when he felt it.

And he felt it again.

He was in full armor this day, complete with hauberk, padded tunics, the de Lohr blue tunic, arm braces, helm, and everything else he took into battle, so he felt something ping against his arm, twice, but just a touch and nothing more. Unfortunately, Alexander had his face plate up and he suddenly put a hand to his eye.

"Damnation," he muttered, rubbing his eye. "Something just hit me."

Peter knew what it was right away. He didn't even have to see the culprit. The aim told him everything he needed to know, so he quickly looked around only to spy Asa and his gang of toughs hiding out behind several barrels that had just been delivered to a merchant along the street. As soon as Asa realized he'd been sighted, he ran, but not away from Peter.

He ran towards him.

"Brace yourself," Peter told Alexander. "We are about to be set upon."

Alexander was blinking his eyes rapidly, trying to clear his vision in his left eye, when several children rushed up to him and Peter. He counted seven, but there were more scattered around, as Peter braced an enormous hand on his thigh and peered down at a boy with a mop of curly, black hair.

"So," Peter said. "You have decided to take on two armed knights with your pebbles? I must say you are braver than I gave you credit for."

Asa shook his head. "I wanted you to see me," he insisted. "I wanted your attention. I need your sword, Saint Peter!"

"I told you that it weighs more than you do," Peter said. "What do you need it for, anyway?"

Asa pointed to a smaller street next to Milk Street. "Saul's Army stole our eggs this morning and I want them back," he said. "Lee-Lee tried to chase them, but they threw an egg at her."

Peter frowned. "They did, did they?" he said, greatly displeased. "Where are these louts?"

"*Saint* Peter?" Alexander said, a glimmer of mirth in his eyes. "Are you going to introduce me to your admirer?"

Peter grinned, pointing to the child. "Sherry, this is the leader of the Maccabees, Asa. Asa, this is Sir Alexander de Sherrington, one of the most elite knights in the entire world. He is not to be trifled with so the next time you shoot him in the eye, you had better be prepared to defend yourself."

Asa turned his big eyes to Alexander, who cocked a disapproving eyebrow. "It was you, was it?" he said. "Excellent aim, young Asa. But do not do it again."

Asa nodded, but he wasn't particularly intim-idated. He studied Alexander closely, noting the enormous broadsword sheathed on the man's saddle. "You have a big sword, too."

"I do."

"Will you help us get the eggs back?"

Alexander looked at Peter for any indication

of how they were going to handle the request, but Peter shrugged. "They have probably already eaten them," he said to Asa. "You would get nothing back but shells."

Asa scowled. "Then we will steal something of theirs!"

"That does not solve the problem."

Asa was in a quandary. He turned to some of his gang behind him, bigger boys who were whispering furiously to him. It was clear that they were in a conference of some kind, but only for a few moments before Asa returned his attention to Peter.

"Will you go down their street with us?" he asked. "If Saul's Army sees you with us, they will be afraid to steal anymore eggs."

"Hold," Alexander put a hand out, looking at Peter. "What is this all about? What are Maccabees and Saul's Army?"

Peter chuckled. "They are two opposing armies," he said as if Alexander was a dullard. "Do you not understand? These are two armies fighting for territory. Asa and his Maccabees are from Milk Street and Saul's Army is from… Asa, what street does Saul's Army live on?"

Asa, and several of the other boys, pointed to the smaller street. "King Street!" he said.

Peter returned his attention to Alexander. "Two gangs fighting one another and now we have egg stealers," he said. "Surely we must help them."

Alexander scowled. "Cease your foolery," he said. "You have business in London to attend to, so let's get on with it."

Peter lifted an eyebrow. "I *am* attending it," he said. "Asa is Liora's brother."

Alexander rolled his eyes when he realized why Peter was being so attentive to the young boy with the wild hair. "I see," he said. "Then, by all means, let us support the Maccabees' efforts so we can get out of here."

Peter grinned. "Indeed," he said, returning his focus to Asa. "We will go with you, but then I must depart. Where is your sister today, anyway?"

Asa pointed to another nearby street. "She is with Papa," he said. "She helps him."

Peter's gaze moved to the street Asa was indicating. It was the Street of the Jewelers, very near to where Liora and her family lived. Up ahead, he could see the top of the Great Synagogue, a two-storied structure with big, stone columns in contrast with the surrounding architecture of London, usually of wattle and daub.

The building caught his attention.

"One more question and we will go with you," he told the boy. "Who is your rabbi?"

Asa scratched his head. "Rabbi Judah," he said. "Why?"

Peter shook his head. "I was simply curious,"

he said. Then, he pointed to King Street. "Lead on. We shall follow."

Excited, and full of revenge against the egg stealers, Asa and his friends began to run, followed by the knights on their warhorses. The boys were whooping and shouting, exciting the horses, who sensed a battle. They were running so fast that by the time the knights made their way down King Street, Asa and his gang were already beating up on some hapless child in the middle of the street.

Peter immediately dismounted and broke up the fight.

"Here, now," he said, pulling Asa off the boy and then pulling the child on the ground to his feet. "What goes on?"

Asa was furious, his little fists balled. "He stole my eggs!" he shouted. "I am punishing him!"

Peter looked at the child, a little boy with dirty blond hair and a dirty face. He was also quite skinny as opposed to the well-fed Asa and his crew. Peter glanced at the street itself – it wasn't nearly as well-appointed as Milk Street, just one block over. More of Saul's Army began to come out of the shadows, bigger children than Asa and his friends, but skinny and not particularly well dressed. Sensing what was happening here, Peter looked between Asa and his victim.

"Stealing is never acceptable," he said to the blond-haired child. "Would you like it if someone stole from you?"

He had to give the kid a little shake because he wouldn't answer. The boy's mouth was working. "Nay," he said. "But… but we need the eggs."

"They're *my* eggs!" Asa shouted.

"Shut your lips," Peter commanded quietly. As Asa frowned, he returned his attention to the other boy. "Why do you need the eggs?"

The boy began to turn red in the face. He refused to answer until Peter gave him another jolt. Then, he seemed nervous.

"Because we need to eat," he said. He pointed to Asa. "They have lots to eat. We take a few eggs. What's that to them? They have money and food. They can always get more eggs."

Peter suspected from the beginning that this was beyond the usual stealing. The boys were hungry. Saul's Army just had that look. He released both boys but when he spoke, it was to the blond.

"Listen to me and listen well," he said. "I do not want to hear about you stealing any more eggs from Asa's chickens. If I hear about that, I will come back to this street looking for you. Is that clear? And you will not like it when I find you. But if you are truly hungry, there is a tavern at the end of this road, by Ludgate. It is called The Farmer's Prick. Do you know it?"

The little boy was looking at him in confusion,

trying to follow along with what he was saying but also not willing to take his eyes off Asa in case Asa should charge him again, so he was off-balance. But he nodded after a moment.

"I… I think so," he said. He pointed west. "That way?"

Peter nodded. "That way," he said. "If you go there every morning around to the kitchens, I will make sure they feed you and your friends a meal. Once a day, in the morning. But in return, you must stop stealing eggs. Do you understand?"

The boy's confusion cleared up and he looked surprised. "Go to the *tavern*?"

"Aye."

"And we will eat?"

"As long as you stop stealing eggs."

The boy's eyes widened and he nodded quickly. "Aye, my lord."

"Then the deal is struck. I will say no more."

Peter lifted an eyebrow at him as if to emphasize what should happen should he go back on his word before turning away, motioning to Asa as he went. Asa trotted after him, followed by the rest of the Maccabees.

"If they continue to steal eggs, you will tell me," he said. "But I have a feeling this will stop their thievery. And you stay away from them, too. Do not antagonize them."

Asa cocked his head. "Ant… ant… *what*?"

"Do not vex them."

Asa looked over his shoulder at the other gang begrudgingly. "As you say," he said. But Peter swung himself back into the saddle and Asa ran after him. "Where are you going now?"

"I have a man to see," Peter said, turning his horse after Alexander, who was already heading down the avenue. "Go home, Asa. Do not stay here where trouble can find you."

Asa was about to shout something after him but thought better of it. He dashed off, running between the houses as his friends followed suit. When Alexander and Peter emerged onto the main road again, Alexander turned to him.

"A brilliant bit of negotiation," he said. "Are you certain that you do not wish to handle the mediation between your father and the king?"

Peter snorted. "Not in the least," he said. "But remind me to visit that tavern before we leave town so I can pay them for the meals they will be dispensing. Those children were hungry."

Alexander nodded, his attention moving towards the Great Synagogue in the distance. "I know," he said. "I could see that. Your actions were noble, Peter. Solomon could not have done better."

Peter gave him a half-grin. "That is why they call me Saint Peter the Rock. I am a noble, immovable object."

"Come along, Rock. Let's get this over with."

They resumed their trek down the road, heading for the Great Synagogue. London was growing busier as the morning deepened, with people going about their business. In the distance, Peter and Alexander could see an armed contingent entering town, bearing the banners of Huntingfield, who was the Sheriff of Suffolk. He was one of the rebel leaders, and had once been close to William Marshal, but he was more than likely coming into town by John's summons. Another warlord to make an offer to because the man had troops inside of London.

Peter reined his steed to a halt.

"See the yellow banner in the distance?" he asked.

Alexander came to a stop beside him. "I do. Huntingfield."

"Do you think The Marshal summoned him on behalf of John?"

"Probably."

Peter sighed faintly. "This is such a strange time right now," he muttered. "I do not think I will ever get over being on the opposite side of The Marshal or Achilles, or Cullen or Bric. It seems so odd to speak of a summons by The Marshal and know that I am no longer an ally in the technical sense of the word. My father feels the same way."

Alexander watched Huntingfield draw closer.

"Claiming sides is only for public perception," he said. "Our loyalty to The Marshal goes beyond politics. It is the moral truth and center of our world, of what is right and what is wrong. Maxton, Kress, Achilles, Caius, Kevin, Bric, Dashiell… we will never be against one another. We will always fight together for what is right. Even Sean, though the man is still sick from the wounds he sustained when the White Tower fell to the rebels. He was always a part of us, even when he was against us."

Peter glanced at him. "Have you seen him lately?"

Alexander shook his head. "Not lately," he said. "Kevin was with him in the beginning, but Kevin has been moved up north by The Marshal. He's keeping an eye on things up there and reporting on it."

Peter thought of his close friend, Kevin de Lara, brother of Sean. Kevin was an excellent knight, a true devotee of William Marshal, and Peter thought of his friend as he scouted the north for signs of rebellion and mercenaries. It was dangerous work in a dangerous time.

"I miss him," he said. "I miss Sean. I miss all of us together, as it should be."

"The only way that is going to happen is if John is dead."

Peter lifted an eyebrow. "And The Marshal still feels that the king needs to be protected? Why would he save the life of a man who has only thrown us deeper and deeper into chaos?"

Alexander had a complicated answer for him, but he didn't speak of it. Peter was young. He was idealistic and he missed his friends. He missed the Executioner Knights as a complete unit. Sometimes men parted for a time only to come back together again, stronger than ever. Alexander was certain this would be one of those times.

Eventually.

"Come on," he said, spurring his horse forward. "We'll speak on all of that later. Right now, we have a rabbi to see."

Peter followed him, but they didn't get too far. He found himself looking down the Street of the Jewelers, knowing that Liora was there, and his entire focus shifted from his fractured friends to the beautiful woman he was increasingly smitten with. He peered down the street, which didn't seem busy at all on this bustling morning, and he found himself pulled in that direction.

Increasingly pulled.

He could hear Alexander calling after him.

"Peter!" he shouted. "Where are you going?"

Peter hadn't even realized that he'd turned his horse down the Street of the Jewelers. One moment, he was looking in that direction and in the next, he was entering that very street. It was narrow, and had the rare feature of cobblestones, so his horse was loud as he passed the various shops that were built like fortresses. The Street of the Jewelers also included gold and silver-smiths, and those were positioned on the edge of the avenue. He could smell the acids and tannins used to smelt the metals.

Alexander was tagging along behind him.

"One more detour?" he said, exasperated. "Peter, if you want to make it to the Great Synagogue before the sun sets, you should probably focus on your destination and stop following your whims."

Peter was looking at the shops as they passed each one... *Betzalel... Ehud... Malkiel... Gil...* all of them with Jewish names, all of them with heavily armed soldiers who postured dangerously when they saw the equally heavily armed knights. A few even unsheathed their swords, but Peter held his hands up, away from the broadsword strapped to his saddle, to show them that he wasn't armed, nor did he intend to draw a weapon.

Behind him, he could hear Alexander grunt unhappily.

"Christ," he muttered. "You are going to get us killed, Peter. Why in the hell did you bring us down this street?"

Peter turned to reply but was cut short when he saw what he was looking for.

Thad.

It had to be Haim ben Thad's shop.

With a smile, he reined his horse over to the shop. "Come with me," he said to Alexander. "I have someone I want you to meet."

Alexander reined his horse alongside him, dismounting and eyeing the armed guards that were on the perimeter of the shop. There was even one on the roof with a crossbow. Alexander kept his hands far away from his weapons as Peter spoke to the man at the door.

"I would like to see Haim ben Thad," he said. "He knows my father. My name is Peter de Lohr."

The man at the door knocked on it and a small, slit window opened. He repeated Peter's words to whoever had opened it and they waited until there was a response, which took a few minutes. Peter fully expected to see a man but was quite shocked – and pleased – when the bolts on the iron door were thrown and Liora appeared.

"Peter?" she said, almost incredulously. "What on earth are you doing here?"

For a moment, Peter couldn't speak. All he could do was look at her, dressed in a shade of blue that matched her eyes. She wore a dark blue scarf over her head and shoulders, looking up at him most curiously.

She was the most beautiful sight he had ever seen.

"Forgive me," he finally said. "I did not expect you to answer the door. You took my breath away for just a moment."

Liora's cheeks flushed and she fought off a grin. "*What* are you doing here?" she whispered, lowering her voice. "My father is here, you know."

Peter nodded. "I know," he said. "I wanted to speak with him on business. Wait... that is not entirely true. Asa said you were here, so I came. But I do want to speak with your father on business while I am here."

"What about?"

"A gift for my father." Before she could reply, Peter indicated Alexander, standing a few feet away. "This is my sister's husband, Sir Alexander de Sherrington. His friends call him Sherry, of which he has many. Sherry, this is Liora, daughter of Haim."

Alexander dipped his head politely. "My lady."

Liora smiled timidly at the very big man with the short, dark hair and a closely cropped black beard. Realizing she had two guests on her doorstep, she motioned them inside.

"Please," she said. "Come in. Let me provide you with rest and drink."

But Peter shook his head. "Nay, Demoiselle," he said. "But I thank you just the same. If your father is busy, I can just as easily come back. I do not mean to interrupt him, as we have come unannounced."

Liora indicated the open door. "It is no trouble," she said. "If you truly have business with my father, do come in."

A smile played on Peter's lips and he took a step closer to her, though he should not have. He simply couldn't help himself. "I really came to see you," he whispered. "I will come back again, I assure you, but I simply had to see you today. I could not sleep last night for thoughts of you."

They were far enough away from the armed men that their conversation wasn't heard, but Liora's cheeks flamed. She was both uncomfortable and titillated by his words.

"I asked you to let me think," she muttered.

"Do you really want me to stay away?"

She opened her mouth to reply but thought better of it. She shook her head reproachfully. "You are impossible," she scolded softly. "Of course I do not want you to stay away. But you should. You must."

"I cannot," he said. "In fact, I am going to the Great Synagogue right now to speak with a rabbi. Asa told me that your rabbi's name is Judah. I intend to seek him."

Liora's eyes widened. "*What*?" she hissed. "Peter, you mustn't, not until I've had a chance to speak with him!"

"And when will that be?"

She was starting to grow nervous, twitchy. "I do not know," she said. "I must finish helping my father today and then I must return home and help my mother. We have a guest for sup tonight and…"

She suddenly stopped, looking at him with big eyes as if she were afraid to say more. Peter's brow furrowed.

"What about it?" he said. "What's wrong?"

She blinked fearfully. "I am afraid to tell you."

"Why?"

"Because… well, you must not come around tonight. Please."

"Why not?"

"Because my father invited the horse trader to sup."

Peter knew exactly what she meant. "The one who wants to marry you?"

He raised his voice and she shushed him, taking him by the arm and pulling him away from the door, out into the street. They were behind the horses now as she faced him.

"Remember that I do not want to marry him," she said quietly. "I have no interest in the man at all, but you are not to come around tonight. You are a very big man with a very big sword and if you cause trouble… it would be very bad, Peter. Do you understand me?"

He did, but he wasn't happy. He sighed heavily. "Aye," he said. "I understand. It does not make me happy, but I understand."

"Good," she said, daring to put a hand on his big arm. "As for the rabbi, please let me speak to him first."

Peter lifted his shoulders. "I am only going to ask a few questions," he said. "I will not even mention your name. I know nothing about your religion or culture, so I want to understand what it is that make Christian and Jew mix like oil and water. I want to understand what issues I face in my quest to court you. There is no harm in asking, is there?"

She eyed him, realizing she would not be able to discourage him. The man was determined and it was so very sweet. Reckless, but sweet. It made her heart leap in both fear and joy. She couldn't decide which emotion was stronger. But she knew one thing.

She *was* glad to see him and, no… she did not want him to stay away.

"Very well," she said, jabbing a finger at him. "But do not mention my name."

Peter smiled broadly, taking that finger and kissing it. "I swear I will not."

She pulled her finger away, giving him a look that suggested he was quite a scamp for daring to give her a kiss. "Good."

"I have missed you."

Her cheeks started to flame again. "You only just saw me yesterday."

"That was a whole day ago. Do you mean to say you have not missed me?"

She grinned, averting her gaze bashfully. "If I did, I would not tell you."

"Why not?"

"Because *you* may act like a besotted fool, but I will not."

His face fell. "You are not besotted with me?"

"Nay."

"You do not even *like* me?"

"I have not yet decided."

He sighed sharply. "You are a cruel woman to toy with me like this. I do believe I shall cry right here and make a fool out of myself. Then you'll be sorry."

She burst into soft laughter, her smile glorious and radiant. Before she could reply, however, Alexander came around the rear of the horse.

"Papa has made an appearance," he muttered, pulling Peter back to his horse.

Liora bolted back towards the front door just as Haim stepped out, looking at the pair of knights curiously. Before he could speak, Liora put her hand on her father's arm.

"This is Sir Peter de Lohr, Papa," she said. "His father is Christopher de Lohr, the Earl of

Hereford and Worcester. The knight with him is his sister's husband, Sir Alexander de Sherrington."

Haim blinked in the bright morning sunlight, peering at Peter as the man mounted his steed. "De Lohr?" he repeated. "Richard's Lion Claw?"

That was a very old nickname Christopher had once had, as Richard's champion. Richard was the Lionheart and Christopher was the Lion's Claw. A lion was only as dangerous as his sharp claws, after all, and Christopher had earned that deadly moniker for his prowess with a sword.

"Aye, my lord," Peter said. "That was his name, long ago. He remembers you as Richard's jeweler."

Haim held up a hand to shield his eyes from the sun, getting a better look at the young man who looked a good deal like Christopher had in his youth. "I was," he said. "Did he send you to see me?"

Peter shook his head. "Nay, my lord," he said. "I came myself. I should like to have something beautiful made for my father for Christmas, which is not so far away. You are the only jeweler I know of, and being the jeweler to the king, I thought you could make something fine for my father. I realize I have come unannounced, but your daughter was being most hospitable. Mayhap I can return at another time and we may discuss something for my father?"

Haim nodded. "I would be honored, young de Lohr," he said. "Return to me tomorrow. We shall discuss it at that time."

"I will, my lord. Thank you."

With that, Peter directed his horse away from the shop, but he only had eyes for Liora, who smiled at him when she thought her father wasn't looking. She watched as Peter and Alexander headed back up to the main avenue, but her father pulled her back inside the shop and her view was cut short.

But it had been enough of a view to feed that giddiness that Peter seemed to bring about.

His appearance may have been unexpected, but it certainly hadn't been unwelcome. *He'll be back tomorrow*, she thought. Somehow, she was going to find more work to do at her father's shop that just might take all day tomorrow to complete. Or, at least until Peter showed up again. That pushy, glorious knight she'd tried so hard to discourage refused to let her sensibilities dampen his enthusiasm and as she thought on it, she realized she was glad.

Glad that the man refused to be dissuaded.

Perhaps there was a part of her that, all along, had wondered if this wasn't some sort of whim for him. He'd met a pretty girl, someone new and different, and he'd become infatuated. Perhaps it would last an hour, a day, and just fade away. But when she'd looked from the window and saw him ride up, it began to occur to her that perhaps this wasn't a whim. Perhaps he'd really meant what he'd said. When he'd mentioned speaking to the rabbi, that only solidified her opinion.

Perhaps all of this *was* real.

It was frightening and exciting. And so very, very wrong. She knew it was wrong. But there was something so very touching about a man who was willing to fight for her with the odds so stacked against them. Try as she might, she had tried to rid herself of him, but he kept coming back. He kept fighting.

Perhaps she needed to fight *with* him from now on… and mean it.

With a smile of anticipation, she bolted the door and headed back to her ledger.

CHAPTER NINE

T HE MAN DRESSED in peasant clothing chugged down an entire cup of fine wine, wiping his mouth with the back of his hand.

"Well?" Walter de Quincy demanded. "What do you have to tell me?"

The man was one of many that Walter had paid to follow Peter de Lohr and report back on the man's activities and movements. There was an entire army of them, about twenty men, who kept track of Peter from the time he left Lonsdale and all around the city. They knew where he ate and where he slept, and who he kept company with. They also spoke to people who had seen him to get even more information, all of it reported back to Walter and Agnes.

Like today.

This particular man was a servant at Lonsdale who was on Walter's payroll. He had followed Peter from Ludgate and to the Street of the Jewelers, and every time he came to Walter with a report, the man gave him a shiny, silver coin. But today… today, he was going to get more than that.

He'd already decided.

"De Lohr came into town very early, m'lord," he said. "De Sherrington came with him."

"The earl's son-in-law?" Walter asked.

The man nodded. "The same," he said. "He's… deadly, m'lord. I didn't want to get too close because de Sherrington is an assassin. Everyone knows he is. He'll kill me and throw my body in the river."

Walter nodded impatiently. "Tell me what you saw and be quick about it."

The man opened his mouth but paused when he saw Agnes enter the well-appointed solar. The room was full of furs and tapestries and valuables, all of it crammed into the small solar of a townhome that belonged to a de Quincy cousin, Saer de Quincy, who was the Earl of Winchester. He also happened to be among the leaders of the rebellion against John and was one more reason why Walter was so determined to make a marriage with de Lohr.

He wanted those connections.

Irritated that his daughter interrupted the spy,

Walter waved the man on.

"Go on, go on," he demanded.

The man was mostly looking at Walter as Agnes eyed him most curiously. "I followed Peter and de Sherrington into London," he said. "They stopped at a tavern to procure food before moving towards Milk Street where he met up with some children. I do not know what happened, or what was said, but they soon left the children and went to the Street of the Jewelers."

Walter's brow furrowed. "Street of the Jewelers?" he said, puzzled. "I wonder why?"

The man lowered his voice. "I do not know why, but I can tell you what I saw," he said. "And it will cost you another coin."

Walter's features stiffened. "You dare to make demands?"

"Not demands, my lord," he said. "What I saw was worth more than the usual payment."

Walter was about to throw the man from the chamber, but thought better of it. He sighed sharply. "Very well," he said. "I'll give you another coin. Tell me what you saw."

Satisfied, the man continued. "He went to the shop of Haim ben Thad. He is the king's jeweler."

Walter recognized the name. "He is one of the most prominent jewelers in all of London," he said. "Peter went there to buy something?"

The man looked between Walter and his

daughter. "I do not think so," he said. "I could not hear what they were saying, but he did not go into the shop. A young woman came forth to greet them and he spoke with her. I was hiding in a doorway, you see, so I could see them clearly. There were other people around, so I did not stand out as a lone man cowering in the shadows and I was able to see a great deal. Peter and this young woman were speaking while de Sherrington was standing off to the side somewhere. He was not part of the conversation."

"*And?*"

The man stepped closer and lowered his voice further, as if divulging a great secret. "And I saw Peter kiss the woman's hand."

"Kiss?" Agnes said, incensed. "Are you certain?"

The man had known from the beginning of his association with de Quincy that all of the spying he was doing was because of Agnes. It was no secret in the de Lohr household that Walter very much wished for a marriage between his daughter and Peter de Lohr, so he knew this news would upset the young woman.

He was right.

Agnes' face was turning as red as her hair.

"Peter was speaking to the young woman, m'lady," he said. "When she lifted her finger to point at him, he took her hand and kissed the tip of her finger. That is not the usual polite kiss. It seemed like there was something more. In fact, it seemed like there was something more through the entire conversation because they were smiling with each other and… and…"

Agnes was ready to explode. "*And* what?"

"And it seemed to me that they were teasing one another – flirting."

Agnes' mouth popped open in outrage. "*Who* is this young woman?"

The man shook his head. "When a man came out of the shop, she called him her father," he said. "I assume it is the jeweler's daughter."

Agnes looked at her father as if she were ready to kill someone. Walter had a sick feeling in his stomach that Peter de Lohr was slipping through his fingers. He quickly paid the man his extra coin and sent him along his way before returning his attention to his daughter.

"A jeweler's daughter," she seethed, pounding her fist on the back of a cushioned chair. "A jeweler's daughter!"

Walter's mind was working quickly. "Not just any jeweler's daughter," he said. "The king's jeweler. There is something significant in that, Agnes. There is something happening."

Agnes stopped pounding the furniture and looked at him. "What could possibly be happening?" she snapped. "That… that whore is to have *my* husband!"

Walter held up a hand. "She's not a whore," he said. "If she is the jeweler's daughter, then she's a Jew and, more than likely, quite sheltered. A Jew cannot marry a Christian and, most importantly, not a de Lohr. Hereford would never allow it."

"If he knows," Agnes pointed out. "He may not know at all."

A thought occurred to Walter. "Mayhap not," he said. "But that will change. I am happy to tell him that his son is allowing himself to be seduced by the jeweler's daughter. The jeweler of John, the very man we are fighting against. Mayhap Peter is even giving the woman information about the rebellion."

"Of course!" Agnes cried. Somehow, it made her feel better to have a reason behind Peter's defection other than the fact he simply didn't like her. "That is the only thing that makes sense. She is seducing him to discover the rebellion's plans so that she can tell her father and he can tell the king!"

Walter looked at her, shocked by his own revelation. Peter de Lohr was leaking information to the king's cause. He clapped his hands together sharply.

"Quickly," he said. "Tell the servants to bring my horse around. I must ride to Lonsdale immediately."

"Can I come?" Agnes begged.

Walter shook his head. "Nay, Daughter," he said. "You remain here. I will tell Hereford personally that his son is a traitor and I do not need you present. I will tell him that I will not inform the rest of the warlords of his son's betrayal if he will immediately consent to a betrothal. After all, I would never betray family. Truly, this is perfect. Young Peter has done our work for us."

Agnes squealed with delight and dashed off, shouting to the servants to have her father's horse prepared. Walter could hear the commotion in the house as he went to collect his cloak. As he'd said, the situation was perfect. Now he had a bargaining chip to use against de Lohr when it came to the betrothal that Hereford was so keen to dodge. If Walter threatened to tell the rebel warlords that Peter was a traitor to their cause, then surely de Lohr would do anything to save his son.

Even marry him to Agnes de Quincy.

Truly… he couldn't have planned it better. Walter was quite happy to gloat about it when a nervous servant brought him a missive that had just been delivered. Annoyed at the interruption, he was about to toss it aside when he saw Pembroke's seal.

William Marshal.

Quickly, Walter broke the seal and read the

contents. He read it twice. Tossing the missive aside, he went shouting for his horse even though the servants were already preparing it. In less than ten minutes' time, Walter was tearing from the small yard of the townhome, riding out to the countryside east of London.

The Marshal's missive had him heading straight for the de Lohr stronghold of Lonsdale.

CHAPTER TEN

P ETER DIDN'T EVEN know where to start.

He and Alexander had just entered the hallowed halls of the Great Synagogue, an enormous building with stone walls and, from what they could see, a great wooden ceiling supported by massive wooden beams in the sanctuary beyond the entry. There was a hard-packed, earthen floor and a riser somewhere in the middle of it. It smelled of dirt and another strange smell which Peter assumed to be incense.

They were standing in a small entry, not particularly well lit, but they could see men moving around inside the sanctuary itself. Before them were four big pillars, reaching to the ceiling, and some kind of symbolic table in the center. They took a few steps towards it, mostly because

Peter wanted to get the attention of someone in the sanctuary so he could ask for Rabbi Judah, but as they moved they noticed there was a second sanctuary to their right, long and narrow. They took one more step and, abruptly, a man wearing a shawl and a hood appeared before them.

"My lords," he said, speaking with an accent. "You are not permitted here."

Peter looked at the man, small and meek, who was rather brave facing two much larger, armed men. "I know," he said. "Forgive us, but I seek Rabbi Judah. Is he here?"

The man looked at him curiously. "Rabbi Judah?"

"Aye."

"You know him?"

"I know *of* him," Peter said. "Is he here?"

The man nodded. "Aye, he is here," he said. "*Shacharit* is finished now. But why do you wish to see him?"

"That is my business," he said, wondering what *Shacharit* was but he was too impatient to ask. "I can promise you that our intention is purely peaceful, however. Will you send him to me? I will wait outside the door if it is more appropriate."

With that, he and Alexander turned for the door, stepping outside to wait. Peter was more focused on the doorway and what was going on inside, hearing the man who had greeted them shouting something in a language he didn't understand. As he stood near the door and listened, Alexander scanned the area, looking for any threats, or worse, someone they knew. They were on a street called Jewry, which was the center of the Jewish neighborhood in London. The synagogue was the center of the district and he stepped down onto the street, looking up at the building, thinking on the synagogues he had seen when he was in The Levant.

"There was a massive synagogue in Jerusalem," he said, looking up. "It is called the Great Temple or the Temple of Solomon, though some called it the Temple Mount. When the crusaders captured the city, the temple was given over to a group calling themselves the Poor Knights of Christ and the Temple of Solomon. They became known as the Templars."

Peter looked at him. "I remember that story," he said. "You were in The Levant, Sherry. You must have seen many Jewish temples."

Alexander nodded. "Many," he said. "And I spent time at the Temple Mount. A great and mysterious place. In fact, all of Jerusalem is a great and mysterious place. It is full of ghosts."

"Indeed, it is."

The voice came from the entry and they both turned to see a rabbi who didn't look much like a rabbi. He was young, with curly brown hair, and a gap-toothed smile. He had a shawl on his shoulders and wore the traditional hood that the Jewish rabbis wore at this time, and he looked at Peter and Alexander in a manner that was both curious and friendly.

"I'm Judah," he said. "I understand you wish to speak with me?"

Peter nodded, suddenly a little tongue-tied. Now that he was faced with a man with answers to his all of his religion-related questions, he didn't quite know what to say. It occurred to him that the situation with Liora had just become real. Until this minute, it had been only talk. Everything had only been sweet talk and implications. But now… now, this was the turning point.

The speculation of a Jewish bride was becoming a reality.

Everything was happening so fast.

"I came to seek you, Father… I mean, Rabbi." He paused, chuckling. "How should I address you?"

Judah chuckled along with him. "Rabbi is acceptable," he said. "Or Judah. Most rabbis are quite formal, but I am not. Children find the title intimidating sometimes and I do like to speak to the children in a way that will not frighten them. But, please – call me whatever you feel comfortable with. I must say that I am surprised to see two

Christian knights on my doorstep, asking for me by name. Did someone send you?"

"Not exactly," Peter said. He opened his mouth to continue, but realized he hadn't introduced himself. "I apologize for my bad manners. My name is Peter de Lohr. This is my sister's husband, Alexander de Sherrington."

Judah looked at Alexander. "I heard you speaking of the Templars," he said. "You were in The Levant?"

Alexander nodded. "I was with King Richard's army."

Judah grinned that gap-toothed smile. "Ah," he said. "The Great Quest. How long were you there?"

"Three years," Alexander said. "But I spent another eight years after that wandering before I came home to England."

"Lost?"

Alexander snorted. "Not literally, but spiritually," he said. "I saw a great deal in The Levant that made me question life in general."

Judah's smile faded. "I am sure your intentions were noble," he said. "But I think many men lost their way during the Great Quest. Battle and corruption has a way of changing a man's heart."

Alexander studied the young rabbi a moment. "That is quite true," Alexander said. "You sound as if you know. But you were too young to be present when I was there."

Judah smiled weakly. "My grandfather was in Jerusalem when the Christians took possession of it," he said. "He both admired and feared them. I heard you speaking of the Temple Mount and I heard my grandfather speak of it, too. It is a most definitely a mysterious place and quite haunted."

"You believe in spirits?"

"Absolutely," Judah said emphatically. "That is something we can all agree on, I think."

Alexander rather liked the young rabbi who was surprisingly friendly. He looked at Peter, who seemed to still be working up the nerve to ask his questions. He hadn't been able to bring them forth yet, so Alexander took pity on him.

"Indeed, we can," he said. "But I am sure you are a busy man, Rabbi, so I will take no more of your time speaking of spirits and mystery. Let us come to the point. No one sent us, but someone who… who admires you gave us your name. We hope you are a man who can help clear up some confusion."

"Oh?" Judah looked between the knights curiously. "What confusion?"

Alexander lowered his voice because what they were about to discuss more than likely should have been done in private, but the rabbi hadn't invited them inside the synagogue for such a discussion, so they were going to have it out on the street.

"As you realize, we were raised in the Catholic faith," her said. "We know nothing of the Jewish religion other than what we have been told, but a situation has arisen that requires answers."

"I will tell you what I can."

"How does the Jewish religion view a marriage between a Jew and a Christian?"

It was apparent that Judah hadn't been expecting that question. He appeared surprised at first, but that expression turned thoughtful very quickly.

"Intermarriage?" he said. "That is certainly a serious topic. Why do you ask? You don't have a Jewish sweetheart, do you?"

Peter nearly choked. He started coughing as Alexander covered for him. "Nay, I do not," he said. "I am a married man. But a… a friend has. He has met a fine woman who happens to be Jewish."

"A fellow knight," Peter put in helpfully.

Alexander eyed the man who couldn't seem to find his tongue. "Aye," he said. "A fellow knight. This man is fond of a Jewess and is considering marrying her. What would have to happen in order to make a marriage recognized by the Jewish religion?"

Judah stroked his chin. "I think this is a question with a complex answer," he said. "There is no simple way to address it."

"It is truly such a difficult question?" Peter asked. "What I mean to say is that a marriage, if consent is given on both sides, should be able to take place, shouldn't it? Can't a Christian man marry a Jewish woman?"

Judah turned his attention to Peter. "In days past, such a thing was forbidden under the penalty of death."

"Is that still the case?"

Judah shook his head. "No longer," he said. "That was mostly in the days of old, when Romans occupied Jerusalem. Today, we consider ourselves more understanding and civilized. But the Talmud declares that any marriage between a Jew and non-Jew is invalid. The Christian Bible also cautions against a marriage between a Jew and a Christian. A passage in the Book of Ezra, I believe, discourages it. So, it is not simply one religion declaring that such a marriage is discouraged. It is both."

Peter knew that was going to be the answer, but he still needed to hear it. "But what if one person converts to the other's religion?"

Judah shrugged. "Then, it is possible," he said. "But only if the Christian converts to Judaism. If the Jewish person converts to Christianity, then the marriage shall not be recognized under Jewish law. The family would be shamed, mayhap even forbidden to worship in the temple."

Peter folded his big arms over his chest, looking up to the synagogue as he pondered what he'd been told. "Is there no exception where a Christian and a Jew can marry and have the marriage accepted by both religions?"

Judah shook his head. "Nay," he said. "There is no such thing. It is one or the other, Sir Peter. Either your friend and his sweetheart are all Jewish or they are all Christian."

Peter drew in a long, thoughtful breath. "Have you ever known any Jewish and Christian marriages?"

Judah shook his head. "I've not known any," he said. "You must understand that our religion is very old, Sir Peter. Older than the Christians. It goes back thousands of years and our laws have been created over those years to protect our people and ensure our survival. We come from the land of Jesus, older than even England and those who walked her shores before the Normans came. Any man, or woman, who breaks faith with us breaks faith with God. Their soul will be lost."

Peter was growing increasingly depressed as he realized there was no gray area, no rules to bend. It was one way or the other, as strict as the natural laws of night and day.

"I do not understand," he said. "We worship the same God, do we not?"

"We do."

"Then why are there different rules for the Christians and different rules for the Jews?"

"Because our origins are different," Judah said. "Our land, our language, our spiritual needs. They are different from Christians, so the laws are different."

"Men make the laws," Peter muttered. When Judah looked at him, surprised, he didn't back off. "The Bible was written by disciples and prophets. Christ did not write the Books of the Bible and I'm certain he did not write the pages of the Talmud. Those were not written by angels, but by men. Men make the rules."

"With God's guidance," Judah said pointedly. "The men who wrote the laws were vessels for God. They did not write them down to suit their own purposes."

"You are saying those men didn't add a law or two because they wanted to?"

Judah smiled, lopsided. "Mayhap," he said. "But if God is watching over your shoulder, are you truly going to write something down that he does not like?"

He made a good case, as a rabbi should. But Peter didn't want to get into a philosophical argument with him. In fact, he'd already said too much. He'd received answers he had already suspected were the truth of the situation and he wasn't happy because of it.

The situation was growing as dire as he thought it would be.

"But what about love and harmony?" he said. "What if the Christian and the Jew love one another? Does that even matter?"

Judah paused thoughtfully before shaking his head. "Marriage is about more than love," he said. "You understand that marriages are made for financial gain or property, to produce children to populate the earth. Love is not a consideration, or at least not a large consideration."

Peter frowned as Alexander reached out to grasp his arm. "I think we've taken enough of Rabbi Judah's time," he said. "We will take this information back to our friend, Rabbi. You've been very tolerant of two non-Jews."

Peter nodded, but it was obvious that he was unhappy. "Of course," he said, forcing a smile at the young rabbi. "You have been very helpful, Rabbi. It means a great deal that you've taken the time to speak with us."

Judah smiled. "I am very happy to do it," he said. "If you have further questions, I am honored to answer them if I can."

Peter's smile turned genuine. "That is kind of you," he said. He paused before continuing. "I will tell you a secret – I have never met a rabbi before."

Judah laughed softly. "And I have never spoken to a Christian knight before," he said. "At least, not like this. I see them come in and out of the city with their big swords and big horses, and they look like death personified, so to speak to two knights who are intelligent and kind… I have learned something today."

"What is that?"

"Never to judge a man by his vocation."

"Then that makes two of us."

As they snorted, Alexander held up a hand. "Three of us," he said. "You've been very accommodating, Rabbi. We shall not forget it. Should you ever need the service of a Christian knight, send word to Lonsdale House. We are in your debt."

Judah simply nodded, waving at them as they turned for their horses. Mounting up, they headed down the street without a hind glance to the rabbi, still standing there, watching them go.

"He knew it was me," Peter muttered. "He knew I was asking for me."

Alexander tightened up his reins. "If he did, he was gracious not to call you out," he said. "Well? Did you learn what you wanted to know?"

"Unfortunately, I did."

"What are you going to do?"

Peter shook his head. "I do not know yet," he said. "I will return home and think on it for the rest of the day and then I shall see Liora tomorrow and tell her of the conversation."

Alexander looked at him. "Peter, far be it from me to say anything about this situation, but you hardly know the woman," he said. "You have only just met her."

Peter looked at him. "How long did you know my sister before you knew she was the woman you wanted to marry?"

The only reply Alexander had would make him look like a fool. He looked away.

"Days."

"And do you regret that you did not court her for years before you made the decision to marry her?"

"Never. She was the best decision I have ever made."

Peter could understand that. More and more, he was feeling like that when it came to Liora. "Sometimes… you just know," he said. "And with Liora, I just know, Sherry. I cannot explain it better than that."

Alexander had no argument for that. He was finished trying to talk Peter out of anything. "Well," he said after a moment. "Not that I blame you. She is astonishingly beautiful."

Peter grinned. "Isn't she?"

Alexander nodded sincerely. "Other than my wife and her mother, I've never seen finer."

Peter laughed softly. Leave it to Alexander to be tactful when speaking of another woman's beauty. But Peter hoped that, now, he at least had an ally in Alexander when it came to the pursuit of Liora ben Thad.

He was going to need it.

After stopping by The Farmer's Prick to pay for several months' worth of food for Saul's Army, they headed back to Lonsdale in silence. However, as they both knew, Peter would be back in London tomorrow.

Back to see his blue-eyed beauty.

CHAPTER ELEVEN

T HEY BEGAN ARRIVING around the nooning hour.

The first to arrive was William Marshal. Christopher had been in the stables inspecting an expensive warhorse that had come up lame when he heard his sentries making noise. Someone had arrived and by the time he got out to the bailey, he saw William dismounting his horse.

But that wasn't what had Christopher surprised. It was the fact that he had several rebel warlords with him – all of The Northerners plus a few others. Puzzled, Christopher went out to meet them.

"William," he greeted calmly, seeing Jax, Juston, and de Longley standing next to the man.

There were others, too, and he looked around the group that was dismounting, sending their horses off with servants. "Evidently I was to host a party today and did not even know it. My wife will be furious."

William grinned. "We will go into the hall and stay there," he said. "She will not even know we have arrived."

More men were coming in through the gates and Christopher cocked an eyebrow. "I doubt it."

William started walking towards the manse. "Come, Chris," he said. "Let us retreat inside. There is much to discuss."

Christopher hung back by Jax, walking next to the man as they headed towards his manse. "What is this about?" he muttered.

Jax eyed his friend. "Trouble, I am guessing."

Christopher grunted. "I assumed as much," he said. "But you do not know what kind?"

"He's not spoken of it yet."

"It looks like he's brought the whole damned north with him."

Jax nodded. "Very nearly," he said. "It started before dawn. I received word from The Marshal to meet him at the nooning hour here at Lonsdale. We all received word, so that is why we've all come."

Christopher pursed his lips irritably. "The least he could have done was tell me since he is using my home," he said. He looked over his shoulder, seeing many faces he recognized. In fact, he recognized all of them, including his brother and Marcus. "The Executioner Knights are here."

"I know."

"So are Daveigh and Cullen. John's allies."

"They are."

"*What* in the hell is going on?"

Jax didn't have any answers. "The Marshal has not been completely forthcoming with information, so your guess is as good as mine," he said. "It must be serious indeed if The Marshal has called us all together."

Christopher couldn't argue with that. He walked with Jax up the stairs leading to the manse and through the massive, reinforced entry door. The hall was to the rear, with windows that overlooked the river. It was a spectacular room, well-appointed and tasteful thanks to Lady Hereford, and Christopher sent servants on the run when he entered. Men were pouring into the chamber and he cast Marcus and David long looks as they walked past him.

They didn't know anything more than Jax did.

Attracted by the noise, Dustin came downstairs only to be faced with a hall full of knights and lords, warlords that were shaping the fate of a nation. Stricken, she looked at her husband.

"What is this?" she demanded. "Did you not

think to tell me you would be entertaining our friends and allies this day?"

Christopher shrugged. "I did not know myself until a short time ago," he said. "It seems that The Marshal has called everyone here to discuss something, so quickly prepare drink and refreshments. I do not care what it is. Anything will be fine. And keep the servants away from the doors and windows. Some of them have big ears."

Dustin nodded, still miffed at the sight of so many men in her hall. Still more were coming in, including Roger and Hugh Bigod, the Earl of Suffolk and his heir. A few other minor barons entered, one of them being Walter de Quincy, who greeted Dustin as if she were a long-lost friend. Not particularly liking the man and his pursuit of Peter, her response was cool. Walter entered the hall after Lady Hereford's rebuff, trying not to look embarrassed.

While Christopher was in discussion with William over near the windows overlooking the Thames, David came over to Dustin.

"Where is Peter?" he hissed. "And Sherry? Are they here?"

Dustin looked at her brother-in-law. "I do not know," she said. "I will send a servant to find them."

"Hurry," David said. "Whatever William has to speak about is serious. He wants all of his knights here."

Dustin dashed off as David, along with Marcus, secured the doors to the hall. David put Bric and Dashiell on the doors to ensure no one entered who wasn't invited as he made his way over to his brother.

"Dustin is sending a servant for Peter and Sherry," he said. "Is everyone here?"

Christopher couldn't even answer that. This was William's party, so he looked at the man who was gazing out over the crowd. When William caught sight of Christopher and David, both looking at him expectantly, he simply nodded his head.

"This will do," he said quietly.

As he held up a hand to silence the buzz of conversation, Christopher whistled loudly between his teeth, which shut the room up almost instantly. Everyone lent an ear in The Marshal's direction, wondering why they had been summoned to Lonsdale.

They would soon find out.

"Good men," William said. "Forgive the secrecy, but it was necessary. John has men all over London and any gathering of note would be reported to the king, so that is why I chose Lonsdale. My apologies to Chris for not telling him sooner."

Everyone grinned as Christopher shrugged, as

if he'd had any choice in the matter. William's yellowed eyes glimmered weakly at the man before he returned his attention to the crowd.

"Late last night, I received word from a man I have in the north," he said. "A trustworthy man who has served me and the House of de Lohr well. His name is Kevin de Lara and his brother, Sean, was the Lord of the Shadows. You all know that name and what it represents, so I will not go into it. Kevin is in the north while two more men who serve me, Achilles de Dere and Kress de Rhydian, are in the south and in East Anglia. Their directive is simple – comb the land, talk to men and discover what they can about the king's allies and their movements. They have been doing this for the better part of four months. But last night, I received a full report from Achilles, who is in Kent. It is disturbing to say the least."

Someone knocked on the hall doors and Bric opened them to admit servants with food and drink. They moved quickly and efficiently, directed by Dustin, who had them set the pitchers of wine on the dais along with wheels of cheese, bread, and great platters of apples and bowls of blackberries. It was the best she could do with such short notice, so she hustled the servants from the hall as Bric and Dashiell shut the doors behind them. Only when they were gone did Christopher turn to William.

"I wasn't aware that Achilles and Kress were scouting for you," he said. "I knew that Kevin was, but I was under the impression that Achilles and Kress were commanding your various holdings."

William nodded. "That is because I wanted the rebel barons to think that they were inactive for the most part," he said, looking out over the hall. "I wanted you all to think that. Today, the king believes he has my support and that is what I want him to believe because without Sean de Lara to keep an eye on him as his bodyguard, our cause is blind. That is why I stand with the king at the moment – because if I am by his side, I can keep abreast of what he is up to. Unfortunately, he does not share everything with me, as evidenced by Achilles' missive. According to Achilles, we have a mess in the south. D'Aubigney, who was positioned at Rochester Castle on behalf of the Earl of East Anglia since it is his holding, has been met with a rush of mercenaries sent by John. The French king, whom you rebels have allied yourselves with, have come ashore in Dover. Dover Castle is under siege as well because it is held by the king."

It was true that the rebel warlords had offered an alliance with the French king in exchange for his military might. That was something Christopher and several others had never been in complete agreement with, but they had been overruled by some of the warlords in Kent, Suffolk, and Norfolk, men who were under more threat than an earldom on the Welsh Marches. Therefore, the arrival of the French wasn't surprising, but the arrival of the mercenaries was.

"So it starts in the south," Christopher said, mulling over the information. "We knew that John had hoarded money to pay for his mercenaries and we knew they were coming to England even as John tried to negotiate peace with us. However, we were told the mercenaries would be flooding into the north."

"They are," William said. "I received a missive two days ago from Kress informing me that thousands of them sailed into Hull, looted the town, and are currently heading north from what he has been told. He's not seen them, but he is told that they are heading for Yorkshire and Northumberland."

He was looking at Jax, de Bourne, de Vesci, and de Longley as he said it. All of them had massive land holdings in Northumberland. But he also looked at Marcus, who had holdings in Yorkshire.

The implications were staggering.

"How old is this information?" Jax asked calmly.

William looked to the old warlord, once the most terrifying warlord in the entire world. Truth be told, he still was. William had used the man last year to accomplish some unsavory tasks because de Velt was the best man for the job. Even at his advanced age, he still was.

There was great respect there.

"Several weeks, at least," William said. "It would be my suggestion that the northern barons depart immediately. If you still have troops in London, withdraw them and go home. Immediately. With thousands of mercenaries overrunning the north, your properties are vulnerable."

That meant de Velt, de Bourne, Marcus, de Longley, d'Umfraville, and even Caius, who garrisoned Richmond Castle. There were several Northerners in that hall, now looking at each other nervously.

"You are aware that Scotland's king has allied with us," Jax said. "You are further aware that I have offered to return Berwick Castle in exchange for this alliance."

William nodded. "I have been told," he said. "Worse still, John knows. Word must be sent to Alexander because the mercenaries will overrun his southern border if he is not there to stop them. John intends to charge into Scotland and take all of the land south of Edinburgh because of Alexander's interference."

There were massive implications on every shore, every border, it seemed, but none so massive as the fact that mercenaries were already in England with the king's blessing.

That was the worst news of all.

"I must return home, too," David said. "Savernake, too. If they are going after properties in Kent, Canterbury will be vulnerable. I must return home and reinforce my holdings."

Bentley de Vaston, the Duke of Savernake, was standing near the windows. He heard David, nodding firmly to the man's statement. "It's not just in the north," he said. "They're going to move through the south, too, like a plague of locusts. I must return to Ramsbury and make sure we are prepared to meet an onslaught."

William realized he was facing men who were close to panicking. They were seasoned veterans, but their families were at their homes in the threatened territories and no man wanted their wife and children to be vulnerable to John's mercenaries. Perhaps the only men not immediately concerned were de Lohr, Wolverhampton, de Quincy, and Maxton because their properties were either on the Welsh Marches or nearby, so they weren't quite so critical.

"I am telling you this so you can depart London immediately and prepare," he said, lifting his voice over the buzz of concern. "I should also tell you that John plans to take the field with his mercenaries and allies. He has no intention of sitting aside while men fight for him. He intends to command from the field."

That wasn't unwelcome as far as the warlords were concerned, nor was it surprising. John had fought with his armies since the days of fighting with his brothers against their father, so not strangely, the king they hated and railed against was a war veteran just as they were.

"Good," Jax said, his voice a rumble. "Let him come north and take the field. I will be more than happy to meet him there."

They all turned to look at the man known as The Dark Lord issue what sounded very much like a threat. No man wanted to hear that come out of Jax's mouth where it pertained to them because he meant what he said. He would find John on the field of battle and kill him. Then, the attention turned to William who had spent the better part of John's reign protecting the king from threats, of which there had been many. That had been The Marshal's job for all those years.

But William didn't openly react.

Perhaps he was finally coming to hope the same thing.

"That is the news I needed to impart upon you, good lords," he said. "Many of you will have plans to make, so I would suggest you do so. The sooner you return home, the better, for England is a pile of kindling and John has just struck a spark.

We must make sure to control that fire or it will consume us all."

It was a neat, concise way of putting things, something quite appropriate. As he went to speak to de Vaston and David, Christopher went over to Marcus and Jax, who were standing in conversation with Caius, Edward de Wolfe, and Alastor de Bourne. Christopher looked between Marcus and Jax.

"Well," he said. "Now we know why The Marshal summoned everyone. I cannot say that I am surprised. We knew this would come."

Marcus nodded. "We did," he said. "But I am concerned that I am not home at this moment. I left Gabrielle and the children behind and I do not like the idea of them being in a castle under siege without me."

Christopher put a hand on his shoulder. "I know," he said. "I can spare men to send back with you, but not many. How many do you have at Somerhill?"

Marcus shrugged. "Around fifteen hundred," he said. "I do not think I need any of your men, so mayhap you had better send them with David to Canterbury. If the mercenaries are at Rochester, it's very possible they will head to Canterbury, knowing it is a de Lohr holding."

That was very true. As Christopher turned to see to his brother, Walter passed in his line of sight. Christopher moved to go around him, but Walter cut him off.

"My lord," he said. "May we speak? I have something important I must discuss with you."

Christopher had little patience for Walter. "I am afraid I must speak with my brother," he said. "I have no time at the moment."

"It is about Peter, my lord, but not what you think," he said, cutting off Christopher again when he tried to step around him. "Something… terrible has come to my attention that you should be aware of."

Christopher didn't want to talk to him and most especially about Peter. "This is no time to discuss your marital aspirations, de Quincy," he said, annoyed. "We will discuss Peter at another time."

Walter still wouldn't move out of his way. "This has nothing to do with marital aspirations, I assure you," he said. "There is something you must know about your son and I do not wish to shout it to the hall. I do not think you want this to be common knowledge."

Frustrated, Christopher was trying not to lose his temper. "Then speak," he said. "But be quick about it because I have business with my brother."

Pleased that he had Christopher's attention, Walter indicated the door. "Shall we go somewhere private?"

"Nay. Tell me now."

Walter's pleasant expression faded. "Very well," he said. "Were you aware that your son is being seduced by a Jewess?"

That caught Christopher's attention. His manner cooled as he looked at Walter. "What are you talking about?"

"Just what I said. He is being seduced by a Jewess."

"Who has told you this?"

"I have my sources, de Lohr. Were you aware of this?"

"He has not been seduced by anyone."

Walter shook his head. "That is not entirely true," he said. "I have it on good authority that your son openly kissed the daughter of the king's jeweler. It was witnessed, only once, but who knows if there have been more incidents that no one has seen. Of course, her father is the personal jeweler to the king, meaning he has the king's ear. I wonder what secrets she is wresting from your son that her father might tell John?"

Christopher had to take a step back from the man because his instinct was to grab him around the neck and throw him out the window. But he didn't; it was sheer, practiced control that he didn't. His eyes narrowed as he sized up a man he hadn't had much use for before, but now... now, he had none.

Absolutely none.

"Who is this 'good' authority?" he asked with a hint of hazard. "Do you mean the spies you pay to follow Peter and report on his every move, including the servant here at Lonsdale? Don't think I don't know about that, de Quincy. I know everything."

Walter didn't like that his upper hand was slipping. His smile began to fade. "But you did not know that your son is cavorting with someone who is not of his faith," he said. "Someone who is loyal to the king."

Christopher's jaw flexed dangerously. "What, exactly, are you accusing my son of?"

Walter lifted his shoulders. "I am not accusing him of anything," he said. "But others might be led to believe that your son was a traitor to you, his allies, and his friends. I shouldn't like a rumor like that to get started, my lord. Not at all. But if he is not being seduced by a woman spying for the king, what on earth would he be doing with her?"

Christopher took a long, deep breath. He was too close to forgetting his decision not to throw Walter out of the window.

"Why are you telling me this, de Quincy?" he asked. "What do you want from me? Be plain."

Walter was trying hard not to smile. "Want?" he repeated. "There is nothing I want, although now that you bring it up, we have been discussing a betrothal between your son and my Agnes. Of course, I would never betray my daughter's husband and any rumors about a Jewess seductress would be firmly met with denial. I would defend him to the death, I swear it."

"*If* he marries Agnes."

"I would have no reason to defend him if he was not."

Christopher had never heard, or seen, such a blatant bit of blackmail. The only thing that kept him from snapping Walter's neck was the fact that he didn't know where Peter was at the moment. He hadn't show up in the hall, and neither had Alexander, so he had no idea where those two were. Since Peter had brought up the jeweler's daughter the day before, he had a sick feeling in his stomach that there might be some truth to what Walter was saying. Not that Peter was a traitor, because Peter was one of the most trustworthy men he knew, but kissing the woman… well, he couldn't be sure that it hadn't happened. And Walter was correct when he said that allied warlords might view that as an act of betrayal given the kiss would be with the daughter of the king's jeweler.

He had to find his son.

"I will think on it," he said as evenly as he could. "But if any of what you have said finds its way to other ears, I will come for you and I will destroy you. Your body will end up in a river somewhere and your daughter will be left destitute. Is this in any way unclear?"

Walter's eyes widened. "Why would I speak of it? That is why I told you in private."

Christopher was a good deal taller and bigger than Walter. He leaned over, posturing over the man threateningly. "That had better be the truth," he growled. "Keep your lips shut or I will cut your tongue out."

With that, he continued past Walter, heading for his brother, who saw him coming. He'd also seen the exchange between Walter and Christopher. By the time his brother reached him, his jaw was ticking furiously and David looked at him with concern.

"What is it?" he asked. "What happened with de Quincy?"

Christopher was so angry that he could barely speak. "I must find my son," he rumbled. "When I do, I am going to send him off to the Marches today. Damn that boy."

David's eyes widened. "Who?" he said. "Peter? What in the hell happened?"

By this time, Marcus had joined them. He, too, had seen the exchange between Christopher and Walter, and Christopher's evident upset.

"What happened, Chris?" he asked. "What did Walter say?"

Marcus knew about Peter's interest in a certain Jewess, but David did not. Christopher tried to remain calm and succinct as he explained the situation to the two men he trusted more than any others.

"Marcus knows this, so the explanation is for your benefit, David," he said through clenched teeth. "Yesterday, Peter informed me that he had found a woman he was attracted to. He was quite enamored with her, or at least he seemed to be. However, the woman is a Jewess, the daughter of the king's jeweler."

David's eyebrows lifted in surprise. "A Jew?" he hissed. "And Peter was serious?"

Christopher sighed heavily. "He seemed to be," he muttered. "And you know how de Quincy has been trying to secure a betrothal between Peter and his unpleasant daughter. Right now, Walter just told me that he has it on good authority that this Jewess has seduced Peter and is probing him for rebel secrets, which she is then passing to her father and, subsequently, the king. He stopped short of calling Peter a traitor if – and only if – he marries Agnes because, surely, de Quincy would not betray his son-in-law."

It was a shocking statement. Marcus' head snapped to Walter, who was over at the table pouring himself some wine. David's eyes were so wide with outrage that they threatened to pop from his head.

"He *threatened* you?" David muttered, incredulous.

"That is my assumption," Christopher said. "If I do not agree to a betrothal, then he'll tell the warlords that Peter is betraying them to the king through the jeweler's daughter."

As David rolled his eyes, infuriated, Marcus' gaze was on Walter as the man calmly drank his wine and spoke to d'Umfraville.

"What do you want me to do with him, Chris?" he rumbled. "Tell me and I shall do it."

Christopher wouldn't look at Walter, but he knew the man was still in the hall. He could smell his stench. "I have overlooked him until now," he said. "He is an ally on the Marches but nothing more. It was important to keep him as an ally, but he has pushed me too far. He's threatening my son. Mayhap someone should warn him that something like that will not be well met in the end."

With that, he broke away from his brother and Marcus, heading over to speak with The Marshal. But both Marcus and David had heard Christopher's reply. There was a message there. It was something they understood clearly, as did the other Executioner Knights who happened to be in the hall once Marcus explained the situation to them.

No one made a threat against an Executioner Knight and got away with it.

Walter made it back to London later that day, but not before he was ambushed while riding alone at the end of a group of warlords and soldiers who were heading back to their respective homes. Walter was pulled off his horse by men who moved swiftly and smoothly, taken into the trees, tied up, and beaten within an inch of his life. Then he was removed from the trees and thrown over the saddle of his own horse, which then wandered back to Lonsdale. When Christopher was told about Walter's beaten body, he instructed his soldiers to take the man back to London and let Saer de Quincy deal with his cousin.

Christopher wouldn't lift a finger to help him.

He hadn't been part of the ambush that broke ribs and knocked out six of Walter's teeth, but he knew Maxton, Caius, and Marcus' work when he saw it. And he wasn't sorry, either. However, the entire incident with Walter had his anger primed and ready for when Peter and Alexander arrived home towards sunset.

He was waiting for them.

One look at his father and Peter knew he was in for it.

CHAPTER TWELVE

"*T*HAT'S WHERE YOU were?" Christopher said, aghast. "The Great Synagogue?"

Standing in his father's sparse solar with Alexander standing somewhere back behind him, Peter was facing his very angry father.

But he stood his ground.

"Aye," he said. "I went to speak to the rabbi so I could understand the challenges in a marriage between a Christian and a Jew."

Christopher was so mad that he was close to breaking his teeth. His jaw was grinding as he struggled not to explode at his son. Knowing that Alexander had been with him only made him madder. His focus moved from Peter to Alexander, back by the solar door.

"I would have thought you would show more

sense where this is concerned," he said, his tone strained. "You are a good deal older than Peter is, Sherry. You have seen the world. How could you, in good conscience, go with him on this... this *folly* and not stop him? At the very least, not stop to tell me what was happening?"

Alexander knew he deserved the lashing. He was prepared to take it. "I am not his father nor his keeper," he said evenly. "I saw him slip from Lonsdale before sunrise and my instincts told me to go with him to keep him out of trouble. That is the only reason I went – to make sure he did not come to harm. He is capable of making his own decisions and it is not my place nor my privilege to tell him what to do. But I would be remiss if I let him go at it alone."

That pushed Christopher over the edge, mostly because he knew Alexander was right. Furious, he grabbed the nearest chair and smashed it against the stone windowsill before tossing the whole broken mess from the window and out to the river's edge below. He did it to release energy, but it didn't work.

He was as mad as ever.

"Of all the damned, stupid actions," he snarled, bracing his fists on the windowsill, his gaze on the river beyond. "Damned, stupid actions that will come back to haunt you, Peter. I told you not to pursue this."

Peter was a little concerned having just watched his father demolish a chair. "Papa, I…"

"Shut your lips!" Christopher whirled on him, jabbing a finger at him. "Shut your foolish lips and listen to me. For once, just *listen* to me. Your little foray into London may very well cost you your freedom because Walter de Quincy's spies saw you. You know the man has people following you everywhere you go. One of those spies saw you in London, with this… this *woman*… and now Walter is threatening to tell the rebel allies that you are giving information to the daughter of the king's jeweler so that her father may pass our secrets on to John. Are you satisfied now?"

He was yelling by the time he was finished. Peter stood there, eyes wide and mouth hanging open. "I did no such thing!" he fired back. "We never discussed you or the rebellion or anything at all. I would never do such a thing!"

Christopher knew that. Deep down, he knew that. His son was trustworthy, but he was so angry that he was bordering on irrational. He struggled to calm himself before he broke another chair, or worse. He took several deep, long breaths before attempting to reply.

"The Marshal called a gathering this morning," he said. "A gathering you both should have been part of, but because of Peter's recklessness, your absence was noticeable. The Marshal has received word from Kevin and Achilles that John's mercenaries are already in England. They have lain siege to Rochester Castle. Dover Castle is also being harassed by French troops which landed and are trying to wrest it from the royalists who hold it. All of The Northerners are removing their armies from London today and departing for home. They have no chance of catching the mercenary army before it reaches Yorkshire and Northumberland, but they are going to try. Sherry, you are to muster all our troops and prepare them to depart by the end of the week. Send a thousand men to Canterbury. David is going to need them."

Alexander nodded sharply. "It shall be done."

"You may leave."

Alexander quit the room without another word, leaving Christopher and Peter alone. Calmer now, Christopher focused on his son.

His golden boy, his eldest, a man he was so proud of that it was all he could do not to shout it from the rooftops. But at the moment, he felt sorely disappointed in the judgment of the man. He'd made a mistake that was going to cost him.

"And you," he said, more quietly. "You will be departing for Ludlow in the morning. I need you on the Marches, taking control of my new properties. Your task will be to secure all four properties and staff them with de Lohr troops pilfered from Lioncross. Do you understand?"

Peter swallowed hard and nodded but had the sense not to argue. He didn't want to leave London, not now, but any resistance to his father's wishes would not be well met. Therefore, he didn't try. He simply agreed.

But his father wasn't done with him yet.

"If you think I am sending you out of London to punish you, you would only be half-correct," Christopher said. "There is a large part of me sending you away for your own good. But there is another part of me who wants you away from the warlords and away from Walter. He intends to leverage your interaction with the jeweler's daughter to get what he wants – if you marry Agnes, he will keep the secret. If you do not, he will tell the warlords what he was told and declare you a traitor to our cause."

Peter rolled his eyes, so incredibly outraged at what he was hearing. "*What*?" he hissed. "But I did nothing wrong, Papa. De Quincy is simply angry because I want nothing to do with his rude, petty daughter."

Christopher knew that, but he couldn't get past his son's bad judgment. "Did you kiss the Jewess?"

Peter looked at him, shocked. "Kiss her? Of course I did not kiss her."

"Did you kiss her hand?"

Peter opened his mouth to deny it, but quickly

remembered that he had. "Her finger," he said as the thought occurred to him. "She stuck her finger in my face and I kissed it. It was playful, innocent. I certainly did not ravage the girl for all to see. Ask Sherry."

Christopher cocked an eyebrow. "I will deal with him later," he said. "Right now, I am concerned for you. Your reckless behavior has put me in a very bad position, Peter."

For the first time since entering the solar, Peter could see the strain on his father's face. The man had gone from angry to stressed in a matter of seconds. He could see what his impulsive behavior had done to the man and he was torn between sorrow and defiance. He wasn't sorry he'd gone to London, but he was sorry it caused his father grief. Marcus' words came back to him at that moment. *Do not mention this to your father, Peter. He has enough on his mind.*

At that moment, he could see just *how* much his father had on his mind.

He began to feel like a very bad son, indeed.

"I'm sorry, Papa," he said, daring to move towards him now that he was calmer. "I never meant to cause you grief. You know I would never knowingly do that. There was no way I could know that The Marshal would call a gathering today."

Christopher looked at his boy. "That is not the

point, is it?" he said. "You deliberately went off without telling me where you were going."

Peter had. After a moment, he nodded. "Aye," he said truthfully. "I did not want you to stop me. And Sherry… do not be angry with him. He tried to convince me not to go, but I would not listen to him. He went with me to make sure I was safe and for no other reason."

Tempers had calmed and Christopher could see his vulnerable boy before him. Slowly, he shook his head.

"This is a fine mess you've gotten yourself into," he said. "I simply do not understand how this situation could have gotten out of control so quickly. Is this infatuation worth it?"

Peter's dark eyes glimmered. "More than ever," he said. "You know I do not say this lightly, Papa. I've never spoken this way about a woman ever before, but there is something about Liora that makes me feel as if I've just awoken from a deep sleep to see the world for the first time. I'm not sure what more I can say about her, but she's the most wonderful woman I've ever met. This isn't a whim that is going to go away, Papa. It's real."

Christopher sighed heavily. Clearly, that wasn't what he had wanted to hear, but his son was a grown man. He could make his own decisions, questionable as they were. "Then tell me what the rabbi said."

With the flurry of anger abating, there was a strained calm between them now. Peter planted himself in the only other chair in the chamber, suddenly feeling weary and defeated.

Very, very weary.

"He was young and surprisingly helpful," he said. "Rabbi Judah is his name. He was quite friendly and answered my questions without judgment, which I found astonishing. But what he told me was much as I expected – he said that marriage between Jews and Christians do not exist, at least any that are recognized by both religions. If Liora were to convert to Christianity, then our marriage would be recognized by our church. If I convert to Judaism, then our marriage would be recognized by her church. But both churches will not recognize the same marriage."

Christopher watched his son struggle with something beyond his control. Part of him felt sorry for Peter, but another part of him felt his son was behaving immaturely. He went to stand in front of Peter, enormous arms folded across his chest.

"Let us look at this logically," he said. "In the matter of who shall convert to which religion, think about who has the most to lose. Having not met Mistress Liora, I do not know anything about her, but I will assume that she does not hold a great social and financial standing in her community."

Peter shook his head. "She is the daughter of Haim ben Thad," he said. "He holds great social and financial status in his community, but she does not. However, her actions will directly reflect upon him."

"Will he lose business?"

"Possibly. If she converts to Christianity, at the very least he may be shunned."

"But his gentile business will not be affected. If anything, it may increase because of his daughter's connections to you."

"That is possible."

Christopher nodded faintly. "Now, let's speak of you," he said. "Should you convert to her religion, you will lose your knighthood. You will lose your command of Ludlow Castle. I alluded to this when we spoke before – employing a dishonored knight will be difficult, if not impossible. I can keep you at Ludlow, but as a dishonored knight, men would have a difficult time following you, which means you would be removed from the chain of command. Do you understand that?"

Peter took a deep breath before nodding. "I do."

Christopher continued. "You would lose your title of Lord Pembridge and the income from those properties," he said. "Mayhap you could still serve with The Marshal as an Executioner Knight, but you would never be a leader, Peter. Only a follower. With your source of income removed because of losing your title and command, you would be solely dependent upon me for any income. I would not let you starve, of course, but your opportunities would be incredibly limited. The best you could hope for is being a mercenary like these bastards who are now overrunning England. You would lose everything you've known and everything you've worked for would be drastically reduced. Are you willing to go this far for a woman you have only just met?"

Peter simply sat there, staring off into the chamber as he pondered his father's words of wisdom. Nothing he said was untrue. Was he willing to lose everything for a woman he'd just met? For a woman who lit him up like a flint and stone ignited the driest kindling? Slouching forward, he put his elbows on his knees and his face in his hands.

"This is so unfair," he muttered.

Christopher sighed faintly, hoping he'd just helped Peter see the light. "I know," he said. "Life is never easy. But the choices we make can define us forever."

Peter sat there with his hands over his face. "I already came into this life with one strike against me," he said. "I was born the bastard of a great English warlord. Everyone knows I am not Dustin's child. Everyone knows you were not married to my mother. They may accept me, and embrace me, but in the backs of their minds they think 'he's not really a de Lohr, not truly'."

"Peter, that's not true."

His hands came away from his face. "Aye, it is," he said strongly. "I will not inherit your title. I should be the Earl of Hereford and Worcester because I was born thirteen years before Curtis was but, instead, the title goes to him and I am given a consolation title of Lord Pembridge. I'm a damned Executioner Knight, Papa. I've proven myself time and time again, but still, I get nothing from you but a courtesy title. Nothing that truly makes me a de Lohr or part of your world other than your name, but I suppose I'm not even really entitled to that. When I first came to live with you, my name was de Vries and you changed it. What's one more strike against me should I convert to Judaism? What, exactly, am I leaving behind or sacrificing should I do that? Is it simply the fact that you don't want such a black mark against your good name?"

He was on his feet by now, pacing and shouting. Christopher watched him carefully. "If I cared about a black mark against the de Lohr name, I would have never acknowledged you as my son," he said. "And nothing you say is true."

Peter came to a halt, glaring at him. "Isn't it?"

"*Nay*," Christopher said. "You are my eldest son and part of this family as much as I am or Dustin is, or Curtis is. You *are* our child."

"If that is true, then have Dustin legally adopt me and declare me her son."

Christopher's eyes widened. "What?"

"You heard me. Have her legally adopt me and make me your heir."

Christopher stared at him a moment. "Are you serious?" he hissed. "You have never once expressed any desire to legally be her son. She has never treated you any differently than the others, Peter. *Never.*"

Peter knew what he had asked was horrible and unreasonable. He was essentially taking away Curtis' inheritance because he was being petty and spiteful. It broke his heart to realize that and to see the expression on his father's face but, then again, this entire situation had him reeling.

His eyes filled with tears.

"Nay, she has not. But the truth is that I am not a full member of the family, not really," he said, his lower lip trembling. "But if I convert to Judaism to marry the only woman who has ever touched me in a way I have never known, then I will destroy what privilege I do have. I know you do not want me as your heir. That belongs to

Curtis. You are the only family I have, but even so, I am an outsider. I have been an outsider since the day I was born. You don't understand that because you have never had to live with it."

Christopher watched Peter crumble in front of him. It had gone beyond the issue of a marriage between Christian and Jew. Now, it had gone into the subject of the isolation Peter had felt his entire life. Christopher and Dustin had always gone out of their way to make Peter feel as if he were one of their family and, for years, they thought he felt the same way. But it was clear that the marital issue had brought up deeper-seated issues as far as Peter was concerned.

Christopher felt as if he'd just had a dagger plunged into his gut.

"Nay, I do not understand," he said hoarsely. "I have tried very hard to understand and I have done all I can to make you feel as if you belong to me. You are *my* son, Peter. You know that your mother did not tell me that she was pregnant with you. Had she told me, the situation would be markedly different. I *would* have married her in spite of the fact that her father, the Earl of Chaumont, did not want a lowly knight for his daughter. Please know that is the truth."

Peter nodded, wiping his eyes, embarrassed at his outburst. "I know," he said. "But you did not love her, did you?"

"Nay."

"Then I was not conceived in love like the rest of my siblings."

Christopher closed his eyes and hung his head. "I do not know what you want me to say," he murmured. "I did not love your mother, but I was very fond of her. She was a kind and good woman, and mayhap with time, I would have fallen in love with her, but we were never given that chance. Her father had hopes for a great marriage with her and, at the time, I was not a great prospect. Were you conceived in love? Nay, you were not, but I cannot change that and if it makes you feel different, know that I would do anything in the world to change how you perceive yourself. I never knew until this moment that you felt as if you weren't truly part of this family and to have that knowledge guts me. It truly guts me."

Peter could hear the pain in his voice. He knew he was making his father feel guilty for something that had happened all those years ago and he knew that it was wrong of him. He was hurting, so he wanted his father to hurt.

It was so very, very wrong of him.

"I'm sorry, Papa," he said after a moment. "I didn't mean to sound spiteful and foolish. I'm not, you know. And I'm sorry to make you feel guilty for your relationship with my mother. I should not have done that. But all my life, I have had the bastard stigma follow me and now that I see happiness within my grasp, to have someone who will belong only to me... to know that cannot happen unless something drastic happens is disheartening."

"I know," Christopher said, feeling deeply hurt for his son. "If I could help, I would. Do you want me to go and speak with her father?"

Peter shook his head, moving out of Christopher's way when the man came over to comfort him. He wasn't ready to be comforted yet. He was embarrassed and unsettled.

"Nay," he said. "I do not want you involved at all. Please, Papa. This is my problem and I must deal with it in my own way."

"You do not have to deal with your problem on your own. That is what I am for."

Peter knew he meant it. But years of feeling like an outsider were difficult to shake. Now, he wanted a marriage that he, an outsider, couldn't have because of family – and vocation – repercussions. He was hurt, confused, and dipping his toes in a sea of grief because of it. When his father moved closer, he simply held up a hand and stepped away.

"Just... leave me alone for now, please," he said. "I have a good deal of thinking to do on the course my life will take from this point forward. But I want you to know that I love you, Papa. I love Dustin and I love my brothers and sisters. I do not want you to think that I do not. But come what may, I must make the decision I feel best for me. However, whatever that decision is, know that I will *not* marry Agnes de Quincy. I am very sorry her father has threatened you, but I have done nothing wrong and I will not marry his daughter."

Christopher watched his son move away from him and it broke his heart. "Nay, you will not marry her," he said. "I will not give in to a threat, but I do believe that de Quincy has learned his lesson the hard way about that."

Peter paused and looked at him. "What do you mean?"

Christopher scratched his head casually. "I mean to say that the man has several missing teeth and broken ribs that suggest to him that threatening me was not the right thing to do," he said. "Before you ask, I never touched him. But there were others more than willing to deliver my message."

Peter's eyebrows lifted and a gleam came to his eyes as he understood what his father meant. "Never threaten a man whose allies are Executioner Knights."

Christopher merely shrugged and turned away. "I suspect he will think twice before doing so again," he said. "But even so, Agnes de Quincy shall not be your wife. This I swear."

Peter watched the man as he turned back to his table cluttered with missives and maps. He was moving more slowly than he had been earlier, the weight of a country and an unhappy son bearing down on him. He'd done just what Marcus asked him not to do – he gave his father more worry than he already had.

Perhaps it was best that his father not be involved in this situation at all.

That would be the kind thing, the magnanimous thing to do. Marcus was right – Christopher's burdens were great. He was, without question, one of the most respected warlords in England and he was, largely, the architect of the rebellion. Not the sole architect, of course, but he'd had a big hand in it. His directives moved mountains, men, and kings. If William Marshal was the driving force, then Christopher was the wheels. And now he had a son who was unhappy with his lot in life.

Peter knew it wasn't fair of him, any of it.

Going to his father, he put his arms around him and kissed him on the head.

"Thank you, Papa," he said softly, releasing him. "And for everything else… I am sorry if I have disappointed you in any way. But I do have a great deal to think about."

Christopher turned to his son, patting him on the cheek. "We both do."

Peter wasn't sure what that meant, but he forced a smile before quitting the solar. Lost in thought, he hit the first step of the mural stairs when his younger brothers, Douglas and Myles, came rushing out of the shadows and grabbed him by the legs with the intention of taking him down. Myles was nine years of age and Douglas had seen five years, so they were old enough to be strong and devious. Peter gripped the wooden railing on the stairs, the one so elaborately carved with lions, as his brothers tried to topple him.

Unfortunately, he didn't last long when Myles pounded on his fingers, causing him to lose his grip, and down he went into a pile on the floor. Myles and Douglas were relentless, trying to steal his coin purse, daggers, and anything else of value on him until he got the upper hand and wrestled both of them over to a lovely, embroidered chair in the entry.

Nearby hung a tapestry with silken cords that could draw it up and down, and Peter yanked off one of those silken cords. He managed to get both boys into the chair and, using the cord, tied them up to the chair as they fought and kicked. Douglas was even biting. It was exhausting and hilarious, but in the end, Peter had them both tied onto the chair, with Myles sitting upright and Douglas upside-down because in his battles, that was the direction he ended up. Out of breath, Peter stood back and surveyed his handiwork as Myles and Douglas yelled and growled.

"There you go, you nasty little thieves," he said, wiping the sweat from his brow. "I'm going to leave you to rot."

"I'm going to cut you when I get out of here!" Douglas said, his face turning red because he was hanging upside-down. "Let me *go!*"

"Never," Peter said. "Today is my victory!"

More kicking and growling until Myles kicked Douglas in the head and the boy began to wail. Peter just stood there and laughed as he felt a presence come up beside him. He turned to see his father standing there, looking at his sons bound to the chair.

"They tried to rob you again?" he asked in resignation.

Peter held up the red fingers on his left hand. "They tried to smash my fingers and steal my money."

"Then you are justified."

As the boys begged for their father to release them and Christopher calmly explained that they deserved to be punished for their thievery, Peter found himself thinking of Asa. That pebble-shooting, boy-sized hoodlum. He wondered how well Myles and Douglas would get along with another boy who was just as ruthless as they were and the thought made him smile. He thought it was quite a pity that two Christian boys and a little Jewish boy couldn't be playmates. But then again, perhaps it was better this way. If those three joined forces, no one in London would be safe ever again.

Leaving his father to deal with the bandits he had raised, Peter headed up the stairs, to his chamber that overlooked the river from the eastern side of the house. Thoughts of Asa turned to thoughts of Liora. Liora, a woman he'd just met, but Liora, a woman he couldn't get out of his mind. Sweet, untouched, pragmatic, beautiful Liora. Now, he had to decide what was important to him – flying in the face of two religions to court a woman that he was told he couldn't have, or turning away and continuing on with his life, such as it was.

There were times that people touched his life that he would never forget – his father and Dustin, for example. He hadn't known them all his life, but he felt like he had. No matter what he'd said about feeling like an outsider, he couldn't imagine his life without them. And then there was Liora – with a look, a smile, and a few brief conversations, somehow, she had gotten under his skin.

Even if he turned away now, Peter wasn't entirely sure he could, or would, forget her. She would always be the one he would wonder about – wonder how his life would have been with her by his side. Wondering if he would regret not standing up for what he wanted against what he was told he couldn't have. His whole life had been dictated for him, planned for him, everything out of his control. Well, this was one thing he could control.

He *wanted* to control.

Reaching the upper floor, he ended up going down the back stairs, the one that led to the kitchens and beyond that, the stables. Liora had told him not to come around tonight, but he couldn't help it. He wanted to tell her about Rabbi Judah and about the discussions with his father. He wanted to see if, in the end, all of this would be worth it. He couldn't make a decision based on only knowing someone for a couple of days, but he was willing to try if she was willing. Perhaps something astonishingly beautiful was waiting for them if they would only show the courage to stand up to convention.

As the sun began to wane in the west, Peter headed off for London again.

CHAPTER THIRTEEN

"HOLD STILL, FATHER!" Agnes begged. "If you do not hold still, the surgeon cannot pull the root out!"

Walter was being held down by two of the surgeon's men while the surgeon used a slender pair of pliers and a hammer and chisel to remove the roots of two teeth that had been broken off at the gumline when he'd been beaten within an inch of his life after leaving Lonsdale.

And he knew by whom.

That's what had him so angry.

Yelling in pain and rage, he strained against the men holding him down as the surgeon removed the roots of the teeth, butchering his mouth in the process. Walter bit down on already-bloodied rags to stop the bleeding, shouting at the surgeon and his helpers to get out. Gladly, the surgeon packed up his grimy tools and shuffled out with his burly helpers, leaving Walter exhausted from pain.

He lay on his bed, grunting, drooling blood and saliva all over his linens.

"Is there anything else I can do, Father?" Agnes asked with concern. "Anything you need?"

Walter just lay there and groaned, staring at the ceiling. He finally pulled the damp, bloodied rag from his mouth.

"Those bastards," he said, his speech odd because he was missing his front teeth. "This is what Hereford's men did to me. He thinks to stop me from telling what I know about his son, but he is wrong!"

Agnes was trying to mop up the blood and saliva that was flying from his lips as he moved around on the bed, restlessly. He was agitated, and in pain, but the words out of his mouth were purely about revenge. He had told her how he'd tried to blackmail Hereford with regards to Peter and the jeweler's daughter and he was convinced that his beating was in retaliation for that.

But Agnes wasn't so sure.

"If it *was* Hereford, then it was a warning," she said. "He is a powerful man. No marriage is worth your life, Father. Mayhap we should try something else."

Walter grabbed her by the arm. "What else is there?" he said. "I must be close to the truth if he is willing to threaten my life."

"If you were close to the truth, I am certain you would be dead."

Walter's gaze lingered on her for a moment before releasing her. "His son is engaged in espionage and he does not want me to speak of it," he said through swollen lips. "And the Jewess… she could have no other interest in Peter than to press him for secrets because her father has the ear of the king."

Agnes had been listening to this inane drivel since her father had been brought back to the London townhome of their cousin, who had seen Walter's injuries, listened to the madness he was spouting, and promptly left the home. The Earl of Winchester held no belief in Christopher de Lohr being behind a beating his cousin had received and considering the man had lost his purse and several expensive pieces of jewelry in the ambush, it was clear that robbers had set upon him.

But Walter seemed to have a different opinion.

Winchester didn't want to hear it.

"Father, it is also possible that Hereford had nothing to do with what happened," she said, picking bloodied rags off the floor. "You did not see who ambushed you – you said so yourself.

Given that men are robbed all the time outside of London, that is more than likely what happened to you. You cannot blame Hereford for that."

Walter didn't like the fact that Agnes didn't seem to be on his side. "Plain and stupid Agnes," he said, eyeing her with contempt. "Ever ready to defend de Lohr, aren't you? You *do* realize the family does not want you. Peter does not want you. If he did, I would not have to resort to great lengths to marry you into that family."

Agnes' cheeks flushed a dull red as she put the rags into a bowl for the servants to take away. There was a second bowl with ingredients for a compress, including arnica. She began to pack the ingredients into a soft, clean cloth.

"I am not defending the family," she said. "But seeking revenge against de Lohr does not work in our favor. Do you think he is going to cower to you? Of course not."

"He will cower to me when I go to the warlords and tell them that de Lohr's precious son is a traitor," he snarled. "I will tell them that… wait… wait just a moment…"

He was on to something. Agnes could tell by the tone of his voice and she turned around, watching him with trepidation as he lay there, staring at the ceiling with the bloodied rag to his mouth.

"What is it?" she asked hesitantly.

Walter held up a finger. "Telling the rebels that Peter is a traitor will not have the desired result," he said thoughtfully. "That will only cause confusion, and anger, and Hereford will be forced to send Peter away for his own good."

"How do you know?"

"Because if I was Hereford, I would send my son away if he was accused of treachery," he said. "I would send him away to remove him from the situation and let suspicions cool. Nay… we do not want him sent away. We want him here, with us, because if he is sent away, arranging a marriage would be difficult. It is not Peter we need removed, but Peter's problem."

"What problem?"

"The jeweler's daughter."

Agnes came over to the bed with the compress in her hand, frowning at him. "She is not his problem, she is *my* problem."

Walter snatched the compress from her. "Peter's attention is not on you because he has the jeweler's daughter to occupy his time," he said. "If we send *her* away, then there is no more problem. We can return his focus in your direction."

"How are you going to send her away?"

Walter tried to sit up but with his broken ribs, it was nearly impossible. He finally shouted at Agnes to help him and she did, pulling him into a sitting position as he grunted and groaned and bled from the mouth. He sat there a moment, eyes closed, holding that compress against his lips until he was able to speak again.

"I need a scribe," he rasped. "Someone who can write a missive for me to be delivered to the king at Westminster. Find me a scribe immediately."

Agnes wasn't sure what he wanted to send to the king, but she hoped it had something to do with the jeweler's daughter. She was more than willing to help him.

"I can write," she reminded him. "Tell me what you want to say and I shall write it down."

"Good," Walter said quickly. "Find vellum and ink. We are going to send a missive to the king."

"What are you going to say?"

A hint of a smile crossed Walter's swollen lips. "We do not want Peter removed, so we must remove the jeweler's daughter instead," he said. "We are going to tell the king that his jeweler, the man he spends a good deal of money with, is harboring a rebel in his bosom. We tell the king that the jeweler's daughter is involved in de Lohr's rebellion and if he wants answers, then he should interrogate her. If she is close to Peter de Lohr, there is no telling what she knows."

Agnes' eyes widened when she realized what he was doing. "But you do not know that for certain," she said. "I am in support of removing this woman, but what if the king finds out you are lying? Won't it go badly for you?"

Walter's head snapped in her direction. "I shall not sign my name to the missive, you fool."

"But won't the king want to know *who* sent the information?"

"Do you want to marry Peter or not?"

Agnes did. She wasn't going to worry about being caught in a lie if her father wasn't. Besides… who was to say if they were lying or not? It would be the word of a Jewess against the word of Walter de Quincy, lord of Astley Cross. Surely her father's word held more weight than that of a common woman.

But it didn't hold more weight than that of Peter and Christopher de Lohr.

Still, she was willing to do it. Anything to get that woman out of her way.

Agnes found her vellum, quill, and ink, and scribed a missive to the king, carefully dictated by her father. He described the treachery of the jeweler's daughter and how she was using her father's place of business to mask her deceitful activities, mostly with the House of de Lohr. By the time the supper hour arrived, the missive was off to Westminster Palace, anonymously. But in the end, Walter used the Earl of Winchester's seal on it. He was afraid an anonymous missive might be cast aside, but one from a rebel warlord would be read with interest.

It was a hope he had.

Walter slept well that night in spite of everything, with dreams of a changed situation come the morning.

CHAPTER FOURTEEN

H E KEPT LOOKING at her.

Liora knew that Gideon was trying to get her attention, to make eye contact with her, but she wouldn't look at him. She didn't even want to be here, but her father had coerced her into eating supper with a guest she didn't want to be around. She'd agreed to do it based on a bargain, but they hadn't even gone to Westminster that afternoon as her father had intended. He'd found something in the golden belt he didn't like, so he'd taken the time to fix it, which meant they'd go tomorrow.

Maybe.

So, Liora had been tricked into having supper with Gideon. It wasn't that he was a terrible man. In fact, he was pleasant enough, kind and accommodating, but he was as bland as water. He was older than she was, having inherited the horse business from his father, but he was very wealthy, with a fine house on King Street. He lived with his mother and grandfather and had made no secret for years that he wanted a wife in Liora ben Thad. Haim wouldn't entertain the suggestion until Liora came of age and even then, he'd waited two full years before he finally allowed Gideon to move past the initial interest phase.

Now, Gideon was a welcome guest in their home.

Liora sat across the table from him, between her mother and grandmother, while Asa sat next to Gideon and stuck his tongue out at the man every time he looked at him. That made Gideon a little uncomfortable, so Asa was excused towards the end of the meal because he was finished and couldn't seem to stop making faces at Gideon. Haim tried to make it seem as if his son were simply lively and full of fun, but Liora knew it was because Asa didn't like Gideon in the least.

It was all she could do to keep from bursting out laughing.

Usually, no one was allowed to leave the table until the last of the meal was finished, so Asa's early departure should have been a harbinger of things to come for Liora. Once Asa was gone, her mother and grandmother departed in quick succession, leaving Haim sitting at the head of the table with his daughter on one side and her hopeful suitor on the other. He poured himself and Gideon more wine but left Liora's glass empty.

"I must speak to you both tonight," Haim said, looking at Gideon. "You know that I have not been willing to let my daughter leave my household, Gideon. You have tried for at least four years to gain my permission, but I have resisted. I wanted to let you know that tonight, I resist no longer."

As Gideon grinned, Liora looked at her father in horror. "*What?*" she cried. "Papa, please do not say anything more. We have not even discussed this!"

Haim looked at her then. "I am sorry, *zeeskeit,*" he said gently. "I know we did not, but it is time. If I told you of my plans today, you would have never come to sup with Gideon."

Liora's mouth popped open. "You... you deceived me?"

Haim merely shrugged. "I believe that Gideon will make a fine husband for you," he said. "You will have your own home and children. Is that not what you want?"

Gideon was beaming from ear to ear, so very pleased to hear that he had Haim's approval, but Liora was out of her chair.

"I will not have this conversation with you,"

she said to her father, angrily. But her focus shifted to Gideon. "This is nothing against you, I assure you. I simply have no desire to marry at the moment and my father does not have my permission to agree to anything."

Gideon's smile faded as he realized Liora was opposed to his suit. "I... I am sorry," he said, genuinely confused. "I thought it was known that I... everyone expects that we will marry. My mother is most anxious to have you as a daughter."

He sounded weak and pleading, with a high-pitched voice that grated on her. All she could think of at that moment was of Peter's deep, honeyed voice, something that sent shivers up her spine.

She wanted a man who sent shivers up her spine.

She'd never realized that more than at this moment. Until Peter de Lohr came into her life, perhaps she would have been accepting of Gideon's suit, eventually. It wasn't as if she had a myriad of attractive prospects. She had merchants and grocers and goldsmiths. That was her world and she accepted that. She'd never known anything differently.

But then came Peter.

He represented something new and exciting, power and passion, bringing forth thoughts and feelings in her that she'd never had before. While her world was rich with beauty and culture and tradition, Peter's appearance hinted at something more out there for her. Something different but just as rich. Perhaps it was wrong of her to think of such things, but she couldn't help it. She was young, beautiful, and vital – and so was her handsome golden knight, Peter.

And then, there was Gideon.

It wasn't his fault. He had been born into the same traditions that she had been. He was a wealthy horse trader. She was the daughter of a jeweler. There was nothing wrong with either of those things provided the people entrenched in them were happy.

Liora knew, increasingly, that she was most definitely not happy.

"I am sorry, Gideon," she said quietly. "You shall have to find your wife elsewhere because it will not be me."

With that, she bolted from the table, hearing her father call after her but unwilling to answer. She was angry and confused, agitated and overwhelmed. It would have been easy to blame Peter for her condition but, truth be told, it wouldn't have been the first time she had longed for a life outside of the world she knew. Every time she saw beautiful women with their handsome lords purchase jewelry from her father, she envied them. She had always envied them.

Now, she had a chance for a handsome lord of her own, an earl's son no less. But was she surrendering all that she was, her entire heritage, to dream about it?

Her bedchamber was a large one, spanning one entire side of the house with the big windows that overlooked the alley and the kitchen yard in part. She entered her chamber and shut the door, bolting it so her father or angry mother couldn't get in. She knew her mother was going to be furious about shunning Gideon, but she didn't care. Jewish girls, just like Christian girls, were raised to listen to their mothers and fathers and to do their bidding. Obedience was smiled upon by God. Liora's mother and father had always given her a great deal of freedom, which would work against them in this case. She wasn't going to marry Gideon no matter how much they demanded it.

She wasn't going to give in.

She lit a taper at the end of her bed, sitting on a table where her sewing was neatly piled. Liora had a knack for embroidery and there were neatly draped veils on the table, one of which was only partially embroidered around the edges. Sitting down, she picked up the veil and resumed her sewing. She found that she could think better when her hands were occupied, as it seemed to ease her mind, which so often would run amok if she let it. She had a busy intellect, something Peter had seen a glimpse of, but sometimes she simply had to sit still and focus on something repetitive – like sewing. It helped clear her mind.

A mind that desperately need clearing tonight.

Silently, she stitched by candlelight, thinking of Peter, thinking of their brief encounters and feeling warm and giddy every time she thought of those intense eyes looking at her. At one point, her father came to the door and knocked softly, begging her to open it, but she chased him away by telling him that she was in bed. He went away only for her mother to come and bang on the door, demanding she open it.

Liora told her that she would see her in the morning.

And on it went for at least an hour. She heard her parents arguing downstairs and then a door slam as her mother went to bed. At one point, she caught a glimpse of shadows down in the alleyway, knowing it was probably Asa playing games with his friends. When all young boys should be in bed, Asa would rather run around with his friends, playing in the dark, until Haim would go outside and yell at him to come to bed. At least, she thought it was Asa until she caught sight of a horse. Startled, she sat up and peered out the window, only to realize that it was Peter's horse.

Peter had made an appearance.

Quickly, she opened the window.

"What are you doing here?" she hissed. "I told you not to come tonight!"

The moon glistened off of Peter's light hair in the darkness. "I know," he said. "And I am sorry, but I must speak with you."

"But… I cannot, not tonight."

"It is important, Liora. Please."

Something in his tone made her heart leap. Puzzled, and the least bit concerned, she shut the window and made her way to the chamber door. Quietly unlocking it, she stuck her head out into the landing to see where her parents were. Her grandmother wasn't a problem, but her parents would be. Sometimes, they prowled the corridors. However, she didn't see them nor did she hear them.

Quietly, she slipped from her chamber and shut the door behind her.

With great stealth, Liora made it down the stairs and through the kitchen, emerging into the kitchen yard beyond. She went to the gate and opened it up, only to see that Peter was standing right next to it. Gazing into his handsome face, she realized how glad she was to see him. Something about him gave her a sense of comfort, of joy.

But his appearance here was not welcome this night.

"What is it?" she whispered. "My mother and father are very angry with me right now and they would be furious if they saw you here. What do you want?"

Peter reached out to gently touch her hand, brushing his flesh against hers in a move that made her tremble so badly that she nearly lost her balance.

"I am sorry," he murmured. "But I spoke with the rabbi today. I must tell you what he said."

Liora's gaze lingered on him, already knowing it was terrible news. He didn't even have to tell her. It softened her edgy manner, now fighting off disappointment and melancholy when she realized this golden dream would be over before it truly began. But she did want to hear what he had to say.

Even if it was only goodbye.

"Tether the horse out here," she said quietly. "He will be safe."

Peter did as he was told, knowing his horse wouldn't go with anyone but him, so he wasn't concerned with leaving it in the alley for a quick getaway. With the horse tied off, Liora grasped his hand and held it tightly as she led him through the yard and into their small stables that smelled strongly of dried grass and goats. In fact, there were several of the little animals corralled up at one end. It was dark, but for a small ventilation window to let in air and light, as she took him over to a pile of hay and sat down.

Peter sat down next to her.

For a moment, they simply looked at each other until Peter lifted his hands and gently cupped her face. Leaning forward, he slanted his lips over hers in a completely unexpected move, a kiss of such power and such passion that Liora couldn't even fight him off. Not that she wanted to, but propriety dictated that she at least force him to behave.

But she couldn't.

It was a kiss like she'd never been kissed in her life. When he finally pulled away, she felt lightheaded. It took her a minute to catch her breath.

"Is… is that what you wanted to tell me?" she whispered.

Peter grinned, his teeth flashing in the darkness. "Nay," he said. "But I simply couldn't help myself. Are you angry?"

Liora shook her head. "Nay."

He took that as an invitation and his lips clamped on to her soft mouth again, kissing her deeply as he pulled her into his arms. The heat from a thousand suns couldn't match the fire she felt when he had her in his arms, her supple body against him, his lips on hers. Her firm, round breasts were pressed against his chest and although he hadn't moved to grope anything, she could feel his fingers on her torso, caressing her. It was wicked and wanton of her, but she wondered what it would feel like for him to touch her body. The more he kissed her, the more heat she felt all over and the more her heart raced.

The man had a touch like lightning.

"Forgive me," he said, pulling away and allowing her to breathe. "I wondered what it would be like to take you in my arms and now I know."

Dazed, she licked her lips. "What is it like?"

His answer was to kiss her a third time, hard, his tongue invading the sweet recesses of her mouth as he pushed her back onto the pile of hay. He was taking charge and Liora was letting him. Everything about the man had her in a fog where she could hardly think and only feel. She felt everything he was doing to her, even when his mouth left hers and began to wander. His left hand was wandering, too, entwined in her hair as he kissed her chin, her neck, her shoulder, before moving down her torso and gently caressing her belly. She could feel his heated palm through the fabric of her gown, and she felt his hand as it moved up her belly to the valley between her breasts. It moved up further and gently grabbed her around the neck as he suckled the flesh of her collarbone. The more he suckled, the tighter his grip on her neck as he turned her head to the side and began to kiss the swell of her breasts.

It was heaven.

But it was also growing increasingly passionate. Liora didn't know enough to stop him. She was loving everything he was doing, every kiss, every touch, letting him do whatever he wished. She had her arms around his head, holding him against her when he pulled back the neckline of her dress to expose one of those full, beautiful breasts. When the neckline didn't give enough, he yanked on it, tearing it. Liora started to come out of her stupor at the sound of a torn garment until he pulled it down enough to expose her left breast. When his seeking mouth descended on a taut nipple, she was lost.

A gasp escaped her lips as he suckled hard enough to bring pinpricks of painful delight. But it only went on for a few seconds before he suddenly pulled away, quickly pulling her bodice up to cover her luscious breasts.

"Oh, God," he breathed. "Forgive me, Liora, please. I wasn't thinking... Christ, everything about you consumes me and I am so sorry... but it was just so natural."

Her head came up, looking at him in the darkness. "You are sorry that you touched me then?"

He could see her, barely, but he shook his head. "Nay," he murmured, leaning down to kiss her firmly, suckling her lower lip before releasing it. "I did not mean it that way. I will never be sorry for touching you. I meant that I should not have taken such liberties. My only excuse is that the moment I touched you, I lost myself. You consume my senses as I've never been consumed before."

Liora smiled faintly at him, reaching down to pull her bodice up to a modest level, noting the tear was only in the seam at her shoulder. "You did not take any liberties that I did not allow you to take," she whispered. "In case you've not yet realized it, I rather lost myself, too."

He smiled timidly. "Truly?"

"Truly."

"Then… then you are feeling the same thing I am?"

"What are you feeling?"

His gaze glittered at her in the darkness. "Things that men speak of but seldom experience," he said. "Attraction and passion towards a woman that blinds him to all else. A pull towards her that is difficult to describe, knowing you'd do anything in the world for her and do it gladly. Hoping for a glimpse of her smile, the sound of her voice, and realizing that it is food for your soul. *Those* things."

She reached up, gently stroking his face. "Then it is the same thing," she said. "It is remarkable that we should have such feelings after having known each other a short time."

"That tells me this is far more than an infatuation, Liora," he murmured. "Sometimes, two people are just meant to be together. There's no logic or reason to it, but it happens. It is *meant* to happen. What we feel... it is real."

She pulled his mouth down to hers, kissing him tenderly. "It is *very* real," she whispered. "But we cannot ignore the truth of our situation. Tell me what the rabbi said."

It was a statement that dampened the mood, but it was the entire reason he'd come. He sat up, pulling her up alongside him. He could see hay sticking out of her hair in the dim light and he began picking it out.

"I spoke to Rabbi Judah," he said, plucking hay from the top of her head. "I rather like him. He was quite surprising."

Liora smiled at him as she shook out her hair. "I knew him when he was much younger," she said. "We have grown up together, Judah and I. His father is a rabbi, too."

"Like father, like son."

"Exactly," she said, picking chaff from the bodice of her dress now. "What did he tell you?"

Peter took the last visible piece of hay from her hair. "I am sure it is no great shock," he said. "The gist of the situation is that my church will not recognize a marriage if you do not convert and your church will not recognize a marriage if I do not convert. We must be all Christian or all Jewish for our marriage to be valid. For us to have any chance of survival."

She finished brushing herself off and looked at him. "Nay, it is no great shock to hear that," she said. "I suppose I knew that from the start."

He put his arms on his bent-up knees, brushing at his boots. "So I sit here with you, speaking on marriage and brushing at my boots simply for something to do with my hands," he said. "All I want to do right now is pull you back into my arms. I feel strangely alone right now even though you are sitting right next to me."

Liora looked at him in the weak light, reaching up to brush some hay from his right shoulder. "That is a sudden change in subject."

"Nay, it is not. When speaking of you as the subject, it is never strange where my mind is."

She smiled at him, reaching out to take one of his big, scarred hands. She held it tightly. "We have only known each other for a few days," she reminded him softly. "If any of my friends had told me that they were mad about a man after only knowing him for a few days, I would tell her that she was daft and lock her up for her own protection. But here I am, sitting with you, speaking of marriage after only a few days. In truth, in our culture, betrothals are often made between people who do not know one another. They will meet only two or three times at most before their families are celebrating a betrothal."

"That can happen in my religion, as well," he said. "Marriages are not made with love in mind, but money or property, or both. I've known men to wed women they've never even met once."

"It does happen," she agreed. "So, you see, it is not really strange at all that we are speaking of this so quickly. At least, not in my experience."

His gaze grew intense. "You *do* want to marry me, don't you?" he said softly. "I am not pressing my suit when you are uncertain, am I?"

She shook her head. "I knew the moment I first spoke to you that you were someone special," she said. "Tonight, my father gave Gideon permission to marry me and all I could think of was you."

He lifted his eyebrows. "What does that mean for us then?"

"I will not marry Gideon."

"Will you marry me?"

She squeezed his hand. "I very much want to," she whispered. "Peter, I know nothing of your life. I do not know your family, your friends, the way you conduct yourself, but I have seen you with Asa and how gentle and kind you are with him. Even though I know little else about you, the way you behave with my brother tells me everything I need to know. You are a man of patience, of a good family, of good character. You look at me and my world is happy and bright. I want the chance to know you better, to see what a fine man you are, but we have a definite problem."

He lifted her hand, kissing it sweetly. "We do," he said. "More than you know. I spoke with my father today about you and told him what Rabbi Judah said."

She moved a little closer to him. "Then you told him?"

Peter nodded. "My father and I are close," he said. "There isn't anything I do not talk over with him, including this."

"And what did he say?"

Peter pulled her closer, into the curve of his torso. He simply couldn't keep his arms away from her. "He feels I am being impulsive and reckless," he said. "Even if you were not a Jewish lass, he would still think the same thing. But because our religions do not mingle, he is quite… skeptical."

"What does that mean?"

Peter sighed faintly, his chin on the top of her head. "You must understand that my father has no issue with Jews," he said. "He spent years in The Levant and his relationship with the Jews was an amicable one, so do not think he takes issue with your religion."

"Then what?"

"He is honest and practical," he said. "He asked me who had the most to lose in a situation like this – me or you. If I convert to Judaism to marry you, then I lose everything. I lose my title, my knighthood, any position of power I might have. He wants me to understand that it would cost me dearly."

She sat up and looked at him. "How could you even consider such a thing?"

He frowned. "Look at the reward, Liora," he said, cupping her cheek. "*You*. You would be the reward. That is how I can consider it."

She gazed at him in the darkness. "You would consider giving up everything for a woman you do not know?"

"I am coming to know her and I like her."

Slowly, she shook her head. "Then nothing Rabbi Judah said discouraged you?"

"Does it discourage *you*?"

Liora wasn't sure how to answer. So very much was at stake. She pulled away from him and stood up.

"Your father is right," she said. "If you think to convert, it will cost you everything. And there is no guarantee my father will even allow us to marry, although he always does what I want him to do. If I want to marry you, it would be with misgivings that he would let me because you are not a born Jew. You would be a convert. My father is trying to marry me to Gideon because he comes from a very old, very prestigious family. That means something to my father, as I am sure a fine wife from a good family would mean something to yours."

Peter stood up because she was, brushing the hay off his breeches. "That is what every parent hopes for his child," he said. "And since you bring it up, there is something else you should know. I am my father's bastard, the result between him and the daughter of an earl. He never married her and when she died, I came to live with him and his wife. I will not inherit the earldom, which I suppose gives me a little more freedom to marry whom I choose."

Liora didn't seem particularly concerned with the fact that his parents had not been married. "Mayhap it does, but you still do not want to give up everything when you marry," she said. "I remember when we walked in the meadow and you told me that your father had given you command of Ludlow Castle. You said it would make you a very wealthy man. You were proud to tell me, Peter, I know you were. I could see it in your face."

He averted his gaze, pretending to brush at nonexistent hay on his thigh. "Of course I was proud," he said. "It is one of the largest castles on the Marches, much coveted."

He was looking at his feet and she went to him, putting her hand on his chin and forcing him to look at her. "And you were given that appointment from your father because you are an elite knight," she said softly. "You have worked very hard for what you have and it would be a waste of all of those years to throw it all away for a marriage. Do you think that would make me happy knowing that you gave it all up for me? Peter, your intention is as sweet and endearing as you can imagine and I am deeply touched, but I cannot and will not let you do it. Giving up your knighthood is out of the question."

He was hypnotized by those pale eyes, that gorgeous face with those ripe lips he'd so recently kissed. "But I want to marry you," he whispered seriously. "I would never ask you to give up your life for me. That would be selfish and wrong to expect you to do it."

She smiled, pressed against him, and his arms went around her yet again. Liora's hands were on his face, looking into those strong, handsome features.

"And that tells me even more about your character that you would not make such demands," she said. "Rather than see me give up everything I know, you are willing to do it instead. That speaks of your honor, Peter. You are very honorable."

"Maybe so, but if I do not give up my world, we cannot be married."

"We can if I give up mine."

He studied her to see if she was serious. After a moment, he sighed faintly. "My father said that if you did that, I would be thrusting you into a world you knew nothing about and eventually, you would grow to resent me," he said. "I could not live with that, Liora. Your happiness would mean everything to me."

She nodded. "I know," she said. "I already know you would make it your life's work to ensure my happiness, but I am telling you that out of the two of us, it makes the most sense that I should become a Christian. I know you will teach me all I need to know so that I would make a fine wife for Lord Pembridge."

He looked at her in disbelief. "Is that what you would want?" he asked. "Truly, Liora – think hard on it. Is that what you would honestly want? What about your heritage and your culture? Do you truly think you could leave that all behind?"

"Would I really have to?"

"What do you mean?"

She shrugged. "I mean that we all worship one God, Peter," she said. "If I worship God as a Jew or as a Christian, I am still worshipping God, am I not?"

"I don't understand."

She patted him on the cheek. "I can still become a Christian and worship at your side," she said. "But in the privacy of our home, would you allow me to observe the Jewish rights? Would you still allow me to say my prayers in Hebrew because it would please my ancestors? Our children would be raised as Christians, but I would still like to teach them where their mother came from."

Peter studied her face as she spoke, trying to determine if she was serious or if she was just telling him what he wanted to hear in an impulsive move. But he couldn't imagine there was any other motive than pure honesty, as she had never given him any reason to think otherwise. And her suggestion wasn't a terrible one. In fact, it gave him hope.

Great hope that this might work out, after all.

"I would permit you to do what you wished," he said. "If it makes you happy, you have my permission."

She grinned at him, her eyes twinkling, when they both heard a door creak and then slam on its hinges. Liora jumped away from him, moving over to the other side of the stable, when a figure abruptly appeared in the stable entry.

Peter and Liora found themselves looking at Haim.

And someone else.

Christopher was standing behind him.

"Papa?" Peter said in disbelief when he realized his father had made an appearance. "How on earth did you find me?"

Christopher came to stand next to Haim. "It was not difficult," he said. "You left your horse tied out in the open. I could see him as I came up Milk Street."

Peter came towards his father, eyeing the man in the moonlight. "You followed me?"

"I followed you."

Peter sighed sharply, realizing his father knew of his intentions back at Lonsdale. He'd already escaped once to see Liora and Christopher, rightly so, had guessed that he would try and see her again before departing for Ludlow in the morning. Peter's gaze moved to Haim, who was looking at him somewhat curiously. He shrugged helplessly.

"This is not how I hoped to be introduced to you, my lord," he said, eyeing her father. "I assume my father told you everything?"

Haim shook his head. "He told me nothing except that you were somewhere on my property," he said. "But, clearly, you should tell me everything. I find you alone with my daughter in the stable?"

"It was my idea, Father," Liora said, coming out of the shadows and looking at Christopher. She bobbed a brief curtsy. "My lord, I am Liora, daughter of Haim. This is not how I hoped to be introduced to you, either."

Christopher's gaze moved over the petite, raven-haired beauty who had his son behaving so irrationally. Within the first few seconds of seeing her, he could understand why Peter was so enamored with her. She was positively exquisite.

"Demoiselle," he greeted her. "It seems there are some odd introductions all around, but I am pleased to finally meet you. Peter has spoken highly of you."

She smiled weakly. "Thank you," she said. Then, she looked to her father. "Papa, I am sorry I became angry with you tonight. I did not mean to be rude, but... but there is a good deal on my mind."

Haim's gaze moved to Peter. "I can see that," he said. "Would you like to tell me what is happening, young de Lohr? Why do I find you here with my daughter?"

Peter cleared his throat softly, glancing at his father, seeing the man's expression. Usually, his father was stone-faced, but in this case, he wasn't. He looked uncertain yet encouraging. It was an odd combination and one that didn't give Peter a lot of confidence, but he cleared his throat softly yet again and proceeded.

"My lord, you know me as Christopher de Lohr's son," he said, improperly addressing Haim but wanting to show respect the way he knew how. "My father stands for truth and honor and I hope to stand for the same. I will therefore be completely honest with you because today when we met, I was not honest at all. I told you that I had come to purchase a gift for my father when, in truth, I had come to see your daughter. I had met her the day before when she so kindly provided me with a hiding place until the danger passed. It was quite by accident, of course, but she was very kind to me."

Haim, fortunately, wasn't the irate type. That was simply his temperament. He nodded to Peter's confession.

"Eh," he said as if it were nothing to be worried over. "I am glad my daughter was of service to you. The Talmud dictates that we always be kind to strangers."

Peter had expected much more of a reaction. Haim's lack of outrage to his admission bolstered his courage.

"I have spoken to your daughter several times since we first met," he said. "She is kind and empathetic, witty and wise, and she is unlike any woman I have ever met before. Please do not think I was sneaking around behind your back and trying to seduce your daughter, because I was not. I have simply found a woman that consumes all of my attention and I have never felt that way before, not ever. There is something so fresh and honest about her, and in the world my father and I live in, finding a woman like that is rare. Liora a very rare jewel."

Haim smiled pleasantly. "She is," he said. "I see that you are trying to explain something to me, but let me explain something to you first. When my daughter started asking questions about your father yesterday, I thought it strange, but now I know why. She asked if knights always marry Christian women and I told her they did, but she wanted to know if I knew any who had married outside of their faith."

Peter looked at Liora, who shrugged apologetically. Now he wasn't so confident because he suspected Haim knew exactly where he was heading.

"I went to speak to Rabbi Judah today," Peter said. "I asked him about interfaith marriages. He told me what I already suspected – that the Jewish faith only recognizes Jewish marriages, and the Catholic Church only recognizes Christian marriages. There is no such thing as a Christian husband and a Jewish wife. I asked him this because I wish to marry your daughter, my lord, but I wanted all of the information I could gather before approaching you. I did not want to appear ignorant and I wanted to be respectful of your faith."

Haim simply nodded as if he'd known this was coming all along, which of course, he did. He looked to Christopher.

"You knew of this, my lord?" he asked.

Christopher nodded, though he was apologetic in manner. "I did," he said. "My son and I have had a couple of serious conversations about it. He understands that in order for a marriage to take place, one of them will have to convert to the other's religion. Either Peter becomes Jewish or Liora becomes a Christian."

"Do you believe he is sincere?"

Christopher looked to his son, looking back at him with such naked emotion in his eyes that Christopher could feel the physical impact. He knew what it was to want something so badly yet be so fearful that it would never come to fruition. In fact, as he looked at Peter, he remembered Peter's mother, Amanda, looking at him in the very same fashion. Peter had her eyes, so looking at Peter was a stark reminder of Amanda from those years ago. Sweet, docile Amanda who would never get what she wanted – marriage to Christopher.

Now, Peter was facing the very same thing. A marriage he could not have.

The irony was not lost on Christopher.

"I do," he finally said. "Haim, you do not know my son, but I can tell you that he is a good man. There is no finer man in all of England and if he wants to marry your daughter, then he is sincere. He is a grown man and can make his own choices, and he will do what it takes to ensure that those choices are best for him and best for your daughter. He knows that he is facing a battle, perhaps the most emotional battle he has ever endured, so do not think he is ignorant about this. But as I pointed out to him, should he choose to convert to Judaism, he will lose everything he has ever worked for – his knighthood, his status, his income. No offense to your daughter, but Peter has much more to lose than she does. This is a much bigger situation for him than it is for her and he is aware of my feelings about it."

Haim was listening to him intently. "And what are your feelings?"

Christopher found himself looking at Peter again, seeing that vulnerability, hearing those words Peter had spoken to him earlier – *all my life, I have had the bastard stigma follow me and now that I see happiness within my grasp, to have someone who will belong only to me... to know that cannot happen unless something drastic happens is disheartening.*

The truth was that Christopher wanted to make his son happy. Even if they weren't choices Christopher would make in order to achieve that happiness, that didn't mean he would disown his son for them. He would stand by him, just as he did now, and he would have to learn to live with those decisions, too.

It didn't make him love his son any less.

In fact, it made him love Peter more.

"He has my blessing whatever he chooses to do," he said hoarsely. "I cannot live his life for him, but I will be by his side no matter what he decides."

Haim was touched by the beautiful devotion, knowing how difficult it must have been for a powerful earl to let his son's decisions be ruled by the heart and not the head. He had only met Christopher once before, years ago, and he didn't know him, but he knew the man's reputation. There was no man more respected in England.

Now, Haim could see why.

"You are a good man, my lord," he said to Christopher. "To allow your son to be something other than what you expect him to be is the mark of a good father. You are to be commended. But I, too, must be a father to my daughter, who may not have as much to lose as your son over this, but she will lose enough. She will lose the respect of her family, of her friends, of those she worships with. She will become an *apostate*, one who rejects her own religion. One who has forsaken everything she knows and loves. Her mother will not see her, nor will her grandmother, nor will I. She will have made her choice and rejected her family."

"That is not true." Liora could no longer remain silent. "Why must you make this sound as if I am willingly and happily leaving the family I love, as if I care nothing about you?"

Haim had such a gentle way about him as he smiled at his daughter in the midst of a deeply serious topic. "Because you would have chosen your own happiness over your family," he said simply. "You will cast us aside in favor of your new family, a family of great knights and great wars. It will be a new life for you, one you have never known. Gone will be the days of peace on Milk Street, *zeeskeit*. You are heading into the lion's den."

Liora was close to tears, trying desperately not to weep. "But I do not want to leave you and Mama behind," she insisted. "You are still my family."

Haim shook his head. "We cannot be," he said. "If we support you in this choice, then it will be as if we have made the choice, too. We can no longer worship in the synagogue. Our friends will not speak with us. We will be exiled, so we, too, must make a choice. I love you very much, *zeeskeit,* but I have your brother to think about. Asa is part of our world and he must be allowed to live in it, to have a family in it, without being damaged by your choices. If you do this thing, you are asking me to choose between you and Asa, and I must choose my son."

Liora closed her eyes and hung her head as the tears streamed down her face and dripped off her chin. Peter watched her with great sorrow. He didn't want to see her lose her entire family because of him. His father had tried to tell him that. He'd tried to tell him that removing her from everything she knew and loved would cause her agony and resentment, and he was right. Already, Peter could see the agony on her face as her father spoke of essentially disowning her for converting to another religion.

It cut him to the bone.

"May I speak to Liora alone, please?" he asked Haim. "Just a brief moment, please."

Haim, as amiable as ever, nodded his head and headed towards the house. Christopher, his gaze lingering on his son and the distraught young lady, followed. When the fathers were over by the kitchen door, Peter grasped Liora gently by the arm and pulled her just inside the stable, just enough so they had a little privacy.

He faced her in the darkness.

"I'm so sorry," he whispered. "This isn't what I wanted for you. I hope you know that."

Liora was sobbing softly. She nodded, wiping at her face. "I know," she said. "I know you would never wish that upon me. Truthfully, it never occurred to me that my father would do that. But he is right, Peter – so very right."

Peter knew that and his heart was breaking for them both. He could see this ending tonight, but he wasn't willing to let it go. He just couldn't. Liora was coming to mean too much to him to so easily walk away. Grasping her by both arms, he forced her to look at him.

"Listen to me," he murmured. "I want you to listen to me carefully. Can you do this?"

She nodded, still wiping at the tears that wouldn't stop falling. "Of course."

He dipped his head down, his face close to hers. "My father is sending me to Ludlow Castle on the morrow," he said. "I have much that I must do for him in securing the property, and others, but it will give us both time to think very carefully about all of this. No matter what happens, I will return for you. I will not forget about you, I will not stay away any longer than necessary. I will be back. Do you believe me?"

She nodded, looking at him with sad eyes. "I do," she said. "But what will you return to? The same situation. It will not change."

"Nay, it will not change, but mayhap I will be able to think of a solution," he said. "There *has* to be a solution, Liora. I refuse to stop trying."

She believed him implicitly. "But I want you to listen to me, now. I will wait for you, no matter how long it takes, and when you return and no solution is reached, know that I will become a Christian and I will marry you. As my father said, he has to make a choice. So do I. I would rather live the rest of my life as your Christian wife than live the rest of my life as a Jewish spinster. When I look at you, it is like looking at the door to my future and all of the wondrous things it will be. I must think of my happiness, Peter, as much as my father's words pain me."

He smiled faintly. "I am willing to convert. I want to be plain."

She shook her head before the words were even out of his mouth. "Nay," she said firmly. "That is out of the question. Your father is correct – you have far more to lose than I do, but the mere fact that you are willing to do it touches me more than you can know. You're willing to give everything up for me and I love you for it, but I will not let you do it."

He stared at her. "You… you love me?"

She smiled weakly when she realized what she had said. "I love that you are so willing to surrender everything because of me," she said. "I am sure my whole and true-hearted love for you, for everything you are, is not far behind."

His back was to the fathers at the kitchen door, blocking their view, so he dared to kiss her swiftly on the lips. "I have never given my heart to anyone before," he whispered. "Take good care of it while I am away. It is the most precious thing I have to give you."

Liora smiled at him, her tears drying up as she realized this wasn't the end. Peter was going, but he would be back. It would do them good to spend time away from one another, he focused on his duties and she focused on her father and family, seeing if she could change her father's mind because she knew one thing – she wasn't going to give up her Christian knight, the archangel who had appeared in her yard those days ago.

He'd appeared for a reason.

To change her world.

"Then I shall see you upon your return, my angel," she murmured. "I will be here, waiting for you."

He smiled at her and let go of her arms. "I'll send you word if I can," he said. "I do not know how busy I shall be or what conditions I'll be facing, but I'll try to send you word. Just... don't forget about me."

"Never."

With that, he nodded encouragingly to her and, together, they came out of the stable and headed to where their fathers were standing. Christopher came over to Peter, taking him by the arm and directing him back towards the alley where his horse was tethered while Haim reached out and took Liora by the hand, taking her back inside the house. The last glimpse Peter had of Liora was her pale eyes, reaching out to him across the darkness of the kitchen yard. Their gazes locked before their respective fathers took them away.

Don't forget about me.

Those words rolled over and over in Peter's mind all the way home.

☙

HE HAD BEEN watching the entire scene.

Asa's bedchamber faced out over the kitchen yard, so he'd been watching the situation with his sister and Peter ever since Peter's father had come to the door, looking for his son. Asa might have been young, and foolish at times, but he wasn't stupid. He knew that something was going on with his sister and the man he'd called a *goy*.

When he saw Peter and his father leave the kitchen yard, he slithered downstairs as his father and sister entered through the rear door. Liora was in tears and she ran past him, up to her chamber, as he hid in the shadows. There was sorrow in the air and even at his young age, he sensed it. As Asa watched, his father sank down into a chair at the table they used to eat their meals.

A big, empty table in a big, empty chamber

with Haim sitting at the end of it, his hands folded in prayer and his eyes closed as he leaned on his hands. He was sitting in the dark but for a small amount of light coming from the banked hearth. Asa crept into the chamber, watching his elderly father from a distance. Haim continued to pray and, little by little, Asa snuck up on him. He was silent in his bare feet against the cold wooden floor, but he could sense that something serious had happened between his sister and the man he knew as Saint Peter.

He was sorry, too. He was coming to like the big knight who was so adept at firing pebbles back at him, yet so compassionate that he recognized hungry children. It was a paradox to young Asa, confused by a man he both feared and admired. He came to stand next to his father, watching the man closely.

"Papa?" he said softly.

Haim opened his eyes, looking at his little boy, the one who was born when he was already an old man. His eyes crinkled and he smiled at the child, pulling him into a hug.

"What are you doing awake, *moyz*," he said, calling his son by his pet name – mouse. "It is very late."

Asa wasn't so old that he didn't like to sit on his father's lap as long as no one was around, particularly his friends. To his friends, he was tough and grown-up. To his father, however, he was still his little boy. He inched his way onto Haim's lap.

"I saw Saint Peter and Liora in the kitchen yard," he said. "That big man who came here – that was Saint Peter's father?"

Haim nodded slowly, wearily. "Aye," he said. "That is the Earl of Hereford and Worcester, a very great man."

"Was he mean?"

"Nay, he was quite kind."

"Why did he come?"

Haim sighed, long and riddled with emotion, setting back in his chair as Asa lay his head on the man's shoulder. "To find his son."

"But why was his son here?"

"He is fond of Liora."

Asa thought on that a moment. "He is her friend," he said. "He talks to her."

"I know."

"He talks to me, too."

"He does?"

Asa nodded his head. "He helped me with Saul's Army when they were stealing our eggs."

Haim frowned, thinking of a fully armed Christian knight against a bunch of small children. "What did he do?"

"He talked to them," Asa said. "He told them that stealing was not acceptable and if he heard that they were stealing again, he would come and punish them. But I saw Eneb – you know Eneb? He is from Saul's Army. Eneb said that Saint Peter arranged for them to be fed every day."

Haim stopped frowning. Asa's words sank in and he sat up in surprise, looking at his son. "He did what?" he said. "He feeds them every day?"

Asa nodded. "A tavern on Lombard feeds them every morning," he said. "Saint Peter feeds them so they will not steal our eggs anymore."

Haim blinked, shocked. "He did that?"

Asa nodded again. Then, he cocked his head thoughtfully. "I know Saul's Army steals because they do not have enough to eat," he said. "I did not like that they stole our eggs, though. But Saint Peter made sure they were fed just so they wouldn't steal. That was good of him, wasn't it?"

Haim was quite surprised to hear all of this. He'd only met Peter twice, and he certainly didn't know that much about him, but what Asa told him... that took a man of great compassion. That was a theme quite prevalent in his religion and culture, the show of compassion, of kindness to strangers. Peter wasn't even Jewish, yet he was showing those traits. Haim had to remind himself that the Christians followed Jesus as the son of God and that Jesus preached kindness to strangers and to the less fortunate.

Some men followed that teaching, some

didn't.

Haim had known many Christian knights and nobles in his lifetime. Some were good, some were not so good, but the same could be said for his religion, as well. The traits of good or evil were not limited to only one religion. Still… Haim was impressed that Peter de Lohr, an elite and seasoned knight, should take the time to feed hungry children.

Perhaps he wasn't just another warmonger, after all.

"It was very good of him, *moyz*," he said after a moment. "You… you know Peter a little?"

Asa nodded. "I tried to chase him away at first," he said. "But I'm glad I did not. He's different from the other men we know, Papa. He's big and has a big sword and he fights in wars. I am glad he is my friend."

"Are you?"

Asa nodded. "Papa, I want to fight with a big sword when I grow up. Can I fight with Saint Peter?"

Haim shook his head. "Nay, little one," he said. "The wars are for the Christians. We will stay safe here, in London."

"But if I wanted to fight when I'm bigger, can I?"

Haim looked at his son, a boy who liked his boy gang and who liked the roughhousing of the streets. He wasn't content to be educated and pious. Asa had a spark in him that was all his own, which could mean trouble when he became older. He'd never shown any interest in knights or battles until now and Haim knew he had to be careful in how he handled it. He wasn't the kind to deny his children and not give them a reason for it, but a small boy might not understand.

He worded his reply deliberately.

"The world of the Jews and the Christian are two different worlds," he said. "The Christians fight to spread the word of God and the Jews are content to live in their world and worship in their faith. We only fight when we have to. It's like the world of the Maccabees and Saul's Army – you never really mix. They have things that are important to them and you have things that are important to you. That is how the Christians and the Jews exist. Do you understand?"

Asa's brow was furrowed as he thought on his father's explanation. "But we can work with Saul's Army if we must," he said. "We have before when boys from Ironmonger Street came here to steal. We came together and we fought them off. We can work with Saint Peter and the Christians, can't we?"

Haim nodded, sort of. "If we must, for the greater good," he said. "But our world is such that only Christians can be knights."

"Can't I fight?"

"I do not think so, *moyz*."

Asa climbed off his lap. "That is not right," he said. "Saint Peter is a good man and if I want to be like him, then I should be allowed to. And Saint Peter likes Lee-Lee; I know he does. What if he wants to marry her?"

Haim shook his head. "He cannot," he said. "Christians and Jews do not marry."

"Who says so?"

"The Catholics and the Great Synagogue."

"They do not like each other?"

Haim shrugged. "It is not a matter of like or dislike," he said. "Is it simply what our faiths dictate. They are different."

Asa pursed his lips, clearly unhappy with that answer. There were apples on the table, left out by his mother in case her children became hungry between meals. They were always welcome to take an apple. Asa picked up the apple, looking at it, thinking.

"I think that we should all be friends," he said. "Papa, what if I wanted to marry a Christian girl when I get big? Would you let me?"

Haim reluctantly shook his head. "You could not," he said. "Not unless she became Jewish."

"Even if she was kind and very pretty?"

"Even so."

Asa frowned. "It seems unfair," he said. "Isn't

it most important that people are kind and love us, no matter if they are Christian and Jewish? The kind of people who will protect you and feed people who do not have enough to eat? That seems to be more important than people who pray in my temple or in a big church. Rabbi Judah told me that God cares what is in our hearts more than he cares about the prayers we give. Saint Peter has a good heart and it makes me feel sad that I will never be able to fight with him. I will never be anything more than a boy on the street to him."

With that, he took his apple and left the chamber, leaving his father sitting in the darkness, pondering the wise, if not naïve, words of a seven-year-old boy. *Out of the mouths of babes*, he thought.

God cares what is in our hearts more than he cares about the prayers we give.

That left Haim wondering if he had broken one of the fundamentals of his own religion. Had he been so fixated on the cross Peter bore in his Christian faith that he failed to see the genuine and noble man beneath?

He wondered.

CHAPTER FIFTEEN

I T WAS QUIET before the dawn.

Liora hadn't slept all night with thoughts of Peter rolling through her head. Her father had been right about one thing – there was peace at the house on Milk Street. There always had been. But since the introduction of Peter de Lohr, that peace had been fractured.

Badly.

But it wasn't his fault. It was hers, completely. Now, she wasn't satisfied with the peace if Peter couldn't be part of her life. After the confrontation in the kitchen yard last night, Haim had brought Liora inside and she had run directly to her bedchamber. She went inside and closed the door, but when she peered into the corridor a couple of hours later, Haim was in a chair next to her door, reading by candlelight. He looked up at her, smiled, and she promptly shut the door.

Her father was on watch duty, making sure his daughter didn't slip out to meet the Christian knight again.

Therefore, Liora went to bed, but she didn't sleep. Clad in her night shift with a shawl around her shoulders, she sat on her bed and gazed from the window, up to the starry night above and wondered just how she was supposed to continue onward with Peter on the Marches, securing castles and fighting for a better England. He was a knight and she knew he had seen battles. It was well known that the de Lohrs were a warring tribe, but now that she was emotionally invested in one of them, the concept of battles and fighting became more real to her.

That kind of thing had never concerned her before.

But it concerned her now. If Peter was fighting, then it was possible he could become wounded. If he became wounded, how would she know? Would her father allow her to help him? Haim had been very polite and quite calm as he spoke to Peter, all things considered, but he could put his foot down if he needed to. She'd seen him do it, especially with Asa. Liora had never given her father a moment of trouble in her life until now.

Evidently, she'd been saving it all up for one major event.

About an hour before dawn, when the chickens began stirring, she finally rose and bathed in the cold rosewater in her chamber before donning a simple broadcloth dress, leather girdle that emphasized her tiny waist, and a broadcloth cloak. She braided her dark hair into two long braids, pulling her hair off her face with a kerchief and looking at herself in her polished bronze mirror, wondering if she looked as different as she felt.

In truth, she felt quite different. Life, for her, had changed drastically in the past few days. The moment she came upon Peter de Lohr in her kitchen yard was the moment her future was forever altered, and she hadn't even been aware of it at the time. She'd never been in love; she'd never even been close. That was something she had never hoped for or expected. But love had showed up in her kitchen yard that night.

She wasn't going to let it go.

Squaring her shoulders, Liora opened her door to see that her father was still there, still reading, and she told him that she was going out to tend the chickens. Haim permitted her to go, but he followed her, watching her from the house as she went out to the coop to gather eggs and feed the chickens.

And so, another peaceful day began on Milk

Street.

The servants were up by the time she came back into the house with the basket of eggs. As they started the fire in the hearth and began the preparations for the day, Liora went back into the stable to release the goats. Feeding them in the morning was her usual task, so she opened the gate on the little corral and out they spilled into the kitchen yard. Using a large pitchfork, she shoveled some of the hay out into the yard for the goats, who provided milk to drink and also to make cheese. It was Asa who would clean up after them, and brush them, and make sure they were well tended at night.

The eastern horizon was growing lighter as the sun began to rise and Liora went about cleaning out the chicken coop. It was yet another duty she had, as the only servants her father had were those who worked for her mother, so she was well-versed in things that took place out in the yard. Both she and Asa were no strangers to work because their father insisted on it. He refused to raise useless children, as he put it. She was sweeping out the straw that the chickens roosted on during the night when the gate to the kitchen yard suddenly burst open.

Royal soldiers appeared.

At first, Liora was too surprised to be afraid. She'd never had a reason in her entire life to be afraid, and certainly not in her own home, so when the soldiers flooded into the yard, she simply set aside the broom to ask what the trouble was.

"Is something the matter?" she asked the first man who had charged in. "Can I help you?"

The man was older, wearing a dirty royal tunic with three golden lions against a scarlet background. When she came out of the coop, he fixed on her, as did the other soldiers in the yard.

They gravitated in her direction.

"Who are ye, girl?" he asked.

She looked at him curiously. "Liora, daughter of Haim," she said. "Whom do you seek?"

A leering smile spread across the soldier's lips. "The jeweler's daughter?"

"Aye."

"Someone wants a word with ye."

"Me?" she said, shocked. "But who should want to speak with me?"

"Ye *are* the jeweler's daughter, aren't ye?"

"I said I was, but…"

He grabbed her by the arm and yanked her towards the gate, cutting her off. Liora's puzzlement turned to fear when she realized their appearance hadn't been random. They seemed to be specifically looking for her, the jeweler's daughter, which she thought quite odd. She watched as two of them went into the house and she could hear screaming from the kitchen servants, but that was the last she saw and heard as she was dragged out into the alleyway and put onto a horse with a man who grabbed her lewdly around the chest. He had one big hand on her right breast, laughing low in his throat, as she beat his hand away so that it ended up around her waist.

Meanwhile, two of the soldiers had wrested Haim from the house and although he wasn't putting up a fight, they were roughly dragging him. When he tripped, they thought he was resisting and someone hit him in the face. Liora screamed at the sight of her father being beaten, rousing the entire neighborhood, including her brother, who had clamored to an upstairs window to see what the fuss was about.

What Asa saw was his sister and father being taken away by armed men. Grabbing his pebble shooter, he ran down to the kitchen yard about the time the soldiers took off, and he chased them all the way down the street, screaming at them. He finally came to a halt at the corner of Milk Street and Lombard Street, watching the group of armed soldiers head west.

And just like that, his father and sister were gone.

Asa was furious and terrified. He could hear neighbors on his street raise the alarm and he could hear his mother screaming. As he stood there, several of his Maccabees came running up, watching the group of armed soldiers fade into the distance.

"What happened?" one of the boys demanded.

Asa realized he was close to tears, trying desperately not to cry and look weak. "The soldiers took my father and my sister."

"Why?"

"I don't know why!" Asa shouted, losing the battle against tears. "But we must go after them! We must help them!"

The older boy shook his head. "We can't," he said. "I know those soldiers. I've seen those tunics. They belong to the king!"

Asa frowned, baffled at the revelation. "Why did he take my father and sister?" he wanted to know. "What does the king want them for? He knows my father – Papa makes his jewelry."

No one had an answer, but Milk Street was growing increasingly agitated as women began to wail alongside Asa's mother. The boys could hear the weeping because some of their own mothers were joining in. Frightened, they began to look at each other.

"What do we do?" the older boy asked. "We need help, but we can't go after them. They'll kill us."

Fighting other boy gangs was one thing, but fighting armed soldiers was strictly another. Even in their wild boyish ways, they knew they were no match for swords.

They only knew one other man who might be.

"Saint Peter!" Asa gasped. "We must find Saint Peter!"

"But where?" the older boy asked. "We don't know where he lives!"

Asa nodded frantically. "I do, I do!" he said. "He told me he lives at a place called Lonsdale, to the west of London and next to the river. That's what he said!"

"Then we'll go to him," the older boy said. "There is a road that goes along the river. We'll go to every house until we find him!"

Asa was eager to move. "You have a horse, Egan," he said. "Get your horse and I will ride with you. Hurry!"

Egan was already on the move, running back to his house as the other Maccabees followed. The boys entered the yard behind the house and pulled the old horse from the stable, all of them trying to put a saddle and bridle on the old beast. Everyone was so eager to help that it took more time than it should have but, soon enough, Egan and Asa mounted the old nag and kicked it to get it going while the other boys slapped it on the rump.

The old horse took off, heading down Lombard Street, aiming for the road the hugged the river in search of the only man they knew could help…

The man they used to shoot pebbles at.

They could only hope he didn't hold a grudge.

 C𝔅

Lonsdale

THE ARMY HAD been mobilizing before dawn.

Peter was among them. The bailey of Lonsdale was lit up with the flames of a hundred torches piercing the mist that had rolled in over the river during the night, and Peter had been up since well before sunrise preparing to depart to the Marches.

Lonsdale was built in such a way that the troop house was built into the wall and into the sublevel underneath the house, so it could conceivably house eight hundred to a thousand men at any given time, and that was only in the troop house. It could also house another five hundred in the bailey alone. Christopher was a warlord and everything in his life had military purpose, including a home he'd built for his wife that was supposed to be for comfort. It was comfortable, that was true, but it wasn't only for show.

It was a fortress in disguise.

Several of his father's friends and allies were in the bailey also, as they had been lodging at Lonsdale while the events went on in London.

Caius was there, preparing to head north to Richmond, along with Maxton, Alexander, Marcus, Jax, Juston, Alastor, and David. David had come to collect the men his brother had promised him because he was departing for Canterbury that morning with the reinforcements.

The talk throughout the morning was about John's mercenaries, now the topic of conversation whenever two or more of the men got together. The concern was in how quickly they were traveling into England and what state their properties would be in when they arrived home. Peter could hear them muttering about it as he helped Alexander muster the de Lohr army with the assistance of the master sergeants. His father and uncle were in private conversation with Jax and Juston over near the entry of the manse, but he wasn't paying attention to them. In truth, he hadn't spoken to his father since leaving Liora last night, mostly because he didn't know what to say.

As the sun began to rise and poke holes through the mist with golden fingers of light, the army was starting to take shape. The quartermaster wagons were mostly loaded and ready to go and the men were properly outfitted. Peter finally stood back and watched the sergeants make the final adjustments, thinking about preparing his own horse for travel. But along with that thought came doubt.

Doubt that he was doing the right thing.

Peter hadn't gotten a good night's sleep since he'd met Liora and last night was no exception. He'd tossed and turned all night, reliving the scene in the kitchen yard over and over. He had told Liora that it would be best for them to spend some time apart, to really think about their devotion and dedication to one another even though she'd told him that she would be willing to convert religions for the sake of their marriage. At the time, he thought a separation was the right thing to do but now he was starting to wonder. He didn't want to be away from her, now more than ever, but it wasn't as if he had any choice in the matter. He had a job to do and she had to make sure her decision wasn't one she was going to regret.

"Good morn, Peter."

Jolted from his thoughts, Peter turned to see Christin standing behind him, wrapped up in a cloak against the cold morning. She smiled at him, her gray eyes just like her mother's, as she came to stand next to him. He smiled weakly at her.

"What are you doing up so early?" he asked.

She cocked a dark eyebrow. "Surely you jest," she said drolly. "I have a toddler son and an infant. I have not slept a full night in two years. I am always up this early."

His grin turned genuine. "That is your fault

for marrying a man you love madly and bearing his children," he said. "Does he at least help you when the boys are up in the night, demanding attention?"

Christin nodded. "He does, actually," she said. "But he is terrible when it comes time to put them back into their bed. He wants them to sleep between us and pouts when I will not let them. The man threatens to weep like an old beer wife."

Peter started chuckling. "I will not tell him you said that."

"I do not care if you do."

"Where are my nephews now?"

"With Mama," she said. "God bless the woman for taking charge of them in the mornings so Sherry and I can have some peace."

Peter grunted. "She has an infant of her own," he said. "I've heard her and Papa arguing about the number of babies she likes to tend to."

Christin laughed softly. "He complains, but he does not mean a word of it," she said. "I've found him dead asleep with both of my children plus our two youngest siblings in his arms. There's Papa, passed out like a drunkard on the bed, with children sleeping all over him. He's really a softhearted man but he does not want anyone to know."

As she and Peter shared a giggle, Christin caught sight of her husband over near the gatehouse. "Ah," she said. "There is my husband. I must speak to him."

Peter could see Alexander, too, in discussion with Caius and Maxton. "Are you returning with him to Lioncross?" he asked. "I heard Mama say something about staying here because she did not want to travel with Olivia just yet."

Olivia Charlotte was their youngest sibling, a late baby for her parents born two months earlier. She had been born at Lonsdale, not Lioncross Abbey like most of the de Lohr children had been, but Dustin wasn't keen on traveling with a newborn even though her husband wanted to return to the Marches.

"It is difficult to travel with an infant that small," Peter said. "Mayhap Papa should leave her here while he goes about his duties. She'll be safe here, away from the turmoil that Papa is sure to face."

"And *you* are sure to face," Christin said, looking at him. "I hope you do not mind that Sherry told me about Liora, but I will confess that he only told me after I heard you and Papa arguing yesterday."

He looked at her queerly. "How did you hear us? We were in his solar."

She lifted an eyebrow. "How could I *not* hear you with his big voice and my big ears," she said, grinning at her own expense. "My husband was gone all morning with you. He wasn't even here when The Marshal called his meeting and I know Papa was furious about it. Then I heard him bellowing at you and Sherry told me why. My husband says she is astonishingly beautiful."

Peter looked at her a moment, hesitation in his manner. "I… I cannot decide if I should tell you that I do not wish to talk about it or if I really *do* want to talk about it," he said. "I do not even know where to start."

Christin smiled faintly. "Start at the beginning," she said. "Where did you meet her?"

Peter shrugged. "I was hiding from Agnes de Quincy and ended up in an alley next to her home," he said. "She hid me until the threat of Agnes passed."

Christin chuckled. "Is this true?" she said. "And you told her why you were hiding?"

"I told her. She called me a coward."

He burst into soft laughter and so did she, seeing joy in Peter's face she'd never seen before. He looked positively giddy. But the laughter soon faded. "Sherry also told me that she is a Jewess," she said. "I have never met one before. What is she like?"

"Like you and me," he said. "She is witty, charming, and intelligent. I cannot take my eyes off her, Cissy. When I am around her, I feel as if I have never felt before. I am happy and joyful, as if

I am walking on clouds. That's what Papa called it and he is right. Does that sound silly?"

Christin shook her head. "It does not because I know exactly how you feel," she said. "So does Sherry. He's quite sympathetic to your cause, you know. We both are. But what does Papa say?"

He cast her a long look. "You mean to say that your big ears didn't hear him?"

She grinned. "Not everything," she said. "Surely he understands your position."

Peter nodded, thinking of what his father had said the night before as they stood in Liora's kitchen yard. The man had been opposed to any liaison between him and Liora until it came down to a critical moment in time.

I cannot live his life for him, but I will be by his side no matter what he decides.

"He does," he said after a moment. "But Papa has a very pragmatic view of the situation. In order for me to marry Liora, either I must become a Jew or she must become a Christian. That is the only way we can have a marriage that will be recognized by either religion. Although he is not happy that I am willing to give up everything that I have worked for to be with Liora, ultimately, he understands."

Christin was watching him intently. "Is she worth so much to you, Peter?"

He looked at her, nodding. "She is worth

everything and more," he said. "Cissy, when you met Sherry, did you know he would be the man you would marry right away? Or did it take time?"

Christin thought back to when she and Alexander had first had any real interaction. Christin had been an agent for William Marshal, one of the best, but she'd never really worked directly with Alexander until an incident at Norwich Castle that involved John and his lascivious attention towards her. She smiled at the memory of coming to know her husband during a fairly turbulent time.

"I was so enamored with him that I was dumbstruck," she said. "He was the famous Alexander de Sherrington, the most elite assassin in The Marshal's stable, and I was just *me*. I had no great background, no great training. I was in such awe of him. But I think even then I knew I would marry him."

"And it happened quickly?"

"Fairly quickly. Ask Papa. I still do not think he is over just *how* quickly it happened."

Peter cracked a smile. "I remember that time," he said. "We were so involved with the king and trying to keep you from marrying his bastard son that it was a very difficult time for us all. The fact that you and Sherry fell in love in the middle of it speaks to the power of your feelings for one another."

There was longing in his tone that Christin

didn't miss. "If your love for Liora is meant to be, Peter, then it *will* be," she said. "But sometimes, you must fight for what you want. Somehow, the victory of it makes it all the sweeter."

Peter scratched his head. "But Sherry wasn't Jewish," he said. Then, he looked at her. "Liora has already told me that she will become a Christian, but as Papa pointed out, we will be bringing her into a world she knows absolutely nothing about. You… you would help her, wouldn't you? And be a friend to her?"

He seemed so distressed about it that she put her hand on his arm. "Of course I would," she said. "I would do anything I could to help her. You need not even ask."

That seemed to ease him a great deal. "I knew you would," he said. "I do not know why I even felt the need to ask that. I suppose it is because the situation is something I've never faced before and I'm simply trying to navigate it the best way I can."

"With your heart," Christin said softly. "Navigate it with your heart, Peter. You cannot go wrong if you do that, but above all else, always think of her first. If she is willing to leave the only life she has ever known just for you, then you must be very considerate of that. But know that come what may, Sherry and I will embrace her with open arms."

He smiled at his sister. She was a few years

younger than he was, but they had practically grown up together. She had never been anything other than devoted and attached to him, and he to her. He reflected on telling Christopher how he'd always felt like an outsider, and that was only of his own doing, because certainly his family had never made him feel differently. Even now, when he was choosing a path that no one else in the family had ever chosen, more and more, it was feeling like the right path.

Right for him.

"Thank you," he whispered, kissing her on the forehead. "That comforts me greatly. And, Cissy… if something happens in these battles were are sure to face against John's mercenaries and I do not make it back to London, will you please go to Liora and tell her… tell her that my thoughts were only of her? I want her to know that I did not forget her."

Christin didn't like it when her brother or husband or father spoke in such ways. She couldn't think of them as anything other than vital, strong, and alive, so to speak of death wasn't something she was comfortable with. But for Peter's sake, and because she knew he was right, she nodded her head.

"If you wish," she said. "I will go to her."

He forced a smile. "Thank you," he said. "That eases me more than you know. You are an excellent sister, even if you are annoying on occasion."

Christin giggled, swatting him on the arm, but she was prevented from sparring with him when a servant found her on the stoop and told her that her mother was in need of her. With children to feed, Christin forgot about seeking her husband and left to find her mother, leaving Peter on the steps of the manse.

But Peter had tasks to attend to, so he headed off to find his father, who happened to be speaking to Jax over near the gatehouse with several other men. As he approached, he could see old Juston de Royans and equally old Jax de Velt, men who had shaped the history of England over the past forty years. Juston, big and burly and with blond hair that had turned mostly to gray, had been Christopher and David and Marcus' mentor back when they were young knights with the world at their feet.

In fact, Juston had been the mentor to many of the Executioner Knights, Maxton and Kress and Achilles included. His seat was Bowes Castle far to the north, close to Richmond where Caius was in command. Peter knew that his father wasn't awestruck or submissive to any man, not even The Marshal, but because Juston used to be his mentor years ago, there was a hint of that submissiveness in Christopher's behavior when he spoke to

Juston. He still looked to the man as if he had all the answers, which he usually did. It was rather touching to see, a glimpse of his father's past in his behavior with a man he respected greatly.

As Peter walked up on the group of men, his caught his father's attention.

"The army will be ready for Canterbury in about an hour, my lord," Peter said, formally addressing his father and his uncle in front of a group of men. "Is there anything else you need?"

Christopher shook his head. "Nay," he said. "In fact, we were just speaking on how we are strapped for knights. Every knight I have is occupied with command duties, including those I left behind at Lioncross. I have none to spare."

Peter looked at his uncle. "You have good knights at Canterbury," he said. "Brickley de Dere is an excellent knight."

David nodded. "He is in command while I am away," he said. "I do not worry with Brickley in command, but we were speaking on the crop of knights coming out of Kenilworth. I intend to get my hands on one or two of those men when they are fully knighted."

Everyone knew that Kenilworth Castle was one of the oldest and most elite training castles for knights in all of England. Many of the Executioner Knights had trained there, men from fine families with skills that been honed by the master knights of Kenilworth. Peter had trained there for a couple of years after leaving Marcus at Somerhill and he could attest to the fact that it was either sink or swim for the trainees at Kenilworth. If you did not succeed, you were doomed to failure.

There was no middle ground.

"I've heard that the de Wolfe brothers are in training," Peter said. "All of Wolverton's sons, including the youngest, William."

That had some of the men snorting. "You mean the Gambling King?" Christopher said. "God help Edward – he's going to have his hands full with that lad. He is either going to be the greatest knight England has ever seen or the greatest outlaw."

The men chortled at Edward de Wolfe's expense. He had three sons, very close in age, the youngest of which was a devious, brilliant, highly skilled warrior even at his very young age. In the siege of London those months ago, William de Wolfe had fought alongside Christopher de Lohr because the lad was just that good and they had needed men to fight. But he also had a penchant for gambling and managed to win money and possessions from almost every man he'd ever served with, Peter included.

"Where *is* Wolverhampton, by the way?" Peter asked, looking around. "I've not seen him this morning."

Christopher sobered as he shook his head. "He has already departed," he said. "He is far enough to the north that he is worried about the mercenaries, so he is already gone."

Peter looked around to the other men gathered, noticing that a few were missing. "Savernake is gone?" he said. "I do not see Dashiell or the duke."

"They departed yesterday, but Dash is heading to Rochester Castle," Christopher said. "It is under siege and we are quite certain that the Earl of East Anglia has sent his army to protect his holding, so Dash went to join up with his father's army."

That made sense considering Dashiell du Reims was the heir to the earldom of East Anglia, an old and powerful holding, but East Anglia was also related to Hereford because Christopher's mother and East Anglia's father had been brother and sister.

"Will we send men, too?" Peter asked. "They are cousins, after all."

Christopher shook his head, looking at David. "I can only spare men for your uncle right now. The bulk of my army is on the Marches, but I will supply men if I am asked. With more men than anyone else on the Marches, I expect the requests to come."

That was very true. Lioncross Abbey had a six-thousand-man standing army, a massive army that was spread between a few garrisons, now to be spread between even more with Peter taking a thousand to Ludlow and, more than likely, Alexander taking another thousand to Wigmore. Men and material were about to be moved all over England in an attempt to protect property and weaken John's mercenary force, but it would take time.

And time was something they didn't have a lot of.

"Hold the Marches, Chris," Jax said quietly. "We can hold the north, but you must hold the Marches. If the mercenaries get control of any castles along the Welsh border, they won't stay there. They'll head into Wales and that will start another war with the Welsh princes. Peace is already a fragile thing there. I do not have to tell you that."

Christopher shook his head. "Nay, you do not," he said regretfully. "But the Marches will hold. Truthfully, John doesn't seem to be interest in Wales. I'm more concerned with his interest in Scotland."

Jax glanced at Juston, John de Longley, Alastor de Bourne, and finally Gilbert d'Umfraville, all of them lords of enormous castles in Northumberland. They had the most to lose and since the revelations of yesterday, that fact had never been more apparent. John, in fact, was brand new to his title because his father had recently passed away, so this was a test of his command skills.

Jax finally shook his head with the absurdity of it all.

"It wasn't even a year or two ago that we were fighting to keep Scotland from invading the north," he said. "There is great irony in the fact that now, we are allying with them to keep John's mercenary army from taking our lands. They will want Northwood Castle, home of Teviot, because it controls a great river crossing and a good portion of the river itself. They will want Castle Keld, home of de Bourne, because it controls a major road in and out of Scotland. They will want Prudhoe Castle where d'Umfraville lives because of its strategic importance. They will want Bowes Castle because it controls a major road that crosses east to west from Cumbria to Northumberland, and they will try to claim Alnwick, where de Vesci lives, simply because Alnwick is a prize. But most of all... most of all, they will come for Berwick Castle and Pelinom Castle, my home, because both are crucial to holding Northumberland in general. Something tells me that out of all the battles I have fought in my lifetime, and there have been many, this may very well be my most important."

By the time he finished, everyone was looking at him with great concern and perhaps even greater trepidation. For The Dark Lord, the greatest knight of his generation, to speak in such a way was unusual, indeed. It was quite unsettling. But Jax had aptly brought the truth of the matter into focus, something all of them were concerned with.

Peter found himself looking around the group of old warriors, the greatest men of their generation, men who had fought for England their entire lives. Men who were legends to all fighting men throughout the known world. Men who, ironically enough, now found themselves fighting against the king of their own country. They were now rebels, fighting an unjust ruler and called outlaws because of it.

It all seemed horribly unfair to their legacies.

"There was an old master knight at Kenilworth by the name of Boone Pendleton," Peter said quietly. "He died the year I was knighted. I'm sure you know the name, but he was someone I greatly admired. Right before I was knighted, there was some trouble over in Kidderminster and Kenilworth was called upon because we were the only available army at the time. I do not remember the exact details, but the master knights, and several squires, including me, took the army over to Kidderminster to face a Welsh incursion. I was absolutely terrified. In fact, I think most of the squires were because we were suited up like knights and expected to fight. I remember Boone repeating an old Viking prayer and it was a cry we all took up. It started out with *Behold, I see those I love, and my relatives who have died before me…"*

He was cut off when Christopher lifted his head and spoke the next line. "*I see my father seated in the great hall, with an empty seat beside him.*"

David continued. "*I see the greatest warriors who have ever lived, surrounding my father, calling to me.*"

Astonished, Peter watched as all of the men took up the prayer, speaking the last few lines –

> *Death is not the end, but the beginning, for a true warrior never dies.*
>
> *He takes his place of greatness beside those who are worthy.*
>
> *Mourn not the glorious dead but rejoice in their legacy.*
>
> *They wait for me, not in this life, but in the next,*
>
> *Where their legends shall live forever.*

There was something so incredibly reverent about that prayer being spoken by some of the greatest men who had ever held a sword. Peter didn't feel as if he should speak, as if the silence after that glorious poem should not be broken. It hung like a spell over them, each man feeling it to his very bones, knowing that today, more than ever, it held true. In truth, it brought tears to Peter's eyes, for it was an emotional moment for them all.

It was Christopher who finally broke the silence.

"Listen to me and listen well, all of you," he said, though he was mostly looking at Jax and Juston. "If any of you fall in battle and I survive, know that I will stop at nothing to avenge you. John has been a thorn in my side for over twenty years. What he is doing now is beyond what I thought he was capable of and if it costs the lives of good men like you, know that my vengeance will know no limits. If William Marshal stands in my way, he will pay the price. I will burn him and all he stands for to the ground if he opposes me. But I *will* avenge you, I swear it."

With that, he reached out to Juston first, gripping the man's hand in a silent promise of his pledge. Juston nodded, his old eyes glimmering, as Christopher moved to Jax and did the same thing. He held Jax's hand just a little longer than necessary, knowing that out of all of them, Jax might find himself the most involved. With two prime properties, he would be a preferred target.

After Jax, Christopher shook hands with Teviot, de Bourne, and d'Umfraville, reaffirming bonds of men who had an uphill battle. They were all preparing to head out when the sentries began to cry out that a rider had been sighted.

The gates of Lonsdale were already open because of the assembling army, so no one seemed concerned over a lone rider. In fact, the group of warlords were breaking up, including Peter, but he noticed that Alexander was going to the gate because, as the commander of the de Lohr armies, that was his job. Peter had never felt ousted by Alexander when he married Christin and swore an oath to command Christopher's armies because it was well known that Alexander was the best commander of men in England. Even when the Executioner Knights went on a mission, it was almost always Alexander in command.

Therefore, Peter was happy to surrender the responsibility. He turned for the manse but ended up running into Maxton and Caius and striking up a conversation, when he heard Alexander shouting his name.

"Peter!"

Peter turned for the gatehouse, but there were so many men between him and the gatehouse that he couldn't see Alexander at all. But he heard his name again and headed in that direction, followed by Maxton and Caius simply because their horses were over near the gatehouse and they were preparing to depart with the rest of the warlords.

The three of them closed in on the gatehouse, finally spying Alexander, and Peter's calm demeanor took a turn for the worse when he saw who Alexander was standing with.

Asa.

Peter bolted.

The little boy was on a horse with another child and Peter could see that Asa had been weeping because there was dirt smeared all over his face. Incredulous, he came to an unsteady halt.

"Asa?" he gasped. "What in the h-… I mean, what are you doing here? How did you find me?"

When Asa laid eyes on Peter, the tears returned with a vengeance. "You said you lived next to the river," he said, wiping his eyes furiously. "You said you lived at Lonsdale. We went to the manse before this one and asked for you, but they told us where Lonsdale was."

He was pointing down the road, speaking of the manse that was about two miles up the river, closer to London. "That's Hurlingham," he said, greatly concerned. "Why are you looking for me? What's wrong?"

Asa thought he could be very brave and explain the situation, but seeing Peter seemed to suck the courage right out of him because in Peter, he saw help. He saw hope. He was so frightened that he couldn't speak.

The sobs began to come.

"They came and took them," he wept. "My papa and Lee-Lee. The soldiers came and took them away!"

Peter was stricken with confusion and terror. "What soldiers?" he demanded, grabbing the child. "What do you mean they took your father and Liora away? Who in the hell were they?"

Asa was off on a crying jag, so the older boy spoke. "The king's soldiers," he said, his voice trembling. "They came and took Asa's sister and father away this morning. We came to find you so that you could help."

For a moment, Peter was frozen with shock. He simply couldn't believe what he was hearing. It was Alexander who asked the question Peter couldn't seem to bring forth.

"Are you certain?" he asked. "You know it was the king's men?"

The boy nodded. "The yellow lions on a crimson tunic," he said. "We've seen it before, many times. They came and took Asa's sister and father."

"Where did they take them?"

The boy shook his head. "I do not know," he said. "But they were heading towards the palace."

Westminster. Peter hadn't realized he'd stopped breathing but, suddenly, he took a big breath, so deep that his head began to swim. "But *why*?" he asked. "Why would they do that? Did they say anything? Make any demands?"

Asa found his tongue. "I didn't hear them say anything."

"But your father is the king's jeweler. Mayhap it had everything to do with that?"

Asa shook his head. "They took Lee-Lee and she screamed," he said. "I heard her scream. Then they came into the house and took my father. They were dragging him away."

Peter looked at Alexander in shock. "Why take them both?"

Alexander shook his head. "I don't know," he said honestly. "It sounds as if John is clearly displeased, but to take them both away? I can see him taking the jeweler, but his daughter along with him?"

Peter nodded, his mind reeling. "It makes no sense," he said. "What they are describing sounds as if they have taken Liora and her father prisoner."

Alexander didn't want to agree with him, but he had no choice. That was exactly what it sounded like.

"Aye," he said. "That would be my assumption as well."

"Saint Peter, please!" Asa begged. "Please help. You have a big sword and you can free them!"

Peter looked at the child, hearing the heart-wrenching plea. Without a word, he bolted, running towards the stable as fast as his legs would take him. Alexander ran after him and because he was running, Maxton and Caius began to run, too. All of them running for their horses simply because Peter was. Maxton and Caius didn't even know why Peter was running, or what the weeping young boy was talking about, but that didn't matter. Peter thought it was serious enough to run and they wouldn't let him go alone, wherever that may be.

Something was badly amiss.

As knights were dashing towards the stables, Christopher caught sight of them. He was over near the manse entry with David, watching men race for their horses. They were scattering through the assembling army, mounting horses and tearing off through the gatehouse. Puzzled, and concerned, Christopher caught Alexander before he could get away.

"Sherry!" he shouted. "What is happening?"

Alexander reined his horse to a swift halt, causing the horse to rear up. "Trouble," he said. "Stay here."

Christopher scowled. "What is –?"

Alexander cut him off. "Stay *here*, Chris," he said in a rare use of Christopher's given name. "If you get involved, it will only make it worse, so stay here."

Christopher had no idea what he was talking

about, watching the man tear off through the courtyard and sprint from the gatehouse. He scratched his head, baffled at what had just happened, as Marcus came up to him.

"What in the hell was that all about?" Marcus asked.

Christopher shook his head, baffled. "I have no idea," he said. "Sherry said to remain here, but he and Peter and Cai and Maxton just flew out of here as if the world were ending."

Marcus looked at David, who shrugged. He returned his focus to the gatehouse, seeing two young boys on a horse still standing there. He pointed.

"Who is that?" he asked.

Christopher's vision wasn't what it used to be. All he could see was a horse and two figures, but not much else. "I don't know," he said. "Who does it look like?'"

"Two children."

The curiosity was mounting. Christopher, Marcus, and David headed to the gatehouse to find out who the children were and what, exactly, they had to do with the flight of the knights out of his bailey. When he finally got close enough to speak to the children, he didn't recognize them, but after a brief conversation with the smaller of the pair, a great deal suddenly became very clear.

Now, he knew why Peter had left so swiftly.

Stay here, Chris. You'll only make it worse if you get involved.

When he told David and Marcus his suspicions, they didn't quite agree with Alexander. Neither did Jax or Juston.

Soon enough, the group of them were heading towards Westminster, too.

CHAPTER SIXTEEN

Westminster Palace

LIORA HAD NEVER been so frightened in her entire life.

Sitting in a lavish chamber, one with carved wood paneling and gold on the ceiling, it would have been beautiful under any other circumstances. But at the moment, all she could see was darkness and unfamiliarity and men all around her. She had been escorted into this chamber or, more precisely, dragged by the same man who had put his hand on her breast and then laughed about it when she slapped his hand. He'd put her in the chair and then stood back as other men came into the chamber.

She had no idea what had happened to her father.

"I do not understand why I am here," she said, her cloak pulled tightly around her trembling body. "Why was I wrested from my home and brought here? Where is my father?"

The man who was doing the questioning sat across from her in a chair that cost more than a rich man would earn in an entire year. He was older, with dark hair that had gone to gray around his face and one droopy eye. He'd entered the chamber with several other men who were now back in the shadows while the man with the droopy eye interrogated her.

The silent eyes watched her, waiting.

But Liora had no idea what, exactly, they were waiting for.

"Something *has* happened," the man said. "I have discovered your treachery. Now I must discover what you know, so kindly answer my questions and your father will remain perfectly safe. Deny me and it is possible that he will not be."

Liora looked at him in horror. "What does that mean?" she said, struggling not to panic. "What is it I have done?"

Someone handed the man a cup of wine. This oddly gentle interrogation session had been going on for the better part of two hours and, at first, it had been relatively benign. The man with the droopy eye had asked her about her family, her father's work, and who her father's rich customers were. Liora had answered him steadily, asking occasional questions of her own, which went ignored.

Now, the tension in the chamber seemed to be growing in intensity. For as roughly as she was removed from her home, she'd not expected this strangely pleasant reception.

But that was about to change.

"You are Peter de Lohr's lover, are you not?" the man asked.

Liora was blindsided by the question. That was not something she had expected to hear and, now, she could feel the stakes of the situation taking an even more confusing turn. Confusing, but at the same time, more focused because if they were asking her a question about Peter, then this entire incident must be *about* Peter.

So she thought.

"I... I do not understand," she said. "Why would you ask that question?"

"Answer me. Are you Peter's lover?"

Liora didn't know what to say. Everything between her and Peter had been private for the most part, certainly nothing to speak of to family and friends. At least, not beyond Haim and Peter's father. She looked at the man in the chair hesitantly before her gaze moved to the men back in the shadows.

"Is that why I am here?" she asked, her voice starting to tremble. "You wish to know about Peter?"

"I wish to know if you are his lover and you are not giving me an answer."

"Nay, I am not his lover."

The man sighed heavily. "I have it on good authority that you are lying," he said. "I have received information to the contrary. I am told that you have seduced Peter and are part of the de Lohr rebellion. Is this true?"

Liora was horrified. "It is *not* true," she said. "I have not seduced him and I would know nothing about a rebellion other than there is one going on. Everyone knows that. Peter and I have only carried on a few conversations, but nothing else. Are you... does this have to do with Agnes de Quincy?"

"What about Agnes?"

"Peter was hiding from her and he hid in my kitchen yard. That is how I met him."

That seemed to bring the man pause. "He *hid* in your yard?"

She nodded. "He said that he was being followed."

"And you let him remain?"

"I did. I did not see any harm in it."

The man looked at his group, having an expression of great confusion. Liora looked at him anxiously until he returned his focus on her and slapped the side of his chair. The sound made her leap.

"You will cease this foolery and tell me what I want to know!" he nearly shouted. "I have tried to be kind to you, but you are making it very difficult. Tell me what things you have told Peter!"

Liora recoiled, sitting as far back in her chair as she could get. "About what?"

The man slapped his chair again and leaned forward, his eyes boring into her. "What information have you wrested from your father that you would tell Peter and his father?"

"I've not wrested anything from my father!"

"Lies!"

It was turning into a shouting match and Liora's eyes filled with tears, having no idea what the man wanted from her. He started to move in her direction but he was stopped when someone leaned over and whispered in his ear. That seemed to visibly calm him and, after a moment, he nodded and rose from the chair. He filtered out of the chamber, followed by his entourage and leaving only one man behind. When the door closed, the lone man sat down in the same chair that the man with the droopy eye had occupied.

Liora found herself looking at an older man with yellowed eyes.

"My name is William Marshal," the man said

in a surprisingly gentle voice. "You do not know why you are here, do you?"

Liora had heard that name. Everyone in London had heard that name. She didn't know if she should be relieved or even more frightened facing the great Earl of Pembroke.

The mystery deepened.

"Nay," she said, wiping at her eyes. "Where is my father? Why were we brought here?"

William held up a hand to quiet her before standing up and going to the door in the chamber. He listened for a moment before putting his hand on the latch and yanking the door open. Liora watched him curiously as he stepped into the corridor and looked around. Seemingly satisfied that no one was eavesdropping, he stepped back inside and shut the door, bolting it.

He returned to the chair.

"Now," he said quietly. "I am going to tell you why you are here, but you must be perfectly truthful with me. Can you do that?"

Liora nodded firmly. "Of course I can," she said. "I swear it. But why am I here?"

William pulled the chair a little closer to her so that he could keep his voice down. "The king wished to continue interrogating you and even wants to turn you over to his personal guard should you not give him the answers he seeks, but I have convinced him to let me try."

Liora cocked her head curiously. "The king?" she repeated. "He was here?"

"He was in this chair."

Liora's eyes widened with the realization. "I did not know, my lord," she said. "I have never even seen him before."

William nodded and put a hand up to silence her. "I know," he said. "But listen to me now. You are here because late last night, the king received a missive bearing the Earl of Winchester's seal stating that you are part of the rebellion against the king because you are wresting the king's secrets from your father and feeding them to Peter de Lohr. Is this true?"

The color drained from her face. "Nay, of course not," she said, terror in her voice. "My father would not know any of the king's secrets and even if he did, he would never tell me. And Peter… it is true what I told you. He hid in my kitchen yard because he was hiding from a woman named Agnes de Quincy."

The Marshal sat back in the chair, pondering her explanation and trying to piece the situation together. "Does Agnes know he hid in your yard?" he asked, but then he answered his own question. "Never mind. I am certain she knew. Her father has spies following Peter everywhere he goes, so she must have known."

Liora wasn't following him. "Spies? What

spies?"

William didn't answer her. He was following a mental trail, putting together scraps of information from what he knew and from what Liora was telling him. What he didn't tell her was that he had spies all over the city, too. That was his business. He knew that Peter had his eye on the daughter of the king's jeweler since yesterday when Peter and Alexander hadn't attended the meeting he'd called at Lonsdale. A few discreet questions to Marcus Burton, of all people, and he was aware that Peter was fond of a certain lovely Jewess.

But that was all he knew until now.

Now, he could definitely see that something was afoot.

"So Agnes and Walter knew of Peter's interest in a young woman on Milk Street because they followed him there," he said, more to himself than to her. "Walter has been trying to force Peter into a betrothal for months but Peter is not interested. So when his spies saw Peter with you, they assumed that there was something between you two."

Liora was understanding him a little more now. She knew the names of Agnes and Peter, of course, and she knew that Peter had been hiding from Agnes. Pembroke was simply elaborating on that. She watched as he stood up and went to the wine that was on a table against the wall.

He poured himself a cup, thinking.

"I have never known Walter to be the vengeful sort, but it is the only explanation that makes sense," he said. "Seeing Peter with the jeweler's daughter, he sent the king a missive about you to remove you from the equation. If the jeweler's daughter is locked up for treason, then Agnes' path to Peter is made clear. Walter can continue to press a betrothal between his daughter and Peter."

Liora was coming to see what William was coming to see. "This… this man has told everyone I am a traitor to the king?"

William turned to look at her. "It has to be him," he said. "The missive the king received about you, though it was anonymous, bore the seal of the Earl of Winchester. That is Walter's cousin and he is staying with the man here in London. If Winchester did not write the missive, and I would be willing to wager money that he did not, then it had to be by someone who had access to his seal – and that brings us back to Walter."

It occurred to Liora that this had nothing to do with her father, or their religion, or any number of factors. This had to do with Agnes de Quincy and nothing more. The realization had her slumping back against the chair.

"Prophets save us," she muttered. "A man I do not even know is trying to ruin me? Worse still, ruin my father in the eyes of the king?"

William came back over to the chair and sat in front of her. "Tell me truthfully what your relationship is with Peter," he said. "If I am to help you, I must know everything, but you must never mention that I intend to help you. No matter what I say or do, you must keep silent on the matter and have faith that I will do all I can to save you. Do you believe me?"

Liora looked into his eyes and realized that, although she didn't know Pembroke, she had no choice but to trust him. She was in a world where men she didn't even know were trying to harm her, so it stood to reason that she would trust a man she didn't know to save her.

She was willing to go on a little faith.

"Peter… he wants to marry me," she said quietly. "He has discussed the situation with a rabbi at the Great Synagogue so that he understands the challenges of such a thing. He has discussed the situation with his father and with my father."

William's white eyebrows slowly lifted. "I cannot imagine Chris has taken this lightly," he said. "What did Hereford say?"

Liora had to force herself to speak it out. The situation was still so very new and, in a sense, still quite surreal. She didn't want to speak out of turn, but if she had already told Peter she would convert to Christianity for him, then she supposed there was no turning back now. The wheels were in motion. She wanted to marry the man and there was no denying the fact.

"He was not happy at first," she said truthfully. "There can be no interfaith marriage between me and Peter. We must be all Christian or all Jewish, and Peter said that he would convert to Judaism to marry me. His father reminded him that if he did so, he would lose everything."

"That is very true," William said quietly. "Peter is the eldest de Lohr son and his father holds a great empire. Peter has a great deal to lose should he renounce his knighthood."

"I know," Liora said. "I told him that I would not allow him to do so and that I would convert. It makes the most sense that I should do so because I have the least to lose."

William found that an interesting statement. "Converting from Judaism is not a simple thing," he said. "Your religion is your way of life. It is everything you know. It is the food you eat and the prayers you give. You would be willing to relinquish that for the uncertainty of a life that you are not familiar with?"

Liora didn't sense any judgment, but simply an honest question. She met it with an honest answer.

"My life has been planned for me," she said. "I

am the eldest daughter of Haim ben Thad. I have been raised to be a good wife, to manage a home for my husband, and to be pleasing and educated. But the truth is that the best I could hope for is marrying a horse trader. It is not as bad as it sounds, because the man my father chose for me is wealthy and kind, but the life as the wife of a horse trader… living my life with a man I do not yearn for… is not something I am willing to settle for, only I did not realize this until I met Peter. My lord… do you know him well?"

William nodded faintly. "I do," he said. "He serves his father and he has served me on many occasions."

"Is it fair to say that he is a good and just man?"

"The finest," William said without hesitation. "Peter is the future of this country. He bears de Lohr blood and that makes him a better man that most. But you must understand that marrying into the House of de Lohr will be quite different from the life you lead now."

"It does not matter so long as I am married to Peter. I am confident I can learn all he wishes for me to learn."

William's brow furrowed because he thought she sounded a bit unrealistic. "I am sure you can," he said. "But living a life with Peter will be as different as if you moved from your home in

London and took up residence on the moon. You are in for a life of great excitement, pageantry, life and death, battles and politics, and with Peter right in the middle of it. It will not be a quiet life, my lady. Your husband will not be as safe as he would be if he were a horse trader."

She smiled faintly. "I have been told that," she said. "It is not that I am ignorant to the fact that it will be very different. It is the fact that I would rather live a different life with Peter than a familiar one without him. My lord, there are things we can control in our lives to a certain extent – our friends, the food we eat, where we live. Basic things. But we cannot control what the heart demands. I am under no illusion that this will be a simple thing, but I am under the belief that, ultimately, it will be worth the risk. If I do not take the chance, then I will never know. And I shall always regret it."

William wasn't going to argue with her about it. Her mind seemed set. In fact, he was coming to respect her because no matter the challenge before her, she was prepared to face it. He could see what Peter had found so fascinating in her because had he been a younger man, he might have found her fascinating, too.

He was rather partial to beautiful, intelligent women.

But they still had an immediate problem.

"Then I wish you well," he said. "But right now, we have a pressing problem and that is the fact that the king believes you are somehow tied to the rebel warlords. He believes you are a traitor to him and, subsequently, he believes your father is a traitor to him."

Liora was back to being frightened. "But how?" she asked. "My father knows nothing. He is simply a jeweler and nothing more. He is not involved in political intrigue."

"That may be, but the moment you harbored Peter de Lohr in your yard, he became involved," William said. "I am not entirely sure how this will be resolved, but I will do my best. Meanwhile, you are going to be a guest of the king for tonight. Your father, too, although I may be able to secure his release sooner. For the fact that I must put you under lock and key now, I do not want you to despair. It must be done until the king forgets about you and moves on to something else. I think I can convince him that you are innocent, but it may take time."

Liora wasn't feeling much hope. In fact, she was feeling rather sick. "Whatever you can do to clear up the misconception is much appreciated, my lord," she said. But then she paused, studying him for a moment. "May I ask *why* you should help me?"

William stood up from the chair. "Because the

moment I heard John speak of the mysterious missive libeling the jeweler's daughter and Peter de Lohr, I was compelled to get to the bottom of things," he said. "What concerns the House of de Lohr concerns me. If that does not answer your question, suffice it to say that if Peter wishes to marry you, and the king holds you, there will be trouble even more than there already is. So what I do, I do to avoid trouble."

She nodded, trying very hard to be brave because she wasn't as bad off as she could have been. At least she had one ally in the Earl of Pembroke and she thanked God for that.

"You have my thanks, my lord," she said. "I am very grateful."

William simply nodded, moving for the door, but something made him pause. He looked at Liora again, his eyes glittering in the weak light.

"Can you scream?" he asked.

She looked at him strangely. "I can. Why?"

"Can you act like you are terrified and hysterical?"

She nodded unsteadily. "It is not far from the truth."

A smile flickered across his lips. "Then you will do something for me."

Leaning in to her, he whispered something in her ear.

A few minutes later, the door to the chamber

opened and the sounds of hysteria filled the corridor. William had Liora by the arm as she screamed and fought against him, falling to her knees and begging him for mercy. He ended up dragging her, on her knees, halfway up the corridor until he came to several royal guards.

"Find me a chamber I can lock her in," he barked.

The guards rushed to do Pembroke's bidding. They ended up locking her in an upstairs chamber that, at one time, had belonged to a former advisor. Now, it simply sat dusty and unused, so William all but tossed Liora into the chamber and slammed the door, using the brass key that was already in the lock to secure her.

He could hear her screaming on the other side.

The guards were happy to leave the hysterical woman in peace, which was exactly what William wanted. John's men had little to no control, and a lovely young woman wouldn't escape their notice. He held the only key, as far as he knew, but guards could be clever. They might try to get to her regardless, so the screaming – and hysterics – were designed to keep them away.

But he knew it wouldn't last forever.

With Liora secured, his thoughts turned to the king. He headed to the ground floor where he found John in the solar he favored, the one that faced Westminster Abbey. The corridors were narrow, long, and high-ceilinged, and the great double-doors opened into a fairly lavish chamber where the king and a few men were gathering. When they saw William enter, all attention turned in his direction.

William held up a hand.

"Be at ease," he said, focusing on the king. "I questioned the lady extensively and I am satisfied that she is not part of any rebel activity. In fact, I found her too dense to believably be part of anything."

The king looked at him seriously. "Are you certain?" he said. "What about her ties to de Lohr?"

The Marshal shook his head irritably. "There are no ties that I can assess," he said. "She has met the man and she has spoken to him, but I do not believe she is a seductress. That being said, I think I know the origins of the missive you received – you are familiar with Walter de Quincy, your grace."

John nodded. "Winchester's cousin."

"Did you notice the seal on the mysterious missive you received?"

"It was Winchester's."

William smiled thinly. "There is dissention in the ranks of the warlords these days," he said, though it wasn't exactly true. He just wanted the king to think so. "Walter de Quincy and Hereford are fighting amongst themselves and I believe that missive was de Quincy's attempt to disrupt Hereford. As I understand it, the jeweler's daughter met Peter de Lohr when he was hiding from de Quincy's unpleasant daughter, Agnes, who wants very much to marry Peter. What better way to get back at de Lohr than strike out at an innocent woman who was caught in the wrong place at the wrong time? Nay, my lord, I do not think there is anything afoot with the jeweler's daughter or the jeweler. I think it is de Quincy causing trouble."

John scratched his cheek as he pondered that bit of information, looking at the other men in the room, one of which was Richard de Percy, a warlord from Northumberland and one of the few from that region who sided with the king.

"What do you hear about that, Richard?" John asked. "Is de Quincy capable of that kind of deceit?"

Richard snorted. "Your grace, the man's veins are full of ambition," he said. "I must say that I agree with Pembroke. I would not put it past him. That missive was too mysterious for my taste."

John eyed him. "It was concerning enough that you agreed I should send soldiers out at sunrise to bring Haim and his daughter here," he said. "Now you say there is no trouble?"

William spoke up for de Percy. "I do not believe so," he said. "The girl is quite hysterical so I was forced to lock her away for her own good. I suggest we release her in the morning along with her father and be more cautious of anything coming from Walter de Quincy in the future."

He was trying to make it sound benign, like it was a situation that wasn't worth the trouble. William thought that if he made it seem casual, the king would think it was as well. John was, if nothing else, pliable to his advisors and, at times, easily swayed.

William wanted this to be one of those times.

"Very well," John said, turning back to his wine, even at this time in the morning. "I like Haim well enough. He does good work, so that should afford him some consideration from me. Release them both and we'll hear no more about it."

William breathed a sigh of relief. "Excellent decision, your grace."

John paused as he picked up a cup. "Although…" he said thoughtfully. "The daughter is quite beautiful. I do not suppose any of you noticed that."

William wasn't so relieved any longer. He knew John well enough to know that tone. The man had no restraint when it came to a lovely woman and it didn't matter who she was. He was vile in his desires, something Sean de Lara had to deal with for the nine long years he was in service to the king. Sean could usually control the damage somewhat, but not always. Now, there was no Sean and the lascivious king had free rein in everything he did.

But William wasn't going to let him if he could at all help it.

"She is lovely, but she is not worth the trouble," he said steadily. "You have an excellent relationship with the Jews of London and they have provided you with a good deal of capital for your armies. Their bankers have helped you with outstanding debts and other things, so I would suggest you leave the jeweler's daughter alone. You do not want to rouse the anger of men who control the finances of the London… and you."

That was very true. John had always worked well with the Jewish businessmen of London because they provided a definite service for him. In fact, under John's rule, the Jews had enjoyed an enormous amount of peace and prosperity. Therefore, John evidently relinquished any thoughts of pursuing the jeweler's daughter and turned back to his wine without another word. William once again breathed a sigh of relief and intended to head out of the solar to release the jeweler when he ran headlong into one of John's guards.

"My lord," the guard said. "I've a message from the gatehouse."

William was still in the doorway, having not quite made it out of the chamber. "What message?"

The guard looked between The Marshal and the king. "Peter de Lohr is at the gatehouse, demanding to be admitted," he said. "He says he wants to see the king."

Seized with apprehension, William put his hand on the guard's chest in an attempt to shove him out of the room so the name of Peter would not be heard by the king, but it was too late. John had heard him. He shouted before William could remove the guard.

"Wait!" he said. "Peter de Lohr is here?"

William closed his eyes for a brief moment before turning to John. "I will deal with him," he said steadily. "You needn't trouble yourself. I will send him away."

John was on his feet. "*Wait*," he said again, more firmly. "Is it a coincidence that he has come, Pembroke? You told me the jeweler's daughter had no relationship with him."

"She does not," William said. "Of that, I am certain. Peter must be here on another matter."

It was clear that John was coming to think that William was trying to deceive him, which he was. But John wasn't quite certain of it, not yet.

His dark eyes took on a faint glimmer.

"We shall see," he said. "Bring him to me immediately. I will speak with him."

William didn't have a choice. All he could do was agree as he pushed past the guard and headed out of the palace, heading for the gatehouse where Peter was waiting. How on earth Peter knew that Liora was at Westminster, he didn't know, but he did know one thing – now it was going to be a hell of a mess. If the king believed that Liora was truly involved with Peter, then all of William's work would be ruined. In fact, a great deal would be ruined.

The situation was about to go from bad to worse, but more than he knew. Just as he went down to admit Peter at the gatehouse, the king sent someone for Liora, who remained behind a locked door.

But not for long.

A few well-placed ax strokes from one of John's household guards saw to that.

❧

PETER WAS A hair's width from losing his control as he stood at the north gatehouse of Westminster Palace.

Alexander, Caius, and Maxton were with them and Alexander had quietly explained the issue because Peter was too wound up to speak. He was pacing around, his face like stone, his gaze on the portcullis, which was lowered. He couldn't see much other than a courtyard and the carefully landscape gardens that Westminster was known for. He finally came to a halt and planted himself right in front of the portcullis, focused on the activity beyond like a hunter focused on his prey. He completely missed his father riding up in the company of David and Marcus, the men dismounting their horses as Alexander tried to call them off.

"I told you not to come," Alexander hissed. "Chris, you are leading a rebellion. John would like nothing better than to get you into the walls of Westminster and lock you in the vault. You *must* leave."

Christopher was looking over Alexander's head at his son, standing in front of the portcullis and being carefully watched by the palace guards.

"I cannot leave him alone with this situation," he said.

Alexander did something then that he wouldn't normally do. He pushed Christopher back towards his horse and indicated David and Marcus to go, too.

"Get out of here before someone in a position of power sees you," he growled. "The last thing we need on the eve of battle is for Christopher de

Lohr to be imprisoned by the king. Do you have any idea what that would do to your allies?"

Christopher knew that. He knew that very well. But he simply couldn't let his son face John alone.

"Sherry…" he said, a hint of hazard in his tone. "I cannot let Peter deal with this alone."

Alexander's eyebrows flew up. "He is not alone," he said. "Look who is with him – me, Max, and Cai. Do you think we will let anything happen to him?"

"Of course not."

"Then get out of sight," Alexander said. "Get out and stay out. I will send you word if we end up going inside. Please, Chris… *go*."

"But I must be near."

"Then go to Hollyhock House," Alexander said, pointing to the river road that would take them right to Hollyhock House, which was less than a mile away. "De Winter will let you stay there until we know more."

Christopher looked at David and Marcus, both of whom reluctantly nodded. Therefore, he mounted up and directed his horse back the way he'd come. David and Marcus followed behind him as they headed off to the de Winter stronghold. When they were out of sight, Alexander turned back to Peter.

Maxton and Caius were standing with him

now, all of them watching the activity beyond the lowered portcullis. It was Maxton who finally hissed at Alexander.

"Sherry," he said. "The Marshal is coming."

That brought Alexander to the portcullis as well, just in time to see William crossing from one of the larger inner gatehouses. Westminster was a maze of chapels, apartments, and administration chambers spread out over a massive plot of land. It was a city unto itself and as The Marshal drew near, he motioned to the gatehouse guards to raise the portcullis. It started to lift and Peter and Alexander ducked under it, but The Marshal threw out a hand.

"Nay, Sherry," he said. "Only Peter. You and Max and Cai wait here."

Alexander backed off, but it was with great hesitation. Once Peter was under the portcullis and it lifted all the way to the top, The Marshal reached out to grab him.

"Why are you here?" he demanded.

Peter's fair face was pale, his jaw ticking angrily. "There is a woman I…"

The Marshal cut him off. "I know of Mistress Liora," he hissed. "I know all about the two of you. She is here with her father and I nearly had the king convinced to release them both when you showed up. Now, John wants to see you."

Peter looked at him, his anger faltering. "You

know?"

"Of course I know," The Marshal snapped. "There isn't much I do not know. But your appearance here has mucked up the situation, Peter. I am very angry with you."

Peter looked at the man, exasperated. "Then if you know as you say you do, you also know that I had to come," he said. "Liora's little brother showed up at Lonsdale, telling us a hysterical tale of Liora and her father being abducted by John's soldiers."

"It is true."

"*Why*?"

The Marshal could see Alexander, Caius, and Maxton standing in an uncertain huddle beneath the portcullis. Lifting a hand, he indicated for the gate guards to close it, which shoved the three men back and away from it. He began to walk back the way he'd come, taking Peter with him.

"This is all speculation, but I believe it to be true," he said as they headed towards the inner gatehouse that led to the royal apartments. "I believe Walter de Quincy is behind this."

Peter's eyes widened. "*De Quincy*?"

The Marshal nodded. "We all know that he has spies watching you," he said. "He must have seen you with the jeweler's daughter, enough to believe that she was a threat to his ambition to marry Agnes to you. So last night, the king received a missive that was not signed yet bore the seal of Winchester. The missive said that the jeweler's daughter was part of the rebellion, purging the king's secrets from her father and passing them on to you. The king believes that Mistress Liora is a spy for you and your father."

Peter came to a halt, his eyes bugging. "My God," he breathed. "It's not true!"

The Marshal nodded. "I know," he said. "But that is why she was brought here. I almost had the king convinced to release her when you showed up, so now we are about to dance a very delicate dance, Peter. You must do everything I tell you or it will go very badly for Mistress Liora and her father."

Peter was pale with shock and realization. Something his father said occurred to him then. "After the meeting you called at Lonsdale yesterday, de Quincy threatened my father with something quite similar," he said. "He had seen me and Liora together, somehow, and told my father that unless he agreed to a betrothal between me and Agnes, then Walter was going to tell the warlords that I was a traitor because I was giving secrets to Liora to pass to her father and, eventually, to the king."

The Marshal grunted unhappily. "So it *is* Walter," he said. "The man wants you for his daughter very badly, Peter, enough to ruin the lives of people he does not even know. That speaks of madness."

"It speaks of an evil, vindictive man," Peter agreed. "What do we do?"

The Marshal started walking again. "The king believes you are here to speak to him about Liora and her father," he said. "He is looking for confirmation that she is, indeed, a spy, but you must not give it to him. Speak to him about anything else, but not Liora. He already knows that you know her, so you cannot deny it, but you must make it seem as if you met her on whim and nothing more. She has told us about meeting you in her kitchen yard when you were hiding from Agnes."

Peter nodded, his mind quickly processing what he was being told. "It is true," he said. "I just happened to end up there and she let me stay until the threat passed, taunting me the entire time. Somehow... somehow, I fell in love with her. We want to marry, you know."

"I know, but you must not bring that up, no matter what," The Marshal said. "Peter, I will tell you something that I told the others when we met at Lonsdale yesterday. With Sean de Lara out of commission, I have taken his place. Do you wonder why I have sided with the king? It is because he must be watched and, right now, I am the best person for that task. My heart, my loyalty, is to the rebellion, but that must not be made known. John must think it is with him."

Peter looked at the old knight. Inarguably, the greatest knight England had ever seen, a man who worked his way up from the fourth son of a minor nobleman to one of the most important men in England. He'd risked his life, all of his life, for the greater good of England. Above all of his fret and strain, Peter could see how much William Marshal was sacrificing. It made his problems seem pale by comparison, but they *were* his problems.

He intended to get everyone out of this intact.

"I understand, my lord," he said. "What do you wish me to tell the king my purpose is?"

The Marshal seemed to visibly relax now that Peter had agreed to be cooperative. "I have thought about that," he said. "The best subject I can come up with at such short notice is this – your father is a fine purveyor of horses and he has more than he knows what to do with, but the king recently came into possession of one of the finest Belgian warmbloods I have ever seen. The stallion's name is Porthos and the king has been speaking about selling him at a great price because his progeny would be worth a good deal of money, so you can tell the king you've come to speak about buying the horse for your father."

Peter looked at him with doubt. "And he would believe that?"

"He would," he said. "Business is business. He may be your father's enemy, but for the right price, he would sell his own mother. Better still, you can tell him that you wish to purchase the animal for yourself because, as your father's bastard, you need to build your own empire since you will inherit nothing from him. I am sorry if this seems weak, but it is the best I can come up with."

They passed through the inner gatehouse with the royal apartments looming ahead. Peter felt a distinct sense of doom run through his veins at the sight, but he squared his shoulders. Liora was somewhere in that structure and he intended to do everything he could to secure her release. But according to The Marshal, he'd fouled that up simply by coming to Westminster.

Therefore, he was going to have to think fast and trust The Marshal.

"Very well," he said after a moment. "I will do all that I can."

"Good," The Marshal said, relief in his tone. "I will release Mistress Liora and her father as I had planned, but only if the king believes you. It is up to you, Peter."

Peter knew that. He didn't know if that made him feel better or worse.

The cool, dim innards of the royal apartments swallowed them up and Peter ended up following

The Marshal down a corridor, into an enormous hall, and then into another corridor. He'd been in the halls of Westminster before, but it had been years ago. He didn't remember it smelling quite so musty or being quite so dark. The Marshal led him into a chamber that, at first glance, had several men in it.

As his eyes adjusted to the dim light, for there was very little natural light in the chamber, he saw the king sitting on a chair on the far side of the chamber. But what he saw sitting next to the king caused him to start.

The Marshal grabbed his wrist, stilling him.

Liora was sitting next to the king, tears streaming down her face and Peter seriously thought he was going to ruin the entire plan then and there. His instinct was to run to her, killing any man who stood in his way, the king included.

But he knew he couldn't.

He was trapped.

Oh, God…

"Welcome, young de Lohr," the king said, a smile playing on his lips. "I was just telling your seductress how much I know about the de Lohr family and how you are the result of your father's lack of restraint. Lady Amanda, was it? I remember your mother, actually. I think she had more than one lover, which means your father could be anyone, but you look so much like

Christopher that there is no denying the bloodlines."

Peter turned to stone, from the bottom of his feet to the top of his head. He tensed up as he had never tensed in his life and there was a retort on his lips that would have started a brawl, so he bit it off. He shoved it down, swallowed it, praying he could keep it down because all he wanted to do at the moment was fly at the man and cut his head off.

That was where he would start.

He wouldn't end until the man was in pieces.

Bastard!

"Your grace," he greeted with far more serenity than he felt. "I realize my appearance is a surprise, but I have come on a business matter."

He completely blew off John's insults, which only made the king laugh. A soft, snickering laugh.

"My, you are pleasant today," he said. "Have you nothing to say about your lover sitting next to me?"

Peter's gaze moved to Liora, who was pale and terrified. It took every ounce of strength not to react to that, but he knew he couldn't, for all their sakes.

"Although she is attractive enough, regretfully, the lady is not my lover," he said, almost callously. "Liora ben Thad, isn't it? Her father is a jeweler."

"You have been seen with this woman, de Lohr," John said, becoming less amused. "Do not pretend as if you hardly know her. I have it on good authority that she *is* your lover."

Peter shook his head. "My father would not be pleased were I to take a Jewess for a lover so, alas, whoever told you such a thing has lied to your royal ears," he said. "No de Lohr takes a Jew for a lover. In fact, I came to speak with you on a business matter regarding my father. Well, actually, it is more about me, but I assume that I must speak to you directly."

Getting no reaction out of Peter whatsoever did not please John in the least. He frowned. "What business?" he snapped. "I have no business with you."

"Not at the moment, your grace," Peter said. "But I understand you have a Belgian stallion you are thinking on selling and given that you own him, I am sure he has the finest bloodlines. Normally, I would not bother you with such a thing, but my father has made it clear that I shall receive little to no inheritance from his estates, so I must build my own empire. Horse breeding is quite lucrative."

John's face contorted with confusion. "You've come to discuss a *horse*?" he said. "Who told you about this animal?"

Peter shrugged, thinking quickly and desperately. He didn't have a planned answer for that question, but he knew he couldn't tell him the truth. "I have spent a good deal of time in London this summer," he said. "I… I heard some of your soldiers speaking of it. They populate the taverns in London, you know, particularly The Pox. I heard someone mention that you had a fine breeding stallion."

It was plausible enough. Barely. He was rather proud of himself for thinking so quickly. But John's features were still twisted in confusion as he looked to The Marshal. "Is it possible you were correct?" he said. "De Quincy is behind all of this?"

The Marshal nodded faintly. "I asked young de Lohr the same questions you have and these are the same answers I received."

That didn't please John at all. This whole situation had turned markedly against him. But he was a sly, cunning man. He knew how to get answers. Something about Peter de Lohr's appearance was just too coincidental for his taste, considering he was holding a woman who was accused of being his lover and spying for the rebellion – and, suddenly, Peter made an appearance.

Nay, it was *too* coincidental.

Either The Marshal was in on it or he was being bamboozled by a clever de Lohr son.

He intended to find out.

"Very well, young Peter. Let us speak on the horse. But since you have denied this woman as your lover, you will not mind if I take her for mine. She has a magnificent figure that will suit my appetites quite nicely." He turned to his personal guard, men behind him. Men of greed and lust, horrific men who had an even worse reputation than the king. "Take her to my chamber and... prepare her. I will not stop you from tasting her, but leave enough of her so that I might have my fill, also."

It was a horrific thing to say. Given John's reputation, there was no doubt that he meant what he said. He didn't bluff. Peter's resolve had been rock-solid until that moment and he heard himself shouting before he could stop himself.

"*Nay!*"

That brought everything in the chamber to a halt.

The only sound was that of Liora, weeping, as John's men yanked her out of the chair next to the king. They were pawing at her and she screamed, biting the hand of a man who had her by the arm. When he yelped and let go, she managed to wrench herself away from those pawing hands and raced to Peter, who wrapped her up in one big arm while yanking a nasty-looking dagger out from his waist.

The message was clear.

For a moment, no one spoke a word. The Marshal had moved away from Peter, realizing the entire charade was finished. He had to think fast to salvage the situation or all would be lost. Peter would be dead, the woman he loved would be a king's mistress, and the situation would horribly deteriorate when Christopher found out.

He'd told Peter that the man's appearance had mucked up the situation.

Now, it was positively a swamp.

"Wait!" he shouted, holding up his hands as John's guard began to unsheathe their weapons. "No swords, do you hear me? Put them away or we'll have Hereford burning this place down around our ears. Do it!"

He boomed it so loudly that the guards began to comply. No one disobeyed an order from William Marshal, not even John's guards. The king hadn't moved except to look at Peter with a smarmy expression on his face suggesting he finally had the answer he wanted.

This was what he'd been hoping for.

"So," he said casually. "Mayhap you were incorrect in your reply to me, young Peter. Would you care to rephrase your stance on this young woman? I must have misunderstood you. I cannot imagine that you would lie to my face."

Peter was caught. He *knew* he was caught.

Liora was in his arms, weeping softly, her soft and warm body clinging to him. She felt so good in his arms that it was a temptation to give in to the joy of it. To hold her – really hold her – was one of the most satisfying things he'd ever experienced. All he knew was that he was ready to fight to the death for her, even against the king's highly trained guard.

He was prepared to die.

"You asked me if she was my lover, your grace, and she is not," he said. "Not technically, at least not yet. She is the woman I intend to marry. When we marry, she most certainly will be my lover. She will be my everything."

John's eyebrows lifted. "A de Lohr marry a Jew?" he scoffed. "What does your father say to this?"

Peter wouldn't take his eyes off the king or the men behind him, but he had to resist the urge to look at Liora. He wanted to look at her to reaffirm his commitment, his dedication, his attraction. All of those things. He wanted to see the look in her eyes when he told the king that, aye, a de Lohr would marry a Jew. They'd spoken of it. He'd declared his intentions to his father. But now, he was declaring it to the king in a very dicey situation. If he was indeed serious about it, now was the moment of truth.

He wanted her to see his truth.

"He says that he cannot live my life for me, your grace," he said. "But he supports whatever decision I make."

John's gaze lingered on him. "Then the jeweler's daughter means a great deal to you."

"She does, your grace. I love her."

John snorted. "With her attractiveness, she could lure many a man to love her," he said rudely. But he gestured to the dagger Peter still had lifted. He hadn't sheathed it when The Marshal had ordered him to. "You realize that you will not leave here alive should you try to escape."

"Mayhap," Peter said. "But I will not let you have her."

John stroked his chin, glancing at the men behind him, seeing guards that would kill and die for him. Men who were close to him, who always did his bidding. They were his mindless animals and there was something to be said for mindless animals, but something was missing among them.

The Lord of the Shadows that he had lost.

He missed Sean even though the man had betrayed him. Nine years of a strong relationship with a beast of a man who had done anything asked of him, and now, he was gone. Sean had brains and skill along with the talent that the rest of his simpleminded guards had. John surrounded himself with brute strength and that was why those men were present, but with Sean, he'd surrounded himself with a man who became a trusted advisor as well. De Lara had been from an excellent family, but he was no de Lohr.

John wondered just how much it would weaken Christopher de Lohr should he remove Peter from his father's stable.

He fixed on Peter.

"I can see that you mean it," he said after a moment. "We do not need to have bloodshed if we can make a bargain. Lower the dagger and let us speak like reasonable men."

Peter hesitated a moment longer before putting the dagger back where it belonged. He didn't dare glance at The Marshal, fearful that John might pick up on the fact that The Marshal was on Peter's side. He'd already implicated himself in a deception, but he wanted to keep William perfectly safe and secure. However, he wanted to take it a step further.

He had to make it clear.

He looked at William fully in the face.

"My lord, my apologies for lying to you about the horse," he said. "Had you known I'd come here to free Liora, you would have never let me see the king."

The Marshal knew exactly what Peter was doing. *Bless him,* he thought. "You are forgiven," he said, but he didn't sound as if he meant it. "But now you must listen to what the king has to offer.

If you do not, you will not leave here alive."

Peter nodded, returning his attention to the king as his grip on Liora tightened. She was no longer weeping, but he could feel her trembling in his arms.

"I am listening, your grace," he said.

John sat forward in his chair. "Tell me the truth," he said. "I shall not become angry with you, but I want the truth."

"I will not lie to you, your grace."

"Did you really use the woman to gain information from her father? From me?"

Peter shook his head. "I swear upon my mother's grave that I never did, at any time," he said. "You said yourself that the jeweler's daughter is beautiful. Would I really want to speak of politics when looking at her? Not hardly. We only spoke of each other, of our families, and of our religions. That is God's truth."

John nodded, seemingly satisfied. "Nay, I cannot imagine you would want to speak of men's games when you are beholding her vision," he said. "What's all this nonsense about Agnes de Quincy? Were you betrothed to her and jilted her for the Jewess?"

Again, Peter shook his head. "She *wishes* I was betrothed to her, your grace," he said. "That is where this whole madness has come from. She wants to marry me and I want nothing to do with her."

"Ugly?"

"Inside, aye. She is not a good person."

John pondered that, sitting back in his chair and scratching his head. "Then I am to assume you came here to free Haim's daughter."

"I did, your grace."

"Just how did you intend to do that?"

"I am truthfully not sure, but I had to come."

John thought about that. For several long moments, there was an apprehensive silence. Then, he turned to the men standing behind him and ordered them out. They filtered from the chamber, eyeing Peter threateningly, but he didn't flinch. He watched them go as The Marshal went to the king, bending over and whispering something in his ear. John nodded, muttering something in return.

Meanwhile, Peter dared to loosen his grip on Liora. He cupped her face with both hands to get a good look at her.

"You are unharmed?" he whispered.

She nodded, struggling not to tear up again. "My father is still here, somewhere."

Peter kissed her forehead. "I know," he said. "I will worry about him after I've secured your release. Come, sweetheart – sit down before you fall down."

He directed her into the nearest chair and she

sat heavily, greatly shaken from the events of the day. He put his hand on her shoulder, both a possessive and comforting move. He stood next to her, watching The Marshal and the king mutter back and forth. Finally, The Marshal stepped away from John and Peter caught a glimpse of the man's face.

He didn't like what he saw.

"Peter," John said. "I have a proposal for you. Will you listen?"

Concerned about the expression on The Marshal's face, Peter nonetheless managed to nod. "I will, your grace."

John folded his hands across his chest in what looked strangely like both a fatherly and thoughtful gesture. "For nine years, I enjoyed the company and counsel of Sean de Lara," he said. "I am sure you know that. I am sure you also know that de Lara is no longer with me."

"I know, your grace."

"What you do not know is that I feel his absence deeply," John said. "For so many years, I could look over my shoulder and there he would be, but no longer. I miss a great knight in a position of power at my side."

Peter didn't know what to say to that. He simply nodded, watching John as he stood up from the chair and stretched his weary body. "Peter, you mentioned something interesting to me when you spoke of my stallion," he said. "You said that you must build your own empire because, as your father's bastard, you shall inherit very little. You realize that your father's own empire is built upon a lucrative marriage and my own brother's generosity."

"I know, your grace."

"Then you understand there is nothing wrong with accepting titles or lands or positions from the king," he said. "We have the power to give such things. I have the power to give *you* such things."

Now, he had Peter's attention, but not in a good way. He immediately wondered what he was going to have to do in order to gain that power and position.

"You are most generous to suggest that, your grace, but…"

John interrupted. "I have given your father a great deal recently," he said. "Ludlow and Wigmore, to name two. The least he can do is give me his son for all I have done for him. Take de Lara's place at my side, Peter. Become my personal protector."

Peter nearly choked. He stared at John, trying desperately not to look too appalled, but he couldn't quite pull it off. He ended up looking at The Marshal, seeing that same grim expression and realizing why the man had looked so displeased.

John wanted Peter to be his new Lord of the Shadows.

The words sank deep. Peter genuinely had no idea what to say other than to refuse him. But if he refused him, it was very possible Liora and Haim would never leave Westminster. He was well aware that this was coercion on the king's part, so he was careful in his reply.

"You honor me, your grace," he finally said. "Truly, what you are suggesting is a great honor. But I am sure you realize that my place is at my father's side."

"Do this for me and Mistress Liora and her father shall go free today," John said in a master stroke. "Refuse me and... well, there is no knowing what may happen to them. To her. Do you understand my meaning?"

Peter was trapped. God help him, he knew he was trapped and there was no way to wriggle out of it. Liora's freedom for his service to John.

He could hardly believe how badly he'd been played.

It was checkmate.

Sean de Lara had spent all those years at John's side and now, William Marshal was picking up the mantle. But he couldn't do it forever. He was an old man and he had more responsibilities than almost anyone in England. That meant, soon, he would have to back away, but someone had to be at John's side, watching him and manipulating him, making sure the rebellion knew of the king's every move.

Right now, knowing the king's plans was more important than ever considering the mercenaries that were now roaming loose in England with the king's permission. A man next to John would be invaluable to people like Peter's father and the rest of the warlords.

Someone had to do it.

To secure Liora's freedom, Peter realized he had to.

With a heavy sigh, he turned away from John and pulled Liora to her feet, leading her over to a corner of the chamber, as far away as he could get so he could speak to her with some privacy. He had a lot to say and little time to say it.

"Listen to me," he said, putting his hands on her face and forcing her to look at him. "You heard what he said. I am telling you what I am going to do and I want you to be brave. Can you do that, Lee-Lee?"

He used her nickname, the one Asa used, and he watched warmth fill her frightened eyes. "I can," she whispered. "Tell me what you want me to do and I shall do it."

Peter smiled faintly at her, trying to show courage in a moment where he felt absolutely none. As he looked at her, his heart was breaking from the uncertainty they were both going to face.

"I am going to agree to the king's terms and he will release you and your father," he muttered. "That is all I care about right now. I will do everything in my power not to swear fealty to him and he probably knows it, so he will be sly. He knows that a knight, and most especially a de Lohr, will never go back on his word, so what I do now is for the immediate release of you and your father. What comes later… no matter what, I will send word to you or I will come and see you myself. You will go home to Milk Street and stay there until you hear from me. Will you do that?"

Liora looked up at him, putting her fingers across his lips and watching him kiss them. "I will," she murmured. "That you would do this for me… Peter, I cannot find the words to describe how I feel. You are sacrificing everything."

His eyes glimmered at her. "There is nothing I would not do for you," he said. "Don't you realize that by now?"

She mouthed the words *Sweet Peter* and he kissed her fingers again, knowing their time was too short for any more conversation. But he had one last thing to say to her.

"Remember that I love you," he said. "I think I loved you from the first moment I met you. Come what may, we *will* marry. Neither a king nor a religion will keep us apart. But for now… keep the faith that I will return to you. This is not the end, not in the least."

She nodded, though she was holding back tears. "My love goes with you," she whispered. "I will be waiting for you, Peter. No matter how long it takes, no matter where you go. I will be right here, waiting for you. Always."

He gave her a brief smile and dropped his hands from her face, leading her back over to where she had been sitting. It was heartbreaking in so many ways that Peter couldn't even begin to grasp the pain. But he could feel it, all of it. As Liora resumed her seat, he summoned his courage and faced the king.

"Very well, your grace," he said. "Release Liora and her father immediately and we shall speak on this position you wish me to assume."

John smiled, revealing yellowed teeth. "Excellent," he said victoriously. Then, he looked to The Marshal. "You see? He is a reasonable man. The jeweler is in the vault, so remove him immediately and take him and his daughter to the gates. They are free to go. Peter and I have much to discuss."

The Marshal nodded at the king's directive. He couldn't even look at Peter as he went to Liora and extended a hand to her. Hesitantly, she took it, and he led her out of the chamber, leaving Peter with John.

Listening to that chamber door shut behind

him left Peter feeling as if he'd just entered the lion's den… and he was the main course.

God help me.

CHAPTER SEVENTEEN

THE MARSHAL COULD see Alexander, Caius, and Maxton still waiting by the portcullis.

In the company of Haim and Liora, who were holding hands fiercely now that they had been released from their mutual imprisonment, The Marshal had the gate guards lift the portcullis so they could leave the compound entirely. Haim and Liora passed underneath the gatehouse and William followed as Alexander and Caius and Maxton swarmed him.

"What happened?" Alexander said, clearly noting Liora but no Peter. "Where in the hell is Peter?"

The Marshal didn't answer him directly. He looked around, to the street beyond the gatehouse. "Where is Chris?" he asked. "I know the man will not be far away if he knows his son is here."

"We sent him to Hollyhock House," Caius said. "He and Canterbury and Burton are waiting there for word. *Where* is Peter?"

The Marshal still didn't answer. His head turned in the direction of Hollyhock House, down the river road that was lined with trees and manses belonging to some of the finest families in England.

"Fetch Hereford to me," he said. "Be quick about it. Something has happened."

It was Maxton who ran for his horse, thundering down the road towards Hollyhock House as Alexander and Caius stood in a tense bunch. They looked at each other, at The Marshal, figuring something awful must have happened to Peter in order to secure the release of Liora and her father.

In fact, Liora and her father were still standing there, just a few feet away. They should have walked away, quickly heading for home, but neither one of them seemed very anxious to leave. When The Marshal realized that, he motioned back towards the city.

"You may go," he said quietly. "There is nothing more you can do."

Liora looked at him seriously. "Please do not think I am being disagreeable, my lord, but I would prefer to remain," she said. "Peter sacrificed himself to secure the release of me and my father, so I wish to remain. I would like to know what is to be done about helping him."

Alexander looked at The Marshal, his eyes widening. "Peter *sacrificed* himself?" he asked in disbelief. "Sweet Mother of Mercy, what did he do?"

The Marshal waved him off. "He is quite alive, Sherry," he said. "Physically, he is fine. But there is a… complication. There were terms for the jeweler's release. When Chris arrives, I will tell you everything."

Alexander didn't press after that. It was clear that something serious had happened, but he would respect The Marshal's request to wait until Christopher arrived.

So, they waited.

The little group moved away from the main gate, over towards the buildings across the dusty road. They were mostly residences, but there were a couple of businesses, a seamstress being one of them. They collected beneath the overhang of the seamstress' place of business, Liora and Haim still clinging to one another as Alexander and Caius stood in a nervous huddle near The Marshal, who was standing out on the edge of the road, watching the gatehouse of Westminster.

Seconds turned into minutes. The minutes began to pass quickly. Finally, nearly a half-hour later, Maxton made an appearance with Christopher, David, and Marcus thundering after him and it was The Marshal who emitted a sharp whistle, catching their attention. They charged across the road to where The Marshal and the others waited.

Christopher was the first man off his horse.

"Where is my son?" he demanded.

It was then that he noticed Liora and Haim standing several feet away, almost at the door of the seamstress shop. His eyes widened when he realized Liora and her father were free but there was no sign of Peter.

"Be calm, Chris," The Marshal said. "I wanted to explain to you what has happened."

Christopher didn't like the sound of that. He looked at The Marshal. "Is my son healthy and whole?"

The Marshal nodded. "He is."

"Where is he?"

"With John."

That brought a ripple of disgust and apprehension across Christopher's face. "I am listening," he said with strained patience. "*Why* is he with John?"

The Marshal looked at him seriously. "Because the king made him an offer he could not refuse," he said. "I am not sure how much you know about the situation but let me review it for you so there is no question. Last night, the king received an unsigned missive declaring that the jeweler's daughter was working for the rebellion. She was alleged to have wrested secrets of the king from her father and then give them to Peter."

Christopher's face screwed up in disbelief. "Who in the hell said that?" he demanded. "That is categorically untrue."

The Marshal nodded, trying to keep Christopher calm. "I know," he said. "As I said, the missive was unsigned, but it bore the seal of Winchester. As you know, Walter de Quincy is a cousin to Winchester and is, in fact, staying in his townhome. I am utterly convinced that it was Walter who sent the missive in order to remove the jeweler's daughter from Peter so there would be a clear path, once again, for Agnes and a betrothal."

Christopher stared at him for a moment as the depth of de Quincy's treachery sank deep. "Christ," he muttered. "Walter tried to coerce me into finalizing a betrothal with Peter yesterday. He told me that Peter had been sighted with the jeweler's daughter and that he had it on good authority that it was *Peter* providing information on the rebellion to her, meaning Peter was the traitor. He threatened to tell the allied warlords that my son was giving secrets to the king if I did not agree to a betrothal with Agnes. Now you are telling me that he reversed his story and pinned the treachery on Liora?"

The Marshal nodded. "Peter told me the same thing about your conversation with Walter yesterday," he said. "That is why I am convinced Walter sent the missive to the king. John ordered the jeweler and his daughter to be brought to Westminster this morning for interrogation and, evidently, Mistress Liora's little brother went to Lonsdale to tell Peter about it."

Christopher nodded, still stunned at the scope of Walter de Quincy's betrayal. "I spoke to the boy myself," he said. "That is why I followed Peter here because I did not want him to get himself killed trying to free her. Now, tell me what happened to my son?"

The Marshal looked around the little group – David and Marcus, his senior warlords. Alexander, Caius, and Maxton, men who had served him for years and men who were the best spies and assassins in the business. There were no men more capable. And then there were Liora and Haim, two people completely out of their element. He felt a good deal of pity for them, to be truthful, sucked into a deeply serious political situation simply because Liora and Peter fell in love. It was a difficult situation on so many levels.

But The Marshal knew what he had to do.

He returned his attention to Christopher.

"John has been lamenting the loss of Sean de Lara," he said quietly. "I have told you that without de Lara, I am forced to take his place. But today, John offered Peter the position as his new Lord of the Shadows in exchange for the freedom of the jeweler and his daughter. Those were the terms, Chris. Peter accepted."

As he feared, Christopher roared.

"Like hell!" he boomed. "My son serving John? I will kill the king myself before I permit this, William. I will bring my entire army into London and burn Westminster to the ground if he thinks, for one minute, I will stand by and let this happen!"

The Marshal knew he meant every word and he also knew before he even told Christopher the news that he would be in the position of calming the man down.

He was prepared.

"I want you to listen to me and listen well, Hereford," he said. It was rare that he used Christopher's title, but he wanted the man to know he meant business. "Peter made this decision of his own free will. Aye, he was coerced, but he decided that the jeweler's daughter was worth more to him than his own pride and conviction. If you go charging in there like a madman, you'll humiliate your son. Do you understand that? He is a man, and he has made a man's decision. Do not ruin it for him by being his father."

Christopher flamed at the suggestion but deep down, he knew The Marshal was right. He knew there was a great deal of truth in what The Marshal had said. He glared at William, his jaw flexing dangerously.

"I *am* his father," he said. "The king is my enemy. Now my son must serve my enemy?"

The Marshal held up a hand. "Nothing will happen to him," he said. "I will see to that. But having him as John's advisor and bodyguard… he is in a perfect position to help the rebellion more than he ever could if he were only your knight. Do you understand that?"

Christopher only saw that The Marshal wanted to use Peter for his own ends. Christopher, however, wasn't willing to let William Marshal do to Peter what he'd done to others, Sean de Lara most of all. In the end, The Marshal was only out for himself – and what he considered the greater good – and he would use anyone he could in order to advance those objectives.

But Christopher wasn't going to let that happen with Peter.

"I understand that is your lot in life to save and protect England," he said, his voice a husky growl. "I also understand that you will do everything necessary, and use everyone necessary, to accomplish that task. I do not fault you, William, but I have known you for many years. I saw what you did to Sean de Lara. Sean's life was ruined because of his dedication to you and, even now, the man lies gravely wounded because of that directive, a directive *you* gave him. I remember another agent from years ago, Garran le Mon, whom you placed within a family that was extremely loyal to John and that position got Garran killed. How about Rhys du Bois? He had to flee England because of the situation you put him in. One of the best men I have ever served with. I could go on and on. I've *seen* what you've done. You're not thinking of Peter now – you're only thinking of yourself and your dedication to England, but I will tell you this – if you think I am going to let you sacrifice Peter, then you are sadly mistaken. Now, gain me entry into Westminster. I want to speak with John."

Everyone lurched at that suggestion. David and Marcus went so far as to speak words of denial. No one wanted Christopher going into the arena with the lions, which was exactly what this would be akin to. He'd be walking into the heart of the enemy. The Marshal was gazing back at him steadily, for nothing he said was untrue. Absolutely nothing.

But he had something to say about it.

"What if I told you that I want Peter there for the ultimate mission."

"What's that?"

"To kill a king."

That brought a strong reaction from Christopher. "What in the hell are you saying?"

William sighed heavily, looking to the trusted men around him. Liora and Haim were far enough away that they couldn't really hear what was being said, but to ensure that, he lowered his voice.

"Do you want this rebellion to go on forever?" he hissed. "Why do you think I had Sean positioned so close to John? One word from me and he could kill John and make it look like an accident. It is true that Sean fed us information and controlled the king to a certain extent, but his position always was, since the beginning, to be my Trojan horse. Do you remember the tale of Troy and how the Greeks, unable to breech the walls of the city, built a great wooden horse that they proceeded to hide in? When the Trojans opened the gates and brought the horse into their citadel, the Greeks broke loose and destroyed the city. That is Peter's position now, Chris. Let him save England."

Christopher stared at him. It was as terrible and terrifying a position as any man could have, much less his son. He kept trying to take his relationship to Peter out of the equation, but he couldn't. He simply couldn't do it. His son had placed himself in grave danger because he loved a woman and should he keep that position with

John, he would become another Sean de Lara.

If he survived.

Christopher couldn't, in good conscience, let that happen. He was still Peter's father no matter how much The Marshal tried to tell him to stay out of it.

To let Peter save England.

He just couldn't do it.

"Take me to John," he asked again, his voice hoarse with emotion. "I want to see him face to face."

"I'll take Peter's place," Caius spoke up. When everyone looked at him, surprised, he simply shrugged his big shoulders and looked at The Marshal. "When you first secured that position with John, you offered it to me and to Sean. Do you recall? Sean took it to save my reputation because he knew what it would mean to any man who assumed it. It would ruin his life, but Sean did it to save me. Now, let me take up the mantle in Sean's place. Please, my lord."

William looked at him, shaking his head. "It would be perfect except for the fact that you are married now and you control the bastion of Richmond," he said. "What would your wife say to you taking this position, Cai? You know what that would do to her. To your marriage. You are brave to offer, but I must decline."

Caius knew that and a massive part of him

was greatly relieved, but he felt as if he had to offer. "I understand," he said. "But you must understand that someone protected me from that position, once. I felt as if I had to do the same."

"If I changed my mind and let you do it, would you?"

Caius nodded without hesitation. "I would."

The Marshal understood a man of honor. "I believe you," he said. "But it is out of the question."

"Then let me," Alexander said. "I have the most perfect life imaginable and I love my wife and family, but if this is a job for an assassin, then you'll want me. Peter does not have the instincts that I do."

Christopher reached out to put a hand of gratitude on Alexander's arm, knowing the man was trying to spare Peter. It was deeply touching. But The Marshal shook his head.

"You would be perfect, Sherry," he said. "But you are too important to the de Lohr war machine. If you had no other responsibilities, I would agree, but I cannot."

Alexander knew that but, like Caius, he had to offer. Peter was young and talented, with his whole life ahead of him. Even though he was a seasoned veteran and a spy, he hadn't suffered the years of missions and degradation that Caius and Alexander had. They'd already gotten their hands dirty with killing and dirty deeds. But Peter hadn't. There was something in both Alexander and Caius that wanted to protect Peter from the seedier tasks in life.

Like killing a king.

It was something Christopher greatly appreciated, but it didn't solve the problem. When Maxton opened his mouth to chime in, Christopher simply held up a hand to silence him. He knew what the man was going to say, but he didn't have to say it.

That was something Christopher had to do alone.

"William," he said quietly. "Must I ask again for you to take me to John?"

The Marshal looked at him, knowing he couldn't deny him. To do so would be to bring all of the House of de Lohr down around John and Westminster, and with so many rebel warlord armies still in London, it could be messy, indeed. All Christopher would have to say was that his son was in danger and his allies would come running.

That was something The Marshal couldn't chance.

"Very well," he said after a moment. "But all of you are coming. I will not let him go in alone."

He was looking to the group of men around him. Heavily armed men who would fight to the death should John try to move against Christopher. It was as dangerous a situation as they'd ever faced, but they were ready and willing to do it. No questions asked. It was Marcus who began to move towards the gatehouse, hand on the hilt of his broadsword, ready to rumble.

The others followed.

Leaving Liora and Haim in safety back by the seamstress' shop, The Marshal ordered the gate guards to lift the portcullis. As the old iron grate creaked and groaned with the old ropes lifting it, the group of men passed beneath it. William took the lead at that point, taking them on the same path he'd taken Peter when he'd escorted the man to the king. The royal apartments were a vast block, built from wattle and daub and with richly carved interiors, but no one really noticed the opulence when they entered.

Least of all Christopher.

He had been here, years ago, when Richard had been king, so this wasn't his first visit. But it could very well be his most important. David was on his right side and Marcus on his left, and he could feel their strength lift him. He was about to go against The Marshal; he was about to go against all of them and he needed that strength for what was to come. When they finally reached the king's private rooms, The Marshal entered first with Christopher right behind him.

Christopher would never forget the look of

surprise on John's face.

John and Peter were on the far side of the chamber, with John sitting and Peter standing against the wall. There didn't seem to be anyone else in the room, which would work in Christopher's favor. He looked over his shoulder and motioned to Maxton to lock the door, which he did and stood in front of it to guard it. With the meanest knight in England watching the door, everyone else spread out, leaving Christopher facing the king and his son.

Peter, seeing his father, twitched his surprise.

"Papa?" he said, incredulous. "What are you doing here?"

Christopher wasn't looking at his son. He was looking at the king, who was equally shocked. In fact, he was out of his seat, walking in Christopher's direction as if he had absolutely no fear of the man.

"Hereford?" he gasped in delight. "My old and dear friend. What a surprise to see you here."

Christopher stared at John a moment before shaking his head. "I wish that was true," he said. "I wish we *were* old and dear friends. We are definitely old friends, but I use that term in the same vein as adversary. We *are* old adversaries and continue to be, John. Some things never change."

He used John's Christian name, something

he'd done since he first knew the prince all those years ago as Richard's younger brother. Richard and Christopher had been friends before Richard was even king, and Christopher had known John since he'd been an obnoxious child and to Christopher, he was still obnoxious.

Deadly, too.

But John grinned.

"That is true," he said. "But we want the same thing. A safe and strong England."

"But we want it in different ways."

John snorted. "I was just speaking to your son about that," he said. "I was explaining to Peter our fundamental differences, one being that I rule this country and you do not, yet you try to control it."

Christopher had a smile on his face, but it wasn't one of humor. It was one of irony. He looked at his son, who seemed rather edgy to see him.

"Liora and her father are safe," he said. "I came make sure you are safe as well."

"He is quite safe." John answered for him. "I will take good care of him."

Christopher resisted the urge to retort. He didn't want this to become a big battle, at least not yet. Not if he could help it. He had something to say and he wanted John in a congenial mood. Or, as much as he could be.

His focus returned to the king.

"Let us forego the pleasantries and cut to the purpose of my visit," he said. "You have my son. I want him back. I will make you an offer that you cannot refuse."

William, who had been standing at the edge of the room between Christopher and John, looked at Christopher sharply. Even David and Marcus looked at Christopher, concerned with what was about to come forth.

But John found it wholly interesting.

"Is that so?" he said. "I am intrigued. Go on."

Christopher paused, perhaps reconsidering what he was about to say, but he thought better of it. Peter had sacrificed something for Liora.

He was about to sacrifice something for Peter.

"My armies are quite large, as you are well aware," he said. "When you look at your opposition, I am at the forefront. Is that a fair statement?"

John nodded. "You always have been," he said. "As far back as the days of Ralph Fitz Walter, the Sheriff of Nottingham. It all seems like so long ago."

"It was," Christopher said. "We were adversaries when Richard was alive and even before. I loved your brother, as you are well aware."

John's gleeful expression faded somewhat. "I know," he said. "I had always wished you would love me the way you loved him."

"You never gave me a reason to."

John stiffened, gravely insulted by a man he'd known most of his life. It wasn't just insult – deep down, it hurt, too. But he would never admit it.

"Then say what you came here to say," he snapped.

The mood was shifting from one that was almost pleasant to one that was becoming unstable. Christopher fixed on John, pondering how he was going to phrase his offer.

"You are facing mayhap some of the greatest battles you have ever faced," he said. "More warlords are against you than are for you. It is going to be a difficult fight."

John's smile returned, though it was humorless. "I believe I shall triumph."

"Your chances will be better if I lay down my sword."

Everyone in the chamber gasped, including The Marshal. John's eyes were wide as he moved towards Christopher.

"What's this you say?" he demanded. "*Lay down your sword?*"

Christopher's eyes narrowed, conveying his sincerity. "I will not fight in these upcoming battles if you return my son to me," he said. "I *am* England, John. I have been fighting in battles as long as you have been alive, but I will not lift my sword against you from this day forward if you return my son to me. But only if you return him to me now."

Peter, unable to keep silent, moved in his father's direction. "Papa… *nay!*"

Christopher held out a hand to his son, a gesture of silence. His focus remained on John. "Well?" he said. "What say you?"

John's face was wrought with astonishment. "I cannot believe my ears," he finally said. "You would not fight against me?"

"I will not fight for you, either," Christopher clarified. "I will recuse myself. Now, you have to decide what is more valuable – having Peter by your side or having me step down."

John stared at him. He was clearly trying to decide if Christopher was serious but quickly realized that he was. Part of the lure of keeping Peter at his side was the fact that it would hurt Christopher, but if Christopher was willing to lay down his sword and not participate in one of the many battles that were looming in the immediate future, then that was perhaps the greatest victory of all.

Removing the Lion's Claw from battle.

I will not lift my sword against you from this day forward if you return my son to me.

Knowing Christopher as he did, the man's word was solid.

It was too good of an opportunity to waste.

"I accept," John said before he could think to negotiate the details of such a proposal. "Take your son but leave me your sword as your word of honor."

Christopher had a magnificent broadsword, one that he'd used for over thirty years. It had the head of a lion on it with two ruby eyes and was truly a spectacular piece, one he was loath to part with because it was part of him. It represented him and everything he stood for, the power of the de Lohr name. But his son's life was more important to him. He unsheathed it without hesitation and handed it to John, hilt-first.

"Take it," he said, trying not to show how painful such an act was. "Peter, come with me."

John took the sword with shock, perhaps not really believing Christopher would actually give it to him, as Peter went to stand with his father. With his son by his side, Christopher turned and headed out of the chamber, followed by David, Marcus, Caius, Alexander, and Maxton. He waited until they were out of the royal apartments and out in the vast bailey of Westminster before he came to a halt and turned to the group.

Everyone would swear, until they died, that there were tears in his eyes as he spoke.

"Before you all come down on me for doing what I did, know that I feel there was no other choice," he said. "Regaining my son was the most important objective and laying down my sword is of little matter. I have Peter and Sherry and a host of other powerful knights to do the fighting, and I shall be as involved as I have ever been. Truly, this means nothing. But giving over my sword… let me just say that I hope to reclaim it someday."

Peter was standing next to his father, heartsick. "Papa, I'm so sorry," he said. "I never meant that you should sacrifice yourself so. I was prepared to stand beside my decision."

Christopher looked at his son, feeling more relief than he could express that he had him back. "I know you were," he said. "William tried to convince me that he needed you in that position, but I wasn't going to let you do it. You are destined for greater things in life and becoming John's henchman isn't one of them."

Peter shook his head sadly. "Oh, Papa…" he said softly. "But what you did…"

He couldn't even bring himself to say it. Christopher put a hand on his shoulder. "It was nothing you would not have done for me," he said, gentler. "It was the same thing you did to free Liora and her father. Sometimes, you must do something that is greater than yourself. But know that my pledge was very broad – I shall not take the field against John's armies, but that does not mean I will not command my armies. I'll be there, just as I always am, without engaging in active combat. When I said I would lay down my sword, I only meant me. I did not mean that my armies shall not fight. Nothing has changed in that regard, so do not fret. But that means that you, Sherry, will now be in charge of my armies when they take the field."

Alexander suspected this would be the case since he heard Christopher utter that fateful offer. "I understand," he said. "But what about Wigmore?"

"It shall remain yours," Christopher said. "I will move Essien over to command it for now, but it shall be yours when the time comes and the battles are over. Peter, you will still take Ludlow and manage the garrisons. Sherry and Addax will be my field command."

There was some relief to the knights, knowing that Christopher didn't intend to back off altogether. But he wasn't finished yet. He looked at Marcus.

"I need you to do something for me," he said quietly.

Marcus nodded. "Anything, Chris."

"I am finished with Walter de Quincy," he said, his voice a threatening rumble. "He is here, somewhere in London, and you shall find him and make it clear to him that my wrath upon him has come. I do not ever want to see his face again. Then, you will go to his stronghold of Astley Cross and you will lay siege until you purge whatever army Walter keeps there. Clean it out of anything de Quincy and claim it for yourself. I'd rather have you as an ally on the Marches than that bastard. He has pushed me too far this time and he is going to pay."

A flicker of a smile crossed Marcus' lips. "With pleasure," he said. "But Astley Cross is far away from my Yorkshire holdings. Are you sure you would not rather have it?"

Christopher shrugged. "I am occupied with a great many other things at the moment," he said. "In any case, de Quincy has made his last move against me. Remove him, shatter him, but do not kill him. I want him to live in his own filth, knowing who it is who has beaten him. Humiliation like that will be worse than death, Marcus. Make it so."

Marcus understood. He looked at Maxton. "You are heading back to Gloucester," he said. "Care to lend a hand to remove de Quincy?"

Maxton cocked a dark eyebrow. "I thought you would never ask."

With Walter de Quincy's future settled, the group resumed their march towards the gatehouse. When the gate guards saw them coming, they didn't have to be told to lift the portcullis this time. They simply lifted it so that by the time Christopher and the others arrived, they passed through without waiting. Perhaps there was something in those gatehouse guards that simply wanted Christopher de Lohr and his allies out of Westminster altogether.

Out they went onto the dusty streets of London.

"Peter!"

A cry filled the air and they saw Liora rushing across the street from her spot over by the seamstress' shop. Now, the focus shifted from Christopher's sacrifice to Peter and the young lady he was so enchanted with. Seeing her coming, Peter ran in her direction until they came together in a crash of flesh and blood, broadcloth and mail, right out in the middle of the street. Peter kissed her deeply and he didn't care who saw him, including her father and his own.

He just didn't give a lick.

"Thank God you are well," Liora wept softly as she hugged him. "Your father must have worked a miracle!"

Peter wasn't ready to let her go even though he could see that his father and the others had caught up to them. All he could seem to do was hold on to her, clinging to her as if he weren't capable of letting her go. For what they'd just gone through, he felt as if he'd righteously earned this moment.

She was back in his arms and she was going to

stay there.

"He did work a miracle," he said. "I am well and, most importantly, you and your father are well. That is all that matters to me, sweetheart."

Liora nodded, realizing there were men standing around her that she didn't know. She was in a rather amorous embrace with Peter and out of propriety, she pulled away from him as her father walked up. But she was still holding Peter's hand, because he wouldn't let it go, as Haim focused on Peter.

"I have you to thank for this, Saint Peter," he said, a glimmer in his dark eyes. "That is what my son calls you, you know."

Peter smiled weakly. "You have a brave son, my lord," he said, using the address as a sign of respect. "He is fearless as few men are."

Haim smiled. "I think the same can be said for you from what I'm told," he said. "When you left my home last night, Asa came to me. He told me about you. He said that you make sure hungry children are fed."

"Saul's Army?"

"The same."

Peter averted his gaze modestly. "That was to keep them from stealing your eggs," he said. "It was either that or Asa and his Maccabees were going to full-scale war against them. I did what I felt was right."

"It *was* right," Haim said. "That shows your depth of character. It shows the capacity for understanding, something that the Lord smiles upon. Asa is enamored with you. He wants to be like you. I have had the unhappy task of telling him that it is not possible."

Peter's smile faded. "He would make a fine knight," he said sincerely.

Haim shrugged. "That is not for him, unfortunately, though he does not quite understand why," he said. "But he will, in time. He will be happy with his life because he will have a good life. But my daughter… I am not so sure she will have a happy life from now on if you are not in it."

Peter looked at Liora, who was gazing at her father with a pained expression. "I will not," she said. "You know I will not. Peter is a good man, Papa, you've said so yourself. He risked his life to save us just now. He was going to give up everything just to save us until his father stepped in. Doesn't that mean anything?"

Haim nodded. "It means a great deal," he said frankly. "The man has saved my life and undoubtedly has saved yours. Peter, just what do you intend to do now? Will you let Liora go home with me and never see her again?"

Peter was still looking at Liora. "Her home is with you," he said. "She will go home with you, but I will not promise never to see her again. I love her, my lord. I could not walk away from her now if God Himself stood before me and demanded it. What I did with John was not to coerce you into agreeing to a marriage. It was because I had to."

Haim looked at Christopher, at David, and at the other men who were standing back, watching this very personal exchange go on. They all knew why Peter had come and, now, Peter's entire future was playing out before them.

A future that was in Haim's hands.

With a sigh, he took a few steps towards Peter so he could look the man in the eyes.

"Asa said something to me last night that has stayed with me," he said. "He said that the most important thing is that people are kind and love us, no matter if they are Christian or Jewish. The most important thing is a man of noble heart, who will protect people and feed children who do not have enough to eat. God cares what is in our hearts more than He cares about the prayers we give, and if I searched for a million years to find a husband as worthy as you for my daughter, I am certain I could not find such a man. Liora loves you and you have proven that you love her, more than anyone else could have. I realize this means I will lose my daughter to your faith, but as I said, we both worship the same God. All I ask is that you allow her to teach your children about her faith. I should like them to know it and understand it. Will you do this for me?"

Peter hadn't expected to hear those words coming from Haim's mouth. As he stared at him, his eyes filled with tears and spilled over. He was exhausted and emotional, and it had already been a hell of a day. His control was cracking and the tears were the result. He had been waiting his entire life to hear those words, only he hadn't known it until that moment.

He nodded his head.

"We will honor your faith in my household," he said hoarsely. "And we will honor you and your family, I swear it. Thank you, my lord. From the bottom of my heart, thank you. But… but this does not mean that you will shun her, does it?"

Haim shook his head. "For my part, I cannot," he said. "She is my child. I could never leave her."

That relieved Peter's heart more than he could express. Quickly, he wiped at his face as he looked at Liora, who was tearing up as well. But she was smiling from ear to ear as she looked at her father.

"Thank you, Papa," she whispered tightly. "I know this is not an easy decision for you, but you have made me very happy."

Haim smiled weakly at his daughter, feeling emotional and hoping he was doing the right thing. In his heart, it seemed right, but he also knew his daughter would be entering a whole new world that she knew absolutely nothing about.

He hoped she was ready.

"Are you certain, *zeeskeit*?" he asked. "This is what you want?"

Liora looked at Peter and, in that moment, Haim saw the joy between them, the growing adoration. It was as fresh and beautiful as a new morning.

"Aye," Liora said after a moment. "This is what I want. *He* is what I want."

"Then you have my blessing."

Liora rushed her father, throwing her arms around him and thanking him profusely. Peter turned to Christopher, who beamed and embraced his son as David and Marcus did the same. In fact, they were all smiling and embracing Peter, congratulating him on his future bride and his future life. It hadn't been an easy path to get there, and it had been a surprisingly swift one, but the moment had come. In a world that was in turmoil for all of them, the moment was especially sweet.

The joy of a new life to come, for Peter and Liora.

When the congratulations died down, Maxton and Caius and Alexander went to gather the horses while Christopher and Haim spoke in a serious huddle, no doubt discussing what was to come for their children. It was Marcus and David who stood off to the side, watching everything unfold.

"Well?" Marcus said to David. "What do you think about that? Your nephew is about to marry a Jewish woman."

David watched Peter and Liora, in a private huddle. Peter was holding her hands against his chest, saying something to her that she clearly approved of. He could see the woman smiling up at him adoringly.

"As long as she loves him and treats him well, I do not care if she is Jewish or not," he said. "You and I knew plenty of Jews while we were in The Levant. And I seem to remember the daughter of a carpenter you thought was quite lovely."

Marcus had a smile on his lips as he remembered. "Ah," he said. "The fair Adaya. Funny, I'd forgotten about her."

"As I recall, you were fairly enamored with her."

"I was, but her father wasn't enamored with *me*."

David grinned. "Fortunately, that didn't hold true with Liora's father."

Marcus watched Peter in the distance. "Young love is always the sweetest," he said. That statement hung in the air between them for a moment before Marcus glanced at David. "And now I intend to destroy the man who tried to prevent it. Peter may be Chris' son, but I raised him. He belongs to me as much as he does to

Chris. Mark my words when I say that Walter de Quincy and his daughter will pay."

David knew that. He wished he could help, but his attention was needed elsewhere. He watched Marcus walk away, heading over to Maxton where the two of them spoke briefly before mounting their horses. Whenever those two were involved, something very bad was about to happen.

David almost pitied Walter… but not quite.

As David went to find his horse, Peter managed to let go of Liora long enough to collect his own mount. But he didn't climb into the saddle. He remained on foot, walking beside Liora and Haim in an unprecedented show of attention, a Christian knight to a Jewish family, as they headed back to the Jewish quarter.

It was a rare moment of religious unity.

Perhaps that was the bright side of this entire situation, David thought as he watched everyone disband. Perhaps the strife of de Quincy's actions had the effect of bringing everyone together, stronger than before. Most certainly, it brought Haim to a decision he probably never thought he would make – allowing his daughter to marry a Christian. But even as David thought on the positive aspects of the situation, he couldn't help but feel that it wasn't over yet. Not in the least.

Something told him that the worst, for Walter and Agnes, was yet to come.

CHAPTER EIGHTEEN

Avington House, Townhome of the Earl of Winchester
Later that day

"HE DID *WHAT?*"

Marcus stood over a man who seemed particularly pale at the moment. Saer de Quincy, Earl of Winchester, was a man from a good family who had used those family connections to achieve his present status. Like most of the de Quincy family, he'd married well and he'd bought, borrowed, and bribed his way into the position he currently found himself in.

One of the more powerful warlords in England.

By virtue of that station, he was also one of the architects of the Magna Carta and he'd spent the bulk of John's reign fighting against the king. Because of this, he had been a ready ally for Christopher when the man had finally turned against John and Saer had valued that alliance more for the prestige than for the actual friendship.

But that didn't matter to Marcus. Whether the man liked Christopher or whether he didn't was immaterial.

He wanted something from Saer and he wasn't going to leave without it.

"Your cousin, Walter, has been sending messages to John," he repeated. "He has sent John a missive regarding Hereford's son, Peter, informing the king that Peter's intended is a spy for the rebellion."

Saer had his hand over his mouth in disbelief. "Christ," he muttered. "Then I did hear you correctly the first time."

"You did."

"Who is his intended?"

"You would not know her," Marcus said. "She is the daughter of John's jeweler, but in spite of that, this young woman has never done anything wrong, nor has Peter. Yet, your cousin is making salacious claims against Peter and, in doing so, got the girl and her father imprisoned. Peter was forced to swear fealty to John in order to have them released."

Saer was trying not to appear too sickened. "Are you certain it was him?" he asked weakly, already knowing the answer. "You're *sure* about this, Burton?"

Marcus sighed faintly. "You know your cousin has been trying very hard to marry his daughter to Peter de Lohr," he said, sounding as if he were scolding the man. "You know he has had Peter followed, spied on, trailed, and otherwise invasively pursued. If you do not believe me, ask him. He will tell you that he has. Only he happened to see Peter speaking with the jeweler's daughter and out of sheer jealousy, tried to have the woman thrown in the vault for crimes she did not commit. Shall I go on?"

Saer held up a hand. "Nay," he said quickly. "I believe you."

"Then bring him in here. I want to speak with him."

Saer eyed him hesitantly. "Speak to him?" he said. "Or beat him? You know that he has already been badly beaten in a robbery."

Marcus fixed on him with an expression that suggested he wasn't surprised. "It was less than he deserved."

It took Saer a moment to realize that Marcus knew something about that beating. He sighed heavily and averted his gaze. "That was a warning, wasn't it?"

Marcus snorted. "He tried to force Hereford into a marriage by threatening Peter. When that did not work, he threatened the jeweler's daughter instead." He took a step in de Quincy's direction, his big body tense. "Hereford has tried to be patient. He has tried to ignore him. But his actions against Peter and the jeweler's daughter, a completely innocent woman, have forced Hereford into action."

"But…"

"Do you know he used your seal on the missive he sent to the king, hoping the man would think it was from you?"

Saer's eyes widened at that revelation. "He did that?"

"Ask him."

"Surely there has to be more to it!"

"There is no more to it than pure greed and wickedness." When Saer tried to resist, Marcus delivered the final blow. "Give me your cousin or any alliance between you and Hereford is finished."

That was enough for Saer. He'd never liked his cousin, but bloodlines had afforded him some courtesy. But no longer. After what he'd just heard, blood wasn't strong enough to protect Walter. Right now, he was in the path of an enraged Hereford and his allies, including the unpredictable and deadly Marcus Burton, for righteously despicable actions.

He wanted no part of whatever that man was about receive.

"Then take him out of here," he hissed. "I refuse to support a man who only wishes to use my good name for his nefarious deeds. He wanted the king to think I was the one sending him missives? We'll just see about that. Of course I knew he was following Peter de Lohr; he tells me so nightly. He tells me how Agnes is going to marry him and become the next Countess of Hereford."

Marcus shook his head. "She will never be the Countess of Hereford because Peter will never be the earl," he said. "Evidently, he is too stupid to realize that. *Where* is your cousin?"

"Upstairs."

"And his daughter?"

"Probably with him."

Marcus nodded faintly. "Take me to your cousin and then get out of here," he said. "I do not care where you go, but get out of this house for a time. And tell Agnes to wait downstairs. She is not to leave with you."

Saer eyed him. "You will not hurt her, will you?"

"Of course not. But she is part of this. Her actions have consequences."

It was a harsh reply, but no harsher than she

deserved. She was just as ambitious as her father and Saer knew she had been quite aware of her father's actions against Peter. As Walter had bragged, Agnes had beamed her approval. Saer had seen it.

Perhaps it was better this way.

With a weary nod, Saer motioned for Marcus to follow him.

"Come with me."

Marcus did. He followed Saer down a very narrow corridor that led to a narrow flight of steps. They went up the stairs, to the floor above, where wood paneling lined the walls and made the corridor even more narrow. Dark, thick wood lined everything – ceiling and floors – in an astonishing display of Winchester wealth. They came to the last door in the corridor and nearly plowed into a young woman coming from the chamber. Before she could say a word, Saer grabbed her by the arm and pulled her away.

Marcus watched Agnes as she was forcibly escorted away but groaning inside the chamber caught his attention.

He stepped inside.

Walter was laying on the bed, a compress to his mouth as he faced the windows. His back was to the door and Marcus stood there a moment, noting the bloodied rags and bed linens. The entire room was a mess.

Just like Walter's life.

There was some satisfaction in that.

"You have failed, de Quincy."

Walter's head jerked around, seeing Marcus standing in the open doorway. His eyes widened and he threw the compress aside, lurching out of bed. There was a table underneath the windows that contained some of his possessions, including his coin purse, saddlebags, and a small arsenal of daggers. He grabbed one of them, a nasty-looking weapon with a serrated edge, and held it up in a threatening manner.

"What are you doing here?" he demanded, his words slurred because of his swollen mouth. "Get out of here!"

Marcus cocked his head with some amusement. "Do you intend to use that dagger, then?"

"I said get out!"

He was screaming and Marcus stepped further into the chamber, slamming the door behind him. He threw the bolt, watching Walter's face turn bright red with fear and fury at the realization of being in a locked room with Marcus Burton.

There was fear in the man's eyes.

"Shut up," Marcus growled. "For once in your life, shut your insipid mouth and listen for a change. You and I are going to have a serious discussion, Walter. Refuse me and I will throw you right out of the window. Is this in any way unclear?"

Walter's red face went pale, just that quickly. He did not lower the dagger, however. He just stood there and panted like a dog.

"What do you want, then?" he demanded hoarsely. "Say it and leave me alone."

"Why?" Marcus said. "Why should I leave you alone when you've not left Peter alone since the moment you decided that you wanted him for your daughter? You've pestered and plagued him. You've had your spies follow him and report to you. You've not left him alone so I will ask you again – *why* should I leave you alone?"

Walter didn't have an answer for him, so his breathing began to quicken. "This is not your business, Burton."

"I beg to differ," Marcus said. "Peter is like a son to me. He lived with my family for many years and, as you know, his father and I are like brothers, so this is indeed my business. I have come to tell you that your pursuit of Peter, and your harassment of him, is at an end. Your lies have finally caught up with you."

Walter's eyes began to take on a shifty quality. They were jerking back and forth, looking at Marcus, at the door behind him, perhaps wondering if he could somehow get Burton away from that door so he could run for his life. His entire body was beginning to shift and twitch, a rat caught in a trap of his own making.

"You're mad," he finally said. "You do not know what you are saying."

Marcus lifted his dark eyebrows. "Unfortunately, I do," he said. "You tried to coerce Hereford into a marriage by stating you believed that Peter was spying for the king. Then you changed your story and sent word to the king stating that you believed that a young woman seen in Peter's company, the jeweler's daughter, was spying for the rebellion against the king. We know it was you because you sent the missive with Winchester's seal and your cousin most certainly did not send that missive. Since a thrashing did not convince you that your lies would not be tolerated, I have come to personally tell you what your latest offense against Hereford will cost you. And it will cost you dearly."

Walter still had that dagger up, still pointed at Marcus. "If you come near me, I will fight you, do you hear? I can use this dagger well."

Marcus grinned; he couldn't help it. "Not well enough to stop me," he said. "But I've not come to kill you, so you can be thankful for that. I've come to tell you that as we speak, Maxton of Loxbeare is gathering his army, part of de Lohr's army, and preparing to march on Astley Cross."

Walter wasn't sure what he meant. "March on Astley?" he repeated. "For what purpose?"

"To evict your army and claim the property for me."

That brought a strong reaction. "What's this?" he hissed. "You are going to lay siege to my home?"

"It will not be your home when we are finished with it," Marcus said calmly. "It will be mine."

Walter was starting to lose his composure as he realized what Marcus meant. "You cannot do that," he said, his voice trembling. "You cannot take a man's home! It is mine!"

"*Was* yours," Marcus said. "And who is going to stop us? You? Your cousin? In fact, Winchester might very well aid us if I ask him to, so you will receive no support from him. He knows what you have done. When I said your latest offense against Hereford was going to cost you, I meant it."

Walter's face was starting to turn red again. "You cannot do this," he snarled. "You cannot do any of this!"

Marcus folded his big arms across his chest. "You should have thought about that before you lied and tried to ruin a young knight and the lady he is going to marry," he said, watching Walter's eyes widen. "You heard me correctly – he is going to marry her. But not to fear – Agnes will find an appropriate husband."

Walter was beside himself as the entire

scheme he had planned involving Peter and his daughter unraveled before his eyes. "You will have nothing to do with my daughter," he said, bloodied spit flying from his battered lips. "You cannot take my home and not expect me to fight back. I will go to the king! I will stop this... this travesty!"

Marcus decided he'd had enough. He had no patience for fools and that was exactly what Walter was – a fool. He rushed the man, so quickly that Walter barely realized he was being charged until it was too late. The dagger in his hand went flying when Marcus smacked it away, breaking bones in Walter's hand when he did so. As Walter screamed in pain, Marcus grabbed him around the neck and slammed him back against those beautiful wooden walls.

His dark blue eyes blazed into Walter's terrified brown orbs.

"For what you have done, for the havoc you have wrought and the lies you have told, this is far less than you deserve," he growled. "Consider the fact that you still have your life to be most fortunate, de Quincy, for if this were up to me, I would have ended you long ago. You have Hereford's mercy to thank for that, though you do not deserve it. Now, are you listening to me? Tell me you hear me."

Terrified, Walter tried to kick out, to strike

Marcus, but Marcus slammed him back into the wall again and knocked the wind from him.

"Answer me, de Quincy," he said. "I can keep pummeling you until you do, so it would be wise for you to acknowledge me. Put aside that monstrous, misplaced pride and answer me."

Walter hated being subservient to any man. He hated to be backed into a corner like this, so Marcus was right when he'd told him to put his pride aside. It was the one trait that caused him the most problems and had, in fact, caused this entire mess. Walter knew that, deep down, even if he couldn't bring himself to admit it. But he also knew he couldn't take another beating from Burton's ham hock-sized fists.

It was quite the dilemma.

Common sense finally won out.

"I am listening," he muttered angrily. "Speak and be quick about it."

He was still trying to control the situation and Marcus could only sigh with exasperation. "You are going to leave England," he said, still clutching the man's neck. "Your family has property in Scotland. Go there and stay there. I do not want to see your face in England ever again. If I do, I will cut your head off and throw it to the dogs. If I hear your name again, I will find you and you will meet your end. If anyone ever comes to England on your orders, for any purpose against Hereford or his allies, I will hunt you down and I will cut you into a hundred little pieces. Am I making my point?"

Walter's red face was beginning to sweat. "I hear you." When Marcus' grip tightened, he squirmed and beat at the man's hand. "I understand you!"

"Excellent," Marcus said, finally loosening his grip. "Now, I will escort you to the river where a cog waiting to sail to Edinburgh is expecting you. I have already paid for your passage. You are going to get on that boat tonight, Walter. You are leaving immediately."

Some of Walter's belligerence began to leave him. "Now?" he said. "But I am wounded. I must rest."

"You can rest on the boat."

"I have not packed my possessions!"

"Pack them now.

Walter's mouth worked as he prepared for a retort, but he thought better of it. He knew that Marcus would follow through with any and all threats, which brought him to the unalterable conclusion that he had been backed into a corner with no way out – except Burton's way.

This was what his blind ambition had brought him.

It occurred to him that he was to blame for all of this, but he refused to accept that. He refused to accept that his actions had brought him to this point. It was Hereford's fault, or Burton's fault, or Peter's fault. It was even his cousin's fault for not supporting him in his time of need. But it was never, ever his fault.

So… he'd go to Scotland. Just like that, he would depart. It wasn't as if he had a choice. But he knew for certain that wasn't going to stay there. He was an intelligent man, one with breeding and connections, and he wouldn't stay in Scotland forever, no matter what Burton said. He'd come back and he'd have his revenge.

But Burton didn't have to know any of that.

Still… for now, he had to do what the man said.

Walter was slow to pack, so much so that Marcus ended up grabbing what was left and ramming it into a satchel, forcing Walter to pull on his shoes and don a heavy cloak, still wearing his bed clothes, before Marcus dragged him out of the house half-dressed. He forced the man from the chamber and down those narrow stairs, to the reception room near the entry where Agnes was waiting. Saer was nowhere to be found and Marcus was told by a frightened servant that Winchester had fled from the stables with several of his men several minutes earlier.

Walter, and Agnes, were quite alone.

But that was the way Marcus wanted it.

Agnes had no idea why Saer had told her to wait downstairs, but she soon found out. Marcus had her father in one hand and grabbed her with the other, making his way out of Winchester's posh townhome and heading towards the river. Walter grumbled and cursed as Marcus dragged him down the avenue but as long as he kept up a good pace, Marcus wouldn't touch him. Yet the moment he slowed down, Marcus had his hand on the back of the man's neck.

That kept him moving swiftly.

Agnes, however, was another matter. She genuinely had no idea what was going on, although she knew Marcus Burton on sight. She'd been around enough of the rebel warlords to know who he was. She also knew that he was quite close to Peter and given the missive her father had sent last night, she had a feeling Burton's appearance had something to do with that. In fact, she knew it did. Finally, her father had pushed too far. She knew that because her father was going along with Marcus without a fight, so she didn't fight back, either.

But something told her that this wasn't going to end well.

She was right.

They ended up down at the river's edge, on a small boardwalk with several businesses fronting the river, including the most notorious tavern in all of London. The Pox was one of those establishments that was legendary, but not in a good way. It was extremely popular with thieves and nobles alike simply because it was a place with no rules, no class, and loads of entertainment. Oddly enough, it was the place to see and be seen in London, notorious as it was.

Marcus paused near the entry of the place and faced Agnes.

"On behalf of Peter and the young woman you and your father tried to ruin, your life of privilege ends here, my lady," he said. "This is where you shall serve your sentence."

Agnes' eyes widened in shock and horror. "What do you mean?" she said, looking around nervously. "Serve what sentence? What have I done?"

"You know what you have done. You needn't deny it."

Agnes' horror grew. Her gaze took on that same shifty appearance that her father's had when he realized he'd been cornered. Now, *she* was cornered. "But I do not understand," she said. "There… there was a betrothal…"

Marcus cut her off. "There was no betrothal between you and Peter."

She drew in a sharp breath as if greatly offended but, wisely, she didn't argue with him. "That is true, but it was implied that…"

"It was never implied."

Agnes sighed sharply and lowered her gaze. "We had hoped that there would be."

Marcus tried to feel some pity for her but couldn't seem to manage it. "I am sure you did, but what you ended up doing was ruining your chances and your life," he said. "As your father has come to realize, there can be no action without a reaction. If you thought that the House of de Lohr would not fight back against all of the hellish falsehoods you have been perpetuating, then you are sadly mistaken. Much like your father, your participation in all of this is going to cost you."

She lifted her gaze, warily. "What do you mean?"

Marcus pointed to The Pox. "Go inside and ask for a woman named Sloth," he said. "I spoke with her recently and have secured a position for you as a serving wench. You are going to work here, sleep here, and eat here from now until such time as a patron of this establishment decides to marry you and take you away. Before you think about returning to your cousin's townhome, know that he will not allow it. Neither you nor your father are welcome there any longer. And you cannot return to Astley Cross because that will soon be my property. You have nowhere to go but here, my lady."

Agnes' mouth was hanging open in shock by

the time he was finished. "I… I am to *work*?"

Marcus could hear the disgust in her voice. "Aye," he said. "*Work*. Consider it a very tame punishment for what you have done, Agnes. A lady who hoped to be the next Countess of Hereford, and mistakenly so, will now find herself working as a serving wench at the most disreputable tavern in town. A small price to pay for the havoc you have wrought."

Agnes could hardly believe it. Tears of hysteria were beginning to fill her eyes as she looked at her father. "You are allowing this to happen?" she screeched. "Father, help me!"

Walter looked away from his daughter. "I cannot even help myself at the moment," he muttered. "Do what you are told."

The tears spilled over and Agnes began to weep. "I cannot work," she sobbed. "I would not know how!"

Marcus was unmoved. "They will teach you," he said. "Go inside."

"I cannot!"

"Aye, you can."

She flared. "How can you be so cruel?"

The corner of Marcus' mouth twitched. "I am sure the girl you lied against is asking the same question of you," he said. "Now you know how she feels. Now you know how Peter feels, as well. Life *is* cruel, my lady. Now you must face some of it yourself."

Agnes looked at him as if he'd just said something horrifically outrageous, but it didn't stop her tears. She simply lowered her head and wept into her hand. Marcus eyed her for a moment before pointing a finger at The Pox.

"If you do not go in by yourself and ask for Sloth, I will escort you in personally," he said, his voice low and threatening. "If you fail to remain here and work as you are told, then I will make sure you spend the rest of your days in a vault, hidden from society, imprisoned for your crimes against Peter de Lohr. Therefore, you have a choice – work for your punishment or rot in a hole. What will your choice be?"

Agnes had stopped weeping, looking at him with disgust and fear as she realized she had no choice at all. The enormous, deadly warrior that was Marcus Burton had made that clear and as of this day, her life would change forever. Her sins had been found out.

But they weren't only her sins.

Her gaze moved to her father.

"Where are you taking my father?" she asked hoarsely.

Marcus' focus never left her face. "Your father is going to Scotland, where he will remain," he said. "And before you ask, you cannot go with him. The two of you together are like two asps.

Your venom is magnified by one another. Separated, you shall be ineffective. Now, say farewell to your father. It is time for him to go."

Agnes looked at her father, wanting to curse him for not helping her, wanting to shout at him for causing this mess to begin with. Certainly, she'd gone along with everything, but the campaign against Peter had been his idea. Well, *mostly* his idea.

An idea that had ruined them both.

Therefore, she felt nothing as she looked at him with nothing other than anger. No affection, no sense of loss. For the first time in her life, Agnes was seeing her father clearly – a little man in a big world. Without a word, she turned for The Pox, timidly opening the door and then pausing when she saw the common room. It was worse than she could have imagined.

Fighting back tears again, she went inside.

Agnes de Quincy, the young woman who wanted very badly to be the wife of Peter de Lohr and a rich, influential woman in her own right ended up working as a serving wench in a vile hovel of humanity known as The Pox. Not exactly what she'd hoped for herself, but given the circumstances, things could have been worse. It was punishment for her own ruthless ambition.

Marcus Burton showed her, in the end, what ruthless really was.

That left Walter, whom Marcus escorted to a rather nice-looking cog with a Scots captain and a Spanish crew. They took Walter on board and, at Marcus' suggestion, tied him up so that he could not escape. Marcus watched them secure the ropes and before he left, he fixed Walter in the eyes.

"Remember what I said," he said. "Stay in Scotland and you shall live. Return to England and you shall die."

Walter refused to look at him. He was beyond humiliated, laid open to the bone with grief and shame. His daughter was to be a common serving wench and he… well, he wasn't sure what he was going to be now. Exiled in Scotland was where his new life would begin.

Where it ended, he didn't know.

But he knew one thing – he'd be back.

"You had no right," he muttered. "No right to do any of this. The day will come, Burton, when you will regret this day."

Marcus's gaze lingered on him. "Probably not," he said. "You brought this on yourself, Walter. What you and your daughter received in punishment is far less than you deserved. Consider yourself fortunate that you escaped with your life."

Walter didn't reply. Marcus disembarked the cog, his last glimpse of Walter being of the man as he sat on the edge of the deck, ignoring everything and everyone around him. Marcus wondered briefly if it really would be the last time he saw Walter, for the man was just arrogant and ruthless enough to be stupid. He would view this entire event as a slight against him. Marcus had to admit he wouldn't be surprised if Walter returned to England someday.

In fact, he was willing to bet on it.

But that day never came.

Walter's ship, as it sailed north past Great Yarmouth, caught a rogue wave that ended up dumping the ship onto its side in a strong gale. Walter, as well as half the crew, went over the side and into the churning sea. Unfortunately for Walter, he was still bound and instead of swimming, he sank to the bottom of the sea. All of that vengeance for the House of de Lohr, for Burton, and even for Peter sank right along with him.

Perhaps justice was served, after all.

Cave sors, it was said. Beware of Fate.

Fate could be a harsh executioner, indeed.

CHAPTER NINETEEN

Three Days Later
St. Martin le Grand, London

"THIS IS MOST… unusual, my lord." A man in woolen robes, well-dressed, spoke calmly. "I've not had a request like this before, ever, that I can recall."

In the small church that belonged to the bishop of St. Martin le Grand near St. Paul's Cathedral, Christopher and Dustin were speaking with the Bishop of London, William of Sainte-Mère-Église. They had chosen this bishop for two very good reasons – Christopher had known William for many years and he was one of the men who had located King Richard when he'd been taken hostage on his journey home from The Levant. Secondly, and probably most importantly, he was the Clerk of the Exchequer, a position that oversaw the Jewish bankers and businesses in London.

He understood the people and the religion.

Haim had come with them to speak to the bishop because in Liora's intention to convert, Haim wanted to understand the process and he also wanted the bishop to know that his daughter had his permission. He had to admit that he was very curious about the church that was part of St. Martin le Grand's liberty, or district, something he'd walked past many times but had never been inside.

The church itself was part of the greater district of St. Martin le Grand, part of a college of secular canons that had a church attached to it dedicated to St. Martin. It was a little church, but important in London, which was also why Christopher had chosen it. He and Dustin had come along with Peter, Liora, Haim, Alexander, and Christin to discuss Liora's conversion and marriage to Peter.

But William the Bishop, or Wooley as his friends called him, didn't seem too certain.

"I understand this is unusual," Christopher agreed. "But these are unusual times and unusual circumstances. I further realize conversion into the Catholic Church is lengthy, and it is a process, but it is something we do not have time for. My son and his lady wish to marry because he is heading to Ludlow Castle imminently. We simply do not have time for the usual conversion process."

Wooley eyed Christopher with what some thought might be annoyance. There was certainly doubt there.

"I see," he said. "You must understand that there is a reason for the process, Chris. The person converting must be certain he, or she, is ready to accept the sacrament. It is not something we can simply hurry along because your son wants to take a wife."

Christopher sighed faintly, looking at his wife, who was about to go into pleading mode. Having met Liora two days earlier, along with Christin and the rest of the family, Dustin had very quickly come to like the beautiful young woman with the quick wit. She could see, quite easily, why Peter was so smitten and Christin positively adored the woman, all after only two days. Christin and Liora seemed to have a good deal in common and the same quick-witted humor besides the fact that they were the same age. Looking over Dustin's head, he could see that Christin was ready to go to battle for Liora, too.

It was going to be a struggle for him to keep control of the situation if the women got involved.

After that, William would be lucky if he survived it.

"Wooley, I understand it is your duty to uphold the integrity of the church, but look at who we are speaking of," he said, gesturing to Liora and her father, standing next to her. "You know Haim ben Thad. You know that he is a fair and just man, correct?"

By virtue of his clerkship, William did indeed known Haim. "Aye," he said. "He has always had a fair reputation. That is not in doubt."

Christopher gestured to Liora. "And his daughter has her father's character and sensibilities," he said. "She would like to convert to Christianity so that she and Peter can marry. She is a pious, gentle girl who would like to become a Christian to be with the man she loves. You can give the Rite of Reception and Acceptance into the church now so that they can be married. She can continue her education once they reach Ludlow and she will be baptized by the Bishop of Hereford at that time. Everything else she must do to be fully accepted can come after that."

William looked at him in exasperation. "It is so much more than that," he said. "There are rites and blessings and a period of Purification and Enlightenment. One does not simply walk into a church and declare they want to be baptized a Catholic and expect it to happen immediately."

"I am," Liora said, stepping away from her

father and from Peter, her pale gaze fixed on the bishop. "My lord, I realize this is most unusual and that we are asking a great deal, but you must understand something – I was born a Jew. I have been content in my religion. I do not disparage it in any way, but God brought Peter to me because I believe He knew I was needed somewhere other than where I was. At my parents' home, I was content to tend to my chores, to talk to my friends, and to worship at temple. But Peter came into my life and coming to know him, and love him, he has shown me a life I never knew to exist. It is a life where I am needed, by his side, because I firmly believe God has brought us together. He has brought me to this church today to ask you to help us begin that process. Will you help us?"

She was well-spoken and articulate, and Peter smiled proudly at her. But William was focused on her, on what she was requesting.

"Conversion is not a simple matter, my lady," he said politely. "It cannot be rushed. It takes time and consideration. There are a great many steps to take."

"And I am willing to take them all if you will simply do as Hereford has asked and give me the rites that will allow Peter and me to be married in the eyes of the church."

"You must be baptized before that can happen, my lady. I am sorry, but those are the rules."

"Then baptize me," she said, growing emotional and trying not to. "You see, three days ago, Peter saved my life and the life of my father. He risked himself with the king in order to save us. If that is not devotion and selflessness, the kind of actions that God Himself preaches, then I don't know what is. Now, he is being sent to the Marches because the king is moving against his own warlords. You know what that means, my lord. You understand that he will be in danger and I will not be by his side to help him and to tend to him if needed. Not only do I love him, but I owe him my very life. If I stand before you and swear to surrender the faith I was born into, will you baptize me and let us be married?"

By the time she was finished, she was starting to tear up. Peter went to stand next to her, putting his arm round her shoulders comfortingly, before looking at the bishop.

"Please, my lord," he begged softly. "We will do whatever you tell us to do, but please make it so that we may marry."

William was starting to weaken and he wasn't happy about it. Christopher could see that by the look on his face and he stepped in for one final blow to the man's resistance.

"I will sponsor her," he said. "You know my reputation and what I stand for. No man will question Liora's faith if I sponsor her. Wooley, we need your help. While in The Levant, I saw priests baptizing men who wished to convert and there was no Catechism or Religious rights. They said a blessing and baptized them, calling them converts. You know this to be true because, I believe, you were one of those converting those men."

William looked at Christopher with a look that suggested the man was utterly ridiculous, but utterly right. "You know I was there," he said, snappish. "You fended off an attack of some infidels and saved my life."

Christopher fought off a grin. "I know."

"Are you saying that I now must repay that debt?"

Christopher merely shrugged, but he was grinning and William knew he was licked. With a growl of frustration, he rolled his eyes.

"Very well," he said. "Since we are the only witnesses here, I will say that she renounced her faith and I will baptize her, but you must make sure she is religiously educated in every aspect. Do you understand me?"

As Christopher nodded, Dustin rushed towards the bishop. "I will see to it myself," she said. "I will make sure she is fully educated and knows everything she must know. But thank you… you cannot know what this means to our family."

He grunted. "I know what it means," he said. "It means that if the truth is made known, I will be in a good deal of trouble and your marriage will probably be declared invalid, so make sure no one knows we did this backwards. Peter gets his wife and I no longer owe your wily husband anything."

Christopher started laughing. "Not to worry," he said. "For all anyone will know, this was done the way it is supposed to be done."

William eyed Christopher with irritation before turning his full focus to Liora. Dressed in a mustard-yellow garment with a beautiful, embroidered belt around her hips and a green scarf around her head and shoulders, he stood in front of her, inspecting her for a moment. He could see why she had Peter so entranced, for there was nothing about her that was imperfect.

Aye, he understood perfectly.

"Take off the scarf," he told her.

Liora did, but she was uncomfortable doing that. She always wore a scarf for modesty, as dictated by her religion. William could see that she was a little uneasy and he understood why. He was a man who understood a great deal about not only his religion, but others. Forgetting his annoyance with the de Lohrs, he focused on bringing yet another convert into the religion he'd dedicated his life to.

"In the Christian world, maidens are usually signified by leaving their head bare," he said. "It is the married women who cover their heads. I know it is different for you, but if you wish to become Christian, then you must start to think like one. This is truly what you want, is it?"

Liora nodded firmly. "It is, my lord."

She didn't know enough to realize that priests weren't addressed in such a fashion, but William let it go. Her education would come soon enough about such things. He looked over at Haim, standing small a few feet away.

"And you?" he said. "Is this what you want for her?"

Haim's gaze moved to his eldest, his elegant daughter. He hadn't yet told Gideon that a knight had taken Liora away from him, but that would come. He knew he had quite a bit of explaining to do when people realized his daughter had left their religion in order to marry a knight. Such things were frowned upon, but Haim loved his daughter enough to want her to be happy.

He'd reconciled himself to such things.

"Someone told me once that although I could not live my child's life for her, I could still support her," he said. "My religion, like yours, dictates harshly at times. But the laws were dictated by men without children, I think. I can condemn my daughter or I can support her, and I do not think God would be disappointed in me if I support her. This is Liora's choice. She is choosing the man she loves and she is choosing to worship God in a different way. As she pointed out, Christians and Jews worship the same God. I do not think He will mind. I hope not, anyway."

William smiled faintly at the pragmatic, if not parental point of view. "It will not be easy on you," he said. "I know that the Jewish community can be… strict about such things."

Haim lifted his shoulders. "It does not make me any less Jewish that my daughter chose to worship God the way her husband will," he said. "God tested Abraham by asking him to sacrifice Isaac, and Abraham obeyed. He loved his God, he loved his child, but he was still willing to do what was asked of him even to the death of his own child. I suppose in my own way, I love my child enough to give her over to God to do with as He pleases. Mayhap she is right – mayhap God did bring Peter to her. If I do not let her marry him, how will we know the truth?"

William laughed softly. "That is a good way of putting it," he said. "God's will is a mysterious thing. Mayhap this is God's will for your daughter."

"Those are my thoughts also. Mayhap He has something great planned for them both."

Satisfied that the young woman's father had given his blessing, William returned his attention to Liora as she stood before him with her scarf around her shoulders.

"Come with me," he said.

Liora looked at Peter hesitantly, but Peter took her by the elbow and they followed William over to the elaborate baptismal font that was in an alcove near the altar. It was a stone font with a stone basin, carved with scenes from the Bible. Christopher, Dustin, Christin, Alexander, and Haim followed as well. William had Liora remove her scarf and hand it over to Dustin.

"Now, my lady," he said. "You are to receive the sacrament of baptism that will enable you to marry Peter before he goes to the Marches. But we must make sure your heart is ready to accept this blessing. Are you prepared?"

"Aye, my lord."

Peter leaned over her. "Call him 'your grace'," he murmured. When she looked at him questioningly, he smiled. "You can address him as 'your grace', not 'my lord'."

Properly corrected, Liora nodded quickly. "Forgive me," she said. "I am ready, your grace."

William fought off a grin at Peter already doing the husbandly thing by correcting her. "Do you relinquish your former faith in exchange for your new Christian faith?"

"I do, your grace."

"Do you renounce all sin?"

"I do, your grace."

"Do you promise to uphold God's holy ordinance, ensuring that your children shall be raised in the Christian faith?"

She hesitated. "Does that mean I can never speak of the Jewish faith to my children?"

William shook his head. "You may speak of it," he said. "You may even teach them if you wish. But they will be Christians. Is that clear?"

"It is, your grace."

He continued. "Do you swear that God, above all, shall be worshipped and honored in the tradition of the Catholic Church for as long as you live?"

"I swear, your grace."

"Very well," William said, motioning her forward over the baptismal font. "Lean your head over the basin, my lady."

Liora did as Peter held her thick braid back so it would not become wet. William put both hands into the basin of holy water and scooped up the liquid, pouring it over her head.

"Liora, child of God, I baptize you in the name of the Father, of the Son, and of the Holy Spirit," he said as he poured water over her again. "May you be welcome into the Christian faith."

He did it a third time, pouring the water over her head as he trickled it down her scalp and hair, and into her face before dripping back into the font.

"You may rise, my lady," William told her.

Liora lifted her head and Dustin handed her back the scarf so she could dry her face and hair with it. Liora grinned as she dabbed at the water, with Dustin coming up to hug her. Christin came up as well, embracing her, welcoming her, as Peter turned to his father.

"Papa," he whispered. "Do you think he will marry us now? We *are* already here. Would it be too much to ask?"

Christopher had his eyes on the priest. "We'd better ask him now while he still feels as if he owes me something," he muttered. Then, he addressed William. "Wooley, one more thing. Peter and Liora wish to be married right away. Will you perform the mass?"

William had been walking away, glad to be rid of the pushy earl and the clandestine thing he'd just done, but he came to a halt. "*Now?*"

"Now. I will pay you handsomely, of course."

Considering Hereford was very wealthy, William didn't resist. He was already into this situation deep, so what was one more out-of-the-ordinary request? With a sigh, he simply lifted his shoulders and motioned them back towards the altar.

"Very well," he said. "The bride has her father's permission and the groom has his parents' permission. Everyone is of age. I assume there is a dowry?"

Haim nodded as he came to stand behind his daughter, who was still drying her head and face. "One hundred marks of gold," he said. "I also have jewelry I have been saving for her, worth a great deal, as well as three fine horses and a multitude of household items her mother has collected for her. She comes well supplied."

It was quite a dowry and William nodded, impressed. "I believe she is," he said, but his focus remained on Haim. "Since you are unfamiliar with a Christian wedding ceremony, I would usually ask these questions at the door to the church before allowing everyone inside, but since we are already here, I will forego that part of the ceremony. Everyone on their knees, please."

Down they all went, onto their knees, including Peter and Liora, together at the front. Peter held Liora's hand as she knelt and continued to hold it even after he took a knee. William stood over them, looking down at the pair.

"Since this entire situation has been highly irregular and somewhat clandestine, this will not be a long ceremony," he said. "I will begin with a prayer, you will say your vows, and I will bless the union. I will also not speak them in Latin for the benefit of our Jewish guest who, I would imagine, will not understand. Are there any questions?"

Peter and Liora shook their heads. William continued.

"Let us pray for peace and happiness as ordained by God," he said.

"Lord, hear our prayer," was the response from everyone but Liora and Haim.

"Let us pray that Peter and Liora are always surrounded by God's love."

"Lord, hear our prayer."

"Let us pray for those in our lives who are sick and healing, may their road to recovery be blessed."

"Lord, hear our prayer."

William made the sign of the cross over the couple and turned to Liora. "Now, my lady," he said. "Do you promise to honor and obey Peter, forsaking all others from this day forward, until the end of all things?"

Liora looked at Peter, a lump in her throat as the impact of his words hit her. She'd been waiting for this moment her entire life, as a young girl looking forward to marriage, but never did she imagine she would take her vows with a man she loved more deeply by the moment. It was all so surreal.

"I will."

William looked at Peter. "And Peter, do you promise to honor and protect Liora, forsaking all others from this day forward until the end of all things?"

Peter was so swept up in Liora's warm gaze

that he almost forgot to answer. "Most emphatically, I will," he said.

William put his hands over their heads in a gesture of blessing. "Father, you have made the union of husband and wife so holy as it symbolizes the marriage of this man and this woman through Christ to God," he said. "Bless this union from this day forward. Amen."

He made the sign of the cross over them as Christopher, Dustin, Christin, Sherry, and Peter crossed themselves in response. Peter looked at his new wife, a smile spreading over his lips as he beheld her. Finally… *his* wife.

He could hardly believe it.

As he got to his feet, pulling Liora up with him, William went to him and kissed him on the cheek, a traditional kiss of peace from priest to groom, which Peter then passed on to Liora, as his bride.

It was a long, sweet kiss, full of the promise of a new future.

When Peter pulled back to look at Liora, she was laughing and weeping at the same time. The joy in her heart had exploded, coming from her mouth and eyes and body. She was happiness personified. Suddenly, Christopher and Dustin were there, hugging the happy couple as Christin and Alexander joined in. All of them, hugging and kissing, so very happy that the union had finally been made. It was a joyful day in the de Lohr clan, none so much exhibited by the couple themselves.

They were pure delight.

And then, there was Haim.

Peter saw him standing there, alone, as Christopher and Dustin monopolized Liora. Leaving his thrilled family to congratulate the bride, he made his way over to the old man.

Peter knew how much Haim had lost when Liora had become a Christian. Their family heritage, their culture, their roots in the religion had all been sacrificed for her happiness. But Peter wanted the man to know that it was not in vain.

"I know this was not a simple thing for you," he said. "You have sacrificed a great deal for your daughter's happiness. And mine. I want you to know that we are family now and I fully intend to keep my promise to you – we will make sure our children are educated in the Jewish tradition. They will understand their mother's heritage and they will respect and defend it because it is part of them. If, when they come of age, they decide to worship as Jew, I will not stop them. I want you to know that. But they will also understand the perils they may face as a result of that choice. It is not an easy thing being a Jew in a Christian England."

Haim smiled weakly. "Nay, it is not," he said. "But I thank you for your consideration and your compassion. I expect no less from you, Saint

Peter."

Peter laughed softly as Haim used Asa's name for Peter. "It is the truth," he said. "And I swear to you that I will do my best to make your daughter happy, always."

Haim patted his big arm. "That is a comfort," he said. But his expression took on a distant look. "I remember looking at Liora when she was born and something told me that she was meant for greatness. I did not know how, or what, but I am starting to see that mayhap it is through you that she will achieve that greatness. She will make a fine noblewoman and bear you strong, intelligent children. Mayhap that will be her greatest legacy, the wife of the eldest son of the Earl of Hereford and Worcester. Mayhap this is where she was meant to be all along."

"I hope so," Peter said sincerely. "When the troubles with the king are over and we return to a sense of normalcy, you must come to Ludlow and bring Asa. I have two younger brothers I want him to meet."

Haim shook his head. "I will keep Asa as far away from castles and knights as I can," he said. "He has a restless spirit. He wants to be like you. It is one thing for my daughter to become one of you, but it is entirely another for my son to become one. I will keep him close to me from now on."

Peter understood, sort of. "Then mayhap someday I will bring my wild brothers to you," he said. "Mayhap running with the Maccabees and Saul's Army will teach them something about a culture and religion other than their own. I would like them to grow up tolerant and thoughtful, as you are raising your son. A little understanding is a good thing, don't you think?"

Haim smiled broadly. "It is," he said. "It is, indeed."

"Will you at least come to Lonsdale and feast with us tonight? We will be leaving for the Marches tomorrow."

Haim's gaze drifted over to Liora, standing with her new family. He didn't think he'd ever seen her quite so happy. After a moment, he shook his head.

"Although I thank you for your invitation, I do not think so," he said. "This is Liora's new world, but I still have mine. I am happy with mine. But my home is your home, Peter. Remember that."

"I will."

With that, he turned and headed to the entry to the church. He was almost to the door when Liora saw him and called after him. As she ran over to her father, Peter went to stand with his family.

"Did you tell him to come to Lonsdale tonight?" Dustin asked. "I will have a feast fit for a newly married couple prepared. Surely he must come."

"I invited him," Peter said. "But he declined."

Dustin looked at him. "Why?"

Peter shrugged. "He said that this was Liora's world now, not his," he said. "He's an old man. He's not used to our vast halls and loud knights. He's a quiet, peaceful man."

As they watched, Liora hugged her father fiercely before the man shuffled out of the church. They could see her wiping at her eyes and Peter broke away from his family.

"I think my wife needs me," he said quietly. "I'll see you all back at Lonsdale."

As he hustled over to Liora, putting his arms around her when he reached her, Dustin and Christopher watched their son and his tender manner. It was clear how much devotion and adoration the pair had for one another.

Dustin sighed faintly.

"And now, Peter is married," she said, looking to her husband. "That makes two of our children with their own families now."

He grinned at her. "Eight more to go."

"Don't rush me."

"Papa, Olivia is just an infant," Christin reminded him. "It will be at least another eighteen years before she will marry."

"Her name is Charlotte," Christopher said.

"*Olivia*," Christin and Dustin said.

It was a running joke in the de Lohr family with the newborn because Christopher had wanted to name her Charlotte and Dustin had wanted to name her Olivia, so the best they could do now was call her by her full name, Olivia Charlotte, because when one name or the other was used, it caused an argument.

Like it did now.

Rolling her eyes, Dustin took Christin by the arm and headed out of the church, leaving Christopher and Alexander to follow. There was much to do on the horizon and little time to do it. With a newlywed couple and an army that was preparing to head back to the Marches, delayed by Peter and Liora's crisis, there was no longer anything blockading future plans.

The House of de Lohr had a job to do and nothing would get in the way.

David, Marcus, and the rest of the warlords had already departed London. They were on the move, preparing to engage John's army, and Christopher's army was preparing to do the same. Most other warlords were also pulling their armies out of London, knowing that they were needed more desperately in parts of England where the mercenaries were running free. Reports from the north had them overrunning many properties and killing many people. Rochester was under siege and early reports had mentioned that Canterbury was in more danger than originally believed. David had taken a thousand of his brother's men and was rushing home as fast as he could move them.

All of it taking place as Peter and Liora found a brief moment of solace to begin their lives together. For this evening, that was all Christopher and his family would care about.

It was what they would celebrate in a world going up in flames.

Lady Liora de Lohr rode behind her husband all the way back to Lonsdale where the celebration of their marriage went on all night.

CHAPTER TWENTY

Ludlow Castle
March 1216

T HE SUN WAS just starting to peek in between the gaps in the oil cloth, one hitting Peter directly in the eyes. Groaning, he rolled over and nearly smashed into his wife, who was curled up at his back. She grunted as his weight came down on her and he pushed himself off, but then thought better of it.

He rather liked being on top of her.

He began nibbling on her earlobe.

"Peter," she groaned, still half-asleep. "You know what that does to me."

He grinned as he began kissing her neck. "I know exactly what it does to you," he whispered. "It does the same thing to me."

She was in a shift but his hands snaked underneath it, pulling it up to her waist, unable to go any further because she was still groggy and he couldn't get it over her head.

Yet.

He propped himself up, awkwardly, and lifted her up so that he could get it over her head, but her elbow caught him in the nose and down he went, falling back on the bed with his hands over his face.

Liora gasped.

"Did I hurt you?" she asked, more alert now as she tried to pull his hands away to get a look at the damage. "Let me see what I've done."

He was grunting and groaning, only it was rhythmic in nature. It took Liora a moment to realize that he was laughing and she peeled his hands away from his face.

"You fool," she said, annoyed. "You use trickery and sympathy to get your way!"

Peter let her pull his hands away but it was a ruse. As soon as his hands were free, he grabbed her and pulled her down on top of him. As she gasped, he rolled onto his side and effectively trapped her between his big body and the bed. His face was very close to hers as he spoke.

"Of course I use trickery and sympathy," he said, kissing her cheeks as he pinned her wrists. "I returned last night from being away from you for almost two months, so I will use any trick I can to get you into my arms."

Liora had stopped fighting him. With a smile, she removed her shift and wrapped her arms around his neck. "As if you need to," she said. "I was in your arms for most of last night. I do not think we've had more than just an hour or two of sleep, which is less than your pregnant wife requires, but I do it gladly. Words cannot express how much I have missed you, my angel. I am so glad you have returned."

He grinned, putting his hand between them, onto her gently rounded belly. "What a joyful surprise I came home to," he said. "But I am disappointed that my father had to tell me first in the missive he sent me. How is it he knew about it before I did?"

Liora laughed softly. "Because he has been with me constantly," she said. "Either your mother and sister are here at Ludlow, or he is. And, to be clear, your mother knew first. She is the one who told your father."

He pressed his lips flat in an irritable display. "*You* could have at least sent me a missive about it."

Liora reached up, stroking his face. "I wanted to tell you personally," she murmured, kissing his lips softly. "I wanted to see your face when I told you that your son would be coming in the autumn."

He closed his eyes as she kissed his chin. "And what did I look like when you told me?"

"If you recall, we had to throw water on you to revive you."

He started laughing but she latched on to his mouth and, in an instant, he responded. Liora gave herself over to him completely because a kiss between them was the most powerful of things. It rarely ended at just a kiss. Soon, his tongue was in her mouth, gently lapping at her, tasting her. He was being so very tender with her, making her heart flutter to the point where she couldn't catch her breath. There was nothing else in the world more important than her husband's lips on hers, his arms around her holding her close.

Nothing else mattered.

For Peter, it was more than that. He'd just spent two months of hell doing battle against John's mercenary army and thoughts of Liora had kept him alive. When he'd come home yesterday after being summoned home by his father from the de Lohr army's position in Leicester, he'd taken her to bed with him and they were still here, still enfolded in the warm, rich miasma that was their love. She had the ability to arouse him like nothing else and as he finally settled between her legs and gently thrust into her, he could feel her soft breasts against his bare chest, taunting him.

Calling to him.

He thrust harder, trying to be careful about her blossoming belly. The last thing he wanted to do was injure the child she carried, so it had taken some practice for him to find the right position where his weight wasn't smashing her. Her legs were wrapped around his hips, holding him fast to her, but he unwrapped them and raised himself up, holding her legs behind the knees to give him more freedom of movement as he continued to pound into her sweet and yielding body.

This way, he could watch her as he made love to her.

Liora had the most amazing body. Her full breasts were perky, the nipples peaked, and her waist still slender. The rounded hips and slightly rounded belly drew his lust, seeing the result of what he'd put into her.

His son.

He could still hardly believe it.

However, given that he'd had her abed every night since their marriage before he left Ludlow and headed out to join his father's army, it wasn't too surprising. He couldn't get enough of his new wife. Even now, Liora reached up and pulled him down to her, her lips fixing to his. She kissed him fiercely as he braced his arms on either side of her, thrusting hard until he could feel her release around him. Then, and only then, did he join her.

Beneath him, Liora was limp with pleasure but still sensitive to the touch. Peter continued to move in her, touching her, fondling her, and she gasped and twitched until she finally grasped his roving hand and kissed his fingers.

"No more," she whispered. "I've not recovered from the last four times yet."

He grinned wolfishly. "I hope not," he said, nuzzling her right breast because it was by his head. "I intend that you should not recover from my touch, ever."

As Liora lay there, he started sucking her nipple gently and she could feel her loins start to tighten again. "Peter, please," she begged softly, trying to cover her breast with a hand so he couldn't stimulate her further. "Your family is coming this morning to greet you and I do not want to be unprepared. We will have all the time in the world tonight, my angel, but right now, I have many duties to attend to."

He came to a halt, sighing heavily. "I know," he said. "I am sorry. I have simply missed you so."

Liora smiled at him, cupping his face. "And I have missed you desperately," she said. "But I also do not want your family to find us still in bed when they arrive."

With that, she kissed him, slapped his bare arse, and climbed out of bed, leaving him lying on the bed with a semi-erection as he watched her gorgeous, nubile form collect her shift.

"*I* do not care if they still find us in bed," he declared.

She threw a tunic at him, landing on his head.

"Purim will be here soon," she said, changing the subject so he could focus on less sex and more getting out of bed. "Next week, in fact. I have invited your family to celebrate with us."

Clearly, she wasn't interested in spending any more time with him in bed at the moment. Disappointed, he pulled the tunic off his head and sat up.

"What's Purim again?" he asked, scratching his scalp.

"It's an event that celebrates the release of Jewish people from a tyrant in Persia," she said. "We celebrate it in London with great feasts and a festival, but we will not have a festival here. However, I do want to have a feast and I will invite all of the villagers to join us."

He looked at her, frowning. "We are feeding the entire town?"

She nodded as she washed her face in a bowl of cold rosewater. "Aye," she said. "That is tradition. To celebrate Purim, we are to donate to the poor, or feed them, or any number of charitable things. Purim is about blessings and celebration. I would like to invite all of the villagers to a feast."

He watched her as she washed. "Sweetheart, while that is very noble and kind, we cannot tell them that we are celebrating a Jewish holiday," he said. "It will only confuse them and, quite possibly, alienate them. Not everyone is as accepting of your traditions as we are. But I know you mean well."

She dried off her face. "Then we do not tell them it is for Purim," she said. "We can simply say it is a feast for the coming Easter. The resurrection of Jesus."

"I know what Easter is. I'm not that much of a heathen."

She grinned at his reply, drying off her hands. "It is important to me to keep with my traditions, even if we cannot tell people what they really are. Please?"

He lifted a hand, indicating surrender, as he climbed out of bed. "I know," he said. "And I will not deny you, you know that. Have your feast, but just do not tell them what it is for. Some Christians fear what they do not understand and I do not need trouble from my vassals."

"I understand," she said, putting the towel aside. "Thank you, my angel. You are very understanding."

He simply nodded, kissing her on the forehead as he went in search of his breeches. Meanwhile, Liora dressed in a simple blue garment that clung to her figure and as Peter pulled on his clothing, he had to take a second look at his wife. He'd only seen her briefly last night, clothed, but now he got a good look at her in the morning light. She'd always had an astonishing figure of full breasts and a tiny waist, but now with the pregnancy, her breasts had filled in and her hips and belly had become more rounded, but her waist essentially remained the same.

She looked a goddess.

"God's bones," he muttered. "You grow more beautiful by the day, Lady de Lohr."

Liora looked at him, smiling shyly, as she brushed her hair and began to braid it. "I have missed your sweet words," she said. "They make me feel much better about the changes I have had."

"What changes?"

She pointed out the obvious, her breasts and belly. "You should be glad you were not here when I first realized I was pregnant," she said. "Everything hurt to the touch."

He pulled his tunic over his head. "I remember my mother becoming ill when she was carrying my siblings," he said. "Have you felt well enough?"

Liora nodded. "Very well," she said. "But everything is still a little sore."

He pursed his lips regretfully. "And I've done

nothing but poke, stroke, pinch, and nibble," he said. "I am sorry. You should have told me."

She laughed softly and wrapped her braid around the back of her head, using big iron pins to secure it.

"I wanted you to touch me," she said. "You did not hurt me, I promise."

He secured a belt around his waist and came up behind her, wrapping his arms around her from behind and kissing the side of her head. "You will tell me if I do," he said softly. "Swear this to me."

She was trying to finish her hair as Peter cuddled her, so she finally gave up and gave in to his sweet embrace.

"I swear," she said. "Do not worry so. I will not break."

He grinned, kissed her one last time, and let her go. "I must check on the men I've brought back with me," he said. "Is there anything you need before I go?"

Liora put in the last pin and turned to him. "I do not need anything, but…"

"But what?"

"I was thinking," she said. "You did not speak of the battles you saw when you came home last night. In fact, you've not spoke of it at all. I am afraid to ask you how the situation goes."

Peter paused with his hand on the door latch.

"It's not good," he said, his mood sober. "I do not want to bring that hell into this chamber, Lee-Lee. That's why I have not spoken of it. I will speak of it in the hall, or anywhere else, but not here. Here – this is our heaven. It's the one place I do not want talk of battle to penetrate."

She smiled sadly at him. "I understand," she said. "Forgive me for asking. You can speak of it when you are ready. I suppose I was asking because Christin said that Sherry is no longer with the army."

Peter shook his head. "Nay," he said. "Addax is in command right now, with the army outside of Leicester. The Marshal summoned Sherry about a month ago and my father summoned me home last week, so here we are while the army is still out there, waiting."

"Do you think Sherry will come home soon?"

"I hope so, for Christin's sake."

"Me, too."

He smiled at her, giving her a wink before lifting the latch and quitting the chamber. They were in the top floor chamber of a block of buildings built by Gilbert de Lacy, a previous owner, built around the gatehouse and the keep. The floors were relatively new, the walls new, and it didn't have that musty smell that so many older stone buildings had. He headed down the stairs, which were mural stairs and not built into the thickness of the wall. Ludlow was a massive place with a good deal of living quarters, rooms, even smaller halls and one enormous great hall, most definitely fit for a de Lohr. But Peter had only been allowed to enjoy them for a short amount of time before his father requested that he join Alexander and Addax out in the field where he was badly needed.

That meant they had to bring another knight in to command Ludlow in his stead and although his father split his time between Lioncross, Ludlow, and Wigmore to the east, it was still important to have a capable knight commanding Ludlow when Christopher was away. That had required a missive to Kenilworth Castle, who was more than happy to send a newly minted knight to their doorstep in the form of Quintus de Garr.

De Garr was from a fine Hampshire family, related to the House of de Nerra, and Peter took to him right away. He was as strong as a bull, very smart, and very capable thanks to his training. He was also deaf in one ear and looked like the hind end of a dog, which pleased Peter to no end considering he had to leave the man in charge of his new wife. He didn't want an Adonis around Liora, so Quintus was accepted purely based on his skills, and on his appearance, and he swore fealty to Peter without hesitation. Peter had been able to work with him for a few weeks before he headed off to join Alexander and Addax, but according to Christopher, Quintus had been remarkable in command of Ludlow.

Now, Peter wanted to speak to his commander so the man could bring him up to date on everything that had happened while he was gone. As he exited the block of apartments, squinting in the bright early morning sun, he could see Quintus at the gatehouse. When the man spied him, he began running in his direction.

"My lord," he called. "Did you sleep well?"

Considering he had just returned to his new wife after a long separation, Peter cast him a long look but realized Quintus had no idea why he was eyeing him so queerly, so he simply nodded his head.

"Well enough," he said. "I am sorry we did not have time to speak last night. You can understand that I was anxious to see my wife rather than speak to you."

Quintus nodded. "Indeed, my lord," he said. "No apologies necessary. I will say that your wife has done me a very great favor while you were gone."

"Oh? What is that?"

"She has introduced me to a woman I am also anxious to see rather than speak to you, too."

Peter looked at him abruptly and started laughing when he realized that Quintus had, indeed, understood the subtleties of a man returning from battle to a new wife. "Cheeky bastard," he muttered. "But I am glad for you, Quintus. Who is this flowering bloom of womanhood?"

Quintus grinned, displaying reasonably nice teeth beneath a heavy mustache and beard. "A daughter of the lord of Rhayder Castle," he said. "Her name is Livia de Gault and her father is an ally of Lord Blackadder, Ajax de Velt."

Peter recognized the name. "Ah, I remember," he said. "They are allies to the west."

"Exactly, my lord."

"How did you come to meet her, though? Did you see her in the village?"

Quintus shook his head. "Nay, my lord," he said. "Your wife has been inviting local allies to come to Ludlow and feast with her and your father so that they will come to know her and she, them. May I praise Lady de Lohr's grace and charm without angering you, my lord?"

Peter shrugged. "Why would it anger me?" he said. "Everything you say is true. Why do you think I married her?"

Quintus laughed softly. "Perfectly understandable, my lord," he said. "She lives for the mere mention of your name. I, too, hope to have a wife someday who worships me the way your lady wife worships you. I have tried to tell Lady Livia that."

Peter scowled. "Do not tell her that before you marry her, you dolt," he said. "What is wrong with you? Are you trying to scare her off?"

Quintus looked stricken but Peter started to laugh simply because the man truly had no idea what he was saying. He was about to educate Quintus when a cry came from the battlements.

Riders were approaching.

Since Peter knew his father was due to arrive, he headed for the gatehouse with Quintus, preparing to welcome his father to Ludlow. He was excited to see the man he hadn't seen in months, so he stood at the raised portcullis, watching the riders approach, but as he watched, the smile faded from his face.

His father wasn't alone.

Peter stood back as the riders flooded into his bailey. He recognized the men, the horses, the standards, and he most especially recognized William Marshal.

Puzzlement filled him.

So did concern.

His father was the first man to dismount as soldiers rushed forward to collect the warhorses that were frothing from the twenty-mile ride from Lioncross Abbey. He was dressed in full battle regalia, something Peter had seen on his father a thousand times. He approached his father, who opened up his arms to him and hugged him tightly. He didn't let him go. He just stood there and held him as others dismounted their horses and approached, including The Marshal. Peter had no idea why his father was holding on to him for so long but when he finally released him, Peter swore he saw tears in the man's eyes.

He peered at him closely.

"Papa?" he asked, somewhat gently. "What is the matter? I'm safe. Everyone is safe. I came home at your summons so that you can see I am safe."

Christopher took a deep breath, pulling off his helm to reveal his graying blond hair. It was starting to turn white at the temples and crown.

"Not everyone is safe," he said, his voice hoarse with emotion.

Peter was seized with apprehension. "What do you mean?" he said. "What has happened? Oh, dear God, don't tell me something has happened to Sherry."

"Nay," The Marshal said, answering because Christopher was so emotional. "Sherry is well enough. I summoned him away from the de Lohr army for a special purpose and he will be here any day now, but I am certain he is well. Have no fear. Let us go into your great hall, Peter. We must speak."

Peter nodded and started to move, but he was

bewildered. He took his father by the arm, leading the man towards the great hall and sending Quintus to tell Liora that great men had arrived. As Quintus bolted off, Peter looked to his father.

"What is wrong?" he asked quietly. "You're frightening me, Papa. Is Uncle David well?"

Christopher nodded, but he was still close to tears. "Everyone in the family is well," he said. "Your uncle, Sherry, East Anglia, Dash… everyone. But we have received word about a major battle at Berwick Castle."

Peter came to a halt, the color draining out of his face when he thought he knew what his father meant. "Berwick," he breathed. "John's armies were there in January."

"I know."

"Please don't tell me that something happened to Cole de Velt."

Christopher shook his head. "Worse than even that," he said, his voice scratchy. "Jax has fallen."

Peter's eyes few open wide and his jaw dropped. "Nay," he breathed in shock. "Not Jax. Not him. Oh, God, Papa… *not him!*"

"Peter, inside," The Marshal instructed quietly but firmly. "Inside and we will discuss all of this."

Numbly, Peter did as he was told. He led his father to the hall and with Christopher heading for the feasting table, he finally took a look at the men who had come with him. He saw Maxton, who was not only his father's ally, but a close neighbor on the Marches. He also saw two men he hadn't seen in over a year in Kress de Rhydian and Achilles de Dere. Those were the original Executioner Knights, men who, along with Maxton, formed one of the core units within the Executioner Knights known as the Unholy Trinity. Peter hadn't even noticed them as they'd ridden in with his father and The Marshal.

That told him that the situation was dire, indeed.

The great hall of Ludlow was a sight to behold. It could easily hold a thousand men and it had, at times, all of them crammed in and sheltered against the elements that were so often terrible on the Welsh Marches. With his father and The Marshal already inside, Peter hung back to greet Kress and Achilles. Kress, a big man with cropped blond hair, greeted Peter fondly and Achilles, high-strung and passionate, greeted him with a hug that nearly cracked his ribs. Rubbing his chest, Peter couldn't help but grin at Maxton when the man patted him on the head.

When Peter reached the table, his father was already into the wine that had been brought. Over near the servant's alcove that led to the kitchens, he could see his wife as she visually inspected the hall to see who, exactly, had arrived. When she saw her father-in-law, and The Marshal, she disappeared again, no doubt making sure that special refreshments were prepared. As Christopher settled down, Peter took a seat at the table beside him.

He couldn't stand the suspense.

"*What* happened to de Velt?" Peter asked, looking around to anyone who could answer him. "I simply cannot believe... God, I cannot even believe I am saying it. It does not seem real."

It was a sentiment shared by everyone and The Marshal replied. "John was in the north in January, but he is heading south again, which is why you were called to meet him with your father's army," he said, looking older and wearier than Peter had remembered. "What happened to Ajax de Velt happened in January. De Velt and his army, along with de Longley and de Bourne, held their section of the border so John and his mercenaries had to make a great detour to cross into Scotland. John did not take kindly to that and lay siege to Berwick Castle, hoping to gain control of it."

"Berwick held?" Peter asked.

The Marshal nodded. "It did," he said. "Cole de Velt and his brother, Julian, held it admirably, but the trouble that Jax ran into was at Pelinom, his seat. From what I have been told, John's army hit it full force, hoping to capture it and use it as a base, but Jax held firm. He met his end when he was pulling injured men out of the range of the archers and was hit himself."

Peter closed his eyes at the mere idea of it, stricken with horror. "God," he grunted. "Please tell me his end was swift."

The Marshal sighed heavily. Moments like this were the worst part of what he did. But things like this happened; it had happened before and it would happen again. It never became easier, however.

This one cut him to the bone.

"He evidently kept pulling the injured out of range, even with two arrows in his back," he said. "He only stopped when his wife forced him to. He stumbled inside and died in her arms. As you can imagine, his family is devastated, as are his allies. As am I. It is a great loss to say the least."

Peter looked at his father, who was sitting there with red-rimmed eyes, struggling to come to terms with the death of a man he was close to. It also brought about the fact that Jax's youngest son, Cassian, had served at Lioncross Abbey for many years. Cassian had been Christopher's right hand at Lioncross with all of the other knights in strategic posts, which had been a great comfort to Peter. Cassian, young as he was, was extremely talented and he was devoted to both his father and to Christopher.

All Peter could feel at the moment was hollow grief for the young knight who had lost his father.

"How is Cass?" Peter asked his father gently.

"Devastated," Christopher said. "He is heading home as we speak. I will go, also, when things are settled here. I must go to Pelinom's chapel and pay my respects to my friend personally. He would have done the same for me."

Peter sighed heavily, thinking of the de Velt family, not unlike his own. A powerful warlord father, a dedicated mother... it could so easily have been his own father. It was shocking to think of their world without Ajax de Velt in it and he could hear the pain of loss in his father's tone. He could see it in The Marshal's face. It occurred to him that it was hitting the older men much harder than men like himself or even Maxton or Kress or Achilles.

They were all younger knights who hadn't shared the relationship with de Velt like those men had. Christopher and Jax had been tight along with Cullen de Nerra's father, Valor, and the Earl of East Anglia, Talus. These were men who had fought together in the before time, when Henry II was upon the throne, and they had a history together.

Now, part of that history was gone. Pieces of that time were disappearing, leaving a hole in their wake, leaving men like Christopher and William growing older as the world they knew dwindled around them.

Reaching out, Peter grasped his father's hand and held it tightly.

"It seems ironic that a man like Jax de Velt should be killed saving men," he said after a moment. "For years, he was The Dark Lord, the man who killed without thought or feeling. There was no man more feared in all of England. But I must say, as I reflect upon the man who was a legend in my eyes, I feel that he met his end in the most noble way possible. Saving lives and not taking them. He died a glorious death in battle. For an old warrior, I would think that is the best possible end."

Christopher nodded dully. "He went the way I would want to go, the way I hope I go," he said. "In the arms of my wife."

The Marshal grunted. "They said that Kellington held him until the end and even longer still," he muttered. "She never shed a tear until he was gone."

It was a beautiful, tragic, and brave suggestion. "Kellington is a great lady," Christopher said. "She is very strong."

"She is."

As Peter watched the older knights struggle, something occurred to him, perhaps something that would give them some comfort.

Something that had happened, back at Lonsdale.

"I am reminded of the last thing I said to him back at Lonsdale," he said. "Remember when I spoke of Boone Pendleton's prayer? When facing battle, you always know there is a chance you will not return, but the fact that I remembered the warrior's prayer at that particular time seems quite meaningful."

Christopher looked at him. "What do you mean?"

"I mean that we've gone into battle before and we've never said it," he said. "We've joined allies in battle before, but we never said it. Yet, at that moment at Lonsdale, we spoke the words. We spoke them while Jax was still alive so that he could say them with us, but mayhap we should say them again now in his memory. Somehow, it seems appropriate."

Christopher had tears in his eyes, nodding but unable to speak for the lump in his throat. It was Maxton who started it.

"Behold, I see those I love, and my relatives who have died before me," he said. "I see my father seated in the golden halls with an empty seat beside him."

Kress and Achilles and Peter chimed in. "I see the greatest warriors who have ever lived, surrounding my father, calling to me," they said.

"Death is not the end, but the beginning, for a true warrior never dies. He takes his place of greatness among those who are worthy."

By this time, Christopher found his voice and he lifted his head, speaking to the ceiling of the hall and the sky beyond. "Mourn not the glorious dead but rejoice in their legacy," he said, his strong voice joining in with the others in the hope that Jax, wherever he was, would hear him. "They wait for me, not in this life, but in the next, where their legends shall live forever."

Peter watched his father as the man said his farewells to his friend, tears rolling down his cheeks, but fortified with that prayer that had meant so much to them. When his father finally looked at him, he smiled at the man, putting his arm around his neck and hugging him. Christopher smiled weakly, patting his son on the arm, appreciating the moment they were sharing. A moment between warriors, rejoicing in the life of one of their own.

One who was now gone.

But there was a reason why they had all come, more than simply to tell Peter that Jax had fallen in battle. He could see that simply by the expressions on their faces.

There *was* a purpose.

"Now," Peter said after a moment. "Let us focus on the reason you are here at Ludlow.

Although I am greatly saddened at de Velt's passing, I know that is not the reason you have come and it occurs to me that I have been called home for a purpose. Am I right, Papa?"

Christopher nodded slowly. "You are."

"You want something of me, I assume?"

The Marshal held up a hand. "Aye," he said wearily. "The Executioner Knights are to attend to their most important mission yet and you are to be part of it."

"I am listening," Peter said.

William collected his thoughts before continuing. "Sherry is due to arrive here very soon, as I said, because I recalled him for a special purpose," he said. "You will notice that I have only called upon Maxton, Kress, Achilles, you, and Sherry for this particular mission because this is a job for my very best."

Peter nodded seriously. "Go on."

The Marshal glanced at Christopher before answering. "I needed your father's approval before I could do this, Peter," he said. "I must use you. I believe you are the only one who can help us accomplish this task as I told your father once before. You are going to be our Trojan horse in the court of John."

Peter's brow furrowed. "Trojan horse?" he repeated, thinking on the term that he'd heard before, something he remembered from his past education. "You mean the horse that the Greeks built? The one that held an army that deceived Troy?"

"Exactly."

He still wasn't clear on how that related to him. "What will you have me do, my lord?

"Kill the king."

The statement came from Christopher, not The Marshal. Peter looked at his father in shock.

"Kill *John*?" he repeated to make sure he had heard correctly. "What do you mean? How?"

The Marshal poured himself more wine into a cup he'd already drained once. "You will remember last year when John wanted you as his new Lord of the Shadows."

"Of course I do."

The Marshal looked at him. "You are now going to assume that post," he said. "You are going to go to John and tell him that your father humiliated you into going back on a bargain. Remember that I was there, Peter. I saw every-thing. I was there when your father offered to lay down his sword in exchange for your freedom. That was not what I wanted at the time, but none of that matters now. You are going to return to John and tell him that your father made you do it and you feel strongly that you must keep your word. Get close to the man. We need you there for what we are about to do."

Peter was quite perplexed. "But… in all of my years as an Executioner Knight, it was our mission to keep the king alive," he said. "We fought, we killed, we lied and cheated and bargained to keep him alive and now we must eliminate him?"

As The Marshal nodded, Christopher turned to his son. "We have come to the unalterable conclusion that England will never know peace as long as John is alive," he said. "We made a deal with the French king to aid us in our fight against John, but that has only brought French soldiers and mercenaries to overrun our lands. We know now that Louis is not the answer, but John's son is."

Peter's eyes widened. "Henry? But he is only nine years of age!"

"And I shall be his regent," The Marshal said steadily. "I have positioned myself with the king that he has appointed me his son's regent in the event of his death. John and I enjoy a good relationship these days. In fact, right now he believes I am at Pembroke, recruiting more men from the Welsh to fight for him, but instead I am with you and your father, plotting his end. I have served four kings, Peter, if you include Henry the Young King. I have seen John grow into the man he is today and it is true that I have fought to keep him on the throne, but the past year has seen my support drastically reduced. A nine-year-old king would be far better than what we have now. At least we would have a chance to survive."

Peter's gaze moved to his father, staring into his cup of wine. "Papa?" he said. "What say you about this?"

Christopher's head came up. "I have hated John since I first met him when I was nearly twenty years of age and he was barely ten," he said. "I have hated him every moment of every day since. I was content to fight against him and defeat him honorably on the field of battle, but hearing of Jax's death has brought me back to a promise I made to him back at Lonsdale. I swore to avenge his death and avenge I shall, but the most painful realization of that vow is that in order to do that, I must place my own flesh and blood in danger to accomplish it. *You*, Peter. If you agree to assume the post of Lord of the Shadows in Sean's place, I will not stop you."

Peter was listening to his father carefully. "Are you asking me to do it?"

Christopher shook his head. "Nay," he said quietly. "You are my son and if I had to choose between your life and vengeance for Jax, I would choose you. But if you wish to accept The Marshal's directive, I will not stop you."

Peter could see how badly his father was hurting, how much he was torn. He didn't like seeing his father so hurt. He didn't like the thought of leaving his wife and heading, literally, into purgatory. He didn't like the thought of any of those things, but he liked even less that if he did nothing, John would continue his reign of terror and his own son would be born into such a world.

He was going to be a father.

For a moment, he pondered a boy with his blond hair and his mother's magnificent eyes. A brilliant lad that he would protect to the death. Avenging Jax was important; there was no doubt about it. His death seemed to be a catalyst for something greater than all of them, the realization that their country needed peaceful rule and thoughtful direction if it was going to survive. And Peter needed to be able to raise his son in peace, not spending weeks or months on the field of battle against a king intent on tearing his own country apart.

Perhaps Peter couldn't do real damage to John on the battlefield.

But he could do it where it counted, as Sean de Lara had.

By John's side.

"I'll do it," he finally said, looking at The Marshal. "Tell me what you want me to do and I shall do it."

A sigh of relief seemed to go up from everyone. They looked at each other, nodding, showing hope in what was coming and what needed to be done.

Their mission was coming together admirably.

"We'll be with you every step of the way, Peter," Kress said. Much like Alexander, he was a leader of men with a natural air of command, and his words brought courage. "Achilles and Maxton and I will defect to John's guard. We were part of his guard once before and we saved his life from assassins years ago, so he will remember that. For all he knows, we've been out of touch with The Marshal. He has no reason to believe differently."

Peter listened carefully. Maxton, Kress, and Achilles were some of the best spies in the business and he trusted them implicitly. "Then you will be close to me," he said.

"Exactly," Maxton said. "Even now, Cullen de Nerra and Bric MacRohan are infiltrating John's inner circle as gifts from their respective lords. You know that Bric is a legacy knight with de Winter and even though de Winter has sided with the king in this matter, secretly, he supports the rebellion, so he has gifted the king with Bric. For an Irishman who hates the monarchy, I can only imagine how Bric is handling this."

That brought some smiles at the thought of Bric, a man who was utterly terrifying with his pale blond hair and blue-silver eyes. He looked like a warrior-god from Irish mythology and he hated John with a passion. But they needed him, and Cullen, as part of their spy ring close to the king. All of them forming a support system for Peter, who would be the closest.

Peter understood that clearly.

"So this plan has been in the works for some time?" he asked.

The Marshal nodded. "Since late last year," he said. "But after what happened to de Velt, we decided to rush forward with our schedule. I'll not let John kill one more man valuable to England. Jax was too much of a sacrifice in my opinion, but his death will not be in vain, I swear it."

Surprisingly passionate words from a man who was usually steady and even in temperament. But it was clear that Jax's death had done something to him.

It had done something to them all.

"Then what is the plan, my lord?" Peter said. "Surely you have something in mind?"

The Marshal nodded. "Indeed," he said. "As we speak, John is heading from St. Albans to Windsor Castle, which is being besieged by the French. You and I will join him at Windsor where you will join his ranks with my recommendation. He is possibly going to Cambridge and Lincolnshire after that, but it's equally possible he will be moving to his allies at Newark because he has spoken of going there and replenishing his armies.

He cannot go to London, as it is currently being held by the French king, so it's my personal belief he will go to Newark instead of Lincolnshire."

"And I will go with him."

"Aye," The Marshal said. "You will be his right hand, Peter, just as Sean was. His wish is your command. Now, John's death must be made to look like an accident, so your fellow Executioner Knights will poison the man's wine. Not his food, but his wine. John is always fearful that his food will be tampered with, but he never makes mention of his wine. You will ensure the wine brought to him is switched out with the wine Maxton or the others will bring you. Do you want to know why I recalled Sherry? Because he is tasked with finding the right poison. He has been in Bath, collecting a terrible toxin made from the smelting of copper and lead. This poison will build in John's system until it finally kills him. Nothing sudden, nothing rushed. One day, the king will simply turn up… dead."

Peter understood. It was subversion of the greatest magnitude and instead of being hesitant or discouraged, he was honored to be part of it.

"Very well," he said. "When do we move?"

"As soon as Sherry arrives," The Marshal said. "In the meantime, we will wait and we will feast and we will plan. But as soon as Sherry arrives, we will head to Windsor."

So that was it. A terrible plan was in the works, but it was a necessary one. Peter was thinking about what lay ahead as his wife entered the hall followed by several servants. They were heading to the table with bread and cheese and warmed-over beef from the night before, placing it on the table so the men could get to it. Peter reached out and grasped Liora's hand, bringing it to his lips for a sweet kiss.

"It would seem that my lady wife has run Ludlow in my absence better than any battle commander," he said proudly, obviously changing the subject away from what they had been discussing. "My lady, you've not yet met some of the men at this table. You know Maxton and Pembroke, of course, but permit me to introduce you to two good friends of mine, Kress de Rhydian and Achilles de Dere. Good knights, my wife, Liora."

Oblivious to the subversion she had just interrupted, Liora smiled at the big, blond knight and the equally big bald knight who seemed rather young for such a bald head. "Welcome to Ludlow, my lords," she said. "Will you be staying with us tonight?"

Kress nodded. "Aye, Lady de Lohr," he said. "Thank you for your hospitality."

Liora smiled prettily. "Our pleasure, my lord," she said. "You are always welcome here. Do you have a family?"

"I do."

"They are welcome, also."

Kress smiled politely, accepting the cup of wine that came his way, as The Marshal spoke up simply to continue to keep the subject away from what had occupied their attention since they'd entered the hall. It wouldn't do for Lady de Lohr to catch wind of it before Peter had a chance to tell her that he was leaving, off to do what he'd been trained to do.

"I meant to tell you that I saw Saer de Quincy in London the last time I was there," he said to Christopher. "He mentioned about Walter losing Astley Cross to Marcus Burton."

Christopher nodded. "It belongs to Marcus now," he said without remorse. "I hope Winchester doesn't hold a grudge against those who took his cousin's property."

The Marshal snorted. "On the contrary," he said. "He seemed rather grateful. I never did ask what happened to Walter. Not that I care, but after the mess he created, the man has all but disappeared."

Christopher shrugged. "Marcus took care of that problem," he said. "He told me that he sent the man to Scotland under penalty of death should he return to England."

"Do you think he'll remain there?"

"If he values his life, he will."

"But what happened to Agnes?"

Christopher's eyes took on an amused twinkle. "Marcus found her a position."

The Marshal eyed him curiously. "A position? What *kind* of position?"

"As a serving wench at The Pox," Christopher replied. "I heard she married a de la Londe, in fact. They are the dregs of polite society, but I have little sympathy for her. Given her history, she'll be right at home amongst that scheming French family."

"You had trouble with them back in the days of Richard, did you not?" Peter asked him, taking a bite of bread.

Christopher nodded. "A rotten barrel of apples, that bunch."

"Poor Agnes," Liora said.

Peter and Christopher looked at her in surprise. "Why would you say that?" Peter asked. "After everything she did, you still feel pity for her?"

Liora shrugged, watching men shovel food into their mouths. "She tried so hard to keep hold on something that was never hers to begin with," she said. "I find that kind of desperation sad."

Christopher, chewing, patted her on the arm. "You are a saint, Lee-Lee," he said. "Now, where is that wonderful cake you make? Do you have some?"

She grinned, putting a hand on his shoulder. "For you, I always have some," she said. "I will return."

She dashed off, heading for the kitchens where she always kept apple cake because she loved it so much. Christopher, in his many stays at Ludlow, had come to love it, too, so much so that Liora taught Dustin how to make it. Apples chopped fine with cinnamon, eggs, flour, and honey created a fabulous cake. It was made without milk or butter, meaning it could be eaten at the table with meat in adherence to Jewish dietary laws. That was the one thing Liora had never strayed from. She still ate in accordance to Jewish dietary laws because she always had and it was a difficult habit to break. Peter never pushed her, of course, and he'd been privy to some wonderful dishes she had made for him because of it. In fact, the entire de Lohr family had been.

As Peter watched her scurry away, his heart grew heavier and heavier. He'd only just come home and now he was going to have to leave her again. He had a myriad of conflicting feelings as he watched her but, in the end, he knew this was something he had to do. There was no question in his mind and putting off telling her wasn't going to help.

She had to know.

Excusing himself from the table, he followed her trail to the kitchens.

He found her in the kitchens that smelled heavily of yeast. The ovens were in full use as the cooks baked bread for the day and he spied her bent over an earthenware bowl. As he watched, she put something from the bowl in her mouth and he grinned.

"Are you going to eat all of the cake and then tell my father there is none left?" he teased.

Startled by his appearance, Liora quickly relaxed, laughing because he was. "I will bring him some," she said. "But it smells so good I wanted a taste for myself."

Peter bent over the bowl, smelling the cinnamon. "It does smell good," he said. "Mayhap I will eat it all myself."

"I think your father would be very disappointed."

He shrugged. "He'll live," he said, his smile fading. "I wanted to speak to you before you go back into the hall, sweetheart. Can you spare me a moment?"

Liora gazed up at him with those beautiful eyes. "I can spare you all the time that you need," she said. "But I have something to tell you."

"What?"

"You're leaving again."

His eyes took on a glimmer. "I am?"

"You are."

"Where am I going?"

"I do not know yet," she said. "But when William Marshal shows his face, it is not simply to visit. He came here for a reason."

It was very astute of her. She had only really come to know The Marshal through Peter and through her father-in-law, but she knew enough to know that the powerful earl didn't simply show up randomly. Every action had a purpose.

She was smart enough to know that.

"He did," Peter said quietly. "He has asked an important task of me and I must comply. I cannot tell you more than that, but I can tell you that I am not going into battle. It is something different."

She nodded, accepting what he was telling her without angst or upset. "How long will you be gone?"

"I do not know."

"Will you return for the birth of your son?"

He stared at her for a moment before pulling her into his arms, holding her tightly. "I hope so," he murmured into the top of her hair. "God, I hope so. But I cannot promise that I will until this task is completed. It is very important, Lee-Lee. It is so important that I must be part of it. But I swear to you that I will return as soon as I can. My thoughts, my hopes, and my dreams will be only of you, every day, until we see each other again."

Liora collapsed against him, trying very hard not to tear up. She was hormonal, and emotional, and tears were close to the surface these days.

"If you say it is important, then I believe you," she said huskily. "You need not explain yourself because I know there are things you cannot speak of. I knew you were an elite knight when I married you. I simply did not know how important you were to a great many people and how often you would be called upon."

He pulled back and looked at her. "I may be important to a great many people, but you are the most important person in the world to me," he said. "There is no one in my life I love more than you. There is no one in my life who means more to me than you do. I am simply sorry that we have spent so much of our marriage apart. I hope that will change after this task because I do not like leaving you. I do not want to leave you ever again when this is finished."

Liora forced a smile. "I will not let you," she said, teasing him gently. "The next time you try to leave me, I shall throw myself upon you and cling to you like a great anchor. You will hardly be able to move as you drag me around."

He grinned. "It would be pleasurable, I assure you," he said. "But until that time… I am afraid I must leave you just once more."

"Will you tell me one thing?"

"If I can."

"Will you be in danger?"

He thought on how to reply but ended up looking at her regretfully. "Do you want me to tell you the truth?"

"Please."

"It is very possible."

She considered that, forcing herself to be brave because she had asked him, after all. She couldn't become upset about it if he'd been honest with her.

"Thank you for being truthful," she said. "I may not like the answer, but I appreciate the honesty."

He leaned down and kissed her, his lips lingering on hers. It was enough to bring tears to his eyes.

"I love you," he whispered. "More than my own life, I love you. You are the heart that beats within me."

She kissed him in return, her hands on his face, feeling his warmth against her flesh. "Come home to me, my angel," she murmured. "Come home safely. I will be waiting."

He kissed her again but was forced to release her because the cooks were pulling out multiple loaves of bread and putting them on a table nearby. Steam and the smell of hot bread was filling up the kitchen. Liora wiped at her eyes and quickly moved around him, picking up a cloth that contained the apple cake and putting it in Peter's hands.

"Take this to your father," she said.

He looked at the cake. "Are you not coming with me?"

She shook her head, smiling bravely. "I have a feeling you and your guests would like to be alone," she said. "But do not worry. I will be nearby if you need me."

He smiled sadly. "I am sorry," he said. "I will finish with them as quickly as I can and we can spend the rest of the day together, just us."

She nodded, suspecting that might not be possible. "Go on," she said. "Do what you must. I will see you later."

His gaze, warm and loving, lingered on her. "Aye, you will," he said. "You most certainly will."

With that, he turned and headed back for the great hall, leaving his wife watching him walk away. Tall, broad, and powerful Peter. Her pride and joy, the breath in her lungs that sustained her. She watched him until he disappeared from sight and then, and only then, did she head out into the kitchen yard to collect herself.

But it didn't work.

Leaning against the wall of the keep, Liora hung her head and wept.

CHAPTER TWENTY-ONE

October 1216
Newark Castle

H E WAS BIG, grizzled, and scarred these days. A growth of beard covered his face and neck, and his hands were raw from where he'd had to beat down a warlord who had displeased the king. He'd stopped short of breaking the man's neck, but his command had been to disable the man and he had.

He had sprays of blood on the front of his tunic and on his face as a result.

There were days when Peter wondered how Sean de Lara had dealt with it all for so many years. Even though John had been on a battle march for months, that hadn't prevented him from behaving as only the king was so capable of behaving. There had been maidens, pretty daughters from local peasants that he'd caught a glimpse of, that Peter had been forced to abduct from their fathers and bring to the king like some kind of perverted offering. John would bed the girls, delighting in deflowering them, and then sometimes he might even let his guards have the leavings.

That left Peter to pick up the pieces.

The horrible, broken pieces.

There were girls he'd had to clean up, sew up, and return to their families. The first time it had happened had been outside of Oxford when he'd abducted the daughter of a merchant. She'd been of age and John had taken his time with her for three days, like a lion toying with his prey, and in the end, he'd seduced the girl and left a mere shell behind. Peter had taken care of the young woman, made sure she was tended to, and returned her to her father.

And then he'd wept.

In all of his years as an Executioner Knight, he'd never had to deal with the female factor. He'd killed men and done other things he wasn't entirely proud of, but nothing had anything to do with women. He was tender hearted when it came to women, but he'd quickly had to toughen himself up because that was now part of what was expected of him as the king's personal protector.

But the warlord he'd just beaten up?

That was nothing unusual…

However, this particular night was unusual, indeed. It was October and the sun was down early, the air with a hint of ice in it, as he traversed the dark, narrow corridors of Newark on his way to the king. He'd spent the last hour in the vault with the unfortunate warlord, but that had been an unexpected diversion to the main event this evening.

It had been in the works for several months, the careful and methodical planning by Alexander, who had infiltrated the royal quartermasters. He'd done it so brilliantly, so unlike anything he'd ever done before. He'd shaved his head and let his beard grow, rolled around in horse shite every day for three weeks without bathing, and then had shown up in the city of Lynn in Norfolk, asking for a job from the king's quartermasters. Because he was strong and good with horses, they'd permitted him to tend the animals. He also pretended to be deaf and dumb, which meant they said things around him that they wouldn't normally say, and he heard every word.

It had been undeniably valuable.

Maxton, Kress, Achilles, Bric, and Cullen found themselves in the king's guard, more on the outskirts of the action than involved in it. The one thing they did do was shield Alexander's movements if they could and keep an eye on Peter in case he needed them. They'd traveled with the king's mercenary army around the south of England, including Lynn and Oxford, finally stopping at Newark Castle because the king's military campaigns were failing and so was his health.

That had been key.

In fact, John had been sick since Alexander joined the royal army at Lynn because the slow poison he was able to introduce went to work on the man little by little. In the beginning, he couldn't get close to the king, so he provided the poison to Peter and to Maxton, who were able to place it in the wine without any suspicion. Meanwhile, Alexander worked his way from the stable hand to a kitchen servant by helping out a dowdy serving maid who tried to get frisky with him. He grinned at her, and avoided her, but he started helping out in the kitchens because of her and that was exactly where he needed to be.

It gave him access to the wine meant for the king.

Since before their arrival at Newark, Peter insisted on personally bringing the king his drink under the guise of keeping it protected from those who might foul it. He meant to protect the king from someone just like him, someone intent to poison the man's wine, so it was a perfect position to be in. Alexander had managed to become in charge of the ale and the wine simply because he was strong enough to lift the barrels, so it was up to him to tap them and provide drink to the king and his men, and it was Alexander who would pour wine into two special pitchers meant for the king.

One was poisoned, one wasn't.

John always drank both.

It took some time for the lead-based poison to leech into John's digestive track, mimicking the symptoms of dysentery. Everyone said it was the dreaded disease of dysentery, including the king's physic, who suggested that John switch to a bland diet that didn't include the heavy foods he was so fond of. John tried, including switching to watered ale delivered personally by Peter, but the ale was poisoned, too, so it didn't help him much. He had good days and he had bad days.

Today was an especially bad day.

The king had been unable to keep any food or drink down for three days. Three long days of vomiting and purging everything in his intestines and then some. He had three physics with him at this point, two priests, and a host of advisors including William Marshal, because the physics had made it clear that the king was dying. The dysentery had badly dehydrated him, so the physics had ordered wine that had been boiled, which was what Peter had in his hands as he entered the great chamber.

It smelled of peppermint and cloves, thought to ward off the bad humors that caused illness, but it also smelled of vomit and feces, a nasty combination. John lay upon a bed of silks and fine fabrics, all of it stained because he could no longer control his bowels. Everything came leaking out as the Groom of the Stool tried to keep him clean. He had sores on his buttocks and legs from so much seepage, something else the physics had to tend to. In truth, the man was a mess, pale and gaunt.

He was dying the slow, painful death that had been planned for him.

"Is that the wine?"

The question came from The Marshal. Peter nodded, handing him the one that was laced with poison. It was nice and hot, with a slightly metallic taste that went ignored because all of the wine that king drank had that slight flavor, which could be leeched from the pewter pitchers he favored. The Marshal handed the pitcher to one of the physics, who poured it into a cup and helped the king drink some of it.

Peter stood back and watched.

The more the man drank, the more poison entered his system.

"William," John spoke listlessly. "William, are you listening to me?"

The Marshal stood next to the bed, gazing upon the dying king impassively. "I am here, your grace."

The king's sunken eyes fixed on him. "You were not with my father when he died."

It was a statement, not a question. William shook his head. "I was not, your grace."

"Nor Richard?"

"Nay, your grace."

"You were with my brother, Henry, however."

William nodded faintly. "I was, your grace," he said. "He was my friend. He also had the same affliction you have."

John closed his eyes, drawing in a breath, but it was greatly labored. The priests in the corner were praying a soft singsong melody, so quiet that they could barely be heard, and the physics were pretending to busy themselves around John even though there was nothing for them to do. Their purpose had been over days ago. The Marshal watched, and Peter watched, as they gave more of the poison-laced wine to the king.

John eventually drained the entire cup.

He lay back and closed his eyes as the afternoon became evening. Candles were lit and the priests continued to pray as John eventually lost consciousness. His breathing was slow and unsteady, his mouth open as he fought for every breath. The physics packed blankets around his body, keeping him warm against the October chill as a fire blazed in the hearth. It was almost too warm in the chamber for those who weren't ill, but they stood by silently, sweat on their brows, as John's breathing grew slower and slower.

Close to midnight, the death rattle began and shortly thereafter, it stopped altogether.

The silence was deafening as everyone in the chamber waited for the king to resume breathing again, but he didn't. Minutes passed and there was no further movement. The physics lifted his eyelids, listened to his heart, before turning to The Marshal and shaking their heads.

"It is over, my lord," one of them said softly.

The Marshal gazed down at the ashen body. "Are you certain?"

"I am, my lord."

The Marshal's head tipped back as if he'd been physically struck. His gaze lingered on the body on the bed, drinking it in, digesting it.

The moment had finally come.

John, King of England, was dead.

The priests came to stand over him, offering a prayer for the dead, as the advisors ushered out of the chamber with shuffling feet and hushed whispers. They were a confused bunch and a useless bunch as far as William was concerned because most of them were mercenary command-ers. There were only a handful that were actually

English warlords.

The rest were scum.

Now, the scum was out of the chamber.

The priests, with their prayers finished, finally departed but the physics remained, poking and prodding the king, making sure he was truly dead before wrapping the body up tightly and laying his head upon a silken pillow. He didn't look quite so miserable that way.

All the while, William stood at the base of the bed, watching. When the physics looked up at him, he motioned them out of the chamber and they silently complied.

There was nothing left for them to do, any-way.

William shut the door behind them, looking over at the king now that they were alone. As he gazed at the man, he was filled with a myriad of emotions, not the least of which was relief. Complete, utter relief. Slowly, he made his way over to the bed, gazing down at the man he'd known since birth.

A tragic, useless, privileged man.

"And so, it comes," he murmured. "You do not know how many times I have protected your life, saving you to rule another day. It was my duty. Nay, it was more than that. England needed a king and I had hoped you would be different from your brother and father, but alas, you were not. I have watched you since you were a small child, the way you allowed yourself to be swayed by your brothers, the way you railed against your mother and begged for your father's love. I know that was all you ever wanted, John, but Henry was incapable of loving his sons. To him, you were either potential allies or potential enemies."

The chamber remained silent but for the popping and snapping in the hearth. William noticed the pitchers of wine on a nearby table and went to them, picking them both up and heading over to one of three large windows in the chamber that faced south. He dumped out the first one, pouring the liquid into the moat below.

"For years, those sworn to me made sure all threats against you were removed," he said. "We swore to protect you but not serve you. You were necessary. At least, you were until we had a better candidate. Your son may only be nine years of age, but with my guidance and the guidance of others, he will learn what you could never learn – and that is how to be a king his people will love."

Finished dumping the second pitcher, he came back over to the table and set them down again, prepared to tell anyone who asked that he drank the remainder of the wine in honor of the king. No one would question William Marshal. No one ever did. He was just turning for the bed again when there was a knock on the chamber door.

"Who comes?" he asked.

"Peter."

William went to the door and opened it, admitting Peter, who didn't look like the Peter he had known all of these years. Serving the king for the six short months he had served him had done something to the eldest de Lohr son. He was short-tempered, burly, and unafraid to throw a punch that could knock a grown man out in one swipe. Sean de Lara had also gone through that sort of change, but poor Sean had been saddled with it for nine years, far longer than Peter. William could see, looking at Peter, just what this particular mission could do to a decent man.

It could change him.

"He's gone?" Peter muttered.

William nodded. "He is."

"It is over?"

"Aye, Peter. It is over."

Peter's eyes glittered as he looked over at the bed, at the man lying there who seemed strangely small. As William stood by the door, Peter summoned the courage to walk over to the bed, gazing down at the man who had been vile beyond any expectations he'd ever had. Vile beyond words. He'd always known it; his father had told him, his uncle had told him, and Marcus had told him. Aye, he'd known how vile the king was.

But now he'd experienced it first-hand. Seeing

him dead was more gratifying than he had expected. What kings and knights and armies had failed to do in fifty-nine years, a group of eight men had managed in six months.

They'd changed the course of history.

Peter leaned over, looking at John's ashen face.

"For all of those you have sinned against," he whispered. "For a country you tried to destroy, and for the loyalty of men you were not worthy of, you have met a just and righteous end. If you can still hear, if your spirit still lingers nearby, know that I rejoice in your death, you despicable bastard. And I shall tell my father that for Jax de Velt, his old and dear friend, justice has finally been served."

With that, he stood up and headed out of the chamber, followed by William, who would now enter an entirely new world as the guardian of a nine-year-old king. The priests who had been praying for the king had come from the nearby church and he could hear the bells ringing, announcing the death of the king. Soon enough, word would travel fast, and everyone would know that the King of England was dead.

A new era was upon them.

A new future was at hand.

As William and Peter headed out into the bailey of Newark, they happened to see a collection of soldiers waiting for them – Maxton, Kress, Achilles, Bric, and Cullen, all of them dressed in the colors of the royal house. They also saw Alexander, clad in his servant's clothing. William and Peter went to stand with them, gazing back at anxious faces, until William broke the silence.

"He is dead," he said quietly. "Henry is now our king. Long live the king."

"Truly?" Maxton said, sounding both surprised and relieved. "John is no more?"

William nodded, feeling his age at that moment. "Truly," he said. "He is gone. The man with many sins is, even now, standing before God to read over the events of his life and I am quite certain that God will not be merciful in John's case. At least, I hope not. And I hope that all of those people John has sinned against are standing there in judgment, ensuring that John's stay in hell will be a long and miserable one. But Peter made sure of one thing."

Heads turned in Peter's direction. "What is that?" Maxton asked.

William looked at Peter, too. "He made sure that Jax de Velt was one of the last men spoken of in that chamber," he said. "If John's spirit still lingers, he heard the name. He knows that his offense against Jax is one of the things that brought him to a painful end. That, my friends, is the true measure of vengeance. It does not seem right that Jax had to be sacrificed in order to save England from her king, but he was certainly one of the last nails in John's coffin. For that, The Dark Lord should be proud. And so should his family."

Maxton, a smile playing on his lips, looked at Peter in approval. "For Jax," he muttered.

"For Jax," the group responded.

They were fateful words, words that sank deep into the souls and psyches of the Executioner Knights. Their most important mission yet had succeeded and, now, they had a new task ahead of them – ridding the country of the French king and healing broken bonds. Their fight wasn't over yet. But at least now, they saw peace on the horizon. England had a great deal of healing to do in general but, with time, peace would come.

But for now, their task was over and that very night, they left Newark together, never to return. When Peter finally arrived at Ludlow a few days later to an extremely pregnant wife, that was exactly what he told her.

Peace will come now.

In her arms, it did.

EPILOGUE

Two months later
Ludlow Castle

S NOW HAD KEPT them inside for two days.

Liora could hear the hissing and fussing as she entered the small hall of Ludlow, one that she and Peter used when family visited, like they were now. It had turned into an all-purpose room because they had so many people visiting for the holidays, so there were women near the hearth while men sat a little further away, talking and drinking. As Liora entered the hall, her gaze fell on Dustin, Christin, Brielle, and young Rebecca over near the hearth, sewing on what looked to be a large, patchwork coverlet, while Christopher sat with his infant daughter sleeping in his arms, surrounded by Peter, Alexander, and Peter's younger brothers Curtis and Richard.

But that's not where the hissing was coming from.

That was coming from her father as he sat in a warm corner on the opposite side of the hearth, a swaddled infant in his arms and several young boys at his feet, including Asa. She paused a moment, watching her father carefully hold his new grandson with one arm while holding out a hand to prevent Asa, Myles, Douglas, and Westley from hurting each other with tiny pieces of kindling they'd found in the wood box. Worse still, Christin's eldest child, two-year-old Andrew, had an enormous stick that he was trying to use on Westley.

It was juvenile bedlam in the hall of Ludlow and, all the while, Haim was speaking softly and steadily to the group of rioting little boys.

"… and the candles burned for eight straight nights even though there was hardly enough oil for them," he said. "It was a miracle from God."

"But tell us about the Maccabees, Papa!" Asa said, trading kindling blows with Douglas. "Tell them how fierce the Maccabees were, fiercer than any knight!"

"Was not!" Douglas shouted.

"Was too!" Asa fired back.

Douglas charged Asa and down they went, rolling around on the floor of the great hall as

Liora rushed up and pulled her brother off her husband's little brother, holding Asa and Douglas by their ears. The boys whined and squirmed, trapped by those pinching fingers.

"No fighting in my hall," she said to them both. "What will baby Matthew think to see his uncles rolling around on the floor, fighting like common fools? You are setting a terrible example for him. He must have uncles he can look up to and be proud of."

Asa's face was contorted in pain as his sister pinched his ear. "But he said –!"

Liora tugged on his ear. "Enough," she said. "If you cannot behave any better than a wild puppy, you can go to bed early. Is that what you want?"

Asa frowned. "Nay."

Liora let go of the ears. "Then sit down, both of you, and listen to Papa Haim tell you of the Maccabees," she said. "And no more fighting."

With that, she collected all of the wood that was being used for swords and made the boys sit down and pay attention to her father, who was cuddling his sleeping grandson. Matthew Christopher Henry Haim de Lohr had been born about six weeks earlier, a big baby who had come quickly in the early hours of a cold, icy morning. He had come so quickly, in fact, that Dustin and Christin, who had come to Ludlow to be present for the birth, had delivered him before the midwife could arrive. Peter had been so overwhelmed by the swift birth that Alexander had been forced to ply him with wine until he could regain his composure but, in the end, he had a fat, healthy son and a wife who had breezed through the birth.

He couldn't have been more grateful.

Even now, he could see Liora over with her father and brother, scolding the boys as Haim tried to protect them. It brought a smile to his lips.

"Haim has the patience of Job with those boys," he said, chuckling when Liora wagged a finger at her father. "He's been entertaining them for two days, God bless the man."

Christopher, with a sleeping baby on his chest, smiled at his daughter-in-law and her father. "He's had Matthew since he arrived," he said. "The man is a fool for a baby."

Peter and Alexander looked over at him, laughing. "Says the man with a baby against his chest," Peter said. "Admit it, Papa. You are a fool for babies, also. We all know it. Admit it. It will be liberating for you."

Christopher peered down at his sleeping daughter's face. "Women do not know how to raise children," he said. "I am the one who molded my children."

"I am going to tell Mother you said that."

Christopher fought off a grin. "She already

knows," he said. "Do not trouble her with such things."

Peter and Alexander continued to laugh as Peter poured Alexander more wine. "That is why my brothers are so wild," he said. "Look at them – fighting like scrapping puppies and now we have Asa, the Maccabee, in the middle of them."

"Am I wild, Papa?"

The question came from Curtis, Christopher and Dustin's eldest son. He was on the cusp of manhood, an intense, intelligent boy who had never had the wild streak that his younger brothers had. He was his father to the bone, in personality and looks, and Christopher smiled at his second-eldest boy.

"Nay, not you," he said, looking at his other son, Richard, seated next to Curtis. "Or Richie. You two are exactly like me and I do not have that naughty streak in me. Your younger brothers are your mother to the core. That is why they are so wild."

Hearing that, Peter and Alexander continued to snort as Christopher blamed his lively boys on their mother. "Do you want me to go over and make them behave?" Curtis asked.

Christopher shook his head. "Nay, lad," he said. "Liora is doing a fine job. She can put more fear into them than you can, especially to her own brother."

"Asa told me he wants to be a knight," Curtis said.

Christopher looked over at the boys now sitting on the floor, listening to Haim as Liora stood over them to make sure they behaved. "I would take Asa into battle without question," he said. "The boy has a fighting spirit, but Haim wants him to become a goldsmith, so I am keeping my opinions to myself."

Peter was the one to respond to that statement. "That is wise," he said. "We've already taken Haim's daughter. I think he is fearful that we will take his son as well and I do not wish to do that."

Christopher wasn't hard pressed to agree. "That is true, but Asa has a restlessness about him that may be trouble when he gets older."

"That's what Haim said."

Christopher watched Asa fidget as his father told stories. "You are to be commended, Peter," he said. "You are doing your best to embrace Liora's family and even now, Haim is teaching your brothers about the Maccabees. By teaching them about Jewish traditions, he is teaching them tolerance and by knowing Asa, they will come to understand a boy who is being raised differently than they are. That is never a bad thing."

"True," Peter said. "I'm only sorry that Liora's mother could not come."

"Why not?"

Peter shrugged. "She does not approve of this marriage," he said. "Haim does not speak of it, but Liora has said that her mother does not approve. It saddens her, of course, but mayhap time will ease that stance."

"Time and grandchildren," Christopher said. "I've not known a woman yet who can stay away from her grandchildren, so give her time. She will accept it, eventually."

"Haim did," Peter said. "He told me that he would never come to Ludlow and bring Asa, but a grandson changed that."

"A grandchild can change many things. Meanwhile, Liora has us. *All* of us."

Peter chuckled at his father before rising from his chair and heading over to Liora, who was still standing over the boys who were becoming increasingly twitchy. He put his arm around her shoulders, and she smiled up at him, putting her fingers to her lips for silence as Haim spoke of the Maccabees and their victory over Antiochus. He made their victory sound quite thrilling, and the twitchy little boys were lured into a good story about a victorious battle. But that fragile peace was shattered when Asa found a small piece of wood that had fallen from the kindling and began to poke Myles with it.

After that, another brawl erupted and Liora gave up.

Taking her son from her father, she and Peter headed up to their bedchamber so she could feed the baby, but mostly, it was just so they could spend a few moments alone. They'd had family at Ludlow for almost a week solid because of the looming Christmas holiday and it was a wonderful time of year, with family and warmth and laughter, but sometimes the young couple with the new baby simply wanted to be alone.

They stole away for just that chance.

Their chamber was warm from the fire in the hearth and an iron bank of tallow candles gave off a warm, comforting glow. Peter held his son as Liora settled in a chair near the hearth, unfastening the ties on her bodice so she could nurse the baby. With an engorged breast exposed, she put the child on the nipple, and he began to feed eagerly. Peter stood over them, watching the sweet scene.

Liora heard him sigh.

"What is the matter, my angel?" she said, looking up at him.

He shook his head, taking a knee beside her chair, his head on her shoulder as he watched her nurse their son.

"Nothing is the matter," he said, pushing his big finger into his son's fist and being rewarded with a tight grip. "In fact, there is nothing on this earth that will ever be the matter again. Look at what we have, Lee-Lee; a healthy son, a beautiful home, people who love us. When I ducked into your kitchen yard last year, I could have never imagined this would be my life just a short year later."

Liora smiled as she gazed down at her blond-haired, blue-eyed son. "Nor I," she said. "You do realize that I never thought I would see you again after the first time."

"I know," he snorted. "Asa tried to chase me away."

"It did not work."

He started laughing. "Was it supposed to?"

She shrugged, grinning at him as he kissed her nose. "I am glad it did not," she said sobering. "It's funny, truly. I think on what we had to do in order to marry…"

He cut her off softly. "What *you* had to do."

She looked at him pointedly. "What *we* had to do," she said, more firmly. "I realize I had to surrender one religion in favor of another, but I truly do not feel like I surrendered anything. I still celebrate the things I have always celebrated, now with my father in our hall, teaching your brothers about the Jewish holiday of Hanukkah. But now, I celebrate Christmas as well, and Martinmas, the festival days of all of those saints I still cannot remember. I feel as if I am richer now that I ever was. Does that make sense?"

Peter nodded, putting his big hand on his son's head, dwarfing it. "It does," he said. "I feel the same way. I never knew about Purim or Yom Kippur, but I do now. I know a lot of things now."

"Like what?"

He shrugged. "I told my father once that I always felt different because I was his bastard, but as it turns out, that was a good thing," he said. "Being different has made me into the man I am today and it has made an unconventional marriage with you much more possible. But it's more than that – it has made me more open to things that are different, I suppose, and I hope to convey that to our children."

Liora nodded, looking at the baby suckling against her breast. "I hope that having a mother who was born Jewish makes them more accepting of differences," she said. "Jews have known great persecution in the past, but mayhap understand-ing our differences will be a greater path to peace. Truthfully, since young Henry took the throne, I feel as if those days are behind us. Days of trouble, I mean. You never did tell me what you did during those months you were away, and I swore I would not ask, but the day you returned, things changed. I feel as if we have you to thank for the dawn of this new day."

Peter kept his gaze on his son. He had made a vow never to tell Liora where he'd spent those months, and what he had done, because that wasn't something he wanted to share with her. In fact, she'd never even heard the term Executioner Knight from him. He'd never mentioned it, but he knew that someday, he would. Someday she would understand just how involved he was in The Marshal's spy ring, but not now. There was large part of him that wanted his new wife to think he was noble and strong and relatively innocent, not a man who had killed a king.

Even if it had been for the just and right cause.

But he would tell her everything when the time was right.

"Things are not entirely peaceful," he said after a moment. "We are still chasing the French from our lands. The mercenaries, too. Uncle David managed to chase them away from Canterbury and most of the allied castles, like Uncle Marcus', held against the mercenary army, but there is more work to do. We are having to flush all of them back to where they came from, so the time of total peace is not here yet, but it will be. Men like my father, Jax de Velt, Juston de Royans, William Marshal... they have given their entire lives so that, eventually, we *will* know peace."

"When does your father plan to pay his respects to Lord de Velt?"

"In the spring when weather permits, I am sure. I may go with him."

"I think he would like that."

"I would like to pay my respects to de Velt, too. He has meant a lot to our family."

Liora switched the baby to the other breast, holding him close as she looked down into his little face, her thoughts moving from Jax de Velt to the child she held in her arms. There was no moment more perfect than this – her husband, her baby, her everything.

"I knew when I married you that you were an elite knight and fighting was your vocation," she said softly. "Your father told me it would be a life unlike anything I was used to, and my father told me, as well. Do you know that it was the first time I did not listen to my father?"

"I hope you do not regret it."

She looked at him, her big, strong husband. Handsome and wise, he was everything she imagined he would be and her life with him was everything she had ever hoped for.

"Sometimes I feel as if I am living a dream," she said. "Do you remember when we walked in the meadow, the first real conversation we ever had?"

"I do."

"Do you remember that I told you that we could not become friends?"

"I remember that very clearly."

Liora smiled at him. "I am very glad you did

not listen to me."

Peter put his arms around her, pulling her close, his lips against her head. "So am I, sweetheart," he murmured. "So am I."

In Liora's arms, little Matthew suckled contentedly, never knowing how close he came to never being born. But the heart of an Executioner Knight is a determined thing indeed, as Matthew's mother discovered. A heart determined to love, to protect, and when necessary, kill for the common good. On this night, with the snow falling softly and a hall full of people, Peter and Liora were of one heart and one soul as they enjoyed their first holiday season with their son, the legacy of two religions, of one love, and of one hope.

It was the dawn of a new generation and a new de Lohr legacy. For the bastard son of an earl and the daughter of a jeweler, theirs was a love story of legend.

Cঙ THE END ঙO

Peter and Liora's children
Matthew
Annalise
Madelaine
Aaron
Ethan
Gabriel
Jared
Nathan
Elisabeth

The Executioner Knights:
By the Unholy Hand
The Mountain Dark
Starless
The Promise (also Noble Knights of de Nerra)
A Time of End
Winter of Solace
Lord of the Shadows
Lord of the Sky
Splendid Hour

AFTERWORD

I hope you enjoyed Peter and Liora's story! It was quite a wild ride. The Executioner Knights stories are always a big adventure, anyway, because of the politics involved, but now add a religion other than Christianity into the mix and it makes for even more dimension.

The one thing I wanted to address, as the author of this tale, is the fact that Liora had to convert to Christianity in order to marry Peter. I touched on that in the author's note, but I didn't want to give too much away. Please note that this was not a slam against Judaism in any way – in fact, I hope that this tale rather conveyed, in very small part, the beauty of the religion. But the simple fact of the matter is that, in 1215 A.D., the only way Liora could have married Peter is if one of them converted – he offered to, but she chose to (and insisted on it) so they could be together. It was simply a choice to be with the man she loved and not a statement that one religion is better than another.

Although Judaism has been around longer than Christianity, the historical fact is that England was a Christian country in the 13th century. Liora chose to convert for her husband's sake and nothing more. As we saw at the end, she remained true to the Jewish way of life in many ways. As she said once, both religions worship the same God, so she was comfortable worshipping as both a Christian and a Jew and in introducing her children to both cultures, which Peter wholeheartedly endorsed. They did the best they could with what was really an impossible situation.

In Medieval times, sometimes the world was far too rigid and clear-cut when it came to religion, so keep Liora's choice in the context of the times. Please keep that in mind. For her to surrender herself for love like that is a testament to her love for Peter – and the fact that he was more than willing to do it, too, was a testament to his love for her.

You can't always help who you fall in love with, but in Liora and Peter's case, they did what they had to do in order to see that love thrive.

On another note, this book brings to the conclusion the Executioner Knight's contentious relationship with John and begins the reign of

John's son, Henry III, who had one of the longest reigns in English history. It's interesting to note that Henry could not be crowned in London because the French king, Louis, held the city. When the rebel warlords brought the French over to help them get rid of John, Louis took it seriously – and he claimed London until they could get him out.

Lastly – just a mention about John's death. Officially, it was dysentery but there were rumors for years that it was poisoned ale or bad food (which it very well could have been), so the Executioner Knights and their thallium poisoning fits very well into the legend. Thallium is one of the most deadly poisons on earth and doesn't leave any trace, so who's to say that John's dysentery wasn't something else? Not me!

Fun historical tidbits during the time of the Executioner Knights.

Oh… and as for young Asa always wanting to be a knight, don't be surprised if he turns up in a future Executioner Knight book. My sweet little Maccabee!

Thank you for reading!

KATHRYN LE VEQUE NOVELS

Medieval Romance:

De Wolfe Pack Series:
Warwolfe
The Wolfe
Nighthawk
ShadowWolfe
DarkWolfe
A Joyous de Wolfe
Christmas
BlackWolfe
Serpent
A Wolfe Among Dragons
Scorpion
StormWolfe
Dark Destroyer
The Lion of the North
Walls of Babylon
The Best Is Yet To Be

**De Wolfe Pack
Generations:**
WolfeHeart
WolfeStrike
WolfeSword
WolfeBlade

The de Russe Legacy:
The Falls of Erith
Lord of War: Black Angel

The Iron Knight
Beast
The Dark One: Dark
Knight
The White Lord of
Wellesbourne
Dark Moon
Dark Steel
A de Russe Christmas
Miracle
Dark Warrior

The de Lohr Dynasty:
While Angels Slept
Rise of the Defender
Steelheart
Shadowmoor
Silversword
Spectre of the Sword
Unending Love
Archangel
A Blessed de Lohr
Christmas

The Brothers de Lohr:
The Earl in Winter

Lords of East Anglia:
While Angels Slept
Godspeed
Age of Gods and Mortals

Great Lords of le Bec:
Great Protector

House of de Royans:
Lord of Winter
To the Lady Born
The Centurion

Lords of Eire:
Echoes of Ancient Dreams
Blacksword
The Darkland

**Ancient Kings of
Anglecynn:**
The Whispering Night
Netherworld

Battle Lords of de Velt:
The Dark Lord
Devil's Dominion
Bay of Fear
The Dark Lord's First
Christmas
The Dark Spawn

**Reign of the House of de
Winter:**
Lespada
Swords and Shields

De Reyne Domination:
Guardian of Darkness
With Dreams
The Fallen One

House of d'Vant:
Tender is the Knight
(House of d'Vant)

The Red Fury (House of
d'Vant)

The Dragonblade Series:
Fragments of Grace
Dragonblade
Island of Glass
The Savage Curtain
The Fallen One

**Great Marcher Lords of de
Lara**
Dragonblade

House of St. Hever
Fragments of Grace
Island of Glass
Queen of Lost Stars

Lords of Pembury:
The Savage Curtain

**Lords of Thunder: The de
Shera Brotherhood
Trilogy**
The Thunder Lord
The Thunder Warrior
The Thunder Knight

**The Great Knights of de
Moray:**
Shield of Kronos
The Gorgon

The House of De Nerra:
The Promise
The Falls of Erith
Vestiges of Valor
Realm of Angels

Highland Warriors of Munro:
The Red Lion
Deep Into Darkness

The House of de Garr:
Lord of Light
Realm of Angels

Saxon Lords of Hage:
The Crusader
Kingdom Come

High Warriors of Rohan:
High Warrior

The House of Ashbourne:
Upon a Midnight Dream

The House of D'Aurilliac:
Valiant Chaos

The House of De Dere:
Of Love and Legend

St. John and de Gare Clans:
The Warrior Poet

The House of de Bretagne:
The Questing

The House of Summerlin:
The Legend

The Kingdom of Hendocia:
Kingdom by the Sea

The Executioner Knights:
By the Unholy Hand
The Mountain Dark
Starless
The Promise (also Noble Knights of de Nerra)
A Time of End
Winter of Solace
Lord of the Shadows
Lord of the Sky
Splendid Hour

Gothic Regency Romance:
Emma

Contemporary Romance:

Kathlyn Trent/Marcus Burton Series:
Valley of the Shadow
The Eden Factor
Canyon of the Sphinx

The American Heroes Anthology Series:
The Lucius Robe
Fires of Autumn
Evenshade
Sea of Dreams
Purgatory

Other non-connected Contemporary Romance:
Lady of Heaven
Darkling, I Listen
In the Dreaming Hour
River's End
The Fountain

Sons of Poseidon:
The Immortal Sea

Pirates of Britannia Series (with Eliza Knight):
Savage of the Sea by Eliza Knight
Leader of Titans by Kathryn Le Veque
The Sea Devil by Eliza Knight
Sea Wolfe by Kathryn Le Veque

Note: All Kathryn's novels are designed to be read as stand-alones, although many have cross-over characters or cross-over family groups. Novels that are grouped together have related characters or family groups. You will notice that some series have the same books; that is because they are cross-overs. A hero in one book may be the secondary character in another.

There is NO reading order except by chronology, but even in that case, you can still read the books as stand-alones. No novel is connected to another by a cliff hanger, and every book has an HEA.

Series are clearly marked. All series contain the same characters or family groups except the American Heroes Series, which is an anthology with unrelated characters.

For more information, find it in **A Reader's Guide to the Medieval World of Le Veque.**

ABOUT KATHRYN LE VEQUE

Bringing the Medieval to Romance

KATHRYN LE VEQUE is a critically acclaimed, multiple USA TODAY Bestselling author, an Indie Reader bestseller, a charter Amazon All-Star author, and a #1 bestselling, award-winning, multi-published author in Medieval Historical Romance with over 100 published novels.

Kathryn is a multiple award nominee and winner, including the winner of Uncaged Book Reviews Magazine 2017 and 2018 "Raven Award" for Favorite Medieval Romance. Kathryn is also a multiple RONE nominee (InD'Tale Magazine), holding a record for the number of nominations. In 2018, her novel WARWOLFE was the winner in the Romance category of the Book Excellence Award and in 2019, her novel A WOLFE AMONG DRAGONS won the prestigious RONE award for best pre-16th century romance.

Kathryn is considered one of the top Indie authors in the world with over 2M copies in circulation, and her novels have been translated into several languages. Kathryn recently signed with Sourcebooks Casablanca for a Medieval Fight Club series, first published in 2020.

In addition to her own published works, Kathryn is also the President/CEO of Dragonblade Publishing, a boutique publishing house specializing in Historical Romance. Dragonblade's success has seen it rise in the ranks to become Amazon's #1 e-book publisher of Historical Romance (K-Lytics report July 2020).

Kathryn loves to hear from her readers. Please find Kathryn on Facebook at Kathryn Le Veque, Author, or join her on Twitter @kathrynleveque. Sign up for Kathryn's blog at www.kathryn leveque.com for the latest news and sales.